AT RISK

Staring at the intruder, Casey slipped her hand behind her, hoping to locate something on the counter to defend herself. A knife, a glass pitcher. Anything.

He lunged for her. "Don't scream," he warned, clamping his hand painfully over her wrist. "I've only come for *you.*" Catching her other hand, he then pulled both of her hands forward. "Make a sound and I'll kill your father now. He's watching TV. He can sit there and continue to watch TV or I can slit his throat. Your choice."

Casey shook with fear. She didn't recognize his voice, which was muffled by the latex mask. It shouldn't be happening. It couldn't be. It had to be a dream. She thought she was making tea, but actually she was asleep. She was having a nightmare. A bad one. Any minute, Linda would appear from the dark corner and start shrieking at her.

He nudged her forward. "If you do anything to attempt to attract anyone's attention while in the yard, or once we're on the road, I'll come back inside and kill your father and you'll have to watch. Then I'll kill you. . . ."

Books by Hunter Morgan

The Other Twin

She'll Never Tell

She'll Never Know

She'll Never Live

What She Can't See

Unspoken Fear

Are You Scared Yet?

Don't Turn Around

Published by Kensington Publishing Corporation

DON'T TURN AROUND

HUNTER MORGAN

ZEBRA BOOKS
Kensington Publishing Corp.
www.kensingtonbooks.com

ZEBRA BOOKS are published by

Kensington Publishing Corp.
850 Third Avenue
New York, NY 10022

All Kensington titles, imprints, and distributed lines are available at special quantity discounts for bulk purchases for sales
promotion, premiums, fund-raising, educational, or institu-
tional use.

Special book excerpts or customized printings can also be created to fit specific needs. For details, write or phone the office
of the Kensington Special Sales Manager: Attn. Special Sales
Department. Kensington Publishing Corp., 850 Third Avenue,
New York, NY 10022. Phone: 1-800-221-2647.

Zebra and the Z logo Reg. U.S. Pat. & TM Off.

ISBN-13: 978-0-8217-7947-7
ISBN-10: 0-8217-7947-8

First Printing: July 2008
10 9 8 7 6 5 4 3 2 1

Printed in the United States of America

Prologue

The Beginning of the End

I didn't start out as a killer. It was not an aspiration. I don't fit the profile routinely shared among law enforcement agencies.

As I reflect, I carefully remove each item from the small duffel bag that I have packed according to Maury's careful instructions. I am taking inventory because I must be careful. I must be careful, not because Maury has warned me to, but because I know. *Inherently,* I know what to do. How to do it. And my heart thumps in eager anticipation.

She never saw me coming.

I am a white male from an upper-middle-class family. I am attractive. Fit. I was never abused as a child, not sexually, not emotionally. In fact, I was loved by my family. I was raised to be a contributing member of society. I was brought up believing that my God-given talents brought a certain responsibility to champion for those less fortunate than me.

Duct tape.

I came into the world without complications. I saw a pediatrician regularly and was immunized against all childhood diseases. I attended good, safe schools. I was permitted to participate in extracurricular activities and often had friends to our home.

A blue bandana.

I was a bright child. I could count to one hundred and recite the alphabet by the time I was three. I was reading by the time I was four. By the time I reached elementary school, everyone around me recognized my intelligence. My *superior* intelligence.

Zip-strips.

I was placed in accelerated classes, and though I was smarter than my classmates and they knew it, I was well liked. I had friends. Mostly males as an adolescent, but then females as I entered my teen years.

A spool of #4-gauge wire.

I dated in high school, and while I was never the most popular boy in my class, I had my pick of girls. Cheerleaders. Field hockey players. Honor Society members. They all admired me. Wanted to be my friend. Wanted to be seen with me.

A box of disposable latex gloves.

As a young boy, I dreamed of being an astronaut. Later, as I grew wiser to the world, an architect. A physician. Perhaps a psychiatrist. I understood people. I could empathize, but more importantly, I could see them for who they really were. Perhaps it was because I always knew myself so well.

Wire cutters.

I always knew what I was. I always knew I was smarter than them. Than all of them; my parents, my friends, my teachers, my professors. I never had my IQ tested, but I am probably a genius.

Garden shears.

For a long time, it was enough to simply know how smart I was. I didn't need anyone else's acknowledgment. I was amused by the fact that others had no idea how truly brilliant I am. But later, as I grew into adulthood, I began to resent the stupidity around me. My amusement turned to anger. Eventually, that anger found a way to channel itself. Now, I am simply amused again.

Hand towels.

As I run my fingers over the cotton fabric and imagine the ample capacity for mopping up her blood, it occurs to me that my resentment probably started earlier than I realize. It likely initiated the early stealing. Just a cookie at the cafeteria when I was a young child. Later, gum from the mini-mart. It was a thrill to steal and get away with it.

Drop cloth.

It was so easy. Too easy. As I grew older, I began looking for a challenge. In prep school, I had a buddy who knew the ins and outs of surveillance equipment. We cased stores together. First it was a Coach wallet. A Fendi tie. Then pricier items. Larger items.

Hacksaw.

My friend got busted. I had been ready by then to move on, anyway. I had outgrown his companionship and there were larger, greater challenges ahead of me.

Disposable coveralls.

I learned how to handle a gun, although I had the forethought to pretend I oppose them and would like to see stronger laws in legislation against handgun use. I became an expert marksman. I quietly made friends among the retired officers at the firing ranges. They were all too willing to talk with me. To share their knowledge and experiences. They trusted me.

Disposable shoe covers.

The first time I held up a convenience store, the exhilaration was incredible. The look on the counter guy's face when

I shoved the barrel of the pistol between his teeth reminded me just how stupid he was. How smart I was.

Hunting knife.

And the first time I ever saw one of my crimes in the pages of a newspaper . . . I experienced an amazing high. *Unidentified suspect.* How I loved that phrase. Still do.

Mentally, I go through the list of items that do not fit in my bag.

Shovel.

That first convenience-store robbery opened up so many avenues to me. B&Es were so much more personal. Sometimes I would steal things from the homes I invaded. Other times, I would just watch the occupants while they slept.

Plastic sheeting.

An accidental meeting with a would-be thief on a fire escape was what really launched my career. By then, I was bored by simple thievery. I wanted to kick the thrill up a notch. But I recognized the need to be safe. I was never one of those mentally deficient criminals who wanted to be caught. Indeed, I hope—I know—that my career will span decades.

A sound taps my attention and I glance down. I pause. Listen. I hear nothing but the throaty voice of Pavarotti.

Just nerves. She is silent.

I place each item back in the bag, gently, lovingly. The bitch won't be silent for long.

Chapter 1

The Beginning

The phone woke her on the first ring. She was used to calls in the middle of the night, either from the hospital or, more recently, from the assisted-living facility, where her father was a resident. As she reached for the phone in the dark, she prayed he hadn't wandered away from Oak Orchard again. One more incident, the director had warned her, and she would have to "seek placement for Mr. McDaniel elsewhere."

Even though she was used to the interruptions of her sleep, her heart still thumped in her chest as her fingers found the cordless phone on the nightstand. Calls in the middle of the night were never good.

"Hello."

"Casey? Oh, Jesus," a female cried on the other end of the line. "You got to help me."

Casey reached for the lamp switch, fumbling. Her heart raced faster. She recognized the voice, but still half asleep, she couldn't put a name to it. "Who is this?"

"It's me! Linda! Linda Truman."

Casey thought she heard a thump in the background. Linda yelped.

"Do you hear that? Did you hear it?" Linda pleaded. Her voice trembled on the verge of hysteria. "Oh, Jesus, Casey. You got to help me. He's back. It's him, I know it's him."

Still trying to find the lamp, Casey threw her feet over the side of the bed. At last, she located the switch and turned it. Light flooded the room.

"Linda, you have to calm down. Talk to me. Who's trying to break in?"

"It's him," Linda gasped. "It's Charlie. I know it's him."

The terror in Linda's voice became Casey's terror. She had seen the woman's battered, bloody face two weeks ago in the ER. She'd held Linda's hand while an intern had applied a cast to her broken wrist. Casey gripped the handset. "Doors and windows locked?"

"Yeah. But it sounds like he's got a crowbar or somethin'. He's tryin' to get in the back door. I . . . I fell asleep on the couch and now he's here, Casey. Oh, Jesus God, he's here."

"Did you call the police? You called the police, right?"

"No. No, I called you." She was crying so hard now that her words were nearly indistinguishable. "You . . . you said I could call you any t-time day or n-night."

Casey's bare feet met the bumpy, soft wool of the rug on the floor beside her bed. "Listen to me. You have to calm down. I'm going to hang up, Lin—"

"No! No, don't hang up," she begged, sniffing. "Don't leave me!"

"I'm going to hang up and call 911. The police will come, Linda." Casey raced across the cold wood floor and grabbed a pair of dirty jeans off a chair. "They'll be able to get there faster than I can."

"No, don't hang up," Linda half sobbed, half shouted. "Don't leave me alone with him. He's gonna kill me. He told me he was gonna kill me if I left him. If I ever kicked him out."

"Linda," Casey said firmly. She cradled the phone between her shoulder and her ear as she stepped into her jeans, hopping on one foot and then the other. "We both have to hang up so I can call 911, but I'll call you right back. I'll call you from my cell phone so I can talk to you while I'm in the car."

"You swear you'll call me back?" Linda's voice sounded smaller than before. Deflated. She didn't believe Casey. She didn't believe Casey would come for her.

"I swear. Now, where are you right now? In the living room?"

"Yeah. Yeah, and he's at the back door. It opens into the hallway. I . . . I live in a trailer."

"Can you get to a bedroom or a bathroom, Linda? Somewhere with a door and a lock?"

There was another loud noise in the background. Casey thought she heard splintering wood and she fumbled to zip up her jeans.

"Linda!" Casey repeated, grasping the phone again, as if she could somehow physically reach the terrified woman. "Are you listening to me? Answer me! Can you get to a room with a lock on the door?"

"No. Yeah. Yeah. I . . . I think so. But . . . the front door. Maybe I should go out—"

"No. No, don't go outside. You don't know where he is."

"He's at the back door!" Linda shrieked.

"But he could run around to the front at any moment. You're safer inside. Go to the closest room. Lock yourself in." Casey gripped the phone tighter. "Now run, Linda. Take the phone with you and run!"

"The bedroom," Linda said almost trancelike. "Run for the bedroom."

"I'll call you right back, Linda. I swear." Casey hit the "end call" button on the phone. Hearing a dial tone, she punched in 911, trying to catch her breath as the call clicked through.

"This is nine-one-one. Is this an emergency?" came the practiced voice on the other end of the line.

Casey took a deep breath. This was not the first time she had had to call 911. She knew how to do this. She just had to stay calm. "Yes," she said. She took another deep breath. "This is an emergency."

For a moment, Linda stood motionless in the middle of the tiny living room, the phone still to her ear, her casted arm hanging heavy at her side. Casey was gone. She'd hung up. There was nothing but dead silence on the other end of the phone.

Linda heard a laugh track come from the tiny TV that sat on the microwave cart under the window. Her gaze shifted to the squiggly lines of the dim picture. *Seinfeld.*

Suddenly, another loud slam against the back door reverberated through the dark trailer. The sound of splitting wood and bending metal shocked Linda out of her stupor.

Casey is coming. The police are coming. Run. Casey had said she should run. She only had to make it as far as the bedroom.

She bolted. Tripped over the damned laundry basket next to the couch. Fell flat on her face, pain spearing up to her shoulder as the pink cast on her forearm cracked against the end table. The phone slipped out of her hand and slid across the carpet, which reeked of cigarette smoke and cat food. "No! No!" she screamed. She felt for the phone with her good hand but couldn't find it, couldn't see it, in the dim light thrown off by the TV. She scrambled to get to her feet. Canned laughter echoed through the cluttered room.

"You bastard!" she shouted down the hallway. "The cops are coming, you bastard. I'm gonna tell. You won't get away with it this time!"

Linda ran. She ran just like Casey told her. She made it to the spare bedroom doorway as he half fell, half leaped through the jimmied back door.

She couldn't scream. She was too scared. She was afraid she was going to barf.

He pounded down the hallway after her. Even in the dark, not able to see his face, she could tell how pissed he was.

Inside the bedroom, she spun around, throwing both hands against the door. It slammed shut and she felt for the lock on the knob. "Don't do it. Don't do it, Charlie," she sobbed.

Casey jumped into her car, sneakers untied and hair uncombed. She hadn't even taken the time to put her contacts in. Pushing her glasses farther up on her nose, she snapped on her seat belt and started the engine. She waited until she was on the road to use her cell phone to call information and have them put the call through to Linda. *Thank God I knew the address*.

The phone rang as she adjusted her Bluetooth earpiece. One ring. Two. Three. It rang and rang. With each passing second, dread began to creep up Casey's spine. Linda didn't pick up, but there was no answering machine either. Stopped at a red light, Casey ended the call and redialed, remembering the number the mechanical voice had provided before putting the call through the first time. Again, Linda's phone rang unanswered.

"Come on, Linda. Come on," Casey muttered. She glanced up at the traffic light that still blared red. There was

no one approaching in any direction. "Come on, come, on."
She tapped on the steering wheel.

Still red. She hung up her cell phone with the earpiece,
tapped it again. "Redial," she ordered.

Still no answer.

Maybe the police had called Linda. Maybe that's why she
wasn't picking up.

But shouldn't there have been a busy tone? Then again,
everyone had Call Waiting these days.

At last, the light turned green and Casey stepped on the
gas. It took her twenty-three minutes from the time Linda
had called until she turned onto the gravel road at the entrance to the trailer park hidden on the edge of town. As she
passed a line of beat-up mailboxes, she saw the flash of blue
lights. The police. *Thank goodness.* She heaved a sigh of
relief. The police were here. The abusive ex-boyfriend
would be cuffed and taken away. He'd go to prison for sure
this time.

He wouldn't hurt Linda again.

Casey pulled over onto the grass between two older cars,
both parked at odd angles. Lights were on in the trailers on
both sides of the street. People in bathrobes stood in their
matchbook-sized front yards and in the middle of the street,
talking excitedly, all staring and gesturing in the same direction. A poodle yipped from the doorway of an adjoining
home. Casey got out of the car and leaned over to tie her
shoelaces, putting her at eye level with a cluster of gnomes
that guarded a dead rosebush. The warm night air smelled
of motor oil, cat urine, and cigarette smoke.

The pulsing blue lights of the police cruisers blended
with the flash of rotating ambulance lights and the blink of
red flashers on the rear of several emergency vehicles. The
street was a cacophony: the bark of voices from personnel
at the scene, the ding-ding warning that someone had left

his or her car door open with keys in the ignition, the neighbors' voices.

Casey's heart was pounding again, another wave of adrenaline kicking in. As she walked up the street, approaching the vehicles, the hard gravel crunched under her feet. She was surrounded by people: men, women, children, all shades of color from pale white to dark brown. But as she walked toward the flashing lights, she felt alone. Alone and empty and scared.

Casey loved her job. But she hated it. Hated the fact that a hospital needed a victims' advocate.

She craned her neck in search of Linda. Linda was thirty-two. Divorced, no children. A clerk at a convenience market. Average height. A brunette with a pretty smile that would have been prettier had it not been for her smoke-stained teeth.

There were police, firemen, and paramedics milling around. Someone opened the ambulance's rear door and cold white light spilled out.

Casey didn't see Linda anywhere. She'd have been hard to miss. There were no other women present except for one chunky paramedic and a black police officer, both of whom she knew from the hospital. How hard could Linda be to spot with that bright pink cast?

"Excuse me, ma'am. You'll have to step back."

A beefy arm barred Casey's way. She looked up at an officer in a bright orange safety vest.

"I'm Casey McDaniel." She fumbled in her back pocket for the ID that she'd had the good sense to grab off her dresser before she left the house. "I'm the victims' advocate at Sussex County Hospital. Linda Truman called me a few minutes ago. I was the one who notified the police of the break-in."

He moved the beam of his flashlight over her ID. "You talked to Ms. Truman a few minutes ago?"

His gaze met hers and Casey felt a trickle of fear. She fought it. "Yes. I need to see her. I promised her I would meet her here. I . . . I was assigned to her case at the hospital a few weeks ago when she came in, beaten by her boyfriend."

He glanced over his shoulder in the direction of Linda's trailer. There was an old Nissan pickup with a tennis ball on the antenna parked in the driveway. He looked back at Casey, not meeting her gaze this time. "Can you come with me? Detectives'll want to talk to you."

"I'll be happy to speak with the police, but first, I'd *really* like to talk to Linda. If that's possible. I promised her—"

"Officer Chatham, this is . . ." The male officer hesitated.

"Casey McDaniel," Officer Chatham cut in. "We've met."

Casey observed the slender young African American woman in the blue uniform. She was no taller than Casey but appeared so in the regulation hat.

"Casey," the female cop murmured.

"Chanel." Casey moved closer to her.

The officer who had escorted Casey walked away.

"The victim was one of your clients?" Chanel looked at her from under the brim of her hat.

Casey felt light-headed. *The victim.* She didn't like the way Chanel said it. But Linda was a victim, wasn't she? Her ex-boyfriend had beaten her half to death a few weeks ago. "Is she all right? She was pretty scared when she called me."

When Chanel didn't answer immediately, Casey knew. *She knew.* "No," she whispered.

"I'm sorry."

"She's dead?" Tears sprang up in Casey's eyes.

"Bled out before we got here. Multiple stab wounds."

"She's dead?" Casey repeated. She looked toward the

trailer, pressing the heel of her hand to her forehead. "He killed her? But I just talked to her. Less than half an hour ago. She said he was trying to break in the back door."

Chanel settled her hand on Casey's shoulder, facing her, then spoke directly to her in the same way that Casey had been trained to talk to her clients. Her voice was calm, soft, but strong. "Did Linda Truman say who was breaking into her house?"

"It was her ex-boyfriend." Casey fought her tears, fought to remain professional. "She said it was Charles Gaitlin."

Chapter 2

Four Months Later

The phone rang and Casey bolted upright in her bed.

"Casey? Oh, God, you have to help me," Linda Truman begged. The room was pitch black.

The phone continued to ring and Casey recoiled against the headboard, pulling the bed linens to her chin.

The phone jangled so loudly that it seemed as if she was surrounded in the darkness by ringing phones.

"Casey? Casey, it's him! It's him. He says he's going to kill me."

Casey drew her knees to her chest, her heart pounding.

The phone still rang. It wouldn't stop. The voice, Linda's voice, was coming from somewhere in the room, but Casey couldn't see her.

"Casey?"

"Linda?" Casey cried. She heard a loud thump and a splinter of wood. Someone was breaking through her bedroom door. No, through the trailer door!

Linda screamed, a bloodcurdling, shrivel-your-guts

scream, and Casey cringed, covering her ears with her hands, trying to make it stop.

But it wouldn't stop. The phone kept ringing.

Casey wakened with a start, the phone still ringing. Her eyes flew wide open. No . . . not the phone. Her alarm. Her alarm clock was buzzing.

She sat up and pressed the button on top of the digital clock with a shaky hand. Taking a deep breath, she leaned back on the pillows and closed her eyes, pulling up the comforter. The room was chilly. Her heart was still pounding.

Just a dream, she told herself, taking another deep breath.

Linda had been haunting Casey's dreams for months, as if calling to her from her grave. But Casey knew it wasn't really Linda haunting her; it was Charles Gaitlin.

"Have a seat." The receptionist motioned to a wall lined with sad metal chairs. "Mr. Preston is taking a call, but he'll be with you in just a second."

"Thank you." Casey managed a nervous smile and walked back to the waiting area. She sat in the chair closest to the door and set her brown leather briefcase on her lap.

The receptionist returned her attention to her keyboard and Casey glanced around. The Delaware Department of Justice office for Sussex County was like any other state office Casey had ever been in: scuffed green floor tile, a maze of narrow hallways and tiny offices, and a sea of over-worked, underpaid employees. From where Casey sat, she could see through a glass partition to a room of cubicles that boasted gunmetal gray desks and outdated computers and fax machines.

A large white clock with black hands and numerals ticked. She'd had a difficult time getting the appointment with Assistant Deputy Attorney Adam Preston III. Even though she was a potential witness in the case against Charles Gaitlin, she'd been told by some nebulous voice on the other end of the line that the county prosecutor didn't meet with witnesses this early in the trial process. Casey had gleaned from a little poking around on the Internet that Adam Thomas Preston III was considered one of the best and brightest in the state and that the Republican Party had great hopes for his future. Home grown in Delaware, he was the son of a retired Superior Court judge, and the grandson of a former state senator.

But Casey didn't care how big a hotshot he was; it was important to her that she speak to him about Linda's case. Unwilling to be deterred by the runaround she had gotten with the Delaware Department of Justice, she had sent Preston an e-mail, and he had responded to it personally, saying he would be happy to speak with her. The appointment had originally been scheduled twice, but both times it had been rescheduled by someone in his office. The clerk who had called most recently to reschedule had been short with Casey, warning her that Mr. Preston had only ten minutes this afternoon before he would have to leave for court for the Gaitlin preliminary hearing.

Charles Gaitlin had pleaded not guilty to the charge of the murder of his ex-girlfriend Linda Truman at his arraignment. Because he had not been able to make bail, he had been held in Sussex Correctional Institute since then. Casey had read in the newspaper that his grandmother had hired an attorney for him. The preliminary hearing scheduled today in the courthouse would determine whether there was sufficient evidence to bring him to trial for murder.

Casey glanced at the clock again, tapping her foot nervously on the tile floor. She only had ten minutes with the deputy attorney and two had already been used up in the waiting room. She inhaled and exhaled, trying to will away her jitters.

Now that she was actually here, she wasn't sure why it had been so important to her to see Preston before Gaitlin's preliminary hearing. Numerous statements had been taken by the police the night Linda was killed. A bloody knife purported to have been seen in Gaitlin's possession a week earlier had been discovered in Linda's yard. What did the prosecuting attorney need Casey for?

She'd told herself that she was here to put a real face with a name on the file. The state's Department of Justice had an overwhelming case load, as did Mr. Preston, Casey was sure. She just didn't want to see this one slip through the cracks. She didn't want Gaitlin getting a ten-year prison sentence, and out in four or five for good behavior. She hoped to see Gaitlin tried on a capital count so that he would receive a life sentence. With a one on one with Preston, no matter how brief, Casey was hoping he would go that extra mile in the case. She was speaking for Linda because Linda could no longer speak for herself.

Or . . . Casey was here to silence Linda, who still called to her in her sleep.

A male voice caught Casey's attention, and she glanced up to see a good-looking man in gray slacks, a white shirt, and a red and black tie striding down the hall toward her, a file in his hand, a cell phone to his ear.

"I understand perfectly, but that's not how the contract is worded," he said to the caller. "The way it's worded, it leaves open the option to hire private nursing as the family sees fit. I can have a copy sent over to your office with the phrases in question marked, if you like." He halted in front of the receptionist's desk. She pointed to Casey. He turned toward Casey, pausing long enough for the person on the other end of the line to speak.

"Great. I'm glad we've cleared this up," he continued into the phone. "Thanks, John. I'll get back to you with details once a decision has been made. Have a great day."

Casey rose as he disconnected.

"Miss McDaniel?" he asked but didn't give her time to answer. "Adam Preston."

"Nice to meet you." She switched her briefcase from her right to her left hand as he offered his hand to her.

Casey was taken completely off guard. This was Assistant Deputy Attorney Adam Preston? *The third?* She'd been expecting an older man and certainly not one so good-looking. He was only in his mid- to late thirties, with short, dark hair and an aristocratic face. Very Kennedyesque.

They shook hands. He had a warm, firm grip.

"I apologize for cancelling our previous appointments. This job has a way of . . . well, getting in the way of the job, sometimes, if you know what I mean."

"That's quite all right. I'm just glad we could meet beforehand," she fumbled, still trying to recover from her total miscalculation. She could usually guess what a person looked like or what kind of person he or she was with very little information. Some might even have accused her of stereotyping. Unfortunately, in her line of work, she had discovered that entirely too often stereotypes were dead on target. People didn't often surprise her, but Adam Preston III had. The idea made her want to smile.

"Unfortunately, I don't have much time." He checked his watch. "The prelim is in forty-five minutes and Judge Trudeau doesn't tolerate tardiness."

"Not a problem. I actually need to be at the courthouse shortly myself," she said. "Another case."

He stopped outside an open door to an office and gestured for her to go in. On the door was an unobtrusive nameplate. His office. "Please, have a seat." He smiled down at her.

She smiled up.

He had to be six two, maybe six three, making her measly five feet two inches seem even shorter.

She sat in a black leather chair in front of his desk, which was cherry, not gunmetal gray aluminum. The walls were painted beige, and on them hung various diplomas and certificates of award, which she quickly scanned. Undergraduate degree from the University of Delaware, law degree from Villanova. Filled with legal tomes, cherry bookcases, matching the executive desk, towered in the room. The office was austere, but warm.

"I appreciate your interest in this case," Preston said as he took a seat. "Our victims' advocates don't get enough recognition." He tented his hands on the desk. They were clean, neatly manicured, but not fussy. "Now what can I do for you, Miss McDaniel?"

She took a deep breath, meeting his gaze across the broad desk. "This case hit me particularly hard, Mr. Preston. I'm sure you've seen the statement I provided the police the night Linda was murdered. I saw Linda when she came to the emergency room two weeks before her death; she had a broken arm and facial bruises and lacerations courtesy of Mr. Gaitlin. I know she told the police that night that he didn't do it, but she was just scared. She was actually considering pressing charges at the time of her death."

Casey reached out, pressing her palm to his desk. "Linda called me the night she was murdered. She told me he was breaking in. If you had heard the terror in her voice—" Emotion choked Casey and she couldn't go on.

"Are you all right, Miss McDaniel?" Preston asked after a moment.

She nodded, feeling foolish. She was too professional for

this kind of behavior. But *someone* had to get emotional, right? Otherwise, who would ever mourn the Lindas of the world? Who would ever protect the next Linda?

Casey pressed her palm to her mouth and nodded. She was impressed by the attorney's compassion. She lowered her hand, more in control of herself again. "I'm sorry. I didn't mean to—" She met his gaze again. He didn't seem uncomfortable with her inappropriate expression of emotion. "I guess I just wanted to put a name with a face for you." She reached into her briefcase and pulled out a Polaroid of Linda she'd taken that night in the hospital. She slid it across the desk.

He picked it up, looked at it, and then slid it gently back toward her. "We have a good case, Miss McDaniel."

"A capital case? He told Linda repeatedly before that night that he was going to kill her if she didn't agree to let him move back in." Casey went on faster. "Surely that's premeditated. Mr. Preston, the only way to stop men like Charles Gaitlin from killing their girlfriends, their wives, is for the state to take these crimes more seriously. The only way—"

"I'm sorry, Mr. Preston," a pert voice interrupted from the doorway, directly behind Casey. "You're going to be late if you don't get to the courthouse."

Casey rose to her feet, tucking the photo into her briefcase as the woman disappeared down the hallway.

"I'm sorry I don't have more time. Really." He stood, taking his suit jacket from the back of his chair. He seemed to be debating whether or not to share something that she guessed was personal.

"You want to know the truth?" He lowered his voice. "It wasn't work that kept me from seeing you yesterday. It was personal," he confessed. "My grandfather has been very ill. He's in a nursing home and I'm supposed to be keeping an eye on him while my parents are in Europe. My father just retired and he and Mother had been planning this trip for years."

"I'm sorry. Is it serious?" Casey walked around the chair, moving toward the door.

"I'm afraid so." He smiled grimly, hesitating again before continuing. "But he's eighty-eight and he's had a good life. He's not going to get better, but I want to be certain he's as comfortable as possible."

He looked at her and she immediately felt a connection to him. As corny as it might sound, she felt his pain.

"My father recently moved in with me," she said softly. "He's only sixty-three, but he has early onset Alzheimer's. I know how hard it is to see someone you love hurting."

Preston came around the desk. "Does he know he's ill?"

Now the grim smile was hers. "Unfortunately, yes. He gets very frustrated with himself sometimes because his memory is so sporadic."

"That must be hard. My grandfather hasn't been conscious in more than a week. He's had another stroke. But thankfully, he doesn't seem to know what's going on. He's on a respirator."

"He's lucky to have family looking after him."

Preston halted in the doorway, seeming reluctant to go, despite Judge Trudeau's opinions on tardiness. "And your dad's lucky to have you. Lot of responsibility, though. You have others to help out? Siblings . . . a husband?"

If Casey didn't know better, she would have thought Adam Preston III was fishing to determine her availability. She was flattered. "No husband. Not even a boyfriend." She grimaced. "My father says I'm a workaholic."

"So does my mother. She says *I'm* a workaholic, not you." He chuckled and held up his bare left hand. "So no wedding ring here. Not even anyone remotely interested."

He glanced at his watch again and winced. "I really am

sorry, but I've got to run." He hesitated, then looked down at her, and in a lower voice said, "This is probably totally inappropriate to ask, but do you think you . . . you and I could maybe go out for a drink sometime? Commiserate on what it's like to be workaholics?"

She smiled. "I'll consider it. In the meantime, you'd better get going, Mr. Preston."

"Adam."

"I'm sorry?"

"Call me Adam." He pointed at her, sounding only a little cocky as he backed his way down the hall, and added, "And I'm not going to take no for an answer."

Casey sat for over an hour in the lobby waiting to see if she would be needed as a witness to an altercation that had taken place in the hospital waiting room a couple of months ago. The case was finally called, and the young man ended up pleading to a lesser charge. The assistant deputy attorney in the case, a young pregnant woman, thanked Casey for her time and said she was free to go.

As Casey left the courtroom, she checked her watch. It was just after three; she could return to work but decided against it. She wasn't expected at the hospital today, and she had some paperwork with her she could see to this evening after she put her father to bed, so the day wouldn't be a total wash. Instead of going to work and ending up staying late, as often happened, she thought she would stop at the grocery store. Then she'd go home and spend some time with her father and make him one of his favorite meals. Maybe they'd even curl up on the couch together and watch one of his favorite movies from his John Wayne DVD collection.

The last two months, since her father had moved in with her, had been difficult for her, but she knew they had been

difficult for him, too. Once a well-respected and popular
English professor at the University of Maryland, he had had
to give up his independent living to move into assisted-
living care. It had been even harder for him to leave his
apartment to move into his daughter's house, because that
had meant admitting he could no longer care for himself. As
she had told Adam, her father was ill, but not so ill that he
was unaware of his state. He knew that his lapses in memory
and judgment had reached a point where independent living
was no longer possible.

Casey followed the long hallway flanked by courtrooms
and turned into the entry hall where she'd had to leave her
cell phone at security. She was standing in line to collect it
when she heard Adam call her. She turned to see him hurrying toward her, tan trench coat and briefcase in hand.

"Miss McDaniel. I'm glad I caught you." He glanced at
the people in front of and behind her in line. "Could I speak
with you for a moment?"

She stepped out of line and followed him to an alcove
down the hall. "How did it go?" She was half smiling as she
spoke, already thinking about that drink he had offered, but
her smile fell as the look on his face registered. "Oh, please,
don't tell me," she groaned.

"I'm really sorry, Casey." He shook his head. "I requested
a continuance because the DNA results aren't back yet on
the suspected murder weapon. Judge Trudeau denied my request so I had to nol pros—"

"Nol pros?" She gripped her briefcase in frustration. How
could this be happening? She'd been in and out of the courthouse enough to know that justice wasn't always done. But
the law couldn't fail her this time. Not today. "I don't understand."

"*Nolle prosequi*. It's a legal term meaning that at this
time, the state chooses not to prosecute."

"You chose not to prosecute?" she demanded, louder than she intended. Two men in suits passing in the hallway glanced in their direction. Casey lowered her voice as she looked back up at the attorney. "How can you *choose not to prosecute?* He murdered her."

"It means we choose not to prosecute *at this time.* It's sometimes a necessary evil of the process. We knew going into—"

"I don't understand how this could happen. You didn't say anything about this when I was in your office." She didn't give him a chance to speak. She wasn't angry with him, but she was angry. Angry with a system that would fail Linda. That would fail women like her. "What about his fingerprints on the knife?"

"Inconclusive," he said. "We need the lab report."

"So now nothing happens until the DNA evidence comes in positive for Linda's blood?" She shouted her last words.

His hand was warm on her arm, even through her jacket.

"I'm sorry." She shook her head as if she could shake off the feeling of helplessness that had manifested itself as anger. She'd been experiencing the same thing at home with her father. "That was unprofessional of me. I just—" She looked away and then back at him. "What can you do now?"

"We can have Gaitlin reindicted. It will take a little time, but—"

"I can't believe this is happening." Casey turned away, still in disbelief. It was as if she didn't know what to do next. What to say. It had never occurred to her that Gaitlin could be set free. No one she had talked to from the Department of Justice had ever brought up the possibility.

"And so that's it?" Casey threw up her hand and let it fall. She thought of Linda calling to her in her nightmares. How loud would Linda be now that Gaitlin had been set free? "That's it?" she repeated. "Charles Gaitlin stabs his ex-girlfriend to death, and after only four months in prison, he's set free?"

Adam steadied her shaking hand. "We'll reindict."

"You can do that? It's not . . ." She searched her mind for the correct legal term. "Double jeopardy?"

"We're still in the preliminary stage. Double jeopardy doesn't apply. We'll reindict. We'll take the DNA evidence into the prelim and we'll go to trial with a strong case for life in prison. Or, after the prelim, maybe he'll change his plea to guilty and he'll still go to prison for life." He squeezed her hand. "I'm sorry. I know this doesn't seem right, but it's the way the system works. It has to. But thanks to that system, we can still make the charge stick."

"And you still think you can make that happen?"

He met her gaze. His eyes were green with little flecks of amber. "Absolutely."

She shifted her gaze to a spot on the wall behind Adam's head, her eyes burning. She'd already made a fool of herself in front of Adam once today. If she cried now, she'd be mortified. "But Gaitlin still goes free, today."

"The judge has already released him." He hesitated. "I'm sorry."

Casey took a deep breath and exhaled, releasing the pain. Suddenly, she was tired. Weary to the bone. "Okay, then. That's that for now." She hooked her thumb in the direction of the security desk, and the outside world. "I'm going to go home, put my slippers on, and have a cup of tea."

"I don't suppose you could be persuaded to join me for a drink?" When she didn't answer him at once, he went on smoothly, "Or an early dinner . . . or a cup of coffee? Tea?"

"No, but thanks." She turned away. "I think I just want to go home and check on my dad. Curl up with a good book."

"Thank you," he called after her as he set his briefcase down to put on his coat. "I'll be in touch."

Casey waited in the long line at the security desk, collected her cell phone, and made a beeline for the door. Out on the sidewalk in front of the impressive brick courthouse, an autumn wind whistled. With her free hand, she drew her suit jacket closer to ward off the chill. She had parked her car two blocks away in a public lot behind the bank. It was a long walk in the cold, but she had purposely left her coat in the car, thinking she would have one less thing to carry all day. Despite her father's warning this morning, she hadn't expected the temperature to drop so fast.

By the time she reached her Toyota hybrid, she was shivering. Standing at the driver's side door, she dug into the side pocket of her briefcase in search of her keys but came up empty-handed. She was sure she had dropped them in that compartment, with her wallet and lipstick. But they weren't there. Aggravated with herself, she started to pull through the other compartments, but with all the files and loose sheets of paper and various pamphlets, she couldn't find them. Her fingers numb with cold, she was having a difficult time picking through the mess.

She walked to the hood of the car and plopped her briefcase on top. "Where the heck could they be?" she muttered under her breath, giving the briefcase a good shake. She was rewarded with the telltale jingle of keys. She hadn't lost them. They were there. It was just a matter of—

A crunch of loose gravel on the pavement behind Casey made her spin around. She'd been so engrossed in the key search that she hadn't heard anyone approach.

"Well looky here, if it ain't Linda's good friend Casey McDaniel."

Instinctively, Casey shrank back, clutching her briefcase to her chest. "Mr. Gaitlin."

Chapter 3

"Guess you're surprised to see me, huh? Out free and clear?"

Charlic was dcfinitcly stcrcotypical of a woman abuscr. Average stature. Bad haircut. Pinched face and watery eyes that couldn't be trusted. He could easily have been cast in a made-for-TV movie.

"They decided not to prosecute me, which is a good thing for me, seein' as how you said all that bad stuff about me. Made up those lies."

"I don't know what you're talking about," Casey managed.

"Sure you do. Tellin' the police that night in the hospital that I hit Linda. Tellin' lawyers. Makin' up lies. Makes a man kind of angry. Know what I mean?" He threw back his shoulders in a bullying posture and took another step toward her.

Casey stared at Gaitlin, her heart pounding. For a moment she couldn't move, couldn't react. All these years, and still she hadn't forgotten that feeling of terror, of vulnerability.

But she wasn't defenseless. No woman was. No woman

had to feel that way. She told her clients that all the time. *Stop feeling and start thinking,* she told herself.

Snapping out of her daze, Casey quickly assessed the area around her. *Damn, damn, damn,* she thought. There wasn't a soul in the parking lot. Cars passed on the street, but from this distance, with windows up, she doubted anyone would hear her if she screamed. She wouldn't have to run far to get someone's attention by stepping out into the street, but she'd put herself in a bad position when she'd moved to the hood of the car. Gaitlin had her backed up against it now. Trapped.

"Don't take another step toward me, Mr. Gaitlin," she warned loudly, using one hand to hold the briefcase against her chest while she held up the other to stop him.

"Or what?" he grunted. "What're you gonna do?"

He had the aggressive male body language that women all over the world were forced to endure every day. He was like a strutting rooster with his chest thrown out, his shoulders back, his fists clenched as if he would strike her at any moment. He was pathetic. Charles Gaitlin was a pathetic man. But a dangerous pathetic man.

Casey had pepper spray. She always carried it with her, but it was on her damned key chain, somewhere in her briefcase.

She couldn't believe she'd been this foolish. She knew better than to enter a parking lot without having her keys ready. It was one of the very first precautions she taught in the safety course she presented to local women's groups.

The engine of a car revved, and out of the corner of her eye, Casey saw the taillights of an old blue sedan light up. One of the taillights was cracked. The engine sputtered as the car backed out of its space, sending loose gravel flying.

Thank God. There was someone else in the parking lot.

Gaitlin saw the car, too.

He shoved his hands down into the pockets of his pants,

the sides of his ugly brown suit billowing out as he relaxed his stance. His thin comb-over came unglued from behind his ear and danced in the wind. He was a ridiculous-looking man. Casey shouldn't be afraid of him. But she was afraid. Afraid, just as Linda had been, and with good cause.

"Guess I best be goin'. Ride's here." He nodded in the direction of the car, which was now pulling behind Casey's car. There was a woman driving. A woman who looked so much like Linda that Casey did a double take. The driver was smaller than Linda, her hair lighter. Upon closer inspection, Casey could see that she really didn't resemble Linda much, except for the look on her face. The woman had the *look* of an abused woman.

"Guess we can't visit anymore today." Gaitlin started around the front of the blue car. "But if I was you, missy, I'd have eyes in the back of my head." He winked at her and opened the passenger-side door. She heard the door groan as it scraped metal on metal.

Still watching the car as it pulled out of the parking lot, Casey fumbled inside her briefcase. She was now shaking so hard that her teeth chattered.

At long last, her fingertips curled around the ring of keys in the bottom of the bag and she yanked them out. Safely inside her car, she locked the doors, turned over the engine, and flipped the heat on high.

Had it been her imagination, or had Charles Gaitlin just threatened her?

He couldn't have. Wouldn't have dared. *Would he?*

As Casey sat with her hands clenched on the steering wheel, the car heater blasting, she slowly began to thaw. When she finally stopped shaking, she put the car into reverse and eased out of the parking lot.

Taking the Georgetown Circle, she headed east toward home. There was no way she was going to the grocery store now. All she wanted to do was get inside her house and lock the doors.

Should she call the police? Tell them what Gaitlin had done?

But what exactly *had* he done? The exchange in the parking lot couldn't have lasted much more than a couple of minutes. He didn't touch her and what he had said was her word against his.

His word against hers.

That was what her father had said about Billy Bosley. Tears stung Casey's eyes and she wiped at them in frustration. All these years and had she not come any further than this?

No, she'd just had a bad day. A bad day in court. A run-in with a loser in the parking lot. There was no need for self-loathing or self-doubt. Casey knew she just had to push through. Push through, enjoy the weekend, and get prepared to do her job again, come Monday morning. Charles Gaitlin might be free right now, but he would have his day in court. Adam Preston III would see he was found guilty of murder and Linda's death would be avenged.

By the time she pulled into her neighborhood, Casey was feeling better. A little less tense. Less self-deprecating. She'd just go home, have a nice quiet evening with her father, and she would feel better tomorrow. Although she hadn't stopped at the grocery store, she was certain she could whip up a decent comfort meal from the pantry, even if it wasn't her father's favorite. It didn't really matter anymore because he couldn't usually remember his favorite foods. Only Casey could.

She turned onto her street. The neighborhood was new, less than five years old and centrally located between Georgetown and Lewes, twenty minutes from SCH, where she worked. A school bus ahead of her flashed its red lights and she braked. Mrs. Cline, a neighbor from across the street, walked on the sidewalk, all bundled in a coat and hat and scarf. Her poodle, also decked out in a coat, trotted in front of her, tugging on its rhinestone leash. Stopping behind the bus, Casey waved to her.

Mrs. Cline waved casually as she walked by.

The bus pulled forward as a little boy ran across a front lawn toward an older sibling waiting on his doorstep. As Casey eased forward, she saw Mrs. Cline, having apparently just realized who was in the car, waving at her. Then waving toward something farther up the street.

Casey braked again, looking back, but Mrs. Cline continued along the sidewalk in the opposite direction.

What in the world? Casey wondered.

She didn't have to wonder long. She made the bend in the road and there, standing on her front lawn, was her father dressed in a pink chenille bathrobe. It was Casey's favorite bathrobe, the one she kept on the back of the bathroom door.

And boxer shorts. Her father was wearing nothing but boxer shorts and an open bathrobe. He was spraying the flower bed with a hose.

She pulled into her driveway, hitting the garage door opener fastened to the visor. But instead of waiting for the door to go up so she could park inside the garage, she stopped in the middle of the blacktop driveway, jumped out, and ran across the lawn. "Dad, what are you doing?"

Frazier, her father's old boxer, barked excitedly, rushing to greet her.

"Dad?" She looked down at the dog, which was bouncing up and down in front of her excitedly. "Hey, boy. Good boy, off," she ordered, trying to pull her suit jacket close against the cold wind while attempting to prevent the big dog from jumping on her with his muddy paws.

"Dad?" She walked up behind him and reached around to take the hose from him.

Frazier continued to bark, now dancing in the muddy flower bed.

Casey's father stared at her for a moment. A half smile of recognition rose slowly on his face. "My daughter."

"Yeah, Dad. What are you doing out here in the cold?" The bathrobe fluttered open in the wind, exposing his bare chest and bird legs. She dropped the running hose and reached around him to grab the ties of the pink robe and fasten them around his waist.

He made no attempt to assist her.

"You need a hat and a coat and shoes if you bring Frazier outside. You know that, Dad." She wrapped her arm around his shoulder and tried to turn him toward the house. "And pants. We wear pants outside."

Ed McDaniel resisted her.

She groaned, praying silently for patience. "Dad, come on. It's cold out." She glanced toward the street at the sound of squeaky brakes.

The bus had turned around in the cul-de-sac and come back. It had stopped to let Jenny Rousseau off directly across the street, and the elementary kids remaining on the bus had their faces plastered to the windows. They laughed and pointed at the old man in the pink bathrobe.

"Dad, you're going to be arrested for indecent exposure. Come on." She gave him a little push. "Frazier, come, boy."

The old boxer bounded past them.

"Dad, follow Frazier." She nudged him, trying to keep her tone even. When her father suspected she was annoyed with him, he could be obstinate.

Her father slowly turned. "Watering the mums. They look dry."

"Dad, they're dead. It's October and we've had a cold

snap. They'll come back next year." Her arm around his thin shoulders, she urged him toward the front porch. "Why are you out here without a coat? You told me this morning high of forty-three with winds at four knots."

"High of forty-three, low of thirty-eight," he said.

"That's right," she agreed, wondering how in heaven's name he could remember the morning forecast but couldn't remember to wear clothes outside.

He shuffled beside her, their progress impeded by his hunched posture, sometimes prominent, sometimes not, for which doctors could give no real explanation. It was all part of the disease, she had been told.

"Up to twelve inches of snow expected in Butte."

"It's cold in Butte, Dad. Glad we don't live there, right?"

He halted and stared at her with gray eyes that had, years ago, been blue. Confusion lined his once handsome face. "We live in Butte?"

She smiled, a lump rising in her throat. This was so hard, still so hard. Ed McDaniel had once been a brilliant man, a renaissance man, able to carry on a lively discussion on nineteenth-century French and American poets. He had known about the flora and fauna of the Amazon River, the history of the Italian government, the genetic makeup of a common housefly. And now . . . "No, Daddy. We don't live in Montana. We live in Delaware, remember? You used to live in College Park in Maryland, but now we live in Delaware. I work here. I work at the hospital."

"Frazier?" Ed glanced around in sudden concern. "Where's that dog gotten to?"

The dog barked in response to his master's voice as he ran up and down the porch steps, waiting for them.

"He's here. He's fine. Come on. Up the steps." She waited as her father took each red brick step with caution and shuffled across the porch. She reached the front door of the quaint Cape Cod to find it locked.

"Great," she muttered. Her teeth were chattering again.

He must have gone out the back door. "Dad, you stay here." She tugged on his hand. "You stand right here on the porch and wait while I go around and let you in." She hurried down the steps, pointing toward her father. "Frazier, keep him there. Stay, boy."

The dog studied Casey with big dark eyes for a moment and then plopped down on the top step, successfully blocking the none-too-spry man's way.

Casey hurried into the garage, through the side door into the laundry room, down the hall past the kitchen, into the living room to the front door. When she turned the dead bolt and opened the door, thankfully, Ed was standing right where she'd left him. The tie on the robe had loosened and, once again, knobby knees were poking out from the pink, fluffy robe.

Casey grabbed him and pulled him through the doorway. "Your hands are like ice." She held open the door for the dog. "Come on, boy."

"Don't forget the mums," her father told her.

"The hose. Right. I'll get it; you're getting into a hot shower." She led him halfway across the living room and then thought of Charles Gaitlin again.

Charles had seen her car. He knew what she drove. Her car was still in the driveway and needed to be put in the garage.

Was she being paranoid?

No, just safe. She practiced the safety steps she taught other women. Lock your doors after dark. If you have an attached garage, use it.

She looked into her father's eyes, getting his attention. "You go on into your bathroom and get into the shower, okay? Can you do that for me?"

"I can certainly take a shower on my own, Daughter," he snapped, drawing himself up to his full height, tightening the tie on the pink bathrobe.

It was good to see her father still had a little fire in him. "Fine. I'll have hot tea ready in the kitchen in a couple of minutes." She was already on her way toward the garage. She probably *was* being paranoid, but she would feel better when her car was in the garage and the doors were locked.

Sunday afternoon, Casey and her father had dinner at her sister's house. When their father moved in with Casey eight weeks ago, Jayne had promised to have a weekly family dinner, but Jayne made a lot of promises. She was one of those women trying to work full-time, be a mother and a wife, and serve on various community boards. She often fell short of her commitments, especially when it came to Casey and their father, but so far, she'd kept her word about having them over. Usually, though she lived only twenty minutes away, it was the only time each week that Jayne saw Ed.

As Casey and Jayne began to clear the table after dinner, Jayne's husband excused himself on the premise of *getting the kids out of their hair.* He took his and Jayne's two children and Ed into the family room.

Casey could hear a football commentator talking on the TV about the Eagles's winning record. She was surprised Ed hadn't protested. He hated the Eagles, loved the Redskins. Maybe today he didn't know that. Ed didn't like Joaquin, either, and *that* he seemed to remember. Every Sunday, there was always the question as to whether or not Ed would be civil to Joaquin. Luckily, Joaquin was easygoing and let Ed's sometimes sharp comments roll right off his back.

"I'm really sorry about your case." Jayne stacked plates

smeared with marinara sauce on the end of the table. "I know it was important to you."

Casey held glasses and cups in each hand. Reflecting her personal life, Jayne's dining room was a mess. The dishes were mismatched, the tablecloth was stained, and stacked around the perimeter of the walls were piles of papers, magazines, boxes of toys, and God knew what else.

"It's just so absurd," Casey said. "How can he be set free when everyone knows he did it?"

Jayne followed her through the swinging door, into the kitchen. "Lucky for us, we can't be convicted for looking guilty."

Casey frowned, setting the glasses on the crowded counter so she could open the dishwasher. There was that tone of her sister's that Casey hated. That high-and-mighty, righteous tone.

Jayne, a psychologist, always seemed to believe that the government, the rich, the white, the Republicans, you name the enemy of the week, was taking advantage of the poor, the uneducated, the minority. She belonged and contributed financially to several citizens' groups with names like *Rights for the People* and *American Coalition of Citizens for the Constitution*. Casey, however, didn't see life that simply; her job had a way of stripping away all those labels. She knew that death and injury, blame and innocence crossed all social and economic lines in the ER. It wasn't that she didn't believe injustices were committed, only that she didn't think being impoverished or uneducated automatically made you innocent.

But that was not a fight Casey wanted to pick this evening. "I was there the night Linda came into the emergency room. She was terrified of the boyfriend. There was no way she was faking that."

"Okay, so maybe he is guilty of assault. Uneducated men

working jobs that can't support their families sometimes strike out at those they love. Sometimes physically. Maybe he did hit her, even though you said yourself that she told the police at the time that he didn't." Her sister stacked the plates in the sink and began to rinse them off under the faucet. "That doesn't make him a killer."

Casey worked her jaw as she lined the glasses up in a row in the top rack of the dishwasher. "You can't imagine how scared she was the night she called me. The night she died."

"You said yourself that no one saw her boyfriend break in the back door. You know what kind of neighborhood that is. They have break-ins all the time."

Finding a meatball in the bottom of a plastic kid's cup, Casey dumped it into the garbage disposal and grabbed the sprayer. The faucet immediately cut off.

"Hey, hey."

"Sorry," Casey mumbled, releasing the handle on the sprayer and restoring her sister's stream of water. "But he had a knife just like the one used in the murder."

"From Wal-Mart, probably. There have to be thousands of them manufactured each year. Who knows, Joaquin may have one. That's not enough evidence to convict him. Thank God."

Casey groaned in frustration, wishing she could somehow make her sister understand. "I don't know how to explain how I know, but I'm telling you, this man is dangerous. He killed Linda and this was not a onetime thing. He has a history of beating his girlfriends, even before Linda came along. I'm telling you, he killed her and I'm afraid he could kill again."

Jayne glanced at her older sister. "A little overly dramatic, don't you think?"

"He stabbed her eleven times. I would say that's pretty dramatic."

"*Someone* stabbed her eleven times. You said yourself

that the initial fingerprinting on the knife came back inconclusive. The district attorney's office did the right thing in
nol prossing. They did the only fair thing. That poor guy had
already been in jail for months for something he really
might not have done."

Casey held Annabelle's blue cup in her hand staring at it.
She looked up at her sister. "Jayne, he threatened me."

Jayne was leaning down to load the plates in the dishwasher, but she straightened up to look at Casey. "The
boyfriend?"

"His name is Charles Gaitlin. He was released from custody as soon as the preliminary hearing was adjourned. He
came up to me in the parking lot as I was getting in my car."

"What did he say?" Jayne placed the two plates in the
dishwasher and reached for a dish towel.

"I don't know exactly. It all happened so quickly." Casey
dropped the kiddy cup into the dishwasher. "He was angry
that I had told the police what Linda said about him."

"Okay."

Jayne didn't sound all that concerned to Casey. In fact,
she sounded a little as if she didn't believe her. *Déjà vu.*

"He warned me that I'd better have eyes in the back of my
head."

Scowling, Jayne tossed the towel on the counter and
headed for the dining room again. "What's that supposed to
mean?"

"I don't know." Casey followed her. She threw up her hands
and let them fall. "You tell me. That he's going to . . . be
watching me? That he's going to do something to me? Get re-
venge for my talking to the police? When the case comes to
trial, I could be called as a witness. The assistant deputy attorney, Adam, said he would need my testimony."

"It's *Adam* now, is it?" Jayne questioned, eyebrows arched.
"You're on a first-name basis after one meeting?"

"Jayne, you're missing the point. I'm talking about Gaitlin." Casey hesitated. "Should I be concerned?"

Her sister thought for a moment as she walked around to the other side of the dining room table. "The boyfriend didn't say he was going to hurt you, right?"

"No, not exactly." Casey balled up dirty napkins. "But you had to be there. You had to see his body language. He acted as if he wanted to hit me. I've seen this kind of behavior dozens of times in the hospital. I know how abusive men posture."

Jayne covered Casey's hand on the table. Casey scrunched the dirty napkins.

"He probably *was* angry with you. When people speak out of anger, sometimes they say things they shouldn't. They don't mean what they say. He's been in jail all this time because he couldn't make bail. What if he didn't kill her? I don't know about you, but I'd be pretty angry if I'd been in jail for months for something I didn't do."

Casey met Jayne's gaze. Jayne had their father's eyes. Pale blue with thick, dark lashes. She didn't even have to wear mascara, her eyes were so pretty.

"I—" Casey sighed and slipped her hand out from under Jayne's, beginning to feel a little silly. Maybe Jayne was right, maybe she was making something out of nothing.

But Casey had seen the look in Charles's eyes. She had heard Linda's screams.

"You always side against me," Casey said softly. She gathered the napkins and carried them into the kitchen. The door behind her swung shut.

From the family room, the sounds of a cheering crowd filtered into the kitchen.

"Touchdown!" Joaquin shouted, clapping.

"Touchdown," little Chad echoed in his baby-boy voice.

Casey was dropping the napkins into the trash can under the sink when Jayne entered the kitchen.

"I'm not taking anyone's side, Casey."

"You're just saying I'm paranoid."

"I'm just saying you have nothing to worry about."

Chapter 4

"Sorry I didn't get here sooner." Adam walked to the side of the bed, rested both hands on the railing, and leaned over to brush his lips against Adam Thomas Preston Sr.'s cheek. The old man's skin was as dry and fragile as one of the autumn leaves that had crackled under Adam's foot as he had entered the nursing home.

"Been at the office. I know. Sunday." Adam pulled the single chair in the stark room up closer to the bed and picked up the briefcase he'd tossed on the floor on the way in. He sat down and removed a brown paper bag from inside. Tuna on whole wheat from the deli, and a diet green tea. He wasn't that hungry, but he knew he needed to eat. He often forgot to eat when time got away from him at the office.

"I really screwed up a case this week." Adam chatted as if his grandfather could understand him. The doctors said he was in a deep coma and probably couldn't hear anything, couldn't comprehend, but who knew for sure?

Adam unwrapped the sandwich. "Well, maybe I didn't really screw it up, but I wasn't as prepared as I should have been. I ended up having to nol pros." He took a bite of the sandwich, half expecting the old man to rise up and chastise him.

"Not the kind of results we're looking for, young man. Not the kind of results that make a state attorney general," he would have said.

His grandfather gave no response, though. The only sound in the room was the respirator, which made a whooshing sound as it pushed air into the old man's lungs.

"I went into a prelim hoping for a continuance while I waited on DNA evidence." The sandwich tasted like sawdust. He was still thoroughly disgusted with himself, even after two days. He knew this kind of thing happened when you were a lawyer; all his colleagues had said so. The good guys didn't always win in the first round; it happened to everyone. But it didn't often happen to Adam.

"Who am I kidding? I went into that prelim needing a continuance. It was Judge Trudeau. You know what a ballbuster she can be." He set the sandwich on the bag in his lap and unscrewed the lid on the bottle of iced tea. "You'd have been better prepared. You'd have gone in there with a plan B." He chewed the dry crust. Swallowed. "I didn't have a plan B."

A nurse stuck her head in the door. She was pretty. Late twenties. He knew from previous observation that she had a nice backside. But more importantly, she was kind to his grandfather. "Mr. Preston, we were beginning to wonder if you were going to make it tonight."

"I know. I'm late. I got tied up at the office." He set his dinner on the nightstand and got to his feet. Men no longer stood when women entered or exited a room, but it was one of those things his mother had taught him that he still did out of habit. "How's he been today?" He lifted his chin in the direction of his grandfather, lying flat on his back in the hospital bed. The old man's face was as pale as the crisp white sheets.

"Good." She entered the room and walked to the opposite side of the bed. "Blood pressure's been steady all day. He had a bit of a temp this morning, but he was ninety-eight-point-seven last vitals check." She smoothed the already smooth sheets, all the while keeping her eyes on Adam. She was flirting with him. She always did. A lot of women flirted with him.

"I'm so glad you're on the evening shift this week, Tiffany. You're a lot more thorough than Diane."

"Diane's okay." She lifted a slender shoulder. Even in her white pants and pale pink scrub top, he could tell she had a knockout figure. "She does her job."

"Yeah, but you're better." He flashed the Preston smile. In old photographs, from the days when his grandfather had been in the state senate, the old man had had the same smile.

Her hands lingered over her patient's chest, her flirty gaze locked with Adam's.

"Tiff, can you give me a hand with Mrs. Sorensen?" A nurse halted in the doorway. It was Maryanne, queen of the nightshift. "Mr. Preston." She smiled. "I told Tiff not to worry. That you'd be here."

Adam looked to Tiffany.

She backed away from the bed. "I wasn't really worried. I just . . . I was afraid maybe there was something wrong. A flat tire or something."

"Mrs. Sorensen is waiting," Maryanne reminded.

"Call if you need anything." Tiffany gave him a big smile and hurried out the door after her boss.

Adam sat down again. He took another bite of his sandwich. The respirator continued to whoosh.

"I wish you were awake; I really do." Adam swallowed the dry bite of sandwich and dug for a napkin in the bag. "I still think I can get a conviction, but I could sure use your help in pointing me in the right direction." He shook his head. "Because the bastard did it. I know he did."

His grandfather didn't respond, of course.

Adam finished his sandwich, balled up the wrapper, and stuffed it in the bag. He thought about Casey. He liked her. She was pretty. Smart. Good at what she did, apparently.

He'd let her down, too.

Someone touched Casey's arm and she woke immediately, her eyes flying open, her heart pounding. Would Linda ever let her sleep again? "Dad?"

Her father stood over her bed, his face only inches from hers. She could hear the dog snuffing. Pacing in the dark room.

"Dad, what's wrong?" She rose on her elbows and flipped on the light. Her father never got out of bed. Once she tucked him in and turned on The Weather Channel on his TV, she never heard a peep from him until the next morning.

He straightened slowly. "Someone's out there," he whispered.

"Someone's where?" She checked the bedside clock. It was twelve-sixteen. She'd been in bed only two hours. "Dad, what are you talking about?" She sat up and gave his flannel pajama sleeve a tug. "What are you and Frazier doing out of bed in the middle of the night?"

"Tornados reported near Galveston today," Ed said. "There should be more on that development in the next hour."

Casey slid her bare feet to the floor and stepped into her slippers. "Come on, Dad, let's go back to bed."

"You're not listening to me, Freckles. I told you there's someone out there." He shuffled toward the door.

Freckles was Jayne. He had called her that when Casey and Jayne were kids because Jayne had a sprinkle of freckles on the end of her cute little nose. Casey had no freckles. Casey had never been the pretty sister. Not the smart one, either, in her father's eyes.

"You saw someone where?" In the hall, she led him toward the stairs, surprised he had dared to climb them. When he first moved in, Casey had intended on putting him in the guest room on the second floor, but he had been afraid of the stairs and when she had coaxed him up them, he'd been wobbly on his feet. In the end, she'd given him and the dog the roomy master bedroom suite and she now slept upstairs, where there was a bathroom down the hall.

"Outside, Freckles." Standing at the top of the stairs, Ed studied her face. "Did you see him?"

"You weren't outside, were you?" She started down the steps in front of him. Frazier bounded ahead of them both. "Please tell me you weren't outside, Dad. I took Frazier out before I went to bed."

"Not outside." He halted on the stairs, looking down at her. "In the window."

"Someone was looking in the window?" Her heart gave a trip. It was totally irrational, yet the first person she thought of was Charles Gaitlin. "Was he an average-height man, Daddy, with thin hair brushed over like this?" She gestured.

Ed shuffled down the steps. "Hurricane season. Already up to Henry. Monitoring it off the coast of Cuba."

At the bottom of the staircase, she grabbed her father's shoulders, facing him, making him look at her. "Dad, this is important. Was there a man looking in the window? What did he look like?"

He thought for a minute, his eyes glazing over, then refocusing on her face again. "Been through a couple of hurricanes in my day. Remember Hazel?"

The dog trotted back and forth in the living room, waiting for them. He didn't seem nervous. Frazier was usually a good watchdog. He barked at delivery men, the garbage truck, and any child who strayed to the front lawn chasing a ball. He usually warned Casey when Ed was straying from the yard, as well.

Ed turned away from her and shuffled toward the short hall that led to his bedroom. Frazier took the lead. Casey followed them. The light was on beside the bed. The TV was on and the accordion shades were still lowered. She had closed them herself when they returned from Jayne's. There was no way her father could have seen anyone through the shades, and he didn't have the dexterity to raise them and then lower them himself without making a telltale mess.

"Sit down, Dad. Take off your slippers. You need to use the bathroom?"

"I'm not a child," Ed mumbled, kicking off his leather slippers and sliding his bony feet beneath the comforter.

She turned out the light.

"Dark," he said.

"Shhh. I just want to have a look."

She crossed the room, located the string on the nearest window shade, and raised the shade. The front lawn was well lit by the street lamp near her driveway. She could see as perfectly as if it were midday. All was quiet on the street. No lights shone in any of the neighbors' windows. The red maple she'd planted in the front yard bent and whipped in the wind.

"Dad. There's no one there." After checking to be sure her father hadn't been playing with the locks on the windows, she lowered the shade and walked back to his bedside.

He leaned in one direction and then the other as she cut in front of his TV. There was a commercial on for a prescription sleeping aid. She hoped she wasn't going to have to start medicating her father to get him to stay put at night.

She sat down on the edge of the bed beside him. Frazier had settled on the floor near the door. "You want me to turn the TV off?" she asked.

"Timer." He stared straight ahead at the TV.

He was right. She had set the timer to turn the TV off at one. He still had more than half an hour left to watch The Weather Channel.

"Well . . . goodnight." Casey left the bedroom, closing the door behind her. She checked all the doors and windows downstairs again, and satisfied, she climbed the stairs to her bedroom.

At the top of the staircase, she looked down, almost expecting to see someone behind her. The stairwell was empty, of course.

She stood there, staring down the stairwell. She didn't know what was wrong with her. She was always careful about doors and windows, about lights, but she wasn't paranoid anymore. Not like she had been once.

Ed listened to the sound of Casey's footsteps on the staircase. He rolled onto his side, his gaze drifting to the TV. The young girl doing the forecast was pregnant. He could see her big belly under her red shirt, even though the cameraman was trying to avoid a belly shot. But he just couldn't get Galveston in on the map without her belly. Tornados in Galveston.

Ed had once read a poem about Galveston. He wished he could remember it. It was silly, he knew, the idea of a poem about Galveston. But he hadn't imagined it. He had known several lines of it. They were there, jumbled up somewhere in his head.

Ed used to like his head, but not anymore. Not the way his thoughts flew around inside, half the time making no sense. Not to his daughters, not even to him. It was the disease, Freckles said. He didn't care what it was; he didn't like it.

This wasn't how Ed had imagined getting old would be. He had thought he would retire and live on a golf course in Palm Beach or somewhere warm like that with his wife. A couple of rounds of golf a week. Playing cards with friends on Wednesday nights. He hadn't expected to be widowed and living with his daughter. Now his favorite pastime was watching TV. His only friend was a dog. Not that he and Frazier weren't good friends—it just wasn't the same.

And Frazier didn't play cards.

The weather girl on TV pointed to Oklahoma. At least Ed thought it was Oklahoma. His geography wasn't as good as it had once been.

He rolled onto his back and stared at the ceiling. Had he really seen someone outside or had it been his imagination?

No, it wasn't his imagination. He'd been there. He had watched Ed. Ed had watched him. He had seemed vaguely familiar to Ed.

But maybe the man wasn't really watching Ed through the blinds. Maybe the man was watching The Weather Channel.

Casey wasn't entirely surprised by Adam's call Monday. He said he wanted to let her know that he was serious about the Gaitlin case. That it was not over and that his office would be in touch with her concerning her statement. They chatted for five minutes about nothing in particular. She asked how his grandfather was doing. He asked about her dad.

When a conference call came in, Adam had to excuse himself. He didn't ask her out, but she had a feeling that the next time he called—and she knew there would be a next time— he'd offer that cup of coffee or dinner and she'd accept.

Nine months previously, after dating for two years, Casey had broken up with the man she had thought was *the one.* Apparently, his other girlfriend had also thought she was *the one.* Since then, she'd been too busy to date, or so she told herself.

But as she hung up from her conversation with Adam, a smile played on her lips. The idea of going out with Adam appealed to her. He was smart and warm, and she suspected he could be a lot of fun. An attorney looking toward politics, he was just the kind of man her father had always thought she should be dating. Ed would like Adam. Or at least the idea of Adam.

Casey was still smiling when she got in line at the hospital cafeteria. Tray in hand, she leaned over the counter, checking out the soups for the day. "Chicken noodle soup or vegetarian chili. What do you recommend, Sarge?" she asked the middle-aged gentleman in the paper hat behind the counter stirring the soup with a ladle.

"Definitely the chili," someone behind her said.

She turned to see a nice-looking guy about her age. He was wearing a green corduroy blazer and he needed a haircut. He reminded her of a slightly older version of Matthew McConaughey. Definitely cute.

"The chili?" she asked.

"Absolutely. Had it yesterday. Homemade. Excellent. The chicken noodle here?" He frowned. "Straight out of a can. Enough MSG in it to kill you."

She turned back to Sarge. "I'm thinking the chili. You have whole-wheat crackers?"

"Just for you, darlin'." The black gentleman began to ladle a healthy portion of the chili into a plastic bowl.

"Hey, what about me, Sarge?" McConaughey moved up beside Casey. "I asked for whole-wheat crackers yesterday and you said you didn't have any."

"Yer not as pretty as Miss McDaniel here." He winked at Casey.

Casey laughed as she accepted the bowl, placed it on her tray, and scooped up the handful of crackers in cellophane Sarge had dropped on the counter.

Casey paid for her soup and a bottle of water. At the condiments bar, the McConaughey look-alike set his tray down next to hers and grabbed a couple of napkins. "I can't believe Sarge said you were better looking than I am," he announced. "I mean, he's right. You are." He glanced at her. "But isn't that prejudice of the worst kind? I'm thinking my rights have been violated here."

She smiled, grabbed several packets of crackers and dropped them on his tray. "There you go, wrong righted."

"Hey, thanks." He had a nice smile.

"You're welcome." She picked up her tray and scanned the room. It was her lucky day; her favorite table was unoccupied. She always had to fight the orthopedic docs for it.

He followed her across the noisy cafeteria. "You eating alone?"

"Uh-huh." She took a table next to the window. Directly below was a parking lot, but beyond it was a tree line. Sometimes she ate lunch in her office, but sometimes, especially in the winter, she liked to sit here and look out over the woods. Most people thought a forest in winter was ugly, but she liked the look of the bare branches and flattened underbrush. She liked the idea of the promise of spring.

"You mind if I join you?"

She lifted one shoulder. "Um . . . sure." She indicated the empty chair across from her.

It had been longer than she could remember since someone had hit on her, and now twice in a week? Her friend Marcy, who worked in hospital administration, said it was the vibes Casey sent out that made her seem unavailable. Her vibes seemed to be working for Mr. McConaughey.

"Casey McDaniel." She offered her hand over the bowls of chili as he sat down.

"Lincoln Tyndall. Nice to meet you."

She shook his hand. "Lincoln, wow, that's an interesting name."

"Yeah, I know, but my middle name is worse. My grandmother named me."

"No, I like it." She nodded thoughtfully, opening her water bottle. "It's nice. Different, but not too strange, you know what I mean?"

He opened a cellophane package and began to crumble the crackers onto his chili.

"My dad likes to do that," she remarked, pointing with her spoon. "Well, he used to."

He must have picked up on her wistful tone because he said, "I'm sorry. Is your dad ill? I saw your name badge and just assumed you worked here."

"My dad is ill"—she put down the water bottle and unwrapped her plastic spoon—"but he's not in the hospital. I do work here."

He took a bite of chili, crunching the crackers. "I'm visiting my grandmother. She broke her hip. She was trying to unload a hundred-pound bag of goat food for my grandfather, who is on crutches, because *he* broke his ankle in the spring and is still healing from it."

"Oh, my." Casey pushed a spoon of chili into her mouth, trying not to laugh.

"It's okay," Lincoln assured her. "It's pretty funny when you think about it. I laughed, too, when my grandfather called me from the ambulance."

"Is she going to be all right?"

"She's going to be fine." He put his spoon down and wiped his mouth with the napkin from his lap. "She's just really pissed right now because her doctor says she can't go home yet. He told her she had to go to a rehab facility, and she thought he was suggesting she had a drug or an alcohol problem. She thought he wanted to send her to a rehab facility like the kind the Hollywood stars are always checking into." He grabbed his drink. "Elsa's a big E! Television fan."

Casey chuckled and took another bite of chili. "You're right. It's good."

"Told you." He picked up his spoon again. "So . . . what do you do? You a doctor?"

"I'm the victims' rights advocate."

"Wow. I hadn't even realized SCH had one. How progressive of them. What exactly do you do?"

For the next forty-five minutes Casey and Lincoln talked. They bounced all around, touching on subjects ranging from child abuse to what kind of goats produced the best milk. Before Casey realized it, her lunch hour was over, and if she didn't hurry she was going to be late to a staff meeting.

"Gosh, I have to run," she said, jumping up. "I'm going to be late to a meeting I can't be late to." She started to clean up her tray, but he rose, waving her away.

"Let me take care of this. You go."

She took a step back, slipping her purse onto her shoulder. She'd had such a nice conversation with him that she hated to leave. "It was nice to talk to you, Lincoln. I hope your grandmother is feeling better."

"It was nice talking to you, too." He set the tray down again, turning to her. "And thanks. I'm sure she'll be fine."

Casey started to turn away, beginning to feel awkward. "Guess maybe I'll see you again, sometime. Sounds like your grandparents are here a lot."

"Hey, wait." He reached into his corduroy suit jacket and produced a business card. "I'm really clumsy with this whole asking-women-out-on-dates thing," he confessed. "But if you'd like to have lunch again. Or dinner, or coffee." He chuckled. "Anyway, here's my card. My phone number's there."

She took it.

"I hope you don't mind me not asking for your number. I . . . do it this way so I don't have to suffer through that embarrassing moment when I call a woman to ask her on a date and it's the Jiffy Lube number, or it *is* her number and she says no, or she tells me to call back and I do and then she accuses me of stalking her."

Casey laughed. He was funny. She liked funny. "Thanks." She waved the card. "I really do have to go."

She hurried out of the busy cafeteria and down a hall, waiting until she was out of his sight to look at the plain white business card. They'd been so busy talking about goat food and soy products that she had never gotten a chance to ask him what he did for a living. She guessed architect . . . or maybe graphic designer. Something creative. She guessed wrong.

He was an attorney. The second one to hit on her in the same week.

Casey walked into her meeting smiling.

Chapter 5

Maury lay on his back on the bottom bunk, his arms tucked behind his head, and stared up at the way the mattress above him poked through the metal bedsprings. The wire frame produced perfect little quilted puffs of blue ticking. Like little square pillows. Or diamond pillows if he shifted his focus. The discovery delighted him. Patterns, textures delighted Maury.

Then his roommate moved and the pattern was, at once, altered. Ruined really, because if TexMex rolled back into exactly the same position, he would never be able to distribute his weight in precisely the same way. The mattress patterns could never be reproduced perfectly. Never. The magic was gone forever.

Maury wondered what blood would do to the pattern.

Annoyed, he rolled over onto his side to study the pale green cinder-block wall of his jail cell. It was a decent pattern, but nowhere near as interesting as the mattress had been.

Closing his eyes, Maury listened to the sounds of the pod. Patterns, he had learned, could be audible as well as visual. Sounds were not as satisfying as images, but not so worthless as to be totally dismissed, either. He listened to the voices . . . of inmates, of guards. Some were low voices, some higher in pitch. Maury could identify the voice of CO Jameson at once. She was a woman. And even though she was pretty butch, her voice was still higher than the voices of her male counterparts.

Maury heard the squeak, squeak, squeak of Corporal Tatter's shoes. Names being called out. Mail call didn't interest him. He had no girlfriend to write to him. No parents. Just a sister who never wrote or came to visit. Her punishment for him getting arrested and sent to jail.

Maury never got mail except from his attorney, and he had nothing to say. Maury would be out of Sussex Correctional in less than four months, and out of this cell within days. He was moving up to work release and a taste of freedom just as soon as there was a place for him. At least semi-freedom. He had no interest in mail.

There were other sounds in the pod. More-rhythmic sounds. Old Man Snort snoring. The guy in the end cell jacking off. The flip, flip, flip of the guy in the next cell over playing solitaire. They were nice, rhythmic noises, noises that drew steady patterns, but just not exciting. Just not as good as the mattress pillows had been.

"Mail call!" Corporal Tatter— Bambi, other COs called him—was an ugly black man with splotches all over his face from a burn suffered as a child. Maury hated ugly, uneven patterns and he hated the name Bambi. The nickname was completely inappropriate. Bambi had had such perfect spots. The Disney animators had done an incredible job, especially for having drawn the character so many years ago, what with all the advances that must have taken place in animation over the years.

"Maurice Pinkerton," Bambi read aloud in a bass voice.
Bambi always did that. He read the name exactly as it was

printed on the mail. He could never just call you by your name. Better yet, pitch the delivery through the cell bars not speaking at all. But Bambi took his mail room job seriously.

"Maurice Pinkerton," Bambi repeated when Maury didn't respond.

Maury contemplated just lying there, eyes closed, pretending he was asleep so he wouldn't have to look at Bambi and his ugly spots. But Maury knew from experience that that was only a waste of time. It was only putting off the inevitable. If Maury didn't take the envelope today, Bambi would just bring it back tomorrow.

"Maur—"

"All right! Christ a'mighty! I'm coming." Maury rose from his bunk. He only had to take three steps to walk out of his open cell door. He held out his hand.

Bambi, face stern, passed Maury an envelope.

Maury was going to toss the envelope on the bed unopened and lie down again. See what he could find in TexMex's mattress again.

But there was something about the envelope in Maury's hand that gave him pause. Something about the texture of paper that tapped his attention. He flipped the envelope over and checked the return address. It was a post office box in Millsboro.

Not from his public defender. Definitely not.

Bambi walked away, leaving Maury to stare at the envelope in his hand. It had been opened across the top with a letter opener. Everything sent into the prison had to be opened by officers in the mail room. But he still couldn't help but be excited by the turn of events. Intrigued. The envelope was clearly addressed to Maury in nondescript print, written with a black Sharpie. His personal SBI number and housing unit were printed plainly. This was no mix-up. The letter was for him.

Maury walked back into his cell and sat down on the edge of his bed, carefully placing the envelope across his prison-white knees. Inside, they wore prison whites day in and day out. It was one of the reasons he was looking forward to work release. In work release, he'd get a uniform most likely. It just depended on what kind of job he got. He was lucky enough to have a skill, his counselor had said. So being an auto mechanic came in handy in ways Maury would never have imagined.

He stared at the envelope in his lap wondering what could possibly be inside. He lifted the envelope to the light to get a better look. It was a generic white envelope that could have been purchased by anyone. Sent by anyone. It was light; he doubted photographs were enclosed. Just a single sheet of paper, he guessed. He closed his eyes and sniffed the envelope. No hint there of where it might have come from.

He wondered for a moment if maybe the letter had come from his old girlfriend Sheila. But last he heard, she was in Baylor Women's Correctional up in Wilmington doing eight to ten for armed robbery. Besides, she hated his guts. She wouldn't send him a letter. A letter bomb, possibly, but not a plain old letter.

TexMex rolled over on the top bunk and Maury was reminded that he wasn't alone. You were never alone in prison.

Maury stretched out on his back on his bunk and laid the envelope across his chest. He watched it rise and fall as he inhaled and exhaled in perfect rhythm. He would save the letter until later to read. He would savor the anticipation of seeing who had sent him the letter.

Casey toyed with the business card on her desk. She pushed it around with her index finger. Flipped it over so she could see Lincoln's name. She was just flipping it back again when Marcy walked into her office.

"So, are you going to call him or not?"

Casey grabbed up the business card and dropped it into the top desk drawer, then closed it soundly. "I don't know." She grimaced. "The idea of calling a guy, asking him on a date—"

"Puh-lease." Marcy rolled her eyes. She was recently divorced but had started dating the moment her ex had walked out on her and their three-year-old son. In less than a year, Marcy had become *the* expert on dating, or at least the expert on the administrative floor of the hospital. "What happened to being a modern woman? You can karate chop a guy in the crotch for being flirtatious in an elevator, but you can't call a guy on the phone and ask him out? *After* he gave you his number?"

"I don't teach women to karate chop guys in elevators. You should come to one of my self-defense classes." Casey frowned at her friend, annoyed that she was making fun of her. "There's not even such a thing as a karate chop."

Marcy stood in the doorway, hand on her hip, giving Casey one of her looks. Marcy was tall, slender and always wore short skirts to work. She had great highlights in her hair. Casey had been thinking about getting highlights.

"So maybe I'll call him."

"Either you call him or I'm calling him." Marcy walked out the door.

"You're not calling to make a date for me," Casey called after her.

"The date won't be for you," Marcy hollered back.

Casey opened the drawer and pulled the card out again. She studied the phone number. It was just Lincoln's office number. She could leave a message. Get him to call her back. Chewing on a piece of nail cuticle hanging off her little finger, she set the card down.

She really liked Lincoln. She wanted to go out with him. But this was so hard—putting herself out there like that. And what if Adam called? What if he called and wanted to ask her out this weekend? Would that make her some kind of slut or something, going out with two different men on the same weekend?

Casey groaned, realizing what a stupid thought that was. She wasn't intending on having sex with either of them. At least not anytime soon. She just wanted . . . She wanted to go out on a real date. She wanted to get away from this office, from her father. She wanted to feel pretty again.

So she would call Lincoln.

She picked up the card to look at it again and realized his e-mail was also on the card.

She'd e-mail him. That was even a better idea. That way, if he had changed his mind and didn't want to go out with her, it wouldn't be so awkward for him—or her.

Casey opened the e-mail program on her computer and typed a couple of short lines. She asked him if he was available tomorrow night, Friday, and then shot the note off before she had a chance to chicken out and not send it. Or revise it to death.

For the next hour, she busied herself returning phone calls to clients. She talked to two different state police officers concerning automobile accident victims who had come into the ER in the last week, one of whom had died. Then she made a call to a local funeral home for another client and made arrangements for the family to drop off the dead man's suit. A teenager killed in a hit-and-run. Another hard case. The family had had to go out and buy a suit for their dead fifteen-year-old son.

Casey forced herself to wait an hour before she checked her e-mail, and even as she was opening it, she told herself not to worry if Lincoln didn't answer right away. Most people checked their e-mail only once or twice a day. He could be in court. He could be downstairs with his grandmother, or at the nursing home she was being transferred to. Casey might not even hear from him until tomorrow . . . or later. And he might already have plans since it took her all week to get up the nerve to contact him. And should she really leave her father all day tomorrow and then all evening tomorrow night?

But there it was, the second piece of new mail in her mailbox, posted only eighteen minutes after she'd e-mailed him. *RE: Goat chow and dinner*

Lincoln said he'd hoped she would contact him. He suggested a nice restaurant in Rehoboth Beach for dinner and offered to pick her up, or, if she preferred, he would meet her there. That way if she was bored or he creeped her out in some way, he said, she'd be able to make a fast getaway.

She e-mailed him back, telling him she would meet him there at seven . . . just in case he creeped her out.

"I think I'm about ready to go, Dad." Casey walked into the living room, running some smoothing gel through her red-blond hair. With the colder weather, it easily got staticky and flyaway. She'd been trying to grow it out long enough to wear a ponytail. She hadn't had long hair since she was sixteen.

"You sure you're going to be okay here without me for a few hours?" She stood at the end of the couch.

He was watching a Discovery Channel show on the Valley of the Kings. Frazier was sitting contentedly at his feet chewing on a stuffed dog toy that looked like a mallard duck. It squawked every time he bit it.

Her flyaway hair tackled, Casey dropped her arms nervously to her sides. *Stop fussing with it,* she chided herself. *Stop fussing. Lincoln already said he thinks you're attractive.*

"Dad? Can you look at me?"

Her father stared straight ahead. Omar Sharif continued his monologue as the miles of desert rolled across the TV screen. The dog toy continued to squawk.

She picked up the remote control and turned down the volume. "Dad?"

"You know the Valley of the Kings is nowhere near the pyramids or the Sphinx?" he said. "I didn't realize how far apart geographically they are. I always wanted to go to Egypt, never made it there, Lorraine and I."

Casey forced a smile, but her throat tightened. Somehow, her father's illness seemed even harder to bear when he was lucid like this. Sometimes it lasted an hour or so, sometimes less. But the new medication for Alzheimer's patients he had just started taking might improve his memory. His doctor was hopeful. Casey was hopeful.

Not that she and her father had ever had a wonderful relationship or anything. Casey's parents had been very career oriented. Pleasant, but removed from their daughters' lives. In her parents' eyes, it was Lorraine's role to provide the finances for the family by means of her inheritance, and Ed, the intellectual stimulation. Beyond that, it had been up to their daughters to find their own way in the world. There had never been tenderness between Casey and Jayne and their parents. Emotion was rarely shown in their home, discussed even less frequently.

But Ed had been a good man. He had contributed to the education of thousands of young, impressionable students over the years, including his own children. It just hurt Casey to know that his time had passed and that he would never be able to teach his grandchildren. He might not even live to see his grandchildren reach school age.

"I suppose I never really thought about how far apart the pyramids in Cairo are from the Valley of the Kings." She sat down on the edge of the couch. She had changed three times, settling on a pair of brown slacks and a pale blue sweater that made her hazel eyes appear bluer. "But the pyramids are actually the burial site of only a couple of kings, right?" she probed. The doctor had said it was important to stimulate her father's brain, to take advantage of the times when he *was* cognizant.

"For five hundred years, from the sixteenth to the eleventh century B.C., tombs were constructed in the Valley of the Kings for kings and noblemen." Ed retrieved the remote from her hand. "King Tutankhamen's tomb being the most famous, of course."

When her father spoke like this, he sounded just like the Professor McDaniel with whom students had come most nights of the week to converse. Not only had her father been well versed in English literature, but numerous other subjects, as well. He had always been a climatology and geology buff, which might be what had led him to his recent interest in meteorology.

"We saw relics from Tut's tomb at the Franklin Institute. Do you remember, Dad? Jayne and I took you."

Her father stared at the TV screen. It was a commercial for another Discovery Channel show, one where real autopsies were shown.

"Dad, do you remember going to the museum and seeing things from Tut's tomb?" she asked again. "There were stone canopic jars and his crook and flail and . . . and you were fascinated by the chair the king sat in as a child."

He repeatedly pushed a button on the remote, changing the channels.

"Dad, the show you're watching will be back on in just a second. Valley of the Kings."

He set his jaw, changing channels faster. The channel numbers blinked on the upper-right-hand corner of the screen. The numbers were decreasing rapidly.

She knew where he was headed.

She rose from the chair and reached for the cordless phone on the end table. "I'm going out for a while with a friend. If you need me, you just push the memory button and the number one, right? Jayne is *Memory Two*. Now if there's a real emergency like a fire or—"

He turned up the volume on the TV until the voice of the weather girl drowned out Casey's.

"Dad, if there's a fire, you need to get out of the house," she said loudly above the prediction for heavy rains in the Dallas–Fort Worth area. "You need to get out of the house, take the phone with you and dial nine-one-one or go to a neighbor's, right?"

"Local on the 8s" began. The local forecast flashed on the screen, accompanied by loud "on hold" music.

She set the phone down beside him on the couch. "You sure you don't want to go to Jayne's? I could drop you off on the way to dinner."

He ignored her, but a response really wasn't necessary. She already knew the answer. He didn't want to go to Jayne's. He didn't like going there at all, and certainly not in the evening. Not when the house was in turmoil with Jayne and Joaquin coming in from work, Chad fussing for his dinner, and the rushing around to get Annabelle off to her gymnastics class or her ballet class or the Children and Art class that Jayne insisted every child needed to attend by the age of five. Casey didn't blame her father for not want-ing to go to Jayne's; she avoided weeknights there too.

"Okay, well. You know how to call me on my cell. If you have any problems, any questions . . ." She rose off the couch. "I left a bag of pretzels on the counter and there's root beer in the fridge for you. Dog biscuits in the cookie jar for Frazier." She looked down at her dad.

He pointed at the TV with the remote. "Going to be windy Monday."

She nodded. "See you later, Dad. I won't be late, but if you get tired, go to bed. I'll lock up behind me." She wanted to touch him, to kiss the top of his gray head, something, but sometimes physical contact agitated him. She didn't want to leave him agitated.

"See you when I get home."

Casey's mood lightened as she drove east toward the coast. She found a parking space on the same block in Re-hoboth Beach as the restaurant and walked in at seven on the nose. Lincoln was already waiting for her in the bar.

"Casey." He waved, climbing down off a stool. "You came."

She laughed, hooking her purse on the brass hook under the bar and taking the stool beside him. "Of course I came. I'm the one who asked you out, remember?" She smiled, pretty proud of herself. "Well, I guess *technically* you asked me to ask you out, but . . ."

He chuckled with her. "A drink?"

He was wearing a corduroy suit jacket again, this one moss green. Beneath it, a navy sweater and khakis. He smelled freshly showered and completely delicious.

She pointed to his wineglass. "What are you having?"

He looked at his glass. "Um . . . red. Shiraz." He glanced at her. "I told you I wasn't good at this. Shiraz. Definitely."

"Sounds good."

He ordered her drink and they waited in awkward silence for it. When the young female bartender brought it, Casey and Lincoln raised their glasses in toast.

"*Cin cin,*" he said.

She smiled over the rim of her glass.

"It's Italian." He sipped his wine, lifting one shoulder in a shrug. "I went to Italy this summer. I'm not that great with languages. It's about the only phrase I came home with."

"Italy? I've been dying to go."

They talked for half an hour in the bar, ordering a second glass of wine, and then were shown to a table. She learned that he was divorced, that he had no children, and that he called his ex-wife, also an attorney, Skitzy-Witzy. Apparently he had called her that even before they were divorced. She learned that he *did* eat raw oysters, which was a definite plus for him, but that he didn't like Brussels sprouts, not even fresh out of the garden.

As the waiter walked away with their appetizer and entrée order, Casey checked her cell phone. She was afraid the bar had been so loud that she might have missed it ringing. Which really was foolish because her father never called her.

"Everything okay?" Lincoln asked.

The waiter had seated them at a table for two. It was covered with a white cloth. Votive candles sparkled in funky glass vases. Seated across from him in such an intimate space, Casey couldn't avoid Lincoln's handsome face.

"Everything's fine." She dropped her phone into her bag. "I just wanted to make sure my dad hadn't called. He insists he's fine home alone. His doctor says he still needs to feel a little bit of independence, but I worry about him. My sister says I'm not happy unless I'm worrying about—" She halted. "I'm sorry. I'm rambling. I'm rambling about my crazy dad and my crazy life."

"Actually, I'm kind of relieved to know that I'm not the only person with a crazy life." He leaned forward. "It's got to be hard dealing with your dad. How advanced is the Alzheimer's?"

"He's somewhere between moderate decline and moderately severe decline, which means—" She cut herself off. "You don't want to hear this."

"You had to hear about my schizo ex-wife." He leaned back in his chair. "I want to hear about your dad."

She exhaled. Actually, it felt good to talk to someone about her problems. She spent so much time dealing with other people's, which usually were far worse than hers, that she felt as if she was whining whenever she said anything. "It means he's moving from early to midstage." She reached for her wine, paused, and looked up at Lincoln. "Honestly, he's in midstage. The signs are all there; I'm just trying to ignore them. He loses track of time, the day, the week, even the month. He has trouble doing even simple math. But he's on a new—"

Casey's phone rang, stopping her in midsentence. The ring tone indicated the call was coming from her house. "I'm sorry. Excuse me." She fumbled in her bag for the phone, located it, and hit the receive button. "Dad? Dad, what's wrong?"

"Freckles?" Her father's voice was uncertain.

"Yes, Daddy, it's Casey." She covered her other ear with her hand so she could hear him in the noisy restaurant. "Is something wrong?"

"He's back."

"Who's back?"

"Richard Nixon."

Chapter 6

"I'm so sorry about this." Casey hurried down the side-walk toward her car.

"Stop apologizing." Lincoln walked beside her, helping her into her wool coat.

She reached her car and hit the remote on her key ring. The car's door locks clicked open. "You should go back in. Have your dinner."

"Yeah. I'll have my veal and your salmon while you chat with Richard Nixon, raised from the grave."

"I know it sounds ridiculous. I know no one is there, but he sounded scared. I have to go home." She opened her door before he could open it for her.

She put her hand to her forehead, feeling so bad for run-ning out on Lincoln like this. She really *was* having a good time. She didn't want to go, but she had to. She had contem-plated calling Jayne, but her sister rarely answered her phone and was slow calling back. Besides, if their father was really upset, Jayne wouldn't be able to calm him down. Only Casey was able to do that.

"At least let me pay for the meal," Casey told Lincoln. "I really am sorry."

"Get in the car," he ordered. "Are you sure we shouldn't call the police?"

She climbed into the driver's side, looking up at him, her hand on the door handle. "And tell them that Richard Nixon is in my backyard? Last week Dad swore there were sheep in his shower stall. When I showed him there weren't any sheep, he said I had hidden them in another room to make a fool out of him."

"At least let me follow you home. If there *is* someone poking around your house, *you* shouldn't be verifying the fact."

"That isn't necessary." She slid the key into the ignition.

"What if it *is* Richard Nixon? I'd like to meet him."

She hesitated. She was careful about giving out her home address and phone number because she liked to practice what she preached. Single women were too free with that information. But she had his personal information, even his office number and partners' names, and this was really a second date. Lincoln didn't seem like the type to stalk an ex-girlfriend.

"Okay?" he asked, taking her hesitation as a maybe.

"Okay," she agreed. "I'm going to take Route One north, then four-oh-four west. I live in Long Meadow Run."

"I got it. I'm parked half a block behind you. I left my credit card with the maître d'. I'll grab it and be right behind you. You go." He closed her door.

Casey sat for a second getting herself together and then started the car.

She pulled into her driveway twenty minutes later. Having caught up with her, Lincoln pulled in behind her in a bright blue Mini Cooper. She raised the garage door, drove into the garage, but left the door up for him. She used her keys to let herself into the laundry room. An entire drying rack of panties and bras caught her attention as she hurried through the room with Lincoln right behind her.

He politely ignored the Victoria's Secret fall collection.

"Dad?"

Frazier gave a bark of greeting and barreled into the hall, meeting Casey before she got to the living room. The Weather Channel was on so loud it was a miracle the dog even heard her.

"Dad!"

Frazier barked and danced a side-step, excited they had a visitor.

Casey found her father sitting on the couch eating from a bag of pretzels. He had two opened cans of soda on the end table. When she picked up the remote and lowered the volume, he glanced up at her as if surprised to see her.

"Dad"—she sat down on the couch beside him—"where did you see the man?"

"What man?" Ed glanced at Lincoln, who stood at the edge of the living room rug. Frazier circled Lincoln, sniffing him. "Him? I've never seen him in my life." He looked back at the TV.

Casey glanced at Lincoln, an apologetic look on her face.

He smiled and put his hand out to Frazier. The dog came to him, tail wagging and tongue lolling.

Casey returned her attention to her father, knowing the big boxer wouldn't harm Lincoln. The dog was all muscle and bark and brawn, but he was sweet as a kitten. "Dad, you called me on my cell phone and said that there was a man looking through the French doors in the dining room." She hesitated. "You said Richard Nixon was watching you."

Ed turned back to her, crunching on a pretzel as he contemplated her words.

Casey waited.

"Yeah," Ed agreed, expressing none of the fear Casey had

heard in his voice half an hour ago. "He was there, but now he's gone. Frazier growled at him and he ran away." His gaze wandered back to the TV. "I thought he was dead," he mused.

Sighing, Casey got up, leaving the remote on the couch. This conversation was going to be pointless. They usually were, and she saw no reason to further embarrass herself or her father in front of Lincoln. "I really am sorry," she told Lincoln.

"Look, you apologize once more and there's no way I'm asking you out again," he warned. "So how about I take a walk around outside the house, make sure everything looks okay, and then we whip up something for dinner, because I'm starving. Unless, of course, you want me to go." He pointed to the door. "I can leave if you want me to."

"No. No, please stay." She grabbed his arm, then shyly released him. "I've got some chicken breasts and bok choy. You like stir-fry?"

"Love it. As long as there's no Brussels sprouts involved. Got a flashlight?"

"Sure." She walked back to the kitchen and took a red heavy-duty flashlight from a drawer. She handed it to Lincoln and followed him to the laundry room.

"Lock the door behind me."

She looked up at him.

"Just to be safe. I'll knock when I come back."

She opened the door to the garage. "You sure you'll be okay? You want . . . some kind of weapon or something?"

"What? You mean like a gun?"

She frowned. "I don't have a gun."

"Good. Because I hate handguns. I think they should be outlawed. I usually vote Democrat. I wouldn't have voted for Nixon even if I'd been old enough to vote. I hope that's not a problem."

She grinned. "Not a problem. My sister's a Democrat. I still speak to her."

He leaned over and gave her a quick kiss. His mouth was pleasantly firm. He was gone before it registered in her mind what he'd done.

Casey locked the door, tossed her clean undergarments in the dryer to hide them, and went to the kitchen to see what she could dig up for dinner. By the time Lincoln knocked on the back door, she was busy slicing chicken breasts.

"Nothing looks disturbed. Windows and doors are all secure." He followed her into the kitchen and put the flashlight back in the drawer. "You think he really saw someone?" He leaned on the counter and popped a chunk of carrot from the cutting board into his mouth.

"Hard to say." She dropped the chicken into the wok and it sizzled. "Probably not. As I said, he gets confused." She squeezed a garlic press over the chicken, and the kitchen filled at once with the pungent, slightly sweet aroma of garlic and chicken.

"Mmm." Lincoln leaned over the stove inhaling. "Smells great. Need help?"

"Nah. I've got it. No recipe. I'm being creative." She waved a wooden spoon.

"You mind if I talk to your dad? I won't scare him or anything, will I?"

"No, it's fine. Go ahead. Just don't be offended if he's nonresponsive. Sometimes he likes to talk, sometimes he doesn't."

"Not a problem."

Lincoln went into the living room and Casey started a pot of quick-cooking brown rice. For an impromptu dinner, she thought the meal was coming together pretty well. She'd found a decent assortment of vegetables in the bin in the bottom of the refrigerator. As she chopped, she listened to the timbre of Lincoln's voice. He was doing most of the talking. She couldn't hear exactly what he was saying because the TV was so loud, but occasionally she could hear her father respond.

At one point, Casey walked into the living room to ask Lincoln if he liked his stir-fry spicy. She didn't want to scare him off with hot pepper flakes the first time she cooked for him. She found him and her father sitting side by side on the couch, both crunching on pretzels as they watched a ski report for Vail.

Lincoln told her he loved spicy and went back to watching the ski report. Casey had to pry him away from The Weather Channel twenty minutes later. They had a nice meal at the dining room table, though her father declined to join them. He had eaten earlier and refused to leave the couch. Lincoln did convince him to check out a special on volcanos on a different channel.

In the kitchen, as Lincoln and Casey washed the dishes, they chatted. They talked about her job, and he seemed impressed by all the community outreach the hospital was doing for women. She found out that he lived on his grandparents' property in a restored farmhouse and that his house was environmentally green. He laughed when she admitted that she didn't know what all that entailed, but that she tried to recycle.

Once the kitchen was clean, Casey wasn't exactly sure what to do with Lincoln. Her father was still watching TV. She didn't want to invite Lincoln in there—the TV was too loud for them to talk. She could ask her father to go to bed, but that process could sometimes be long and tedious.

Casey ended up not having to decide what they should do, because after starting the dishwasher, Lincoln walked into the living room and told her father good night. Ed didn't respond, but Frazier escorted Lincoln to the door.

Chuckling as they stepped out onto the front porch, Casey ordered the dog back into the living room. Then she stood in front of the door hugging herself for warmth.

"Thanks," Lincoln said. "For dinner. For the evening."

She started to say something but he held up his hand, silencing her. "You think I'm kidding. Don't apologize again. I want to ask you out again, but I'm a man of convictions."

She exhaled. "Thank you," she whispered. He was standing less than an arm's length from her and he moved a little closer.

"This is the dating part I'm really not good at. Do I kiss her? If I do, does she think I'm moving too fast?" he mused aloud. "If I don't, does she think I don't like her?"

Casey was shivering with cold. She moved closer to him, smoothing the corduroy of his jacket lapel. "In this case, you kiss her because she wants to kiss you," she said softly, looking into his blue eyes, "but she's too chicken to make the first move."

He took her in his arms and kissed her lightly. When her mouth lingered over his, he went with his gut feeling and kissed her harder. His gut had been right. Another kiss and Lincoln stepped back. Casey's mouth was tingling. Her whole body was tingling.

"Can I call you tomorrow?" he asked as he cut across the porch.

"You'd better."

He walked down the steps backward. "Go inside and lock the door behind you. I'm not going until I know you're safe inside."

Casey went into the house and locked the door. From behind the sheers in the living room windows, she watched Lincoln back out of her driveway.

* * *

Angel sat on the couch in front of the TV. Everything was fine, but then all of a sudden, Charlie got up, went into the bedroom, and came out with his jacket on. "Where you think yer goin'?" she asked suspiciously.

"What's it to you?" Charlie shoved his wallet into his back pocket.

"Come on, baby." She sat on her knees on the couch facing him. "I'm just askin'."

"It's none of your damned business!"

She glanced down the hall. Her little boy's door was shut, but he'd screamed on and off for an hour when she'd put him to bed. She didn't want him up again tonight. "You don't have to holler like that! You're gonna wake up Buddy."

He balled up an empty package and threw it at her. "Goin' out for cigarettes."

"You already went out for cigarettes."

He yanked open the door, and sounds spilled into the living room. Kit, next door, and her old man arguing. Somebody's baby crying. Kit's dog barking. They weren't allowed to have pets, but people had them anyway. Angel lived in public housing. The place was small and loud and ratty, but it was all she could afford, working at the flea market with her sister.

"Come on, Charlie. Come sit next to me." Angel patted the lumpy place beside her on the plaid couch. The couch was new—well, new to her. She and her best friend, Shonda, had borrowed a truck, and gone all through Georgetown the night before garbage pickup. It was amazing all the good stuff people put out on their sidewalks to get rid of. Angel got the couch. Shonda got a rocking chair and a bookcase for her little girl's room. The couch was a little stained, but she knew that with a bedspread or a sheet or something thrown over it, it wouldn't be bad at all.

"We got two more beers. I don't want anymore. You can have 'em." She pointed to the two cans, still in the plastic

ring, on the coffee table. She'd had to trade WIC coupons
for the beer because she didn't have any cash, and she felt
bad about that because the coupons were for milk for her
little boy. But Charlie liked his beer. He said after being in
jail all that time, he needed his beer.

"I don't want that warm piss." Charlie walked out.

"You better not bring that good fer nuthin' brother of
yours back here!" she shouted after him.

He slammed the door.

Angel reached for another beer.

I wait at the red light, fingers tapping lightly on the steering wheel to the tune on the radio. I rev the engine. I am
wired. Eager to go. To get moving, though where I am
headed, I don't even know. Just away from here. From my
life. From the person I profess to be. I think about the project I am working on and wonder if it's ready for a test run.
Bomb making can be tricky. One can read a great deal of the
particulars on the Internet, but it's also about using your
hands. When I am ready, I am considering carrying the task
out myself, rather than hiring a messenger. No one will suspect me, I know, even if I walk right into a school or other
public building carrying it under my arm.

I am a good actor. My voice, my body language, the way
I talk; sometimes I even convince myself that I am that man
others see.

But I know the truth.

And the truth will set me free.

I smile at the thought of the words learned decades ago in
elementary school.

My life has recently taken an interesting turn. I have met
a woman. I like her in ways that I have never liked anyone
before. To me, Casey is not just a sexual object, as women

generally are. I am certainly attracted to her, but I sense there could be something more between us than I have experienced with other women, even those I shared so-called long-term relationships with.

I watch her when she doesn't know I'm watching. When she doesn't even know I'm there. Like the other day in the cafeteria at the hospital. She was so pretty, so flirtatious in an innocent sort of way. I watched how the plastic spoon touched her lips, how her tongue darted out to lick the last drop of chili.

Even though she does not see when I'm watching, I wonder if she senses my presence.

At last, the light turns green and I shift, hitting the accelerator.

My attraction to Casey has put me in a bit of a dilemma. I really don't have time for her right now. Time for a relationship.

And the truth is, I don't entirely trust myself with her. Sometimes, when I lie in bed at night thinking of her loveliness, I have dark thoughts. I think about blood. Hers, spilling onto my bed sheets. Her life spilling into my hands, flowing over the sides of the bed like a great fountain.

These sinister thoughts startle me.

Mistakes in judgment lead to prying questions. Watching eyes. Watching eyes will end the fun and I have no intention of ending the fun. The only watching eyes must be mine, and mine alone.

Another red light and I tap my brake pedal.

Against my will, images of Casey flash through my head. The blood again.

I see myself holding her in my arms, her head thrown back as the last droplets of blood fall.

I think about her father and I wonder what the old man would think.

Chapter 7

"So, how's it going?"

"Good." Casey smiled, putting her hands together, entwining her fingers.

"Yeah? You still seeing the new guy? What's his name, Lincoln?" Mandy sounded more like a girlfriend than a psychotherapist.

"I am."

Mandy stood near the window watching Casey, who sat in a comfortable chair in front of Mandy's desk. "And . . ."

"And what? We're dating. He's nice. I'm nice. We're nice together."

"Casey, you know how I feel about wasting your time or mine." Mandy picked up a copper watering can that had a long spout and tipped it over one of the many potted plants that grew in her office windows. It was the south side of the building, perfect for growing indoor foliage. "You've dated a total of one guy since you were sixteen. This is a big deal."

"But I was with John for two years. That should mean something."

"It should." Mandy nodded. "But it took you sixteen

years to really give dating a chance again after Billy. That's why you started coming to me in the first place."

Casey glanced at a little clay pot on the desk. Molded from a single rope of clay, the crude creation had obviously been made by a child. "Jacqueline or Dannine?" She ran her finger along the delicate edge.

Mandy, the same age as Casey, thirty-four, had twin daughters six years old. She was expecting another child, a son, in three months.

"Dannine made it. Now back to the boyfriend."

"He's not really my boyfriend." Casey sat back. "I mean, I really like him. I think he likes me. We've been going out once or twice a week, talking on the phone, e-mailing. But nothing's been . . . you know, formally said."

Mandy poured water over another plant, and the office was instantly filled with the pleasant, pungent scent of rosemary. "Would you *like* Lincoln to be your boyfriend?"

Casey pressed her lips together. "I don't know. I'm so busy with work and Dad. Lincoln's an attorney. He's busier than I am, if that's possible. And he's got his grandparents to care for."

"Some say this will be the burden of our generation, caring for the elderly. So that's a common bond between you?"

"Yeah." Casey thought about it. "I guess it is. We both take our responsibilities seriously."

"And what about the other guy you mentioned? The one who's also an attorney? Have you heard from him?"

"Actually, he left me a message this morning. I haven't had a chance to call him back."

"Two men interested in you at the same time. You're doing nicely," Mandy said, with a smile.

"Thank you."

"So are you going to go out with him too? If he asks you again?"

"I don't know." Casey fiddled with the cuff of her sweater sleeve.

The sweater was new. She'd bought two whole bags of clothes last week at the Ann Taylor Loft outlet in Rehoboth Beach. She never bought herself new clothes, but Lincoln had remarked how pretty bright blue was on her, so she'd gone out and bought several more shirts and sweaters in the same color. She was wearing new slacks, too, and kitten-heeled shoes.

"I like Adam too," Casey went on. "But . . . the case he . . . we were both involved with," she said evasively. She never liked to talk to anyone about specific cases she dealt with at the hospital. Not even with her therapist. It was just too easy to cross the lines of privacy. "The case is still pending," she finished.

"When the case is settled, will you go out with him then?"

"I've thought about it. I like him. He's the kind of man my father would have chosen for me."

"You let your father choose once for you," Mandy said evenly. "And we both know how that turned out. You need to date men *you* want to date. Not whom your father wants."

Her father had liked John well enough, but Casey knew it wasn't John that Mandy was referring to. She ignored the door her therapist presented to her and took a second door. "Honestly, I'm not sure I could handle dating more than one guy at a time. I've already started a relationship with Lincoln. I think I should just stay with that for now."

"Have you had sex?"

Casey made a face, surprised Mandy would ask such a thing. Doubly surprised that Mandy would allow her to pass the Billy Bosley door without so much as a knock. "That's a heck of a question! We've been dating all of . . .

two weeks. Do people really have sex after dating for two weeks?"

"Sweetie, they have sex after one date," Mandy said with a big-sister tone to her voice. "Sometimes a second date *starts* with sex."

"Oh," Casey groaned. "I am *so* not a part of this world. You know, I have a laptop, a cell phone with a Bluetooth headset, even an iPod nano. I'm down with technology, but as far as social practices, I really would have fit in better a hundred years ago. Even fifty."

"So, would you *like* to have sex with Lincoln?" Mandy set the watering can down and leaned back against a shelf, crossing her arms over her chest. She wore a tight, pale blue shirt over black slacks. The shirt accentuated her perfectly round tummy.

Casey felt a pang of jealousy. No, not jealousy, something else. Sadness, maybe. For herself. She was happy for Mandy, but she wanted a baby of her own. Despite her unorthodox upbringing, she had always wanted to be a mother, and now . . . she was beginning to wonder if that was ever going to happen. If she was ever going to be ready to let it happen.

Casey realized Mandy was waiting for an answer on the whole sex with Lincoln thing. "Yes. I guess I would like to have sex with Lincoln." She threw up both hands. "Maybe. I mean, not yet, but . . . *if* the relationship keeps going the way it has . . ." She let her voice trail off.

Mandy moved to her desk, then took a seat in her cream-colored leather chair. She folded her hands. "Do you trust him?"

Casey glanced away. She looked back at Mandy. "I think I can trust him."

"And how do you feel about that? About trusting yourself?"

Casey exhaled. "You know, you could have warned me.

When I come in here, you should have some sort of flag system, like . . . green for this is going to be an easy day, yellow if you intend to pick and prod, red if we're going to really rehash the past and bring back all the ugly feelings."

"My job is to pick and prod. You've made tremendous progress, Casey. You're handling an incredibly difficult career, the care of an aging, ill parent, and you've actually found a social life. I'm here to pick at the wounds to be sure they're healed."

Casey met Mandy's warm brown gaze across the desk. "I *feel* healed."

"Any anxiety?"

Casey gave a humorless laugh. "Every day."

"You know what I mean," Mandy intoned.

"Nothing like before, no. Just the daily stresses, nothing I can't handle." She placed her hands in her lap. "You know, I feel as if this thing with Lincoln. . ." She tried to choose her words carefully. "It's too early to say for sure—I mean the man is a Democrat—but I see possibilities."

"Good." Mandy smiled, glancing at her computer screen. "So is two weeks from now good for you for your next appointment?"

Casey grabbed her purse off the floor and rose from her chair. "Same time, same place. Ciao." She gave a little wave over her shoulder as she went out the door.

On the way home, Casey called Adam's office. She was placed on hold. He picked up in less than a minute.

"How are you?" His voice was warm. He sounded genuinely happy to hear from her.

"I'm good. Busy." She chuckled. "Sorry it took me so long to get back to you. Busy day."

"I understand. Things are crazy here, too. I guess you saw

the headlines this week. The Jameson case has been moved
to Sussex County. Looks like I'm going to be lead prosecutor."

Casey *had* read the news in the paper. The Jameson case
was big. Due to the defendant's notoriety in Kent County,
and belief that he would not get a fair trial, he had been
asking to have his case moved. A judge had agreed to his petition. The Kent County state's prosecutor could have kept
the case, but the paper had indicated that the attorney general's office wanted Adam Preston III on it. It was a big
feather in Adam's cap.

"I did hear. Congratulations, I guess. I mean, attempted
murder, racketeering, attempted bribery of state officers—
sounds like it's going to get intense."

"Just the kind of case I like," he told her.

She laughed at his bravado. On him, it worked. "I just
hope this doesn't mean you'll be too busy for the Gaitlin
case."

"Absolutely not," he said firmly. "We're still waiting on
the lab. Turns out, the lab was waiting for a trial date before
they ran the evidence."

"You've got to be kidding." Casey tapped her brake. A
little boy ran down the sidewalk along the street with what
appeared to be a big sister chasing him down.

"It happens more often than you think," Adam continued.
"Labs don't work like the ones you see on the TV crime
shows."

"Yeah, I know. But still, you don't expect delays like this,
not when a woman was murdered."

"Don't worry, Casey. We're going to get the evidence we
need. I promised you, remember?" Adam said, his voice
more intimate. "We're going to get Gaitlin. It's just going to
take time."

Hitting the Georgetown Circle, she waited to merge with

traffic. Lincoln's office was only two blocks off the circle. She considered stopping by unannounced. He'd invited her to come by anytime. She just hadn't taken him up on it. It seemed as if going to his office would change the dynamics of the relationship. Going to see him would almost make her his girlfriend.

"Listen, I know you're busy," Casey said into the phone, feeling guilty that she was talking to Adam, practically letting him flirt with her, while she was thinking about Lincoln. Adam was too nice a guy to do that to. "I was just returning your call."

"I really didn't need anything. I just wanted to touch base with you since it had been a few weeks," he said. "Your dad okay?"

"Yeah. Yeah, he's good. He's okay. How about your grandfather? Any change?"

"Unfortunately not. He's still in a coma."

"I'm sorry to hear that." Casey finally saw an opening in the traffic circle and hit the gas.

"I appreciate your concern. Say, we never got to have that cup of coffee, glass of wine, whatever. You busy Friday night?"

Casey had known this was coming. It was why she had put off returning his call all day. "Actually, I am. Sorry."

"Saturday night?" he pushed gently.

Although she and Lincoln had not made definite plans, for the last two weekends, she had seen him on both Friday and Saturday night. She thought about just telling Adam she was busy both nights, but that wasn't really very fair to him. Even if it weren't for Lincoln, she wasn't sure she would want to date Adam right now, not if there was even a chance the situation could be misconstrued in some way. There was no way she wanted to jeopardize Linda's case. "Listen, Adam, I . . ." She should have thought this conversation out better. "I would love to go out with you, but with this Gaitlin case still open, I think we'd better hold off." *No sense closing doors completely.* "You mind?"

"So if I passed the case off to someone else, you'd go out with me?" he teased.

"Please don't do that. We . . . *I* need you on this case. Linda deserves the best."

"It was good talking to you, Casey."

"Good to talk to you too, Adam."

He hung up and checked his wristwatch. He could still work another forty minutes or so before leaving for the nursing home. He reached for his cup of coffee and took a sip. It was lukewarm. He set the cup down and searched for a document on his desk.

Adam was disappointed that Casey hadn't agreed to go out with him, but he wasn't ready to give up on the idea. He liked her and he thought they would get along well. His mother was still giving him a hard time about being a bachelor. She said she couldn't overemphasize the fact that in the political arena married men made out far better than those who were single. Citizens trusted married men more.

Adam could imagine Casey making a good wife to a politician. She had the looks, the education, the smile. She was definitely wife material. Of course, he couldn't marry her if she wouldn't even agree to go out with him.

She'd change her mind, though. It was just going to take some time to wear her down. It wasn't as if he had time to seriously date right now, anyway. Not with his caseload. With his grandfather so ill and his parents not expected back in the States until after Christmas.

Finally locating the document he'd been looking for, Adam slid it in front of him to peruse the wording and reached for another sip of cold coffee.

* * *

The next day, Casey went out to run errands during her lunch hour. She went to the bank, the dry cleaner's, and the drugstore, where she picked up her father's blood pressure medication. She took a late lunch, so by the time she returned to the hospital, the parking lot was full of afternoon visitors. She ended up having to park in the rear parking lot near the woods line that she could see from her favorite table in the cafeteria. She didn't mind the walk across the parking lot, even though it was cold and the wind bit at her bare neck. It felt good to stretch her legs.

As Casey approached the rear entrance, she passed a light blue car. It appeared to be the same one she had seen in her rearview mirror the day before when she'd been talking to Adam. How did she know this car? She stared at the cracked taillight on the driver's side thinking. She didn't recognize the license plate. From where she stood she could see nothing inside that would identify the driver. Nothing inside but a car seat.

Then it hit her.

Charles Gaitlin. She immediately scanned the parking lot.

The woman who had picked up Charles in the parking lot the day he had been released from police custody had been driving this car. An old blue boat with a cracked taillight.

Was Charles following her? Watching her? Was the girl-friend?

Casey dug into her purse, removed a small notebook and pen, and quickly scribbled down the plate number. She noted the date on the sticker on the upper right side of the blue and gold plate. The tags had expired.

Suddenly feeling as if she *was* being watched, Casey hurried to the brick staircase that led up to the rear public entrance. At the top of the steps, a full story up, she gazed out

over the parking lot. The blue car hadn't moved. She spotted a woman removing a toddler from the rear of her minivan to deposit him in a stroller. Casey turned at the sound of
a loud crash. Over the railing she saw a black man, dressed
in a cafeteria employee smock, with his back to her. He was
throwing bags of trash into a Dumpster. From above, it
looked like it might be Sarge, her soup guy, but she couldn't
tell for sure.

No one was watching her.

Slipping out of her coat, she hurried through the pneu-
matic double doors and straight to the elevator bank. She
took an elevator to the second floor, exited, and followed the
corridor to her small office.

"Looky here. Small world."

Casey looked up from the bottom file drawer of her desk,
where she was putting her purse. Charles Gaitlin stood in
her doorway. She flinched at the sight of him.

"Mr. Gaitlin, what are you doing here?" She closed the
drawer with her foot, afraid to take her eyes off him.

"Guess this is your office, ain't it?" He looked at the
name sign on her desk. "Casey McDaniel," he read.

Casey's heart raced. So she'd been right. Not paranoid.
The car in the parking lot *was* connected to Charles Gaitlin.
Had he been following her yesterday? If so, why? "How can
I help you, Mr. Gaitlin?"

"Don't know that you can help me at all." He was wearing wrinkled khaki work pants and a uniform-style navy
blue work shirt that might have once sported his name above
the breast pocket. The patch had been ripped off, leaving a
tear in the worn fabric. He carried a nondescript navy jacket
over his arm.

She realized that there was no need to be afraid of Gaitlin
here in her office. There were plenty of people in the hall,
in nearby offices, but the fact that he was here at all un-

nerved her. "Then what are you doing here, Mr. Gaitlin?" she asked pointedly.

He slid his hand into his pocket, taking a step into her office. "Guess I got off the elevator on the wrong floor. Came to see this buddy I got. Wrecked his bike. Hit a tree. Ruptured spleen. It's bad. " He looked around. "Nice office."

"Mr. Gaitlin, I'll have to ask you to leave." She pressed her fingertips to the smooth desktop, refusing to suggest in any way with her body language that she was intimidated by him. Men like Gaitlin fed off intimidation. "You can't be here."

"I ain't doin' nothin' wrong. No signs or anything when you get off the elevator sayin' this floor's off limits to the public." He studied the diplomas on her wall. "You talk to a lot of women in here? Try to get 'em to make up shit about their old men?"

Casey reached for her phone. "Mr. Gaitlin, I really must insist you leave. I can't talk to you. Your case is still pending."

"So I'm right, am I? This where you put crazy ideas into women's heads?" He picked up a small plaque one of her clients had given her as a thank-you gift. It read "Hope Is the Thing Dreams Are Made of." "You a man hater, Casey McDaniel?" he asked. "That why you wanna get me back in court? That why you *wanna* see me get thrown in jail for the rest of my life for something I didn't do? I loved Linda. What would make you think I'd wanna kill 'er?"

"I'm calling security." She picked up the handset and punched in the extension.

"All right. All right." He raised both hands, palms toward her. "I'm goin'. Crazy bitch," he said under his breath as he walked out the door. "Just got off on the wrong floor is all."

"SCH security," a male voice said on the other end of the phone line.

"This is Casey McDaniel," she said, her hand shaking as

she drew the receiver closer to her mouth. "I need you to send someone to the admin floor."

Ten minutes later, Casey was called to the security office in the basement of the hospital. It was right down the hall from the morgue. The gentleman who had called had been curt.

Casey now stood face-to-face with Charles Gaitlin in the security office. It looked little different from her own except that here there were no windows.

"Mr. Gaitlin says he doesn't understand what the problem is, Miss McDaniel. He says he just got off on the wrong floor looking for a patient's room. The patient's name checked out," the rail-thin security officer said from behind his desk, checking his notes on a notepad. "We do have a patient by the name of William Pusey."

The security officer was the daytime shift supervisor, apparently. Casey recognized his face, but she rarely saw him in the hospital halls. He was a smoker. She saw him regularly from her window huddling with other hospital employees against the building, in a tiny courtyard, grabbing a cigarette.

"Mr. Gaitlin says he recognized your name on your door and just stopped to ask for directions. He said he didn't mean to disturb you."

Casey glanced at Gaitlin. He was staring straight ahead, hands tucked behind him, looking quite the part of the victim. "Did Mr. Gaitlin tell you that I'm a witness in a murder case against him?"

"With all due respect, sir," Gaitlin said to the security officer, "I was falsely accused and the charges were dropped. You can check if you want. I ain't got nothin' but a few parkin' tickets maybe need payin'. Don't we all?" He chuckled.

The officer chuckled with him, which pissed Casey off. This was so typical of the way women were treated by society.

The security officer didn't think Gaitlin was a threat to him, so he made the assumption that he was a threat to no one.

"I'm real sorry if I scared you, Miss McDaniel. I didn't mean to." Gaitlin looked back to the officer, who was now leaning back in his springy chair, tucking his hands behind his head.

"Is it okay if I go now, sir? I told my girlfriend I'd be home as soon as I stopped by to see Willy."

The hospital employee looked to Casey. "You have anything else, Miss McDaniel?"

She glanced at him. At Gaitlin. They were both looking at her as if she was the one with the problem. Truthfully, there was nothing else to say. She thought maybe she'd seen his car in the rearview mirror of her own car yesterday? He had come to the hospital where she worked to see a friend? Neither were crimes.

But Casey knew how Gaitlin had looked at her that day in the parking lot. Again, upstairs in her office. He was angry with her. Resentful.

"Miss McDaniel?"

"Just stay away from me, Mr. Gaitlin," Casey warned under her breath as she turned to go. "I'm not the kind of woman you want to mess with."

Chapter 8

"Another letter for me?" Maury had to hide his delight. It was never a good idea for men like Maury to draw attention to themselves, not in the outside world, not in prison. It was one of the keys to remaining undetected. Had Maury stuck to that rule, he wouldn't have been here for the last year. The drug bust had been a mistake; he'd been off his game. But at least it hadn't been a fatal mistake.

"Got your name on it," Tatter grumbled. "I'm assuming it's yours."

It was the fifth letter he had received, and with each one, Maury became more excited. More . . . pumped.

The letters were so shrewdly run-of-the-mill. Chatty. The sender signed her name Danni with an *i* and she always made hearts instead of dots over her *i*'s.

Only *she* was a *he*.

Despite the name and the attempt at female handwriting, Maury knew from the very first letter that his new friend was a man, not a woman. This person was an admirer, but not one of the romantic types. "Danni" wanted something from Maury, but it wasn't sex. He hadn't yet come out and said so, but Maury suspected it was something much more intimate than sex.

It was that thought that thrilled him the most.

Seated on his bunk, Maury carefully pried the two staples out of the envelope. A guard in the prison mail room always slit the envelopes across the top, shook them to search for contraband, and then sealed them back up with a stapler.

Danni's letters were getting more interesting. Each one building on the previous. Maury had a feeling something was about to break. He had a feeling that Danni, who had been testing the waters, would speak his mind soon. Maybe today.

"Don't let me down," Maury whispered under his breath. Somehow he knew Danni wouldn't.

The letter was carefully folded into thirds and Maury suspected, by the soft lines of the folds, that it had not been inspected by anyone inside the prison facility. Guards in the mail room weren't supposed to read the inmates' correspondence, but they were supposed to check for contraband: photos, drugs, and the like. No one had even bothered to open Maury's actual letter, he suspected, because he had been receiving mail from the same "woman" for weeks, the same innocuous letters.

Some women had a thing for men in prison. Everyone knew it. Prisoners. Guards. Administrators. Some women got off on the idea that the man they so-called loved had committed a crime. The bigger the crime, the more obsessed women were. It was not uncommon, Maury had once learned on a TV news program, for women to pursue incarcerated murderers. Death row inmates. Even serial murderers who murdered women.

The weaker sex. A mystery, for sure.

Maury lay back on his bunk, lifted his knees, and smoothed the folds of the paper. He read through the letter once quickly, but was left unsatisfied. There was nothing here. No secret message.

But there was no woman named Danni. He was sure of it.

Maury stared at the words on the lined paper for a moment, then let his eyes go out of focus. He sensed Danni was trying to tell him something, something beyond the trivial chatter about her boring job and a neighbor's cat getting into her trash cans.

Suddenly, letters, then words began to take shape on the page.

How clever. How fuckingly, unbelievably clever.

Heart racing, Maury retrieved a pen from under his pillow and circled letters in a familiar pattern. When connected, the letters became words. A different letter from that which the untrained eye could read began to emerge.

I have admired you for a long time. I know your work, your _real_ work, and you are my hero. I wish that I could be more like you. I hope that we can be good friends. I hope that I can learn from you.

Astounded, Maury read the note twice more to be sure he had made no mistakes in the translation. He had not. He knew he had not because the stranger, this new *admirer,* was using Maury's own secret code.

Something woke Casey in the middle of the night, but it wasn't a sound. It wasn't Linda's voice in her dreams. It wasn't her father or the dog whining to go out. It was a feeling that woke her. *A bad feeling.*

Eyes wide open, Casey gripped the blanket with both hands as she took deep, shaky breaths. Mandy had just asked her about her anxiety and Casey had told her it wasn't an issue. Casey had been telling the truth. She hadn't had any anxiety attacks, but it had only been a half-truth. The anxiety was here again, somehow lurking just beyond her consciousness, in a place where she could sense it but not really see it. Feel it. It was almost as if it was taunting her.

But Casey would not give in to it. Not ever again.

She listened to the house. She heard nothing but familiar sounds; the whoosh of warm air blowing through the heating vents and the low hum of the fan Ed had left on again in his bathroom.

She breathed a little easier, forcing herself to relax. Nothing was wrong. She was fine. Her father was fine. The house was quiet.

Her fingers loosened from the blanket. Lincoln was right. She was too jumpy. He was just telling her at lunch yesterday at the hospital—he'd run in for a quick bowl of Sarge's chili—that she needed to relax a little. Enjoy life more. "I *am* enjoying life, *damn it,*" she had told him. They had both laughed.

Although she and Lincoln now talked every day, she had not told him about Linda's case. Or about Gaitlin. About him following her. About the incident at the hospital. It sounded paranoid, even to her. She didn't want Lincoln to think she was more uptight than he already thought she was.

Now positive that there were no unusual sounds in the house, Casey got out of bed, headed for the bathroom down the hall. As she crossed the room, however, she felt drawn to the window. The pull was so strong, it almost seemed magnetic. After walking across the cool hardwood floor, she parted the heavy drapes and leaned forward to look out over the Cape Cod's roofline. There was a car parked along the street positioned just right between two street lamps so that it remained in a shadow.

That was odd. Her neighborhood was quiet in the middle of the night. No one on her street worked a nightshift. None of them were the late-night-partying type.

Casey watched the car for a moment, squinting. Her heart rate increased. Was the car light blue?

She couldn't be sure. Without her contacts, she could hardly tell it was a car.

She darted to her nightstand, grabbed her glasses, and pushed them onto her nose. She considered turning on the light but quickly nixed that idea. If someone was watching her, if it was Gaitlin, she wouldn't want him to know she was on to him.

Casey was back at the window in less than thirty seconds, but by the time she pulled back the drapes again, the car was pulling away.

Casey let the drapes fall and leaned back against the window covering her mouth with her hand. Maybe the car hadn't been blue. Maybe it had been white.

It had looked so familiar.

Beginning to shake, she wrapped her arms around her waist. Old emotions, old terrors began to wash over her in thick, suffocating waves. She always read about people feeling as if they were drowning in water when they began to suffer anxiety attacks, but it had never been water she had felt she was drowning in. It had always been something thick. Like oil. Suffocating her, dragging her down.

The car had looked similar to Charlie's but it had looked *just like* Billy Bosley's.

Which, of course, was ridiculous because he and the car had gone to a watery grave eighteen years ago.

Angel read the price tag off each object and rang it up on the cash register before adding it to the bag.

The lady bought a Redskins football, a NASCAR car model that included all the pieces and the glue, a used *South Park* DVD, and a "grab bag" of candy that Angel made up herself in the back. Her sister ordered big bags of candy wholesale, and then they would divide it and put it into brown paper lunch sacks and staple them shut. Most of it was crappy, cheap candy. Sticky taffy. Tasteless sour balls. But they always threw in a pack of snack-sized Skittles or Nerds, or a little toy, just to keep customers coming back.

"That'll be twenty-three fifty." Angel ripped the receipt off the top of the cash register. "Your kid's birthday?"

"Yeah. He's gonna be ten," the proud mother said, digging into her purse for the money.

Ten, Angel thought. There was no way she was going to let Buddy watch shows like *South Park* when he turned ten. She was going to raise Buddy right. Raise him better than her mom had raised her and Amber.

As Angel accepted the crumpled one-dollar bills from the customer's hand, someone beat on the bongos near the doorway. "Hey," Angel called, not looking up, "read the sign. No playin' the bongos."

"You rather I played you?"

Angel looked up to see James, Charlie's brother. She groaned to herself. James was the last person on earth she wanted to see today. Any day the rest of her life. James was only a year younger than Charlie, but he had none of Charlie's charm and he was twice the trouble.

"Sorry, but all I got left is change," the customer said, giving Angel the last five dollars in quarters, dimes, and nickels.

"That's okay." Angel dumped the coins into the cash register drawer without counting. Women like this one never tried to cheat her out of fifty cents. Not poor working women. It was the ones with the expensive purses and jeans you had to watch. Angel handed her the plastic bag of toys and candy. "Have a nice day. I hope your boy has a good birthday."

James slapped the bongos.

Angel watched the customer walk out the door, which wasn't so much a door as a gate. Amber rented the space at the flea market in a big warehouse. The good thing was, the rent was cheap; the bad thing was, you had to open and close the same hours as everyone else, because there weren't any walls to the booths, just chain-link fence, so there was no way to secure your own store. Everyone walked out at the same time every night, and one old watchman was left to keep an eye on everything.

James rapped his knuckles on the bongos again.

"I said knock it off." Angel walked around the counter. "Get out of here."

"What's the matter with you?"

"I told you before, I don't want you hangin' around here. Amber said if you stole anything else, she was callin' the cops on you and she was firin' me. I can't lose my job. I got a boy to feed."

James pushed his long, thinning hair out of his eyes. He looked so much like Charlie that some people believed they were twins. But Angel thought James looked a lot meaner. It was something about the way his eyes slanted at the corners.

"Come on, Angel," James said in a sweet voice, trying to put his arm around her. "Come on, sugar pie. Tell the truth. You're glad to see me. You miss me comin' around."

Angel stepped out of his reach, grabbing the bongos. She put them back on the shelf where they belonged. "What do you want, asshole? I don't have any money."

"Aww, come on, sweet lips. How can you act like this?"

"And you can't borrow my car again. I gotta have my car to get home when Amber gets back. I gotta pick Buddy up at the babysitter's. She's got a date tonight. She says I'm late again, she's leavin' him on the step."

"Just an hour," he begged. He picked up a little rubber hammer thingy and hit a xylophone.

The kiddy instrument made a ping.

"Take your truck." She snatched the hammer out of his hand.

"Fuel pump's gone up in it."

"Again? You lie. The last time you said that, it was workin' just fine. You just wanted to use up my gas instead of your own."

Following her down a narrow aisle, James picked up a pink feather boa from the costume area and wrapped it around his neck. He looked stupid in a flannel shirt and pink boa. "I can't believe you're bein' so mean to me. Why you bein' so mean to me, Angel baby?"

When she turned to look at him, she saw that he had taken a rubber mask from a whole bin of them and pulled it over his face. It was Freddy Krueger. A cheap copy of the good ones you saw in costume stores and on TV. They had sold a lot of them in the last week for Halloween.

"I'm not kiddin'. Get out of here, James." She turned her back to him and began arranging a stack of coloring books. "I'm not loanin' you my car."

"Sure you are." He came up behind her, putting his hands on her hips. He thrust his crotch against her butt. "Otherwise, big brother and I will have to have a little talk. A little talk about what you and me were doin' when he was in jail."

She spun around in his arms and yanked the mask off his face. "You wouldn't do that," she said, fighting tears. "Me and him were barely goin' out when he got arrested."

James thrust his face into Angel's. He had bad breath. She'd known it was a mistake to sleep with him. Her mother had always said if you climb into bed with filth, you climb out filthy. It was just that she had been so lonely and James had been nice to her. Kinda. "You can't tell him," she said.

"He moved into my place. He's my old man now and I'm his old lady."

James held out his hand.

Angel looked away, her eyes filling with tears. She hated feeling like this. Like she was trapped. But she loved Charlie. And he loved her. She couldn't let James screw that up. What would she have then? She'd be all alone again and she hated being alone. "You better be back in an hour," she warned, thrusting her hand into her pocket for her keys. "You're late and I swear to God I'll take my car back and then I'll chase you down in it and run your sorry ass over."

He took the keys and walked away with a smirk on his face and the pink boa still around his neck. "Thanks."

"You better not be stickin' up a liquor store or somethin' stupid like that in my car!" she hollered after him.

He gave her the finger.

"Dad, don't pout." Casey hit her signal before decelerating to turn into Jayne's neighborhood. "You've always liked seeing kids get dressed up for Halloween. Remember the kids who used to come to the door at the house in Baltimore? Neighborhood kids. Kids of your colleagues. You would give them toys instead of candy. Neat toys like little abacuses and calculators."

Ed sat stiffly on the passenger side, his arms crossed over his chest. He wore a leather and sheepskin hat with the earflaps snapped on top. Once upon a time he had been handsome in the hat; now, it sat askew, looking a little silly. Casey reached out and straightened the hat. "Hey, Dad, do you remember . . ." She gripped the steering wheel. "Do you remember what kind of car Billy Bosley drove?"

"Billy Bosley?" He slowly turned his head to look at her. It was obvious he had no idea who she was talking about.

Casey looked at the road again. How could she have been so stupid as to have brought up Billy Bosley? Now what should she say?

"Billy Bosley," he repeated. "I had him in Shakespeare, The Comedies, fall semester."

She was fascinated that her father could remember Billy Bosley had taken a Shakespeare class from him almost two decades ago, and that that was what stood out in her father's mind. Maybe the medication was working. His doctor said it could be weeks, even months before they saw any change.

"A LeSabre," Ed said suddenly. He grabbed her arm, startling her. Her father never voluntarily touched anyone but Frazier.

"He drove a white Buick LeSabre."

Casey pulled into Jayne's driveway. Joaquin's car was there, but Jayne's van wasn't. She was obviously running late. Nothing new there.

"I think you're right, Dad. It was a white LeSabre."

"A white LeSabre," Ed said, obviously pleased with himself. He unbuckled his seat belt and opened the car door. "Nice car for a young man that age. Got a B in the class, I think. He—" Her father slammed the door and his voice was lost to her.

For a second Casey just sat there. She remembered the feel of the upholstery of the car. She remembered the smell of Billy in it.

Ed cut in front of the car and started down the driveway. Casey waited until he passed her door to open it. "Dad, this way. You're going to walk around and go trick-or-treating with Jayne and the kids." She grabbed his arm and gently turned him, then led him back up the driveway toward the house.

"Are you going?" he asked.

"I was thinking I'd run over to my friend's house and say hi while you're with Jayne."

"Billy?" He shuffled beside her. "Nice young man. Biology major."

He can remember Billy Bosley's college major, but he can't always remember to put on underwear. "With Lincoln, Dad. You remember Lincoln? He likes to watch The Weather Channel too."

Ed stopped at the front door. "I should go home. Frazier is at home."

She reached around him and rang the doorbell, then opened the door. "Come on, Dad. You stay a while, see your grandchildren in their Halloween costumes, and then Jayne will take you home."

Joaquin met her in the foyer with a thread and needle in one hand, a tiny pink skirt in the other, and yards of pink tulle wrapped around his neck and tumbling over his broad shoulders. He opened his arms and grimaced. "Can you tell Jayne's running late?"

Chapter 9

"More wine?" Lincoln reached for the bottle.

They were sitting in his eat-in kitchen just finishing up a delicious lamb stew that he had cooked inside a pumpkin, of all things. His house, located on the family farm, was nothing like she had expected. She had anticipated sleek, modern lines; cool, light woods; and solar panels. She'd guessed right on the solar panels, but they were completely out of view. The two-story, three-bedroom house was a restored eighteenth-century frame farmhouse and the home his grandmother had grown up in. The ceilings were low with dark, exposed beams; the walls were painted warm fall colors; and the floors were stained walnut and had colorful handmade rugs thrown all over the place. Lincoln had a cat, not a dog, and his grandparents talked to him via a walkie-talkie, from their new modular house across the pasture from him.

"No, thank you, no more wine." She covered her glass with her hand. "After two, I start to get silly."

"Do you, now?" He poured himself a glass and sat back in his chair studying her. "That's something I'd like to see. You silly."

"My father never approved of silly."

Lincoln lifted his glass in toast. "I'd say he's pretty silly now."

He offered a boyish grin.

She laughed. It was nice he could make light of the situation without disrespecting the man her father had once been. She knew that was all Lincoln was doing, just making light of it.

"How about dessert?"

"You made dessert?"

"Of course I made dessert." He walked the three steps to the refrigerator and removed two parfait glasses.

"Pudding?" she questioned.

"Mousse, smarty-pants. Homemade." He grabbed two spoons from a drawer and carried the beautiful dessert glasses to the table.

"How did you work all day and still have time to do this? Weeknights, Dad and I are lucky to get hot dogs and steamed broccoli."

"I have to confess, I made the stew last night and just reheated it in the pumpkin." He pushed her mousse across the table to her. "My plan was that if it tasted awful last night, I could stop for steamed shrimp on the way home tonight."

She dug into her mousse with her spoon and sampled it. "Mmmm."

"But I made the mousse after work." He pointed at her with his spoon. "Found the recipe on the Food Network."

"Homemade dinner, wine, chocolate dessert." She looked at him over the dessert glasses. "You trying to romance me, counselor?"

He narrowed his gaze. "Is it working?"

She smiled, suddenly feeling shy. This was always the hard part for her. The intimacy. Not sex, but the talk that came before and after. The opening up, that was what was difficult. But she really did like Lincoln and she really was ready for another relationship. "I think it's working," she told him.

After dinner, they cleaned up and then went into the small, neat living room. There was a working fireplace and Lincoln had it all ready to start; all he had to do was strike a match.

"Homemade dinner, wine, dessert, *and* a fire?" She curled up on the couch, tucking her stocking feet under her. "Who are you kidding? You're not trying to romance me; you're trying to get me in the sack."

The crumpled newspaper on the fireplace grill caught and leaped upward, licking at the kindling.

Lincoln waited to be sure the wood caught and then he sat down beside her, wrapping his arm around her shoulders. She snuggled against him.

"What time do you have to go?" He drew his mouth along her cheek, making contact with her lips.

"Not for a while. Jayne's having Daddy over for dinner and then she's taking him trick-or-treating with them. She told me she didn't think she'd possibly get him home before nine." She turned her head to meet his mouth.

He tasted wonderful. His arms were warm, secure. Casey could feel herself relaxing. As they kissed again and she parted her lips, she thought about what she and Mandy had been talking about. Casey really *did* want to sleep with Lincoln. It seemed soon, but she wanted to. Obviously, he wanted to. But he wasn't being pushy. He wasn't making her feel uncomfortable about it in any way.

Casey turned so that she could lie back in Lincoln's arms. She slid her hands over his chest and around his neck. "You hot in this?" she whispered, tugging at the wool sweater he wore.

"You hot in this?" He pulled on the collar of her shirt.

She could feel her cheeks growing warm. "But I'm not wearing anything under this."

"Not a problem for me." Keeping eye contact with her, he grabbed the hem of his sweater and pulled it over his head, then tossed it on the couch beside them. Beneath the sweater, he wore a tight, black, cotton T-shirt that was pretty damned sexy. "Nothing under that a problem for you?"

She leaned forward to whisper something witty. As she toyed with the top button of her blouse, the walkie-talkie on the kitchen counter suddenly squawked. "Base Camp Two, come in. Over."

"Holy hell," Lincoln muttered.

Casey crawled out of his lap, cracking up.

"Base Camp Two, this is Base Camp One. Do you read me? Over."

Lincoln jumped up off the couch and dashed for the walkie-talkie.

"We need to add tart cherry juice to the grocery list, Base Camp Two, do you copy? Over."

Lincoln snapped up the receiver and walked back into the living room, raising one hand to Casey in abject apology.

Casey reached for his wineglass and took a sip, still giggling.

"Grandma, I'm not going to the grocery store tonight. Over."

"You can take Blue Bessie. Over."

"I don't need your old gas-guzzling car. I have my own. Over."

"Save you on your gas. Over."

Lincoln rolled his eyes. "You're supposed to be in bed. Are you in bed? Over."

He waited.

"That's an affirmative, Base Camp Two. In my bed in the living room. Your grandfather says he's sleeping in his own bed tonight. He's not sleeping on the couch. Doesn't care if I die out here, he's not sleeping on the couch another night, he tells me. Over."

There was the sound of a deep voice in the background mixed with the static before the walkie-talkie cut out again.

"Grandma, you're not going to die in the middle of the night unless Grandpa or I smother you with a pillow."

The walkie-talkie crackled. "That's not funny, Base Two. This is your grandmother you're speaking to and—"

"Grandma," Lincoln interrupted, "Casey's still here. Dinner. You weren't going to disturb me unless you or the house was on fire, remember? Over."

"Oh, my, you have a girl. Porter, our Lincoln has a girl in his house." The receiver crackled. "Over," his grandmother came back on and said.

Casey covered her mouth with both hands trying not to laugh, but she couldn't help herself. Lincoln looked so pathetic.

"Anything else but the grape juice, Grandma? I'll get it tomorrow. Over."

"Tart cherry juice," she corrected. "Over."

"Good night, Grandma. Grandpa. Over and out."

"Over and out, Base Two."

Casey was still chuckling to herself when Lincoln returned the walkie-talkie to its base charger on the kitchen counter and walked back into the living room. He added two logs the thickness of his wrist to the fire before joining her on the couch again.

He picked his sweater up off the floor and covered his face with it. "I would apologize," he mumbled, "but I'm already so mortified, I'm not sure I can speak in a coherent sentence."

Sitting on her knees beside him, Casey tugged the sweater away from his face, then looked into his warm, blue eyes.

"You shouldn't be embarrassed. I think it's very noble of you to be taking care of your grandparents like this."

"Noble, huh?" He took a sip of wine from her glass and placed it on the end table. "Well, it doesn't feel noble. Good days I feel like I've been taken by two clever con artists with arthritis. Bad days . . ." He didn't finish his sentence.

Casey drew her palm across his cheek. He had the barest amount of beard stubble. It felt good beneath her fingertips. "On bad days?" she prodded softly.

"I wanted a family, Casey. I wanted a wife. Children. A life beyond work and"—he ran his fingers through his slightly disheveled blond hair—"tart cherry juice." He let his hand fall. "I'm lonely. Thirty-five years old and I'm all alone."

She took his hand in hers, turning it, smoothing it. "No brothers or sisters?"

He shook his head.

She knew that he'd been raised by his grandparents and that he had never known his father, but she didn't really know what the story was with his mother. When she had tried to ask him about his mother the week before, he had smoothly moved on to another subject.

"And your mother—"

"Is a crackhead, Casey." He drained the last of the wine. "We haven't heard from her in almost two years, and for my grandparents, that's a good thing. She only shows up when she needs something. Money. She's been in and out of jail. After me, she had at least two more children; we have no idea where they are. We don't even know for sure my mother's still alive."

Casey rubbed his hand between hers. "I'm sorry, Lincoln. I shouldn't have asked."

"No, it's okay." He raised her hand to his lips and kissed it. "I should have told you sooner. It's just that some people don't like the idea of dating a—"

She silenced him by pressing her fingers against his mouth and then replaced them with her lips. His fingers found the top button of her blouse. She curled against him, closing her eyes as he slid his warm hand inside her blouse and cupped her breast.

Their mouths met hungrily and the flush from her cheeks seemed to flow outward, first warming her face, then her torso, then her limbs. Her lips, her toes, her fingertips tingled and then the slow burn began in the pit of her stomach.

It had been a long time since someone had kissed her this way.

Who was she kidding? No one had ever kissed her this way. Made her feel like this. Not John. Certainly not Billy.

Casey could feel herself melting in Lincoln's arms.

She wasn't afraid. Not of Lincoln. Not of herself. Mandy was right. She really had come a long way, hadn't she?

The faint sound of musical notes penetrated Casey's lust-fogged brain. Art Garfunkel.

Lincoln drew his mouth from the corner of hers to her cheek. "Hey," he whispered in her ear, "isn't that your phone?"

Casey looked at Lincoln for a second. Blinked. It *was* her phone. Art was singing "Homeward Bound." "My bag," she managed. Her lips felt love bruised. Her head was swimming.

"I'll get it." Lincoln was back in a second carrying her stone-tumbled, brown leather purse.

Casey dug inside for the phone and hit the receive button. "Dad?"

"He's gone," her father said into the phone. He didn't sound scared this time. This time he sounded angry. Worried.

Not the man-in-the-window story again. Not Richard Nixon standing in the flower bed. "Who's gone, Dad?"

"Frazier. I sicced him after that lying bastard Richard Nixon," Ed said clearly. "And now they're both gone."

Casey threw on her coat as she rushed out of Lincoln's house, her purse flung over her shoulder. She didn't bother to apologize. He didn't bother to ask if it was okay if he followed her home. On the way, Casey called Jayne.

The phone rang. And rang. Eventually, the answering machine picked up, and Casey listened to the corny recording made by Jayne, Joaquin, Chad, and Annabelle: "You've reached the Mendez family. Sorry, we can't come to the phone right now. We're out making a difference. Leave a message."

"Leave a message," Annabelle repeated in the end in her sweet little-girl voice.

Casey groaned as she checked the digital clock on the dash. Eight-forty. It was past the kids' bedtime. Where could they be? The answering machine beeped obnoxiously loudly in her ear.

"Jayne? Joaquin? Could someone pick up? Dad just called. I thought you weren't taking him home until nine." She tried not to sound annoyed. "Is anyone there?" When still no one picked up, she hung up.

She had almost reached home when her phone rang to the tune of Sister Sledge's "We Are Family."

Casey thought she liked the new ring tones she had added to her phone plan, but tonight they were annoying her.

"Jayne," Casey said, not giving her sister a chance to speak, "Dad says Frazier's run away. I thought you were keeping him until nine."

"Casey, you need to calm down."

Jayne's tone annoyed Casey even further. It was her "now don't get hysterical, Casey" voice. It was the same voice,

Casey suspected, that Jayne used with her clients who were prone to hysterics.

"I *am* calm." Casey tried not to sound quite so waspish. Why did her sister always do this to her? Why did she make *her* the bitchy one? "I'm also concerned. I thought Dad was with you. Apparently, he thought someone was looking in the window at him so he let Frazier out the door and now Frazier's run off." She decided to leave out the Richard Nixon part. It was just too bizarre for a cell phone conversation.

"Is Dad all right?"

"I don't know, Jayne. He's home. I thought he was all right because I thought he was with you."

"I'm just putting Chad into the tub. He's got gum in his hair. You want me to send Joaquin?" Without bothering to cover the phone, Jayne hollered, "Joaquin, can you put down what you're doing and run over to Casey's?! She needs help with Dad *again*!"

"No, it's all right. Joaquin doesn't have to come." Casey was caught between being annoyed with Jayne for suggesting she couldn't handle their father, and wishing Jayne had offered to come. Maybe sit with Dad while she and Lincoln looked for the dog. "I'm sure Dad's fine. He's just upset about Frazier taking off. I'll find him."

"I think we need to start thinking seriously about our options with the dog, Casey," Jayne said.

Casey could hear water splashing and the sound of Chad's laughter.

"Options? What options? Frazier's no trouble. He just—" Casey pulled into her driveway. "Look, I'm home. Dad's standing on the front porch *in my bathrobe*. I have to go."

"Call me if you need me," Jayne said cheerfully.

Casey hung up. Lincoln reached the front porch before Casey did.

"Hey, Ed," Lincoln said casually, as he walked up the steps. "It's chilly out here. Why don't we go inside? Get warmed up." He put his arm around the old man.

"It was Richard Nixon," Ed insisted. "He took my dog."

"I know, but we're going to get him back." Lincoln ushered Ed through the front door. "I promise."

Chapter 10

In the end, Casey agreed to stay with her father while Lincoln searched for the runaway. Leaving Ed in his bedroom to get dressed in his own pajamas, Casey walked out on the front porch with Lincoln. "He never runs away." She wrapped her arms around herself for warmth. A cold wind whistled through the shrubbery, tugging her hair from its ponytail. "He can't be far."

"I'll find him." Lincoln gave her a quick kiss. "Go inside, make us some hot tea, and I'll be back in a few minutes, one slobbery boxer in tow."

He started to walk away, but Casey grabbed his arm. "Lincoln, keep your eye out for an older blue car." Then she added quickly, "Or white."

"What?"

She wondered, at once, if she should have said anything. It sounded crazy coming out of her mouth. It was going to sound crazy to Lincoln. "I'll tell you later. It's probably nothing." She waved him off as she stepped back into the house, shivering. "Call me if you have trouble getting Frazier into the car with you. He can be skittish with strangers."

"Inside," Lincoln ordered.

Casey locked the front door behind her. She helped her father put his flannel pajama top over his white T-shirt, rather than the other way around, then led him into the kitchen and made him sit at the table. She gave him a couple of cookies to keep him occupied while she made tea.

"So Frazier just took off, Dad? That's unbelievable. He never goes out of the yard."

"You think I'm lying? Do you see the dog?" He gestured with his cookie.

"No, Dad, I don't think you're lying. Obviously, Frazier isn't here," she said patiently, knowing she shouldn't be hurt by his resentful tone of voice. "I was just remarking how surprised I am by his behavior."

"He didn't just take off, you know." Ed still spoke as if Casey was stupid. "I told you, I sicced him after Richard Nixon. He was doing as he was told." He took a bite out of a chocolate sandwich cookie. "I knew I should never have voted for him. I told Lorraine there was something suspicious about that man. I should have seen Watergate coming."

"No one saw Watergate coming." She filled the electric teakettle with water. "And he's dead, Dad," she said gently.

"Frazier's dead? My dog died?"

The pain in her father's voice made her instantly contrite. She put the electric kettle on the counter and flipped the switch on. "No, Dad." She sat down in the chair next to him and looked into his gray eyes. "Frazier's not dead. *President Nixon* is dead. He died in nineteen ninety-four. You were still at the university teaching. We've been to the Richard M. Nixon Presidential Library in California, you and Jayne and I. Remember the life-size bronze statues of world leaders there? You particularly liked the one of Mao."

He picked up another cookie and nibbled on an edge, the lines on his face sharp with concentration. He seemed to be trying to wrap his mind around what she was saying. "Frazier's not dead?"

"I don't think so, Dad. He's too smart to get hit by a car. I think he just went for a walk around the block." She rested her hand on his. It was warm and bony, the skin wrinkled. "You know how he enjoys his walk."

Ed pushed the cookie into his mouth, crumbs sticking to his lower lip. "But President Nixon is dead."

"Yes, Daddy."

The teakettle whistled and Casey got to her feet.

"Then who the hell was that looking in my window?" Ed demanded.

"I'm really sorry again about bein' late." Angel got out of Shonda's car, hauling Buddy with her. He was fussing and he smelled like poopy pants, but she didn't dare complain about Shonda not changing him. Not after she screwed up Shonda's night like this.

James had never shown up with the car. Big surprise there. After work, Angel had ended up having to catch a ride to Shonda's with the pothead from the pizza place at the flea market. Her friend had been furious, but she hadn't put Buddy out on the step like she had said she would. Shonda would never endanger Buddy's life like that because her cousin was Buddy's daddy; they were family. Then, to make things worse, Angel had had to ask Shonda to take her home, making Shonda even later for her hot date.

"I told ya, ya need to get a new set a wheels." Shonda flipped on the interior light of her car so she could look at herself in the rearview mirror. She was all done up with new hair extensions, a low-cut white sweater, tighter-than-tight red pants, and four-inch heels. She wore a big necklace around her neck that said "Shonda" in gold and rhinestones.

Her baby's daddy had given it to her in the hospital after the birth of their daughter. Shonda and Darrell didn't go out anymore, but he had let her keep the necklace.

"I know. I know I need a better car." After shifting Buddy on her hip, Angel grabbed the two plastic bags of groceries she got at the flea market off the seat of the car. "I'm just glad I got a friend like you, Shonda. A real friend. I don't know what me and Buddy would do without you."

Buddy grabbed at her hair and screamed.

Angel had to grit her teeth to keep from smacking his little hand. She was cold and she was tired and she was pissed as hell with James. She never should have loaned him the car. She *knew* she shouldn't have let him take it.

But what was she going to do? She couldn't let him tell Charlie she'd slept with his brother when Charlie was in jail. It didn't matter how drunk she'd gotten, she should have known better than to sleep with him. It wouldn't matter to Charlie whether he and Angel were really together back then or not—he'd still be angry. He'd still slap her around.

"You have a good time with Tyreek," Angel told Shonda, trying to sound upbeat. "And thanks again. I owe ya."

Just as Angel was about to shut the door, Shonda leaned all the way over, looking past Angel, a lip gloss wand poised over her full mouth. "Hey, I thought you said your car broke down at the flea market?"

"I—" Angel turned around to see her car parked in the handicapped spot near the back door to her apartment. "Son of a bitch," she muttered, slamming the car door.

"S'pitch," her little boy repeated.

Casey had just settled her father on the couch in front of the TV with the ski report for the Midwest when she saw headlights in her driveway. Lincoln was back. She went through the laundry room, out onto the garage steps and opened the automatic garage door.

The passenger-side door of Lincoln's Mini Cooper opened and Frazier bounded out. He ran up the driveway, made a pit stop at a rhododendron bush, and then raced into the garage.

"Frazier!" Casey called, thankful to see the big oaf.

The dog bounded by her and a second later Casey heard her father. "Good boy. Where you been, boy? You been to the presidential library in California?"

The dog barked wildly. Something fell and crashed.

Lincoln walked up the driveway, hands stuffed in his coat pockets. He was so stinking cute. "Get me your keys and I'll put your car in the garage."

She waited while he pulled her car in, and when he walked into the laundry room, she threw her arms around him. He was wearing a soft, navy peacoat and an interesting blue and green scarf that was woven from alpaca. "Thank you so much," she said. "Where did you find him?"

Lincoln held her close, kissing her forehead. He was making it so easy for her. Easing her so seamlessly into a relationship.

"Edge of the neighborhood near a big drainage ditch. I think he had a rabbit or something on the run, but he came right to me when I called him."

Casey felt a weird little shiver. She pushed back in his arms and looked up at him. "He was chasing someone?"

"I didn't see anyone. It was something in the brush. It was dark; I couldn't really see anything but a big dog lumbering in the tall grass." He held her in one arm. "So what's this about a blue car?"

"Nothing. It was silly." She unwound his scarf. She could still hear Frazier jumping around in the living room barking. Her father was trying to get him to sit, apparently, but the dog was still too excited.

"I made a pot of tea." She draped his scarf on a hook near the door and unbuttoned his coat. "You're freezing."

He shrugged off his coat and hung it over his scarf. "Ed says we're expecting a cold winter."

"Ed would know." She went into the kitchen.

Lincoln passed through and went into the living room. "Hey, Ed. Guess you found your buddy," Casey heard Lincoln saying.

Frazier barked.

"He doesn't start behaving himself, he'll have to go on a leash. Won't you, big boy," said Lincoln.

Casey stood in the kitchen listening to Lincoln talk to her father and the dog. The sound of his voice made her warm and not just in a sexual way. Suddenly, she couldn't wait to get into bed with him.

"No, Father, everything is fine." Adam rested the telephone on his shoulder. He was too tired for this conversation. Conversations with his parents took a lot of energy. It was nine-thirty at night and he had just walked in the door a few minutes ago. He'd left for the office at five-thirty this morning.

He entered the kitchen and flipped the light switch. Bright light glared off the polished stainless steel appliances and glossy marble countertop. "Honestly, there's nothing that can be done for Grandfather. I think you and Mother should stay with your itinerary and continue on to Brussels."

Adam's leather slippers made a tapping sound on the Italian tile. He'd left his dress shoes and his tie in his bedroom.

The gourmet kitchen he'd had remodeled the previous year was phenomenal. It was too bad he didn't have time to cook. It was too bad he didn't have anyone to come home to cook for.

When he'd bought the oceanfront house ten years ago with money he'd inherited when his grandmother had passed away, it had been as an investment. Then, when he'd been appointed a prosecutor for the county, he'd made the decision to move into the house, which was nearer his office. It was important, he thought, for a man in public office to stay in touch with those he served. Adam had moved into the house with the intention of bringing a wife home one day, and later, babies from the hospital.

Nights like tonight, when he was beat and still had hours of casework to pore over, he wondered if his dreams were nothing more than that—*dreams*. Tonight, a wife and children seemed a far-fetched possibility.

"No. That's all been straightened out, Father. He has private care, just as we discussed."

Adam opened the refrigerator and pulled out a plastic take-out dish. He popped off the plastic lid and slid the meal into the microwave. He punched the buttons and the light came on. His dinner turned as it reheated.

"I used the company you suggested, Father. They were pleased to work for the Preston family again." Seeing a spot on the microwave door, Adam tore off a paper towel from a roll on the counter and rubbed at it.

The maid had been here today. She was usually pretty good. He wondered how she had missed something like this. The toilet paper had also not been replaced in the master bath and a mirror in the entryway hadn't been cleaned.

Adam tossed the crumpled paper towel into the trash can under the sink. He hoped he wouldn't have to fire the maid. The poor Latino girl needed the job; a single mom with two little kids trying to makes ends meet. He liked being able to help her out. He'd even once given her an advance on her pay when one of her kids had been sick and needed an expensive inhaler for his asthma. But he had been clear with her from the beginning that he was a little obsessive and that he paid well. He paid well enough that he could be obsessive.

"No, Father. I don't need to speak to Mother. The decision's already been made," Adam said into the phone.

The microwave beeped.

"Any changes in Grandfather's status, good or bad, and I'll call you. I promise, sir. Good night."

Adam hung up the phone and retrieved his dinner from the microwave. He carefully set a place with a place mat, a knife, a fork, and a spoon in the correct place and a real plate. He ate at the counter in the cold, quiet kitchen and gazed out the floor-to-ceiling French doors that led out to a deck. In the distance, he could see the silhouettes of waves crashing white on the beach.

Though it had come from an excellent restaurant in Rehoboth Beach, the veal was a little dry. Adam added some freshly ground pepper and pushed another bite into his mouth.

He wondered what Casey McDaniel was doing tonight. He thought about her eating home all alone, too, without a companion to share her meal or the happenings of the day, and it made him sad.

The following Friday afternoon, Casey escorted her elderly client, Mr. Jansen, to the elevator door and promised to call him next week. He and his wife and his ninety-seven-year-old mother-in-law had been involved in an automobile accident Halloween night. Casey was trying to help him through the red tape of auto insurance claims. While he had not been charged in the accident, he was terrified he would lose his driver's license if he contacted the insurance company of the man driving the other car.

Mr. Jansen walked away from the accident with only a broken arm and a cut above his eye that had taken eight stitches, but his wife and her mother hadn't fared so well. Their injuries were extensive enough that they would both require a stay in a rehabilitation center after their hospitalization.

"Thank you so much," Mr. Jansen said, getting stiffly onto the elevator. "I don't know how I could have done all this without you, Miss McDaniel."

"I'll call you as soon as I know something. By next week's end for sure," she promised as she reached around and pressed the first-floor button for him.

The old man moved to the back of the elevator and placed his plaid, wool cap on his bald head. The shiny doors closed. Her father had once had a cap very similar to Mr. Jansen's. One of his students had brought it back from Ireland. Ed had always liked wearing caps. Maybe that was something she could order him for Christmas, perhaps from an Irish import shop.

On her way back to her office, Casey stopped in the copy room and grabbed her mail from one of the keyhole boxes. They called it the copy room, but it was really a multipurpose room. There were copy machines, fax machines, a table for meeting with patients who brought too many relatives to fit into the tiny offices. There was also a little kitchen area with a refrigerator, a microwave oven, and a gigantic coffeepot.

"Hey, you." Marcy leaned against the counter, making herself a cup of coffee in a big pink mug that said "#1 Mom" on it.

"Hey." Casey started to thumb through her mail.

"Nice skirt."

Casey looked up, swishing the skirt a little. "Age appropriate?" It was a little short for what Casey normally wore, but nowhere near as short as Marcy's.

"Absolutely. Very cute." Marcy licked her plastic spoon as she looked Casey over. "And cute sweater. Got a date tonight?"

"Actually, I do. My sister's taking Dad to Annabelle's ballet recital and then they're going out to dinner. I'm making dinner for Lincoln."

"Nice. Very nice." Marcy reached for her coffee mug, nodding approvingly. "So he's good in bed, your attorney?"

Casey turned around, keeping her smile to herself. If things worked out as planned, she might know the answer by tomorrow morning. "That's none of your business."

"Does that mean yes?!" Marcy hollered after her as Casey went down the hall.

Back in her office, Casey returned a phone call and then attacked her mail. She was amazed by how much junk mail a person could receive at her or his place of business. This was what she got for forgetting to pick up her mail the day before. She tossed several items into the circular file.

Why on earth is a department store sending me a sales flyer at work?

Three quarters of the way through the pile, Casey opened an envelope that was hand addressed to her, no return address. She set the letter opener down, then pulled a folded piece of paper out of the envelope and opened it. She froze. On the half sheet of what appeared to be plain-white copy paper was a large blue eye drawn in colored pencil. It was looking at her.

Watching her.

Casey glanced up at her open door. There was no one there. She heard voices in the hallway. Marcy was still in the copy room. Talking to someone. Laughing. Flirting, it sounded like.

Casey looked down at the eye looking up at her. She was almost afraid to pick up the paper.

But it was just a piece of paper.

She flipped it over. It was blank on the back. She stared at it again. Checked for a return address on the envelope again. There was nothing but a Millsboro, Delaware postmark.

A blue eye. Who would send me a drawing of an eye?

It only took her a moment to make the connection.

Was I you, missy, I'd have eyes in the back of my head.

That was what Charles Gaitlin had said to her in the parking lot the day of his prelim.

Casey stared at the eye, her heart pounding. What did she do now? She couldn't help but think of the past. Had she confronted Billy sooner, could she have changed anything? Over the years, she had come to the conclusion that maybe she could have.

Casey's fear turned to anger. Billy had robbed so much of life from her. She had survived, but where was the learning curve? History repeated itself unless someone changed. Truly changed.

She got out of her chair, pushing it back harder than she needed to. It hit the wall with a heavy clunk. She crossed to the single file cabinet and squatted to find the right file in the bottom drawer. She laid her hand on it at once, then carried it back to her desk, flipped it open, and searched the top page, where she always noted contact information.

Sure enough, beside Linda's home phone number, there was a cell number. As Casey angrily punched the buttons into her phone, she remembered what Linda had said while sitting right in that chair across the desk from Casey.

"I ain't got a cell, but Charlie does. You can get me on his, if ya need to."

Casey took a chance that someone had paid Gaitlin's cell bill while he was in prison. Maybe the same grandmother who had hired his lawyer.

Casey got lucky. Someone picked up on the third ring.

Or maybe, in retrospect, she would wonder if this was the moment in time when luck really turned against her.

Chapter 11

"So what you wanna do?" James asked. He'd pulled his truck off the blocks but it wasn't sounding so hot. Charlie figured it'd be broken down again before the day was out. "We got an hour to kill before I have to pick Drina up at the place she's cleanin' in Dewey Beach."

Charlie stared at the window, watching the houses fly by. "New job?"

"Yeah. Sorta. Doin' it as a favor to one of her friends who was too hungover to go. I walked around inside when I dropped her off. Some pretty sweet shit in there. Some rich-assed doctor's summer house. He's comin' for the weekend from Washington or something." James shuddered. "Man, it's too freakin' cold to be at the beach."

Charlie rolled his eyes. James was always up to no good. Scamming some old lady or pretending to be hurt and trying to get money from auto accidents. He did a little B&E on the side when he needed quick money.

"You can't swipe stuff out of the house your girlfriend cleaned today," Charlie said. "The first thing the cops do is ask who's been in the house the last week, appliance repair guys, maids and shit. You'll be in jail before Angel gets home with the fried chicken for us for dinner."

"I didn't say I was goin' back. I told ya, I'm layin' low, bro."

Charlie glanced at James and then back out the window again. "Yeah, right."

Charlie's cell phone on the car seat rang. He could find the phone only half the time, but Angel had given it to him this morning. Apparently it had been in the couch cushions again.

James stopped at an intersection, looked both ways, and pulled forward. The phone rang again. "You gonna answer that?"

Charlie stared out the window. "What for? It'll just be Angel bitchin' about something." Then he imitated her: "Did you put the job application in at Wawa? Did you put in the application at the chicken plant? Did Mom-Mom send the check?"

"It might be Mom-Mom." James picked up the phone. "'Lo."

"Hello."

Charlie could hear a woman's voice, but it wasn't Angel. She was at work, anyway. She never called when she was at work. That bitchy sister of hers wouldn't let her talk on the phone.

The woman on the phone said something.

"This is him," James said. "This is Charlie." He grinned at his brother like he was some kind of ape.

Charlie tried to grab the phone, but James pulled it away from him. The car swerved. The driver of a minivan coming toward them in the westbound lane laid on its horn as the minivan veered to the shoulder.

"This is Casey McDaniel. I just got your letter in the mail and I don't know why you sent it, but I want you to know that I am not going to be intimidated."

"That right?" James said.

"That's absolutely right. I'm warning you. I see you again, I see you following me, you show up at my office, I get any more of these letters in the mail, and I'm calling the police. I'm calling the police and I'm having you arrested for harassment."

"Wait. Who *is* this?" James asked, suddenly more interested.

Charlie swiped at his brother. "Gimme the phone."

James leaned against the driver's-side window, out of Charlie's reach.

"You know very well who it is. Casey McDaniel," she said. "I was Linda's counselor at the hospital. You can't intimidate me, Mr. Gaitlin. You're going to be arrested again for Linda's murder very shortly, and I intend to be a witness against you at the trial. I intend to see you go to jail for the rest of your life for what you did to Linda."

The other end of the line went dead.

"Who was that?" Charlie asked.

James threw the phone down on the seat beside him. "You sendin' shit in the mail?" James asked. "Some friend of Linda's? Casey somebody."

"She wasn't Linda's friend." Charles pushed his hair out of his eyes. "She was that woman at the hospital who tried to get Linda to tell the cops that I punched her. That bitch is crazy. She says I'm, like, following her and shit."

"She does, huh?"

"Yeah. She called the security cops on me at the hospital the other day when I went in to see Willy. She told them I was harassin' her."

"Did she?" James stared straight ahead, both hands on the steering wheel. "That's funny, Charlie, because it sounds to me like it's the other way around."

* * *

By the time Casey got home with her groceries, she was feeling a lot better. After talking to Gaitlin, she'd called Adam's office and left a message for him to call her about Linda's case. She wasn't going to ease up on Gaitlin; she wasn't going to let him slip through the system.

She put a homemade marinara sauce on to simmer and Jayne showed up only half an hour late to take their father.

"Call me when you're on your way back," Casey told Jayne as she helped their father into his coat.

"I'm thinking it'll be close to ten. I told the babysitter ten."

Casey placed her father's hat on his head. He adjusted it.

"Call anyway," Casey said.

Jayne lifted an eyebrow. "Oh, yeah?"

"Oh, yeah," Casey murmured, leading Ed to the door.

"And here I was trying to think of a way to delicately bring up your emotional well-being. You know, the holidays approaching and all. 'Tis the season for depression," Jayne said cheerfully.

"I'm not depressed and I have no intentions of becoming so."

"Be sure Frazier has water," Ed instructed as he tottered toward the door. "And keep an eye on him when you let him out to urinate. I don't want him running off again."

"I'll keep an eye on him, Dad. You have a good time." Casey rested her hand on his shoulder before letting go. "Enjoy the ballet. You and Mom always liked the ballet."

"Come on, Dad. Joaquin is waiting. He's got the car running." Jayne, all bundled up, glanced at Casey. "Is he always this slow?"

"Always." She waved at them from the front door.

Half an hour later, Lincoln arrived with two bottles of wine.

"Whoa, there," Casey said, meeting him at the door.

He wrapped his arms, the bottles in his hands, around her and kissed her long and hard.

Breathless, she pulled away and laughed. "Two bottles? I told you, I'm a two-glass girl. You give me more than that after a long day at work and I'll be asleep before eight-thirty."

"Can I watch The Weather Channel while you're sleeping?" He gave her a quick kiss, then released her and closed the front door.

Casey locked it. "Absolutely not. I'm seeing rainfall reports in my sleep. I helped a client fill out a form for his insurance company today and wrote 'heavy snowfall expected' where I was supposed to print his address."

Lincoln followed her into the kitchen. "Smells great." After putting the bottles down, he took off his coat. "Sounds like you had a long day. Want to talk about it?"

Casey picked up a wooden spoon to stir the marinara. "Nah," she said, ever the cheerful one. Her job was to listen to people's troubles; she wasn't that comfortable talking about her worries, certainly not with a new boyfriend.

"You sure?" He reappeared from the laundry room, minus his coat and scarf. He wrapped his arms around her waist as she stood at the stove still stirring the pot. "I'm a good listener."

Casey shook her head, dead set against talking about work. But when Lincoln turned her around, took the spoon from her hand, and gazed into her eyes, something inside her crumbled.

"I really did have a bad day," she said shakily. "I had this client, Linda . . ."

The next thing Casey knew, Lincoln had taken the sauce off the stove, poured them glasses of wine, and they were sitting on the living room floor in front of her gas fireplace, their backs against the couch. He took her high-heeled shoes off her feet, made her slip her black tights off from under her skirt, and massaged her bare feet as she talked.

She told him about Linda. About the horrible night Linda had called her. About the nol pros and Gaitlin being released and about how nice Adam Preston had been to her. How hard he was working on the case. But she didn't tell him about her suspicion that Gaitlin might be following her or her fear that her father might have seen him in the window or about the drawing she received in the mail. She didn't want him to think she was paranoid or crazy. And she didn't mention Billy, who was probably the real reason why she *was* paranoid about Gaitlin. Sleeping with a man was one thing; telling him about your stint in a mental ward was something entirely different.

Lincoln was a good listener. He rarely interrupted. He let her take her time telling him about Linda's case, didn't seem to mind how neurotic she must have sounded, or how much she skipped around, inserting little tidbits about her father here and there.

"Well, I'd say you had a bad day, all right," he said when she was finally done. He brushed his lips against hers.

"You think?" She lifted her chin and met his mouth with hers.

"Yeah," he whispered.

With the shoes and tights already off, it didn't take that long to shed the sweater. Casey and Lincoln sat face-to-face, knees to knees as she slid the sweater over her head. He pulled off his.

He kissed her hard, taking her breath away. He rubbed her back, her shoulders, her bare arms, covered with goose bumps more from desire than from being cold. By the time he slid the strap of her lacy bra over her shoulder, her breasts were aching so badly to be touched that she thought she'd rip her bra off herself if he didn't hurry.

Lincoln was a gentle lover, but certainly not a dull one. He seemed to know when to kiss softly, and when to push her down into the carpeting. He didn't say much, but the few words he spoke came off sexy and sweet, not silly the way it always seemed in books she read.

He gave her time. He definitely understood foreplay and a woman's body. He stroked her, kissed her. He let her set the pace.

Eventually, it was Casey who was tugging at his clothes. He removed his cord jeans and boxer briefs before helping her shimmy out of her new skirt and the pale teal panties that matched her new bra.

Casey was so glad she had taken advantage of the Victoria's Secret fall catalogue sale. She wouldn't have been caught dead lying in the living room in front of her fireplace in nothing but her old, beige, cotton Wal-Mart panties with the saggy elastic.

Casey stretched out on the carpet under Lincoln, her arms over her head. She closed her eyes, enjoying the feel of his hands on her body, the scent of him. She let herself relax every muscle, set every worry aside, every thought free.

It had been too long since she'd made love. It was funny the way she had forgotten just how much she enjoyed it. Or was it just better with Lincoln?

When he finally pushed inside her, she was practically clawing at his back. Suddenly, she couldn't get enough of him. Enough of the feel of him, and she lifted her hips again and again against his.

Balancing his weight over her, he covered her face with kisses, forcing her to slow down. "It's not a race," he teased in her ear.

But in a way, for Casey, it was. She had needed this for so long. Maybe her whole life.

She was so afraid to be hopeful.

And yet she was.

Maybe saying her orgasm was earth shattering was an exaggeration. Maybe it wasn't. Casey sank her nails into Lincoln's bare shoulders, wrapped her legs around his, arched her back. Tears filled her eyes as the waves of pleasure lapped over her. A second later, he was done.

Lincoln gently slid out of her and rolled onto his side, beside her. He pulled her into his arms and she rested her cheek on his bare chest.

"Are you sad?" he asked, stroking her temple.

Not trusting herself to speak, she shook her head.

"Too soon?"

Again, she shook her head no.

"Just 'great sex' tears?" he ventured.

This time Casey laughed. "Yeah," she whispered, holding him tightly. "Just 'great sex' tears."

Emma stirred, rolled onto her side, and reached out to put her arm around Richard. She was met with nothing but a tangle of blankets. Half asleep, she remembered he was still out of town at the conference. Usually, she went with him on his trips; she didn't find lectures on new technology in urology all that interesting, but she did enjoy exploring new cities, revisiting old ones.

But their youngest daughter was overdue with her first baby and Richard and Emma had agreed that Emma should just stay home and wait for "the call." She'd be too nervous to have a good time in Vegas, anyway. Once the baby was actually on its way, Richard would fly home.

Now more awake, Emma rolled onto her back and checked the clock beside the bed. It was two-thirteen. She closed her eyes and rearranged her pillow, refusing to give in to any form of insomnia tonight. She had a busy day tomorrow.

A sound in the hallway startled Emma, and she sat straight up in bed. It sounded like the lamp on the table at the top of the stairs. If you bumped into the table, the lamp rattled. Richard was always running into it in the dark, always complaining that his wife needed to move it.

Had Richard come home early? It wasn't like him not to call. But maybe he had called and she hadn't heard the phone.

As Emma listened, her heart raced.

She heard nothing but the hum of the heat pump. The drip of the water faucet in the master bath. Two more weeks and they would close up the beach house for the winter. It was really already too cold down here—the rooms were drafty—but Emma enjoyed the house so much that she always dragged her feet in the fall when Richard said it was time to pack up and return to Dover for the winter.

Hearing nothing more, Emma took a deep breath. Had she imagined the sound of the lamp?

She lay back on her pillow and closed her eyes.

But there was no way she was going back to sleep. She sat up, threw her feet over the side of the bed, and pushed her feet into her sheepskin slippers. Richard teased her about her slippers because she never took them back to Dover with her; they were her beach slippers. She didn't just wear them with her pajamas. When it grew cool in the fall and she dragged them out of the closet, she wore them to the bakery in the morning to get fresh croissants. To the grocery store. To the neighbor's house. In the summer, they would be replaced with her favorite flip-flops, also worn only at the beach.

Emma walked halfway across the bedroom, in the dark, then considered turning on the light. But she knew the house with her eyes closed. If there was an intruder, which she certainly doubted, wouldn't she be safer in the dark? She would know her way around and the stranger wouldn't.

The door was partially open and she listened through it. Later, when she'd pick Richard up from the airport and tell him about creeping around in the house in the dark looking for burglars, he would chastise her, saying that a sixty-two-year-old woman who was about to be a grandmother for the fourth time shouldn't be walking around the house in the dark.

Richard had always been like that, so protective. It was one of the reasons she had always stayed with him, even in the years when they worked entirely too hard building his practice and made love entirely too infrequently.

Emma pushed the door with her finger. It glided noiselessly.

The hall was very dark, even darker than the bedroom; it didn't have the benefit of the glow of the bedside digital clock.

Emma didn't see anything. She didn't hear anything. But something in the hallway didn't *feel* right.

The little hairs on the nape of her neck stood up and she rubbed her hand against them. She kept her salt-and-pepper hair, now mostly salt, in a short, fashionable haircut. Richard called it the sassy grandmother look. Emma wondered now if her beautician had shaved the hair on her neck closely enough. The hairs felt prickly.

Emma took a step toward the staircase. The phrase "inky black" came to mind. There must have been no moon tonight, no stars, because very little light shone in through the skylights over the vaulted living room ceiling.

She moved along the open, loft hallway squinting.

She thought about calling out, but what would she say? And if there was somewhere there who shouldn't be, did she really want to talk to him?

Emma's slipper hit something on the floor. Something that didn't belong there.

Her heart leapt upward, lodging in her throat. She froze. Still no sound.

She wiggled her toe in her slipper. The something on the floor in the middle of the hallway was lumpy, hard. Stuff in a cloth sack of some sort. She started to lean over to feel what it was but halfway through the motion realized how stupid that was.

Someone was in the house!

Emma knew she had to get to the phone. She had to dial 911! But first, she needed to get into the bedroom and lock the door.

Just three or four short steps and she would be back in the bedroom.

Emma almost made it.

She heard an odd swish. Felt the air move at her cheek.

Suddenly her head seemed to explode with pain. Lights flashed behind her eye sockets. She grunted, fell forward, crying out in agony. In terror.

He hit her again and she tried to protect herself with her arms, attempting to curl into a fetal position on the floor. She lost one of her sheepskin slippers. Her flannel pajama top rode up, exposing her breast.

"No, please," she sobbed. "Take what you want. Take it all."

She still couldn't see him. Blood stung her eyes.

"Please," she moaned. He hit her again. Kicked her. Emma screamed once more, maybe twice. But he kept hitting her, kicking her. She didn't know how long it went on. But thankfully, the pain began to fade until at last it was gone and she sank into a black abyss.

Chapter 12

"I appreciate you meeting me." Casey walked to one of the small, wrought-iron tables in the coffee shop, carrying her soy latte. "I apologize for bothering you; I know how busy you are." She took a chair.

Adam sat across from her, setting down his double cappuccino with a shot of hazelnut syrup.

"But I really needed to talk to you about Linda's case."

"And I thought this was a date," he teased. "I thought you called me because you couldn't live another moment without me."

She met his gaze across the table, giving him her best "I'm being serious" look. Fortunately, he had a good sense of humor. He smiled. "I'm sorry. You were saying . . ."

"I needed to see you because I need to know what kind of progress you've made. How soon do you think Gaitlin can be arrested again?"

"Soon." He sipped his coffee.

"How soon?"

"Casey, these things take time. I warned you of that. We've got to have our ducks in a row when we go to prelim next time. No more screwups in my office. Because there won't be a third chance. Judges don't appreciate lawyers or the state wasting their time. I absolutely have to get the indictment the next time we stand before a judge."

Casey held the thick paper cup of coffee between her palms, savoring the warmth. It was bitterly cold outside for November in Delaware. She'd actually seen snowflakes this morning on her way to work. She had even tried to call her father to tell him, but he hadn't answered the phone. She rested one hand on the table, then slid it toward him. "I have a bad feeling about this man, Adam. I know that sounds ridiculous. I know you deal with facts, but he . . . he's a bad person. I . . . I'm scared to death he's going to do it again."

He watched her carefully. "You all right?" He slid his hand across the table, covering hers. "Because you don't quite seem all right. Has something happened?"

When she told Lincoln about her concerns about Gaitlin, she didn't tell him that she also suspected he might be harassing her, stalking her, whatever you wanted to call it, but sitting here, she wanted to tell Adam. He knew Gaitlin. He knew what kind of man he was and she sensed that he would understand. She felt as if she and Adam were in this together.

"Casey, what's Gaitlin done?" Adam questioned. His hand was warm and reassuring.

She hesitated.

"Casey, please."

"I think . . ." she began slowly. "I think it's possible he's following me."

He picked up his cup of coffee. "Have you called the police?" He set the coffee down without taking a drink. It was obvious he was trying to restrain his anger. "That son of a bitch," he said under his breath, making a fist.

"Adam"—she laid her hand on his clenched fist—"I have no proof, but I also got this hand-drawn picture in the mail."

She quickly explained about the drawing of the eye and what Gaitlin had said to her in the parking lot.

"You have to go to the police," he said.

"I could be wrong. That time he showed up in the hospital, security checked on him. He really did have a friend who was a patient. It really was a coincidence that he was in the building." She hesitated. "The other thing is . . . my dad says someone is watching him through our windows."

"Casey—"

"But, Adam, Dad says it's Richard Nixon." She gave a little laugh, then sat back in her chair. "Would you want to go to the police and tell them your father thinks Richard Nixon is looking in your windows, but you think it might be this slug of a guy who you think might have killed this woman you never really knew but who haunts your dreams at night?"

He crossed his arms over his chest. He was wearing a navy suit with subtle pinstriping. His dress shirt was pale blue, his tie a navy and red paisley. The man knew how to wear a suit. He was nearly the antithesis of Lincoln, in his khakis and corduroy jacket, yet she couldn't decide who was better looking.

"Would you want to call the police and tell them about Nixon?" she asked again.

"Okay, good point," he conceded.

"I'll sound like a nut job, and I don't want this to negatively affect the case against Gaitlin." She sipped her coffee. "I just want him arrested. I want him off the street. I want him to pay for what he did to Linda, and I don't want another woman to be endangered by him ever again."

Adam checked his watch. "Oh, hell." He opened his hands. "I'm sorry, Casey, but I—"

"No, it's okay." She rose from her chair, taking her coffee with her, her bag slung over her shoulder. "I really appreciate you seeing me. I know you're too busy for this kind of nonsense."

"It's not nonsense and I'm glad you called. I'll see what I can do to speed things up with the case." He had stood, leaving his coffee on the table. He was close enough that she could have reached out and smoothed his already impeccable tie.

What was wrong with her? She'd just had sex with Lincoln the other night for the first time. She wasn't available. And she really liked Lincoln.

So how could she be attracted to Adam like this?

"Thank you," she said, looking down, her cheeks growing warm.

"I guess I'd better go." He grabbed his cup. The coffee shop had exits on two different streets. He had to go one way, she the other. "Thanks for the coffee. I still owe you that glass of wine."

Maury lay on his back in his new bunk in one of the dormitory rooms in the work-release building. He'd been moved earlier in the week and already had a job lined up as a mechanic for one of the local chicken plants. Monday morning at six-thirty he'd be on his way in a prison van to his first day of work, and his first taste of freedom in more than a year.

He studied the envelope on his chest. Danni had known exactly what day Maury had been moved, and he had properly addressed the mail so that it would go to his new friend in a timely manner. How had he known? Who was he? One of the guards?

The latest envelope was thicker than the others had been. There was something more inside than just a single sheet of paper. Maury looked up at the ceiling over his head. Inmates fought over who had to take a top bunk. Everyone wanted the bottom bunk. They went to the infirmary and got notes saying their back was too bad to climb up. But Maury liked the upper bunk because of the ceiling tiles. They were a new pattern to study. The tiles were exciting. *Life* had suddenly become exciting again.

And not just due to the change in his surroundings or to the taste of freedom he'd soon experience. Danni had made life exciting for him. He had opened a door of possibilities, although where that door would lead, Maury still didn't know.

He picked up the envelope, drew it under his nose and sniffed. If he was going to open it in privacy, he'd have to open it now. His roommates had gone to the mess hall to get snacks out of the machine. That was the routine here: the inmates lined up for mail call at about nine P.M., and then they were free to get candy and sodas out of the vending machines before they had to retire to their room for the night.

The envelope smelled of paper, of sticky adhesive. Maury even thought he could smell the staples the guards had used to reseal the envelope. But beneath all of that, he smelled the very faint scent of newspaper print.

Danni had sent him a newspaper article!

What would it be? He couldn't guess.

Suddenly, Maury was too curious to wait a moment longer. He carefully pried the staples out one at a time and straightened them out, then placed them on the bed beside him. He slid the folded sheet of paper out of the top of the envelope.

Sure enough, inside was a small newspaper clipping. *Poor Aunt Emma,* Danni had handwritten in the margin.

Maury eagerly read the clipping.

At approximately 2:00 A.M. Saturday morning, an unidentified male broke into a private home in Dewey

Beach. The suspect entered the home through an unlocked window and brutally beat homeowner Emma
Truman (62). Robbery is believed to have been the
motive. Approximately $10,000 worth of jewelry and
electronics were removed, as well as an antique silver tea
service. Anyone with information on the robbery and assault should contact the state police. Mrs. Truman is in
guarded condition at Christiana Hospital.

Maury read the article a second time. A third. Then he
read Danni's message handwritten in the margin. Maury had
no Aunt Emma. Did Danni?

No. Danni was sending a secret message.

Maury's heart began to beat a little faster.

Danni was boasting. Danni had beaten the old woman
half to death and he wanted Maury to know it.

Casey stood at her bedroom window, peered through the
opening in the curtains, and studied the car parked across
the street. This time, she had her glasses on and she hadn't
been to bed yet. She wasn't sleep muddled. She was clear-
headed and quite certain of what she was seeing. The car
was blue. Not white. It did not belong to a ghost boyfriend.
In the night shadows, she couldn't tell for sure, but she was
almost positive it was Charles Gaitlin in the front seat
behind the wheel.

Casey glanced at the cordless phone in her hand. Adam
told her if she saw Charles near the house again, she should
call the police.

The question was, Why did she doubt herself? Why was
she still standing here in the dark holding the phone?

She thought she had good instincts. She thought the years
of therapy had taught her to trust herself and her feelings as

much as her logic. Hadn't her instinct been right about Billy all those years ago? Why did she question herself now?

Casey leaned her forehead against the window frame, taking care that she couldn't be seen through the window. She was close to tears. What was wrong with her? Why was this so hard? Did she *want* to be a victim? Some people did, on some level.

No. She closed her fingers tightly over the phone. She did *not* want to be a victim. *Not ever again.*

Casey called 911 and was told a state police car would be sent immediately. She wanted to call Lincoln . . . or maybe Adam, since he knew she was worried about Gaitlin following her, but she refrained. She didn't need a man to come to her rescue. That had been part of her mistake with Billy. She had expected her father to protect her.

Casey followed the police dispatcher's directions exactly. She did not turn on her bedroom light or any other lights in the house. She did not walk out of the house in her bathrobe to confront Gaitlin. She waited at her window. Seven minutes after she placed the call, the blue car pulled away. Eleven minutes after the call, a trooper rang her doorbell. She knew from experience at the hospital that that was actually a good response time. Big county. Not enough police to patrol at night.

She had watched the police cruiser pull into her driveway. She met the trooper at the front door in sweatpants, a sweatshirt, and slippers. Frazier barked like crazy from her father's bedroom; fortunately, she had thought to shut his door before the police arrived.

"Miss McDaniel?" the tall trooper in a tall hat that made him appear even taller asked from under the front-porch light.

"Yes, I'm Casey McDaniel. Thank you for coming."

"I'm Trooper Brown. I understand you saw a suspicious car."

"I think I'm being watched. Followed. The car was over there." She pointed across the street. "It was parked between those two cars. I couldn't quite see the driver, but I know who it was. His name is Charles Gaitlin."

Trooper Brown took out a note pad and pen. "Gaitlin. That's spelled how?"

She spelled it for him.

"Old boyfriend?" he asked.

"No." Instinctively she wrapped both arms around her waist. It was cold outside. She thought about inviting the officer in, but Frazier would really go nuts if he heard a strange man's voice in the house. Besides, didn't Trooper Brown need to be on his way? Obviously Gaitlin wasn't here now. Wouldn't he want to go looking for him?

"I'm a victims' advocate at SCH. I was supposed to testify against Mr. Gaitlin in a trial. He was accused of murdering his girlfriend."

"You think he's trying to intimidate you so you won't testify against him? When's the trial?"

Casey exhaled. "The trial date's not been set yet." She brushed her hair off her forehead, trying not to get flustered. Now that Gaitlin was gone, it seemed a little silly to be standing at the front door in the middle of the night talking to a state policeman. "It's complicated. He was released, but any day now the county prosecutor intends to have him arrested again. Gaitlin must know that."

"You witness the alleged murder?"

"No." She pushed her hair out of her eyes again. She was tired and she had a headache now. "I worked with the victim. She called me the night she died. She told me he was breaking into her home. I called 911 for her. By the time the police arrived, she was dead."

He looked down at her. "You get the tag number of this car parked in front of your house?"

He didn't believe her. Or wasn't all that interested. She could hear it in his voice. "No. It was too dark. I couldn't see it because of the way he was parked, facing out of the neighborhood, and when he pulled away, it was too fast."

"But you say the car was blue?"

She thought about Billy's white car that looked so similar. She wondered why that first night she could possibly have thought Gaitlin's car was Billy's. "Yes, blue. Older. Kind of big. And . . . and it had a taillight out on the passenger's side."

"Well, ma'am, I'll get your information and take a drive around the neighborhood—"

"But there's nothing you can really do," she said, suddenly feeling deflated. Why hadn't she listened to her own instincts and *not* called. Now she looked like an idiot.

"Not if I can't find the car, ma'am, and you can't identify it by the driver or the license plate."

But I know it was Gaitlin, she wanted to shout. But she kept her mouth shut, told the officer what he wanted to know: her full name, where she worked, phone numbers where she could be contacted. As she recited the information, she contemplated what she would do the next time she saw Gaitlin. Her instincts told her there would be a next time.

Chapter 13

"You haven't said much about work." Jayne stood on the other side of the kitchen table from Casey and dried her hands on a towel.

Casey was peeling sweet potatoes to make their mother's famous sweet potato soufflé, a staple in the McDaniel family every Thanksgiving and one of the few things her mother had ever baked. The kitchen was filled with the tantalizing aroma of a free-range turkey roasting in the oven. The sound of a football game seeped from under the closed door between the dining room and the kitchen.

She wondered how Lincoln was faring in the family room with her brother-in-law, niece, nephew, and father but assumed since she hadn't seen his car back out of the driveway, he was surviving. Sometimes that's all a person could ask for with family holidays—survival.

"You know, it's work." Casey made a noncommittal shrug.

"So, no more trouble from the dead woman's boyfriend?" Jayne turned her back to Casey and emptied a gigantic bag of frozen green beans into a rectangular casserole dish. "See. I told you it was nothing to worry about. Some of these poor souls, they just can't get a break." She tossed the bag into the trash can under the sink and walked to the refrigerator. "They were born to uneducated parents. Poor. Their parents had to work so hard just to put food on the table that the children didn't get the nurturing they needed. We see it repeated generation after generation."

Jayne continued her diatribe. Casey continued to peel sweet potatoes, barely hearing what her sister was saying. She debated whether or not to mention the latest incidences with Gaitlin or her visit from the state police the other night. A part of her needed to talk it out with someone, but what would be the point in that someone being her sister? Jayne would tell her she was imagining things. She would explain to Casey, yet again, how men like Gaitlin were always being falsely accused. How society, how *Big Brother,* was holding back the poor, uneducated man. She wouldn't believe Casey.

"You see it every day in the newspapers. In my office, in yours," Jayne rattled on. "What's it going to take? That's what I want to know. When are people going to stop being so selfish and look at the plight—"

"He's been following me," Casey interrupted. She couldn't stand it anymore. She just couldn't stand her sister being on her soapbox another minute. "Gaitlin has been following me." She carried the colander of potatoes to the sink and flipped on the faucet.

"You really think so?" Jayne dumped canned soup on top of the green beans. "You're sure you're not just—"

"He was in my office, Jayne. I had to call security." She pulled the sprayer from the sink and squirted the potatoes viciously, angry that Jayne could never be more supportive. "He said he was in the hospital visiting a sick friend. He said he just got off on the wrong floor, saw my office, and stopped to ask directions, but he was lying."

"You still see your therapist?" Jayne set the two soup cans

in the sink to be rinsed before they were tossed into the recycling bin.

Casey shot the cans with the sprayer. "Yes," she answered testily. It was so like her sister to bring up Casey's years of therapy. "What's that got to do with Gaitlin being in my office? With him sending me possibly threatening notes in the mail?"

"You're getting notes in the mail?"

"It was just a picture this time. An eye. But I think he's trying to warn me that he's watching me. I think he might be following me in his car, too."

"What's your therapist say?"

"We haven't really discussed it. It's an open case. Linda's. I probably shouldn't even have told you." Casey frowned, shutting off the water. She picked up the colander full of potatoes and shook off the excess water. "We've mostly been talking about my dating again."

"Aha." Jayne began to stir the green bean and soup mixture with a wooden spoon. As she added milk, she nodded in the direction of the family room. "He's nice looking. Pretty relaxed for your taste."

"What's that supposed to mean?" Casey began to cut up the potatoes at the kitchen table and dropping them into a pot of water. "And yes, he is pretty cute. You don't think a nice-looking guy would want to go out with me?"

The minute the words flew out of her mouth, she wished she could take them back. They were unfair. That wasn't what Jayne said and she knew it. But Jayne made her crazy. She made Casey say things she didn't mean to say.

"I said he was nice looking, that's all," Jayne defended.

"And you said he seemed *pretty relaxed*. You don't think someone who's relaxed might be interested in me?"

"No, I did not say that. But, honestly, he's not the kind of man you usually go for."

"Jayne! How many men in my life have I ever *gone for?*"

"You have to admit John was pretty uptight." Jayne pointed the wooden spoon accusingly at her. "Talk about falling for a guy just like your father."

Casey cut the potatoes faster. Harder, if that was possible. Jayne had never liked John, not from *day one.* But he had been good to Casey. Good *for* her—at least for a while. Before the lying. The cheating.

Casey paused in the middle of slicing a potato. She had to hand it to Jayne; she really had hit home that time, hadn't she? John had been just like her father—distant, superior. Hadn't he?

Casey stared into the pot. "I really like Lincoln," she said quietly. "I wish you could be happy for me. I wish you could be just a little bit supportive." She glanced up at her sister. "I'm lonely, Jayne. Even with Daddy in the house, I'm lonely."

"I like him, Casey." She opened her arms. "I never said I didn't. I was just expressing my surprise that he's the kind of guy you would date seriously. You like men more clean-cut, more . . . I don't know . . . driven."

Casey immediately thought of Adam. Had she made a mistake throwing herself completely into this relationship with Lincoln when Adam would have been a better bet? *Would* they be more compatible? Adam was certainly driven. Certainly more clean-cut than Lincoln. She doubted the assistant deputy attorney ever let his hair get too long, and she knew there was no way he owned a corduroy jacket.

But she liked Lincoln. And she liked the fact that he liked her. "Let's talk about something else," Casey said.

She grabbed another potato. She needed to get them on the stove and boiled if the soufflé was going to be out of the oven by four. It was a good thing Jayne's kitchen had two ovens. Most of the year the second one was used to store cookie sheets, but it came in handy at Thanksgiving and Christmas.

"How's Annabelle's art class going? You said you were afraid you weren't going to like her teacher's methods."

Jayne turned around to face Casey. "Casey, I didn't mean to—"

"It's okay. Really." She waved the paring knife. "I'm seriously PMSing today. Ask Frazier," she joked. "I practically bit his head off this morning when he took too long at the rosebushes."

Jayne hesitated a beat, then picked up the conversation. "I think I'm going to like Miss Cerise. Annabelle already loves her." She covered the casserole dish with tin foil. "I'm wondering if Chad should start in the toddler class. He really does seem to be artistically talented, compared to other children his age."

Casey smiled and nodded. She knew better than to bring up the irony of Jayne spending her days fighting for the rights of the poor and the uneducated and her evenings sending her preschool children to dance classes, art classes, yoga classes. As it was for their own childhoods, the list was endless, as was the excess, in Casey's mind. If she ever had children, she wasn't going to do it this way. She knew she wouldn't be the perfect mother, she knew she wouldn't make all the right choices, but she was pretty confident she could make better choices than her parents had made and her sister was making.

Dinner went off without a hitch. The turkey was cooked perfectly. The sweet potato soufflé was a mile high. Lincoln was practically the belle of the ball. He sat next to Casey and laughed and chatted, completely at ease with her family. He complimented both Casey and Jayne multiple times on the fantastic meal and said how sorry his grandparents would be that they had decided to go to his grandfather's cousin's house for dinner instead of coming with him.

He teased the children. He talked sports scores with Joaquin. And again and again, he took the time to draw Ed out of his shell. As the children were excused and the adults pushed back from the table to have a second glass of wine, Lincoln actually got Ed to talk about what it had been like to be a professor. Ed began to tell stories of the old days, and he spoke fondly of Jayne and Casey's mother, Lorraine.

Casey was proud of her new boyfriend, proud to show him off to her family. She was touched that he went beyond the perfunctory boyfriend conversations with her father to really engage him. As Ed sat at the head of the table and wiped his mouth repeatedly with the cloth napkin from his lap, he became more animated, recalled more memories, and seemed to be enthusiastic about relating them to Lincoln.

At last, Casey stood and began to collect dirty plates. She was stuffed to the point that she was considering unbuttoning her jeans. She needed to stretch her legs before she sat down again to dig into the pies lined up on the kitchen counter.

Somewhere between her first and second trip to the kitchen, the conversation between the men turned to wild game and Joaquin made the mistake of asking Lincoln if he ever hunted. Lincoln's eyes lit up with a fire, and Casey groaned, quickly grabbing half-filled water glasses. She should have warned Joaquin to avoid any discussion involving firearms. Joaquin, an avid hunter locally, had even made a couple of trips out West to hunt elk. Jayne didn't hunt, but she didn't mind that her husband did as long as he donated the game he killed to the local charity that distributed the meat to the poor.

"I'm appalled, Joaquin. A man of your intelligence, a father?" Lincoln said, shocked. "Do you have any idea how many guns get into the hands of children each year in this country?"

"Pie? Anyone up for pie?" Casey asked, making a beeline for the kitchen door, her sister leading the way.

"He'll be fine," Jayne assured her as she entered the kitchen with an armload of dirty plates. "He can hold his own. And if he's serious about you, he needs to learn to get along with his future brother-in-law."

"*Please,*" Casey groaned, carrying plates to the sink. "We're not anywhere that far along."

Jayne tapped Casey on the shoulder. "You stay here and start rinsing and loading dishes. I need to check on the kids and then I'll make another pass by the dining room table. Once the dishwasher is full, we can just let the rest of them soak," she said as she went through the swinging door into the dining room.

Casey heard bursts of Lincoln's impassioned voice. Joaquin was equally fervent.

She mechanically rinsed, loaded, and rinsed some more. Her father wandered into the kitchen carrying a plastic bag of tub toys he must have found on the perimeter of the dining room.

"Dad, give me those."

"Thought I'd help." He glanced at his wristwatch. "Getting late. Joe will be wondering where we are."

Casey smiled to herself. Her father didn't often remember that the dog's name was actually Joe. She had nicknamed him Frazier because of the heavyweight boxer her father had admired. They started calling him Frazier, and eventually Ed forgot what the dog's name actually was.

"It was nice to hear you talk about Mom." She put the

plastic bag she had taken from him on the counter. "You don't speak of her often."

"Lorraine was a lovely woman. Soft wrists." He sat down at the kitchen table. "Her father refused to bless the marriage, but we got married anyway."

Casey smiled. The dishwasher full, she added soap, closed it, and turned it on. "That's right. But after we were born Granddad came around a little, didn't he?"

"I wasn't from the right kind of family. Worked my way through college. Not like your mother, who had her trust fund. She liked to wear red. Red was a good color for Lorraine."

Casey's throat tightened. She loved hearing her father talk so kindly of her mother. The memory of her mother's dissatisfaction with the man her father had warned her not to marry seemed to have faded. Either Ed no longer remembered his wife's unhappiness or he chose to forget. Casey liked the idea that bad memories faded with time. She only wished the same could have held true for her mother before she passed.

"Red *was* a good color for Mom, wasn't it, Daddy?" She sat down at the table across from him. She could hear Jayne talking in the dining room. The heated conversation between Joaquin and Lincoln on gun control seemed to have died down. Her sister had been right. Lincoln had been able to hold his own.

"Do you remember that little red convertible she bought herself on her fortieth birthday?"

Her father half smiled, seeming to recall. "I told her to take the damned thing back." He hooked his thumb in gesture.

Casey clapped her hands. "You did. But then she convinced you to take it for a drive before she took it back to the dealership. You guys were gone for hours. Jayne and I didn't know what had happened to you."

"Drove to Annapolis," he told her. "We stopped at this little place along the bay for cocktails."

Lorraine had always been one for cocktails. Of course, apparently so had Ed. The first time Casey's mother had caught her father cheating on her, it had been in the middle of the day in a bar just off campus. To this day, Casey didn't know what her mother had been doing there at that time of day either. Maybe she never really wanted to know.

"Mom loved that car," Casey said. "You guys used to take it out every Sunday afternoon in the summer. I remember you backing out of the driveway, top down, Mom wearing one of those silly scarves so her hair wouldn't blow."

"You got pie?" Ed asked, craning his neck. "I thought I smelled pie."

And as quick as that, the moment was over. The light of memories died in Ed's eyes, and the only thing he was concerned about was immediate gratification.

"Yeah, Dad, we've got pie." Casey rose. "What would you like? Pumpkin? Apple?"

Casey ended up staying in the kitchen and sharing a piece of each pie with her father. Jayne carried the pies into the dining room for the men. Casey tried to get her father to take his pie into the dining room, but he would have no part of it. Suddenly he became crabby and obstinate; he wanted to eat and get back to his dog. Apparently he'd had enough of memories and family for one day.

Casey was stacking dishes in the sink to soak when Lincoln walked into the kitchen carrying what was left of the pies. "Delicious. Everything was amazingly delicious," he told her, then gave her a quick kiss. "It's been a great day."

"Yeah?" She looked up at him. "Sorry I couldn't join you for dessert, serve as a mediator or something, but Dad wouldn't budge. I think we're going to have to take off shortly."

"It was fine. I'm an attorney, Casey. Arguing is what I do

best." He winked at her as he grabbed plastic wrap off the counter and began to wrap the pies. "I need to get home, too. Goats to feed." He arched his eyebrows.

With his grandmother still somewhat incapacitated, Lincoln had been helping his grandfather take care of the few animals still left on the farm. Casey knew he had tried to convince them it was time to find good homes for the chickens and goats, but to date, the old folks had refused to even consider the matter. In the meantime, several mornings and nights each week, Lincoln put on rubber Wellies and a barn coat and played farmer.

"I'm glad you joined us," Casey told him, smiling. "You made it a perfect day."

"Oh, yeah?" He leaned down to press a kiss to her neck, plastic wrap still in his hand. Then in a low voice he said, "Too bad I can't make it a perfect night, too."

Jayne pushed through the swinging door and Lincoln backed away from Casey.

"Hey, hey, hey, you two. Let's keep this kitchen a general audience rating. I've got young, easily influenced children in this house."

Casey laughed. "Dishwasher's running." She pointed. "Dishes in the sink are soaking. We probably need to get going. Dad's already gone to find his coat. He's worried about Frazier being home alone."

"I'm amazed he was willing to stay this long." Jayne turned to Lincoln. "We're glad you joined us, Lincoln. It's nice to have someone else to talk to at the dinner table. Someone new for my husband to argue with."

"Well, I appreciate you inviting me and I appreciate the engaging conversation." Lincoln smiled as he moved toward the kitchen door. "I'll check on Ed. Whenever you're ready, hon, I'll walk out with you."

Jayne barely waited until the kitchen door swung shut.

"*Hon?* Whenever you're ready, *hon?*" She grabbed Casey's shoulders in a rare show of affection. "I think he's already half in love with you. What a great guy. And right there in plain view. Why didn't you tell me you met him while working on the Gaitlin case?"

Casey, who was sweeping pie crust crumbs off the counter into her hand, turned to her sister. What was she talking about? What had she and Joaquin and Lincoln been talking about while Casey was in the kitchen with her father? "Gaitlin didn't have anything to do with me meeting Lincoln."

"He didn't?" Jayne scowled. "But he said his firm had represented Gaitlin. I just assumed—" Seeing the look on Casey's face, she halted midsentence. "Oh, gosh, I'm really sorry. Did I screw up here somewhere?"

Chapter 14

Maury lay on his back on his bunk, one arm tucked beneath his head as he studied the cartoon drawing of the turkey on the greeting card Danni-with-a-heart-over-the-"i" had sent him for Thanksgiving. He'd only written "Thinking of You! Love Danni" on the bottom.

No letter.

Maury had been thinking about Danni, too. Waiting. Enjoying the anticipation of how the relationship would unfold. Waiting to see what Danni wanted from him. A part of Maury desperately wanted to know, but another part of him didn't. Not yet. And Danni seemed to recognize that. Understand. The anticipation, for Maury, was painfully sweet.

Pain was like that. It hurt. Sometimes it hurt a lot, but at the very end of each wave of pain was a pleasure so pure. . . .

He closed his eyes thinking of the dead woman in the barrel. His last before he wound up here. What agony she had been in before she had died. How sweet that agony must have been for her. It certainly had been for Maury.

He opened his eyes and looked at the turkey again. With the day off from work and nothing to do since his sister had refused to have him for dinner, he had been contemplating for hours whether or not it was time to write back to Danni. Something simple, of course, just to test the waters. Maybe he would practice his secret code. It had been, after all, nearly two years since he had used it.

He had been thinking a lot about the code he had once used early in his career in a couple of letters to a newspaper. About who knew about it. Only the FBI, as far as he knew. Just that dyke cop and whoever she had told. Whoever believed her. Maury had sent those letters just for fun. For his own personal amusement. To tease the cops. The media. He had never expected anyone to actually be able to read them for what they truly said.

So was the dyke sending him the mail? Was *she* Danni? He supposed that could make sense. She wasn't really a woman, was she?

But Maury didn't think it was the dyke writing to him. She didn't know Maury was responsible for all those women; otherwise, he'd be on death row right now, instead of the work-release program. If she *really* knew his identity, even suspected it, he wouldn't be looking at walking out of this place.

He looked at the turkey on the card and then lifted his gaze higher to the ceiling tiles. The pattern was off in the far corner of the shabby dormitory room. Maury had discovered it the first night here. Shoddy workmanship. He hated it when patterns were screwed around with. Some people didn't understand their importance. People like that, he just wanted to . . .

Maury clenched his hands, feeling his blood pressure rise as his heart beat faster, his pulse quickening. . . .

But then he took a deep breath. He let his hands relax. He consciously lowered his heart rate. A man had to have control. Control was what allowed him to do what he wanted. Allowed him the pleasures.

He reached under his pillow and retrieved the half a candy bar he had saved from last night. He unwrapped the paper slowly, inhaling the heavenly chocolaty scent.

Again, he thought of the young woman in the barrel. He thought about her pretty red hair and how it had stuck to her temples wet with blood.

He wondered what Danni would think of the woman in the barrel. . . .

"Your firm represented Gaitlin?" Casey demanded, hanging on to her car door, putting it between her and Lincoln.

Casey had managed to get her coat on and say good-bye to Jayne and Joaquin and the kids. She had gotten her father in the passenger's side of the car and buckled him in. Now, standing in the cold driveway, in the dark, she stared at Lincoln.

"What?" He looked totally confused. Then, by the light from the car interior, a flash of guilt. "Yeah, my firm did represent him. Casey, what's wrong?"

"What's wrong? What's wrong?" she repeated in amazement. "I told you almost three weeks ago that I had a problem with this guy. I told you his name and you didn't feel it necessary to tell me your firm was representing him in the case that I'm supposed to testify in?"

"Casey." He looked at his feet.

Bad sign.

He looked up. "Casey, this is complicated. He wasn't my client."

"Are we going?" Ed demanded from the other side of the car. "We should be going."

Casey leaned over to speak to him. "Dad, we're going." She straightened up and turned back to Lincoln. "But your firm represented him. His grandmother hired you to defend him. To defend this *murderer.*"

"Casey," he said entirely too calmly, "it's what attorneys do. And I wasn't his attorney. One of my colleagues was."

Her lower lip trembled. She felt betrayed. And she felt stupid for feeling that way. Of course that was what attorneys did. Gaitlin had a right to an attorney, no matter how guilty he was.

This wasn't personal. That's what Lincoln was saying.

She didn't care. It *was* personal. It was personal because Gaitlin had invaded her privacy. He had made people doubt her. Doubt her word. He had made her doubt herself.

"I want to go home," her father repeated petulantly. "Take me home. Snow flurries in the forecast. I have to check the forecast."

"I need to go," she told Lincoln. She climbed into the car and tried to pull the door shut, but he held it so she couldn't.

He walked around the door and crouched so that he was eye level with her. "Casey, I'm sorry. I should have told you, but honestly, I don't talk about our firm's clients. I didn't think—"

"You didn't think I would want to know that you had represented the man I'm trying to have thrown in jail for the rest of his life?" *The man she feared was stalking her,* she wanted to say. But of course he didn't know about that.

"I didn't think it was that important to our relationship."

She wasn't going to let him off that easily. "I told you who it was. You acted as if you didn't know him. As if you didn't know *of* him."

"I should have told you," he offered, with a shrug. His emotion seemed honest. "I'm sorry. Okay? I don't know what else you want me to say."

So, no real explanation. "I have to go," she said.

"Casey, don't go like this. Angry."

"I'll talk to you tomorrow." She tugged on the car door he was still blocking. "Excuse me."

Lincoln was quiet for a moment. He just stood there looking down at her. Then he stepped out of the way.

Casey slammed the door shut and started the car.

"Snow flurries," Ed said, folding his arms across his chest as she backed out of the driveway.

"Snow flurries," she echoed.

Casey didn't call Lincoln that night and when she saw his name on the Caller ID, she didn't pick up. She didn't listen to the messages he left, either.

On Black Friday, she left the house at six A.M. to shop with Jayne at the Rehoboth Beach outlets for a few hours. The two sisters followed this tradition annually, not so much because they were big shoppers, but because it had been an institution with their mother. Jayne and Casey didn't get dressed up, they didn't go to department stores with escalators, and they didn't have a girls' lunch at an expensive white-tablecloth restaurant, but they shopped for Christmas gifts.

As the sisters picked through super deals on winter sweaters and cute outfits for the kids, Jayne didn't ask about Lincoln and Casey didn't offer any information. They totally ignored the subject, as if Casey had not brought her boyfriend to Thanksgiving dinner the day before, as if she wasn't dating anyone at all. A part of Casey was annoyed that her sister didn't ask how things now stood with Lincoln, but she thought maybe Jayne was just giving her some privacy.

The crowds at the stores started to be overwhelming by midmorning, and Casey was home by noon. When she walked into the laundry room from the garage, her father startled her. He stood solidly in the doorway between the kitchen and the laundry as if planted like a tree.

"Hey, Dad," she greeted, wrestling an armful of shopping bags into the room and resting them against the dryer.

Frazier was lying on the floor in the kitchen just behind Ed. The dog's posture suggested they had been there a while, that they had been waiting for her. Casey closed the door behind her, locked it, and unwound her scarf. She could hear the sound of the TV in the living room. A commercial. "Everything okay, Dad?"

"You were gone a long time." He removed his handkerchief from his pants pocket and wiped his mouth. This was a new habit he had developed recently; he was continually wiping his mouth with a handkerchief, a tissue, his napkin, the arm cover off the couch if he could find nothing else.

"Not so long. Five hours, maybe. Not as long as I'm gone when I'm at work."

"Frazier missed you."

"Oh, he did, did he?" Smiling, she hung her scarf and then her coat on the hook. "And how about you? Did you miss me?"

"That's ridiculous. I'm your father." He turned and shuffled into the kitchen.

Casey took a deep breath, exhaled, and followed him. "You hungry? I thought I'd make a salad with some of the turkey Jayne gave us yesterday. Would you like one?"

He sat down at the table. "Don't like salad. Rabbit food. You think I live in a hutch?"

"Then a sandwich. I could make you a turkey sandwich with lettuce and pickles and mayonnaise. You like it that way."

"I do?" He looked up at her, the lines around his mouth heavy. He wasn't just contrary today; he was . . . sad.

"Dad, are you okay?" Casey pulled a chair out next to him and sat down. "Has someone been here?" She hesitated. "Has Richard Nixon been back?"

"President Nixon is dead, Casey."

She had to fight a smile. It wasn't that she wanted to laugh at her father, just the bizarre situation they both found themselves in these days. What was that saying? It's better to laugh than to cry?

"I know Nixon is dead, Dad. But was someone here? Did you see someone looking in the window again?"

"I don't want to talk about it." He snapped his fingers and the dog rose and loped over to him. "I'll take that sandwich. You want a biscuit, boy?" He fished a dog treat out of his pocket and tossed it.

Frazier caught it midair.

Casey considered grilling her father further. If someone had been here, she should probably call the police. But what were they going to do? Question her father? Check for shoe prints in the flower bed? This was beginning to play out like a broken record.

Frustrated, she got up to make the sandwiches. "Dad, what do you think about Lincoln?" she asked.

"He understands the importance of our climate. How it affects our day-to-day lives."

She set the mayo and lettuce on the counter. "What do you think about him as a person? I mean . . . for me?"

"You planning on marrying him?"

She found the turkey wrapped in waxed paper and closed the refrigerator. "Actually, right now I'm not sure I'm even speaking to him, so no, no plans for marriage this week."

"Why aren't you speaking?" Ed harrumphed. "You have a fight?"

"A disagreement. I got angry because he didn't tell me something he should have told me."

"You like honesty," her father observed, scratching the dog behind his ears.

She wanted to say, "Doesn't everyone?" but she knew that

wasn't true. Her parents had had secrets and it appeared, in hindsight, that, at some point in their lives, they had agreed that honesty and disclosure were not necessary to their relationship. It had to be true; otherwise, why would they have stayed together? Even though things had been bad in the house, never in the twenty-two years she had lived at home had there ever been even the suggestion that either of them might consider divorce.

"What'd he lie about? Another woman?"

As Casey pulled slices of bread from the bag, she turned toward her father, surprised that he was initiating conversation. Sensible conversation. He actually seemed interested in what was going on in her life. "It was something about work that sort of spilled into personal." She spun the bag from the end before clipping it with a clothespin. "It's kind of complicated."

"You think I'm stupid? You think I can't understand?"

She put the bread in the cupboard. "No, I don't think you're stupid." She felt her temper rise a little, but she kept it in check, reminding herself that he couldn't know how he was now and she couldn't punish him for who he had once been. "That was my polite way of saying I don't want to tell you what the fight is about. Some things are private."

He sat back in the chair, crossing his arms over his chest. He had pulled a sweater vest over the oxford shirt she had left out on the bed for him. He looked nice today. Like his old self, sort of.

He scowled, wrinkling his forehead. "So why didn't you just say that?"

She took a second before responding. "I wanted your opinion on what you thought about Lincoln. I might be making more of this issue than I should. I didn't want to go into the details about the disagreement. I just wanted to know what you think about the man I'm dating. I wanted to sort of talk it out with someone. With you."

"Frazier likes him."

"Do *you*? Do you think he's good for me?" She hesitated. "Do you think I can trust him?"

Her father didn't answer but seemed to be thinking.

Casey spread the mayo on the last piece of bread, screwed the lid on the jar, then put the jar in the refrigerator.

"I liked Billy Bosley. He drove a white car."

"Dad, Billy hurt me," she said stiffly.

"He had a nice car."

She arranged the lettuce on two slices of bread. "I just wanted to know what you thought of Lincoln," she repeated. "We're not talking about Billy."

"Because you're fighting with him."

"Yes, I'm fighting with Lincoln and I don't know what to do. I want to be cautious. I want to be sure he's—"

The doorbell rang and Frazier leapt to his feet, barking wildly.

Casey grabbed a kitchen towel and wiped her hands, then walked out of the kitchen. The dog followed. If that was Lincoln she wasn't sure she wanted to let him in. She didn't know if she was ready to talk to him. And how juvenile was that?

But as she passed the living room window she saw that the car in her driveway was not a blue Mini Coop. It was a silver BMW.

She put her eye to the peephole to see who was there. Surprised, she flipped the dead bolt, signaled for the dog to sit, and opened the door. "Adam."

Chapter 15

"How 'bout some cereal, honey bunny?" Angel leaned over to put her face right in front of Buddy's. "Brunch, they call it. Breakfast and lunch together."

The little boy squealed and grabbed at her nose. She pulled back and he laughed again.

"Can you catch me? Can you get Mama's nose?" He grabbed again and this time she let him catch her. "What a smart boy!"

He laughed. She laughed.

"Told you, you was smart. Smart enough to go to college, I'd say." She looked into his dark, liquidy eyes. He had the skin color and eyes of his daddy, but his smarts came from her family. She was sure of that. No offense against Shonda, whose cousin was Buddy's father, but the man was stupid. Stupid enough to try to buy crack from an undercover cop in Wilmington. Enough to make it look like he was dealing—which he was. Buddy wouldn't be seeing him for at least five years, which was fine with Angel.

"Mama!" Buddy hollered, shaking his little hands.

"Mama," Angel echoed.

She heard the familiar groan of her car door open, then

heard it slam shut. She dropped a handful of Toasty O's on Buddy's high-chair tray. The other car door banged shut. Leaning over him, she pulled back the curtain. The Asshole Brothers were back.

"Be right back, honey bunny." Angel kissed Buddy's short, wiry hair and walked out of the kitchen. She met Charlie at the front door, one hand perched on her hip. "Where have you been all night?"

Charlie walked past her. James followed, slamming the door so hard that a photo of Buddy, taken at Sears on his first birthday, rattled on the wall. The men both stunk of beer, their clothes were wrinkled, and James had the makings of a black eye. Charlie's lip was fat and there was dried blood at the corner of his mouth. One of them smelled like puke.

"I said, where you been, Charlie?" Angel demanded. "I told you I had to go to work and Shonda couldn't baby-sit. You said you would watch Buddy so I could make us some extra money. You promised." She gave him a little push. "My sister's called me three times wantin' to know when I'll be there. She's swamped at the store."

James brushed past her and went down the hall to the bathroom.

Charlie walked into the cluttered living room. The toe of his boot caught the end of a big plastic dump truck and he almost tripped. He kicked the truck hard. It hit the wall next to the TV and exploded into a million plastic pieces.

The sound scared Buddy and he started to cry. Or maybe it was just the sound of Charlie's voice. Buddy cried a lot when Charlie was around.

"Mommy'll be there in a minute, Buddy," Angel called toward the kitchen. She looked back at Charlie, who had plopped himself on the couch and was digging around for the remote between the lumpy cushions.

"I wanna know where you been all night," she repeated stubbornly. "I make a nice turkey breast dinner. I peeled potatoes and everything, and before I'm even done eatin', you and James are pullin' out of the parkin' lot in *my* car." She crossed her arms over her chest. "I waited up half the night for you. I thought you was dead in a ditch somewhere."

"I told you we was goin' for cigarettes." He pulled the remote out of the couch and hit the power button.

"It don't take all night to get cigarettes." She moved in front of the TV, blocking his view.

Charlie leaned one way and then the other. "Move."

"You been drinkin' all night, haven't you? Sittin' in some trashy bar talkin' to trashy girls."

"You're drivin' me crazy. I just had to get out of here. I just wanted to have a quiet beer with my brother. That a big crime?"

"Bars close at one. It's noon. Where were you after that? Where were you spending my money?"

"I got money."

"You don't. You don't have any money. That's my money you're drinkin' at the bar and my food stamps you're eatin'. You *and* your brother are eatin'."

"I'll get money."

"How? How you gonna get money if you don't get off your lazy, fat ass and apply for a job? Your granny's not gonna keep sendin' your sorry asses money. You know how much she paid that lawyer to get you off? She had to mortgage her house to get that money."

Charlie changed the channel. Angel was getting angrier by the second. She was pissed that he had been out with James instead of here with her and Buddy after she went to all that trouble to make him a nice Thanksgiving dinner. She was pissed that he had spent money at a bar, money they didn't have. And she was pissed mostly at herself for ever telling him he could move in when he got out of prison. Amber had warned her not to. So had Shonda. At the time, Angel had reasoned that both of them had worthless boyfriends living with them, so who were they to be giving advice? Now she was thinking she should have listened to them in the first place.

She snatched the remote out of Charlie's hand.

The second she did it, she knew it was a mistake. Charlie came off the couch in a rage. Angel backed up, but not far enough, not fast enough. He hit her across the cheek so hard that the remote flew out of her hand. She screamed as she went down on one knee, grabbing her face. As she hit the stinky carpet, she instinctively curled up, protecting her face. Just in case there was more to come.

In the other room, Buddy was crying so hard that he was gagging.

James hollered something from the bathroom.

"You hit me," Angel accused, choking back a sob. Even though Charlie had hit her only with his open hand, the whole side of her face throbbed and her neck felt like it had been stretched too hard and snapped back like a rubber band.

"I didn't hit you." He picked the remote up off the floor and went back to the couch. "If I had hit you, you'd have known it." He sat down again.

Still on the floor, Angel sat up, drew her knees up, and hugged them to her chest. Buddy was still bawling in the other room. She wiped her runny nose with her sleeve.

"Make him shut up," Charlie warned, changing the channel.

"Okay," she sniffed, starting to get up.

"Make him shut up!" Charlie shouted. "Or I'll shut him up!"

Angel scrambled to her feet and hurried for the kitchen, her own pain forgotten. She had to protect Buddy. Buddy was her baby. She couldn't let Charlie hit her baby, because if he did, she knew she'd have to kill Charlie.

"I hope it's okay that I stopped by. I tried to call from my cell." Dressed casually in khakis and a dark green jacket, Adam held what appeared to be a homemade pie in a blue pottery pie plate. "There was a lot of static, though. I couldn't get the call to go through. I don't think the towers are great around here."

"Happens all the time. No rhyme or reason. Some days I have three bars in my driveway, some days one. " As she backed up to open the door for Adam, she pointed to Frazier and said, "Stay, boy." She motioned to Adam. "Come on in. He's big but he's friendly."

"I . . . I brought pie." He held it in both hands, showing her. "Someone in my office made it. Staff gave me, like, five homemade pies," he explained almost bashfully.

She laughed. "What kind?"

"Apple. I thought I should play it safe."

"Come on into the kitchen and meet my dad. We were just sitting down to have lunch. Leftover turkey sandwiches. Would you like to join us?" Casey led him through the dining room. Frazier followed on their heels, sniffing Adam's coat.

"I'd love a turkey sandwich. If it's not too much trouble. You have a nice home," he said, looking around. "Real turkey sounds great. I think we had 'turkey product' at the nursing home yesterday."

"Oh, I'm sorry." She turned back, grimacing. As she made eye contact, she was glad she was dressed and had on make-up. She would have hated for Adam to see her in sweatpants, a stained T-shirt, and her glasses, her usual day-off attire when she wasn't going anywhere.

"Dad, look, we have a visitor." She gestured toward

Adam, then introduced them. "Adam Preston, my father, Dr. Ed McDaniel."

"Dr. McDaniel, it's very nice to meet you." Adam nimbly switched the pie to his left hand and offered his right. "Are you a medical doctor?"

Ed's mouth was full of turkey sandwich. Mayonnaise oozed from the corners of his lips.

"Retired professor. A PhD in American literature."

Chewing noisily, Ed stared at Adam.

Casey held a napkin out to her father. "Adam and I know each other from work," she explained. She was nervous and she didn't know why. "He's a prosecuting attorney for the county, Dad."

Ed took the napkin, looked back at Adam, paused, then looked at Casey, obviously dismissing their guest. "Got any chips?"

Casey felt her face grow warm. "Sorry," she mouthed to Adam.

He smiled, dropping his hand and walking to the counter to set the pie down.

Casey grabbed a bag of chips and a wooden bowl. "Here you go." She carried the bowl of chips to the table. "Let me take your coat, Adam." She glanced at the counter. "The pie looks great."

"I'll take care of my coat. Where should I put it?" He slipped out of his coat. He was wearing an oxford shirt, but it was obviously a weekend shirt, dark blue with a subtle red pinstripe. Dressy for a holiday weekend, but nice. Very nice.

"Laundry room around the corner. Pick a hook, any hook." She pointed in the general direction. "Would you like mayo, lettuce, and pickle on your sandwich?"

"Anything. Sure, that'll be great. Real turkey and *anything*."

Casey took the loaf of bread out of the cupboard and grabbed another plate. As she picked up the knife from in the sink, she realized her heart was beating a little fast. She felt silly, almost giddy. It was nice of Adam to stop by. *And* he brought pie. She was surprised by how pleased she was to see him. Pleased bordering on thrilled. But how had he known where she lived? She didn't recall having discussed where her house was.

"You just driving by?" she asked him as he walked back into the kitchen.

"Yeah, passing by." Adam sat in the chair across from Ed. "No. Actually, I have to confess . . ." He hesitated, then chuckled as if caught in some mischief. "This morning when I got out of bed, I decided I absolutely was not going to the office today. I wasn't really sure what to do with myself. I had all these pies and I was sort of driving around wondering what to do with them. I remembered you lived in this neighborhood so I took a chance."

She spread mayo on his bread. "I told you where I lived?"

"You should be an attorney, Casey. You're good at extracting confessions. *And* you're good at remembering important details." He took a chip from the bowl. "No, you did *not* tell me where you lived, because, I suspect, a woman in your business knows not to share personal information with a stranger. Truth is, I saw your address somewhere in the Gaitlin records. I remembered it," he finished sheepishly.

He was so charming. So good-looking. And so *honest*.

Casey carried the third sandwich to the table and sat down, then popped up again. "Drinks. I have bottled water. And green tea."

"Water would be fine," Adam said.

Ed continued to crunch potato chips.

Casey grabbed three water bottles and sat down.

"So you took the *whole* day off?" Casey asked, pretending to be shocked. "Thanksgiving *and* Black Friday? Do you take Christmas and Easter off too?"

Adam picked up his sandwich. "Actually, I worked yesterday. Before I went to the nursing home to have my turkey product Thanksgiving dinner with my grandfather."

"He's better, then?"

Adam took a bite of sandwich and reached for his water bottle. "No. Not really. He can't eat or anything, but I feel like I should be there anyway. Doctors can only guess what goes on in the mind of someone in a coma, but for all they know, he could know when I come by and when I don't. He might hear what I'm saying to him." He held the sandwich in both hands, looking down at it. "He probably doesn't. I know that, but . . ." He let his voice trail off.

Casey's chest tightened. She could tell how much Adam loved his grandfather. How he was hurting for him. "I think it's good that you went," she said, empathizing with his sadness. "I know he'd be happy to know you'd eat turkey product for him."

They were both silent for a moment and Casey felt a connection between them. A warmth that seemed to emanate from Adam right into her very bones. He seemed to be a man who wasn't afraid of his feelings and she liked that. Admired it.

Ed, done with his lunch, and not in the least bit interested in Adam's compassion for his grandfather, pushed away from the table, his chair squeaking as it dragged across the tile floor, the table rocking as he got up.

Casey steadied the table. "You done, Dad? Wipe your mouth. Here." She handed him his crumpled napkin. "Wipe your mouth."

Ed removed a handkerchief from his back pocket and wiped his mouth as he shuffled out of the kitchen. "Come on," he told Frazier.

A minute later, Casey heard the TV come on in the living room. The DVD she had left on this morning was still playing—*True Grit*. When he couldn't remember how to switch the DVD to video, sometimes he would just watch the same movie over and over again. Sometimes she fixed it for him, but sometimes she let it go; she figured it gave them both a break from The Weather Channel.

She turned back to Adam. "My dad doesn't mean to be rude."

"Of course not." He motioned with his sandwich. "This has got to be the best turkey I've ever had in my life."

She laughed.

"I'm not kidding. I can't tell you how nice it is to have homemade food, even just a sandwich. I'm so busy at the office that I don't have the time to cook. Or the energy, by the time I finally get home from work at night. I miss it."

"So you cook?" She sipped her water.

"I like to think so. I took some culinary classes once upon a time."

For the next half hour, Adam and Casey sat at the kitchen table and talked about food, about favorite restaurants, about some place his parents had always taken him for his birthday when he was a kid. They sampled the pie, too, which was delicious.

"You don't have to do that," Casey told Adam as he rinsed off the sandwich plates.

"It's the least I can do." He turned to her, grabbing a hand towel to dry his hands. "Listen, I have a benefit dinner I have to go to next week. I know it's short notice, but do you think you could possibly go?"

Before she had a chance to think or respond, he went on.

"My cousin was supposed to go with me but she called and cancelled. It's black tie, at the DuPont Hotel." He moved closer to her, taking her hand. "You'd be doing me a huge favor if you'd go. It's not the kind of event a man can show up at without a date. Not from my family. People start to talk, if you know what I mean."

Casey only had to think for a second. In fact, she purposely didn't let herself think too long on the matter. Why not? She didn't know right now how she felt about Lincoln. And they had made no agreement about dating exclusively anyway. And she would be doing Adam a favor. "I'll have to make sure I'm not on call. I take one weekend a month. I share with other advocates in the county. But if my calendar's clear, I'd love to," she said. "I'll also have to check with my sister to see if she can come stay with my dad, but if I can make that happen—"

"Great." He grabbed her arms, surprising her, and brushed a quick kiss on her cheek.

Her cheek tingled as he stepped back. He smelled of expensive cologne. Different from Lincoln's cologne, but nice. Casey suddenly felt a jumble of emotions.

"So I'll call you Monday about Saturday night? It's a long ride, but I have a limo reserved."

Casey followed him into the laundry room, where he was getting his jacket. "Limo? I don't know." She hesitated.

"Come on, it'll be fun. Most of the women wear long gowns, but you don't have to."

Long gown, she thought, trying not to panic. She didn't have a gown. But Jayne did. Jayne had several she wore to charity balls. Casey might even go shopping and buy her own.

"Thanks so much for the sandwich, and the good company, and agreeing to get me out of not having a date."

They walked to the front door. Adam's good-bye was quick and not at all awkward. Casey watched him back out of her driveway from behind the curtain in the living room window and then grabbed the phone, trying to decide if she should call Jayne or Marcy first.

Chapter 16

Dylan checked the surveillance camera; yellow VW Bug with a cute chick in a short denim skirt pumping gas. She looked to be about his age. Eighteen, maybe nineteen. Old enough not to be jailbait.

In the corner of the screen he saw the blue car that was parked there when he arrived for his four-to-twelve shift. If it was still there in the morning, the boss, Mr. Cain, would call the cops or have it towed. He did it all the time.

Dylan wondered when people would learn they couldn't just leave their cars in parking lots when they broke down. That was customer parking. Someone might need that space.

Not that they were ever that busy anymore. Not with the new Wawa so close.

Dylan went back to loading cigarettes in the trays that slid up over his head in the racks over the cash register. Half the stockroom was full of crap: cigarettes, chips, cases of Coke products. The store shelves all needed to be stocked before morning, and it looked like Dylan would be doing a lot of it himself. Pete was supposed to be working with him, but the dick called in sick again. Probably hungover. Dylan was thinking Pete wouldn't have his job for long. Mr. Cain was going to fire him for sure.

The girl with the VW shut off the pump, grabbed her keys, and sashayed toward the mini-mart door. Dylan turned away from the surveillance screen, pulled his black beanie down farther on his head, and started loading cigarette packs again, playing it cool. "Hey," he greeted when she walked in.

She glanced in his direction. Smiled. She had a nice smile.

"Hey."

"Cold out?" he asked, sneaking a peek at her legs as she went down the candy aisle.

"Freezing. Calling for icy rain tonight or some such craziness as that." She walked to the soda cooler and took out an orange Fanta. As she came up the chips aisle, she grabbed a bag of Doritos. "I hate driving when it's icy."

"Yeah. It gets kinda crazy. People swervin' all over. Old farts drivin' like five miles an hour."

She laughed, setting down her chips and drink. "Exactly." She looked at him. She had thick black eyeliner around her eyes and pink sparkly lip gloss. "You new?"

"Been here about seven months." He shrugged, then rang her up. "Sucks, but it pays the rent."

"There used to be this other guy here. Tattoo of a bowling ball on his cheek." She tapped her cheek.

"That would be Pete." He took his time getting a bag for her.

"Weird guy. Trying to, like, give me free food and stuff if I'd go out with him."

"Yup, that would be Pete." He put her chips and drink in the plastic bag, can in first so it wouldn't squish her chips. "Goin' out?"

"Not partying or anything. Just a girlfriend's house." She reached for her bag, still looking right at him.

She liked him. *Definitely.*

"What's your name?" she asked. Her tone wasn't like, "What's your name because you're in big trouble." It was like, "What's your name because you're cute."

He tried not to look stupid. "Dylan."

"Like the singer." She bobbed her head in approval. She had long, pretty, brown hair, shiny. Didn't even look like it had been dyed. "Very cool. I'm Ashley." She started to back away from the counter.

"Ashley." He bobbed his head the same way she had. "Well, you be careful out there on the ice tonight, *Ashley.* Watch out for the old farts."

She laughed, turning away.

He watched her walk out the door. Then, on the surveillance screen, he watched her get into her yellow Bug, start it up, and drive away.

Ashley, he thought, grinning as he turned up the radio on the back counter. Very cute. And *definitely* into him.

Dylan went back to stocking cigarettes. When he emptied the case of Slim Lights, he checked the cameras. Parking lot was empty except his car and the abandoned blue one. He ducked under the counter and went down the bread aisle, grabbing a pack of Zebra Cakes as he went by. He walked into the stockroom, tucked another case of cigs under his arm, and tried to open the snack cake cellophane package with one hand and his teeth as he went back into the store.

A guy standing just inside the door checking out the newspapers startled Dylan. He hadn't seen the car in the parking lot. Hadn't heard the store door open. The guy was wearing baggy jeans and a black hoodie, the hood pulled up over his head.

Dylan hurried down the aisle, threw the case up on the

counter, and ducked under the counter. He wasn't supposed to leave the cash register, not to go into the stockroom, not to take a piss. If he had to leave the counter for any reason, he was supposed to lock the cash register and the front door.

"Hey," Dylan greeted, moving the case of cigarettes to the back counter. You never knew when some nutcase would try to steal something. "Cold night, huh?" He pulled the cellophane package on the cakes the rest of the way open and dumped one out into his hand. He took a bite.

The guy looking at the newspapers didn't say anything.

Dylan, feeling a little weird, checked the surveillance camera again. Definitely no car. The guy had to have parked on the street or walked in. Neither seemed likely. There weren't really any neighborhoods nearby. This wasn't the kind of place where you saw many walk-ins.

Chewing on the sweet cake, Dylan scooted over a little, trying to get a better look at the guy in the hoodie. In his training, that was of one the things Mr. Cain had emphasized— always getting a good look at the customers. When people know you're watching them, they're less likely to steal or rob you. You *are* robbed, you'll have a better chance of telling the police what the dude looked like.

From here, Dylan couldn't tell anything about the guy. Black, white, old, young. His hands were covered by the sleeves of the hoodie. He could have been a *she* for all Dylan knew.

The guy picked up a local paper off the rack and walked toward the register. Dylan still couldn't see his face. Hood was too big.

"Marlboro Lights. Box," he said.

Definitely a *he*.

"Anything else?" Still munching his cake, Dylan turned around to get the cigarettes out of the overhead rack behind him. When he turned back, the customer was pointing a big-ass pistol at him.

The cake in Dylan's mouth suddenly went dry. He felt like he was going to puke. The pack of cigarettes fell to the floor as he raised both hands over his head. Dylan swallowed the cake in his mouth. He didn't know what to say. God, he really did want to puke.

The guy waved the gun at the cash register. "All of it. In a bag."

Dylan was shaking all over. He kept his hands over his head as he moved toward the cash register. *No sudden moves. Just do what they want. Give them whatever they want.* That was what Mr. Cain said. Pete said Cain was an asshole, but Dylan didn't know if that was true. He had to be a pretty good guy to tell a high school dropout, minimum wage employee how to keep from getting killed in a mini-mart stickup.

"Come on," the guy barked. It didn't sound like his real voice. It sounded like he was trying to disguise it. Like Dylan would be able to identify him when he couldn't even see his face. Which meant the cameras hadn't gotten his face either.

He waved the gun again.

"Don't shoot. Don't shoot," Dylan said. Mr. Cain said not to talk to them. Not to get them aggravated. Just give them what they want and then get them out.

Dylan's hands shook as he tried to hit a button to make the cash register open. It wouldn't just open, though. You had to ring something up. "Gotta . . . gotta ring something up to open it," he said, sounding all scared and girly.

Without thinking, Dylan rung up his Zebra Cakes. He wasn't allowed to eat them without paying for them. He ate a pack every night. Never rung them up. That made him a thief. Just like this guy. He got out of this in one piece, he swore he would pay for everything he ate from now on.

Bile rose in Dylan's throat and he choked a little as the door on the register popped open. He reached under the counter to get a plastic bag. Some big mini-marts, nicer ones, had one of those red buttons you pushed to call the police. Not this one. Dylan was just supposed to call 911 if he got robbed. Lock the door behind the robber and then call the police and wait behind the counter. Those were his instructions.

"Hurry up. You want me to hurry you up?" the guy in the hoodie threatened.

"I'm hurrying. Don't shoot me." Dylan stuffed the money into the bag. "You want anything else? Carton of cigarettes?" The minute the words came out of his mouth, he realized how stupid they were. The guy was stealing cash out of the register and Dylan was offering him cigs, too? Mr. Cain would fire him for sure.

"You getting mouthy, boy?"

"No. No." Suddenly Dylan had to piss. He had to piss and puke. "That's it. That's all the money." He shoved the bag across the counter and stepped back, raising his hands again.

The guy grabbed the plastic bag bulging with bills with his left hand, pointed the pistol with his right. It had a really long barrel for a pistol, longer than a cop's gun. More like a six-shooter in those old cowboy movies or something.

"Hey, man, it's cool." Dylan stared at the gun as he stepped backward. "I'm cool." Why was the guy still standing there? Dylan had done what he'd asked. He had the money. Wasn't he afraid someone was going to pull up to the gas pump? Walk in for a pack of cigarettes?

"You look stupid in that hat," the guy in the hoodie said, lowering the barrel of the pistol, but still pointing it.

A part of Dylan's mind registered that the gun had fired

even before he felt the explosion of pain. His ears were filled with the sound of the gun going off and then the sound of his own scream as he flew backward under the impact, then down as his legs crumpled.

As Dylan hit the cement floor behind the counter, his hands instinctively went to his balls. His whole body felt like it was on fire, but his crotch was an inferno. It seemed to take forever to tilt his head. Look down.

There was blood everywhere; his jeans were soaked. There were bits of red stuff. Flesh.

Dylan's head spun. He was dizzy. Sick to his stomach. It hurt so bad that he couldn't find the strength to scream again. His eyelids fluttered, and the last thing he saw before he blacked out was the surveillance screen, empty except for the gas pumps and the blue car.

"Frazier doesn't want you to go." Ed sat on the couch, his hand on the dog's head. Both of them were looking at her as if she had just eaten their last cookie.

"Dad." Casey grimaced, fiddling with the hook and eye on the back of her gown. She had to contort herself in all sorts of ridiculous ways to reach it. She could have used some help, but her father was useless when it came to this sort of thing, and Jayne was in the kitchen on her cell phone. Her sister had been on her phone since she'd arrived half an hour ago, on time for once. She and Joaquin were fighting.

"Why don't you want me to go, Dad?"

"I don't care if you go," he harrumphed. "It's the dog."

Finally satisfied with how the back of the gown was laying, Casey let her arms fall. She'd tried on all three of Jayne's gowns, then shopped for two evenings, then decided her favorite gown was the teal satin she'd tried on a week ago in her sister's bedroom, the same gown Jayne had worn to the Heart Ball last year.

She ran her hand over her hair, which she'd already smoothed several times. She had enough straightening serum in it to keep it stick straight through a windstorm. "Okay, Dad, so why doesn't Frazier want me to go? Jayne is going to be here and you're going to have a really nice evening. She brought a John Wayne movie that you don't have. She's going to make popcorn on the stove. The real stuff, not microwave. She's even staying the night so we can all have breakfast together in the morning." She opened her arms. "What possible complaint could *Frazier* have?"

"It's not safe." He scratched the dog behind the ears, not making eye contact with her. "You go, he can't protect you."

Ed seemed worried. Scared. But he wasn't really making sense. She wondered if she needed to make an appointment for him with his doctor. She knew that one of the symptoms of advanced Alzheimer's could be unreasonable fear, paranoia, but her father was still functioning pretty well. He was still caring for himself personally, still eating, still showing interest in his dog and the things he liked, even if they were now limited. And his memory was improving; that wasn't her imagination.

"You'll be fine, Dad."

"Not me. You," he mumbled, not looking at her.

"I can take care of myself, Dad. I don't need Frazier or you to protect me. I'm an adult. I've taken care of myself for years. And I'm going with Adam." She sat down on the couch beside him, taking care not to wrinkle the gown. "Didn't you like Adam? He brought pie."

Her father cut his eyes at her. "I like Lincoln. Where's Lincoln? He understands weather patterns. He'll want to know about the low system gathering over the Great Lakes."

She exhaled. For days, her father had been asking where

Lincoln was. She'd finally talked to Lincoln midweek. They had talked a little bit about why she was so upset and he had apologized again. He seemed sincerely remorseful. And he still wanted to see her. He said he thought they could get past this "little bump in the road."

She hadn't broken up with him because she wasn't convinced that was what she wanted, but they were definitely in a time-out. She hadn't mentioned to him her date with Adam. Lincoln was taking his grandparents to an anniversary party tonight and would be staying all evening with them. She reasoned that she wasn't obligated to tell him what she was doing on a night they hadn't made plans together.

A bit of a stretch, but so far, her rationalization was working for her.

Casey looked at her father. "Lincoln had something else to do tonight, so I'm going with Adam to a charity dinner and auction at the DuPont Hotel in Wilmington. Dad, you should be happy for me. Adam is a very well-respected man in the state. He could be attorney general some day. Or a senator."

Ed scowled.

She sat there for a minute. She could hear Jayne talking rapidly, tension in her voice. Obviously, this wasn't a good night for her to come and stay with their father.

Maybe this was a bad idea all around, Casey going out with Adam. Somehow, now that she was dressed, all the rationalization in the world just didn't feel right. When she had talked to Lincoln on Wednesday, she had realized how much she missed him. How much she wanted to trust him. Be with him.

She was so confused by her emotions. Adam was a great guy for her. Almost perfect. She really liked him, but Lincoln . . . she felt as if she could *love* him.

She groaned inwardly. What was wrong with her, even thinking *that* word? Surely the word *love* was the kiss of death in modern dating. She wasn't *in love* with Lincoln. They hardly knew each other yet. She had slept with him because she was lonely. Because he was lonely.

It was just that compared to Adam, Lincoln just seemed more right. His edges were a little less sharp. He was less like her. Casey felt as if he brought a balance to her day. To how she felt about the world and herself.

The doorbell rang.

Frazier barked.

"He's here," Ed pouted, sitting back on the couch, arms crossed over his chest. "You'll be late. I won't sleep a wink."

"Won't sleep? Whom are you kidding? Daddy, you never sat up waiting for me when I was a teenager." She went to the door. "Now, please be nice."

Adam was dressed in a classic black tuxedo and a real bow tie, and his hair was combed back off his face in dark, shiny waves. He looked as if he'd just stepped off the pages of *GQ* magazine, and he smelled even better than he looked.

"Wow. Wow, Casey, you look incredible," he said, still standing in the door. He didn't seem to be able to take his eyes off her for a second, and she could feel herself flush from her toes to her hairline.

"Thank you."

"For you." He offered an exquisite nosegay of white roses and lily of the valley. "I hope it's okay. My assistant said not, under any circumstances, to order you a corsage. She said women didn't like them hanging on their gowns."

Casey couldn't stop smiling as she accepted the flowers. No one had ever given her such amazing flowers. Such expensive flowers. "They're beautiful." She brought them to her nose, inhaling the sweet fragrance.

"Come on in." She waved Adam into the living room, smiling. "Let me tell my sister we're going and I'll grab my coat."

She hurried for the kitchen, turning around halfway there. "Thank you for the flowers. They really are beautiful."

Leaving Adam to say hello to her father, Casey went into the kitchen. She hated to interrupt Jayne's phone call, but there *was* a limo waiting for her in the driveway. "He's here. I'm going," she announced.

"Hang on," Jayne snapped into the phone. She lowered it, reaching for a business-sized envelope on the counter. "I forgot. This was stuck in your front door."

The moment Casey's fingertips touched it, she knew what it was. Who it was from. A thick lump rose in her throat. For a moment, she felt a flutter of panic that made her light-headed. She remembered the squeak of the bed she had slept in at the hospital.

It's not safe, her father had told her a few minutes ago. He didn't want her to go.

"Have a great time. Don't worry about us. We'll be fine." Jayne raised the phone to speak to Joaquin again.

"Lock the doors behind me. Dead bolt, too." Casey hurried out of the kitchen. "I have my key."

She left her flowers on the dining room table and went upstairs to add one more swipe of lipstick and get the dress coat she kept in the upstairs closet and her handbag. As she climbed the steps, the satin of her gown gathered in one hand to keep her from tripping, she gripped the white envelope in the other hand. She didn't even want to look at it.

But the smooth paper felt hot. Almost menacing.

In her room, she dropped it on the antique white dressing table that had been her mother's. She wouldn't even open it tonight. She wouldn't let Charles Gaitlin ruin her evening, which was obviously his intention.

She grabbed her tube of lipstick, popped off the cap, and leaned down in front of the etched-glass mirror to carefully trace her lips.

Against her will, her gaze fell to the envelope.

He had no right. He had no right to scare her like this. To invade her life this way.

She put the cap on the lipstick, then looked down at the envelope again.

Maybe it wasn't another message from Gaitlin. Maybe she was getting all worked up over nothing. Maybe the oil company had started leaving bills in envelopes. It was certainly classier than stuffing the rolled-up bill in the door. And considering the price of fuel oil, customers certainly deserved an envelope.

She dropped the lipstick into her satin handbag on the table and snatched up the envelope. The envelope made her angry. What was inside made her even angrier.

It was another hand-drawn eye. Blue, and almost identical to the last. No note. But the details were better than those of the last drawing. The previous one, though in color, had been more like an outline. This one seemed more real.

You better have eyes in the back of your head.

Casey threw the drawing down on her dressing table and strode to the closet, her high heels tapping on the hardwood floor. By the time she had her coat on, she had decided she wouldn't tell Adam about the envelope tonight. She didn't want to spend the entire evening talking about herself, about Gaitlin. She didn't want Adam fussing over her, treating her as if she needed to be defended or protected. Treating her like a victim.

A long time ago she had vowed never to be a victim again. Tonight, she would pretend Gaitlin didn't exist, and tomorrow, she would decide what to do about him.

Chapter 17

When Casey had arrived at State Police Troop first thing this morning, Detective Martin had listened to her story politely, even checking on the trooper's response to her house the night she had seen Gaitlin's car out front. He seemed sympathetic, but it had rather quickly become obvious to Casey, once she began telling her story, that the detective didn't believe she had enough evidence to have Gaitlin charged with stalking. In fact, he had just delicately pointed out that she didn't really have any evidence at all. He said that in cases such as these, with no evidence and no witnesses, it was basically one person's word against another's.

Casey shifted her purse on her lap, thinking there had to be something the detective could do. Then an idea came to her. "If Gaitlin *did* send these drawings to me and his prints are on them, it wouldn't be hard to get a match. You've obviously got his prints on file."

"I can give it a try." He held up the piece of paper to the light as if he might be able to see fingerprints. "But I doubt I'll be able to lift anything off this. We don't have the kind of technology you see on TV, ma'am. For the most part, we're still doing things the way we did them years ago.

Computer system is better, but it's more about funding than anyone would like to admit."

He glanced at the clock on the wall.

She was wasting his time. Wasting her own.

"What I could do is send a car to Mr. Gaitlin's residence to check on him. I could have an officer speak to him regarding his contact with you. That sometimes does the trick in these cases. Guys like this see we mean business, they lay off." He rose. "In the meantime, you should take safety precautions. Have your keys in your hand before you enter a parking lot. Keep doors and windows locked. Commonsense stuff."

Casey knew when she was being dismissed. She got up from the hard metal chair, trying not to be resentful. This wasn't Detective Martin's fault. She shouldn't have come. She knew there was nothing the police could do. It wasn't their fault or hers. It wasn't anyone's . . . except Gaitlin's.

"I'd like to hang on to these, if you don't mind, Ms. McDaniel."

She glanced at the drawings on his desk. She wanted them back. Why, she didn't know. Of course she couldn't ask for them. How weird would that seem? "Of course," she heard herself mumble.

"I'll walk you to the door."

She smiled up at him. He was a nice man. Late fifties, had probably been on the job a long time. She was sure he was following protocol. For all he knew, *she* could be the stalker.

Still, it guiled her. Despite the increase in stalking in the United States, in the injuries and deaths of women, abusers were still, across the country, not being taken seriously enough.

"Thank you for your time, Detective."

"I'll give you a ring in a couple of days." He buzzed her out.

Casey walked out into the small lobby, out the front door, knowing chances were she wouldn't hear from Detective Martin.

In her car, doors locked, she started the engine. Her cell phone rang. The Caller ID indicated Lincoln's cell phone number. She hesitated before answering it.

"Hey," he said. His voice was warm.

"Hey." She was glad she had picked up.

"Have a good weekend?"

He was trying so hard to be patient with her. To earn a second chance.

"Yeah, I did."

And Saturday night *had* been fun; the limo ride, the amazing Golden Ballroom at the DuPont Hotel, the extravagant dinner. Adam had been charming, attentive. He had been the perfect date. But even though Casey had enjoyed herself thoroughly, all evening she had found herself thinking about Lincoln. She had caught herself daydreaming, wondering how he was faring with his grandparents at the anniversary dinner at the fire hall. She had enjoyed the night of dazzle and hobnobbing, but she would have been just as happy to have had dinner at her house or Lincoln's and played backgammon.

So that was it, she realized suddenly. The final truth. She was in love with Lincoln. At least *falling* in love with him. It didn't matter how perfect Adam was or how much she liked him as a friend; he wasn't perfect for her.

"I had a nice weekend," she said into the phone. "But I missed you." She hesitated. "I still think you should have told me about Gaitlin, Lincoln, but—"

"But you're willing to give me a second chance," he cut in, obviously pleased. "This one time."

"This one time."

"So are we going to kiss and make up?" he asked.

She still sat behind the wheel of her car in the state police parking lot. She glanced up at the traffic rushing by on Route 13. "We are. But you have to promise me that if something like this comes up again, you'll tell me. I don't want you doing anything illegal, of course, but . . ." She halted, then continued, "Lincoln, I want you to know . . . this is probably as much me as you. I have . . . 'trust issues.'" It sounded so lame, but it was the easiest explanation. And it was the truth.

"Lesson learned," he said. "Let me make it up to you. Maybe we could do something more than *kiss* and make up?"

She smiled. She appreciated the fact that he didn't push her at that moment on her "trust issues." Her appreciation quickly turned to guilt. Should she tell him about her date with Adam? After all, they were discussing honesty and that whole idea of lack of disclosure being honest or dishonest was a slippery slope.

"Shoot. Casey, can I call you back? I have a call I've been waiting on and I really have to take it."

"Sure." She felt a little relieved. She did need to tell Lincoln about her date with Adam, but she didn't necessarily have to tell him this minute. "We can talk tonight?"

"Can I come over?" he asked.

"Dad would like that." The fact that she would too went without saying.

"I probably can't make it by dinner, but I'll bring dessert."

She hung up and shifted her car into reverse. Her meeting with the detective hadn't been all that great, but the day was still turning out pretty well.

Maury sat on his bunk, hunched over, legs dangling. He rubbed the back of his neck irritably. He'd had a hard day at work. His boss had ridden his ass hard. The stench of the chicken plant didn't usually bother him, but today it had. Work release was definitely better than Phase IV incarceration, but Maury was beginning to get antsy now that he'd had a taste of the outside world again. He needed to get out of here. Out of the chicken plant. Back to his "life's work."

There was a young woman who worked in the maintenance office, ordered parts and stuff. She was short and a little pudgy, Guatemalan probably. But she spoke English good. She was pretty, in a dark way. Maury liked his women pretty. He wondered if Martina would go out with him if she didn't know he was a con. He wondered if she could be lured by pretty baubles, plied with alcohol and drugs. He wondered how large her dark eyes got when she was terrified.

Maury looked at the folded letter beside him on the bed. He'd had it since last night but he'd just opened it. Danni was getting to be a bit of a dilemma for Maury.

Enclosed in the letter was a newspaper clipping with a blurry high school photo of a young man named Dylan Polanski. He had been robbed at gunpoint at a mini-mart near the beach and shot in the groin. He was expected to live, but when the story went to press, his condition was unknown. According to the paper, it was the third mini-mart robbery in the area in the last six weeks, but the first time anyone had been injured.

Danni had written in the margin, "Poor Dylan!"

Maury didn't know Dylan. He suspected Danni didn't either, until that night. He suspected it was Danni who had been in that store that night. Danni was the shooter.

Which led to the dilemma. Maury wasn't sure what to make of Danni now. Obviously he was trying to impress Maury. But Maury suspected he was also trying to draw him into something. Otherwise, why the request for the drawings of the eyes?

Maury was flattered that Danni cared what Maury thought.

That he obviously admired Maury, obviously wanted his approval. Otherwise, why would he be sending the clippings?

Maury just hoped Danni wasn't expecting any kind of "partnership" when Maury got out in a few months. That happened sometimes. There was an underground network few people knew existed. Men like him, a few women, communicated. Sometimes bragged. Admirers, younger, less experienced, occasionally hoped to latch on to those with more notoriety. Even participate.

Maury would certainly encourage Danni in his "activities," support him in any way he could. Offer guidance, even. But Maury, like most serial killers, was a loner. And he was a smart loner. He didn't mess with petty crimes like armed robbery, which could get you caught. The drug bust had been a mistake, bad error in judgment, but that wasn't who Maury was.

His life's work was important to him. He had definite likes and dislikes. Needs that had to be fulfilled, and they had to be fulfilled alone, just he and the women.

Maury fingered the news clipping. According to the paper, the boy had been shot after he had handed over the money in the cash register. There had been no reason for the robber to shoot the kid. Except that he had wanted to. Danni liked the violence, Maury could tell. First the B&E and the old woman. Now the kid. A shot to the groin. That was cruel. Maury would never do anything like that to another man.

He thought of the woman in the barrel.

He pushed the thought aside.

The issue right now was whether or not to continue his relationship with Danni. Maury was flattered Danni appreciated him, but he was also cautious. No adulation was worth jeopardizing his own efforts. As long as Maury had been in prison, he was eager to go back to see the woman in the barrel. He was eager to . . . provide her company, emotionally if not physically.

So maybe Maury should just end it with Danni here and now.

He unfolded the letter and read the message Danni had written using Maury's code.

And who was he sending Maury's drawings to? Always eyes. Blue eyes.

Maury was really tempted not to send another drawing. But . . . what harm could it do? He was committing no crime and Danni was obviously being careful: the post office box, the secret code, even his cover of Danni with an *i*. And Danni was so grateful for Maury's attention. He always said so in his letters.

Maury liked the idea that someone knew who he was. Appreciated him for what he could do. So many couldn't understand the skill, the intelligence it took. Danni understood.

He picked up the new colored pencils he'd purchased. One more drawing couldn't hurt.

Casey's office phone rang. "Casey McDaniel," she said, glancing at a police report on her desk. A battered woman who had come into the ER this morning.

"Miss McDaniel, Detective Martin with the state police."

Casey lifted her gaze from the sheet of paper in her hand. She hadn't expected to hear from Detective Martin.

"Just wanted to let you know one of our troopers paid a visit to Mr. Gaitlin." He paused.

"And?" she said into the phone.

"He says he's not harassing you."

There was something about his tone of voice that irritated her. "Don't most stalkers say that, Detective?"

He was silent. Now he was annoyed with her.

Perfect, she thought. *Now I've got the police angry with me.* "I'm sorry, Detective. That was inappropriate." She had seen Tiffany Reynolds, the abuse victim, in her hospital room half an hour ago. The twenty-two-year-old mother of three had a broken nose and possibly a ruptured spleen. She was getting a CAT scan now. "I appreciate you having someone speak with him."

"You should know, Miss McDaniel, that Mr. Gaitlin filed a complaint against you."

She sat back in her chair. "He *what?*"

"He filed a complaint saying you're harassing him by calling the police."

"That's ridiculous."

"These things happen, ma'am."

"So now what?" she asked.

"His claim will be investigated. You might be contacted by a third party, a state investigator. Nothing will come of it, most likely, but we have to keep these checks in place. You understand?"

"I understand." Casey exhaled, feeling a little defeated. "And what about Mr. Gaitlin?"

"The trooper suggested he keep his distance from you."

"And that's it?"

"It's all we can do for now, ma'am."

Casey's gaze fell to the police report on her desk. Tiffany's boyfriend had been questioned. The police had been to their house several times in the past six months. He denied laying a hand on his girlfriend. In his statement, he said she had been taking amphetamines and was hallucinating. The police had requested a tox screen. The results hadn't come back yet.

"Thank you for your time," Casey said, feeling slightly disembodied. She remembered standing in the doorway of her father's study a few nights before she accepted the ride home with Billy. She remembered trying to tell him that she was afraid of her ex-boyfriend. Her father had asked her to make him another martini.

"Have a good day, Detective," Casey finally said into the phone. She hung up, feeling as if she could cry. Instead, she headed downstairs to Tiffany's hospital room.

"You gotta get a job, Charlie." Angel pulled clear tubes shaped like candy canes filled with lip balm from a box. She stacked them on a shelf. "We can't make the rent, pay for the gas in my car, and buy groceries. I can't even pay Shonda this week for watchin' Buddy, and he's been there more this week than he's been home."

Charlie munched on chips from a bag he'd taken from a display near the cash register. Angel would have to remember to put fifty cents in the drawer later.

"Quit ridin' my ass. I'm lookin'."

"You can't just look. You have to put applications in. You have to follow up." She eyed James, who was one aisle over. He was pulling the trigger on a plastic pistol over and over again. *Click, click. Click, click.* It was getting pretty annoying. "You can't stay out all night, then sleep 'til three, then start thinkin' about lookin' for a job."

Click, click. Click, click.

"You know, Angel, you used to be fun," Charlie said, his mouth full of chips. "What happened to you?"

"What happened?" she snapped, yanking the candy canes out of the box faster, slamming them down on the shelf. "You moved in." She glanced across the aisle. "He moved in."

"Ah, Christ a'mighty, here we go again."

"He don't work, either!"

Click, click. Click, click. James walked around the end of the aisle toward them. He had two plastic pistols drawn firing both. *Click, click. Click, click.* "Man, she ridin' you about the job thing again?"

Charlie tipped back his head, poured the chip crumbs from the bag into his mouth.

"You didn't tell her our idea?" Lowering the plastic weapons, he looked at Angel. "He didn't tell you?"

"Tell me what?" She glared at Charlie.

"Keep your mouth shut." Charlie crumpled the bag in his hand. "She don't need to know."

Angel picked up the empty cardboard box. She had to go into the back room for another case, but she was afraid to leave the two brothers alone for a minute. They'd steal half the stuff in the store in the time it'd take her to get back. God, she needed to get Charlie out of her house. She needed to get both of them out.

"You better not be doin' anything illegal," she warned. "No drugs. You swore you wouldn't. Too many people needin' my place, Charlie. I told you that." She hugged the cardboard box as she looked at James. "You're supposed to be lookin' out for your brother, not encouragin' him to get into trouble."

James scowled, tucking the pistols into the front pockets of his jeans.

There went another dollar.

"We're not selling weed out of the house. You think we're stupid?"

She wanted to answer, but the bruise on her cheek had just finally faded. She didn't want to piss off Charlie too bad today. She just wasn't up for the fight. Maybe it was the holiday spirit. Maybe she was just tired. "You talkin' about a real job or you two rippin' off old ladies again?" She started to walk toward the cash register. "I hope this isn't that heater inspection scam idea of yours again, because—"

"Come on, baby." Charlie grabbed the hem of her shirt.

"You worry too much. You want me to bring in some money? I'm going to bring in some money. Maybe some serious money down the road." He winked at James as he put his arm around her. "Maybe get you something nice for Christmas."

Holding the box between them, she looked at him. She hated it when he sweet-talked her because she couldn't resist him.

"You know I love you, baby," he crooned.

She groaned. Every time he said it like that, it was like all her troubles melted away.

"You love me, don't ya, baby?" He leaned toward her for a kiss.

He could be sweet when he wanted to. She gave him a quick kiss on the lips. "I love you, baby. Now get out of here. I gotta get some work done."

"How about if we pick up Buddy, James and me? I'll put him to bed. Make James stay and watch him when I come to get you after work. That way, you can go home, put your feet up."

She smiled. She still had another five hours. She'd be exhausted by closing time. "That'd be nice, Charlie."

"Let's go," Charlie told his brother. "Let my Angel get back to work."

She headed for the curtain to the storage room, her back to the brothers. "Leave the chips!" she hollered.

She heard the crunch of bags as they each grabbed one on their way out the door.

Chapter 18

Casey pushed the grocery cart through the fresh-produce section, tossing in broccoli and a bag of carrots. She had a list, but she'd left it on the kitchen counter this morning . . . or on her desk at work. Somewhere.

She tried to remember what they needed. Tried not to think about the envelope in her purse.

She'd had a lousy day at work and ended up leaving early, but she had plenty of personal hours.

She'd had a bad start this morning with an argument with her father. He'd gotten it in his head that he wanted to take the DART bus to the local senior center to play cards. He'd seen an advertisement on TV. He didn't play cards. He'd never been to the senior center. When she'd suggested she look into it and they discuss it later, he'd accused her of smothering him. He wanted to go play cards *today*. Fortunately, she discovered after two phone calls, reservations had to be made twenty-four hours in advance for the bus to pick him up. With that information, she'd been able to stall him, but she had a feeling that wouldn't be the end of it.

These last couple of days, she had noticed an improvement in his cognitive skills, as well as his memory. Nothing definitive, but she was seeing small glimpses of the person he had once been. She wondered if he was noticing too, if this was what was giving him the confidence to even consider leaving the house without her, but she was afraid to ask.

After her argument with her father, she'd arrived at work to bad news. Her abused client, Tiffany, had gone into surgery two days ago for a ruptured spleen. There were complications now. An infection. The doctors weren't sure if she was going to pull through.

And to top off the day, Gaitlin had sent her another one of his stupid drawings. This one came to work, again. It was in her bag now, practically burning a hole in the leather.

She passed the organic foods section and grabbed a tin of Irish oatmeal. A bottle of salad dressing. She didn't know what to do about Gaitlin. She had a call in to Adam's office. He had promised her the last time they had spoken, right after the fund-raiser, that he was close to having Charles arrested again. She was beginning to wonder if that was true or he was just paying lip service to her. After seeing him in action at the fund-raiser that night, she had learned that he was definitely a player. Was he just playing her?

Casey stopped the cart, then leaned over the packaged chicken. She liked breasts; her father liked thighs. She was just going to bake it. Both?

A male voice behind her caught her attention and she immediately lifted her head to listen. She knew the voice. *Better have eyes in the back of your head,* he had said.

She whipped around. Charles Gaitlin stood next to her, leaning over an open cooler. "Five-ninety-five for the bag," he called to someone.

Casey felt her heart leap in her chest. Her face grew warm. Walk away or face him? She turned to him. "Are you following me?" she demanded.

He looked up, a bag of frozen meatballs in his hand. "Scuse me?"

"Nah, don't get 'em," another male voice said. *The same voice, but not the same man.*

Casey watched a second Charles Gaitlin approach the frozen-meat cooler. That was impossible, of course . . . unless he had an identical twin. But on closer scrutiny, she realized that the two men looked similar, but not identical. They had to be fraternal twins, or at least brothers.

She stared at the two men. They were dressed similarly in dirty jeans and sweatshirts. The second one, the one wearing a navy down vest over his shirt, was Charles.

He halted at the meat case, a box of generic cereal in his hand.

"What are you doing here?" she said. "The police told you to stay away from me."

The brother looked at her, looked at Charles. He seemed to be amused. "Charlie's got a right to buy food," he said. "He wasn't doin' nothin' but mindin' his own business."

Casey grabbed her purse and pulled out the envelope. "And what about this?" she asked, shaking it at them. "I don't suppose you know anything about this, either?"

Shoppers were starting to stare. Casey could feel them watching her. Hear them whispering. Her voice was high-pitched; she was on the verge of losing control.

"I don't know what yer talkin' about," Charles grunted. "I didn't send you anything. I told the police that."

"Harassment," the Charles lookalike said. "I'm tellin' you, Charlie, you've got serious harassment here. You've definitely got a case."

Casey suddenly felt as if the walls of the store were closing in around her. The shoppers' voices, though the words indistinguishable, were getting louder. The room spun. Wobbled.

She walked away from her cart, stuffing the envelope back into her bag. She headed straight for the doors in the front of the store. She went out into the cold fumbling for her keys. Locating her pepper spray. She made it into her car and locked all the doors. Then she just sat there shaking all over.

She squeezed her eyes shut. She knew this feeling. She *hated* this feeling.

Her heart was pounding so rapidly that she felt as if it was going to burst from her chest. She was breathing hard, yet she couldn't catch her breath.

An anxiety attack, she told herself. *It's just an anxiety attack.* She was still functioning. Still thinking. It wasn't like before. Not like the breakdown. That had happened only once.

But it felt like only yesterday. . . .

Breathe, Casey told herself. *Don't give in to it. Breathe.*

She'd been walking back from the campus library. Because her father was a professor at the university, she'd had borrowing privileges. She'd been working on a paper for her American government class. She'd heard Billy's car pull up beside her. He'd been following her around for weeks. Showing up at her school. Even at church. Calling over and over again. Hanging up when anyone else in the house answered the phone.

That night she'd kept walking. He had put down the passenger window of his white LeSabre. He had talked to her through the open window.

He had wanted her to get into the car.

It had started to rain and she didn't have her backpack with her. If the books got wet, if they got ruined, she'd owe a ton of money to the library. Money she didn't have . . .

Casey took a shuddering breath as she gripped the steering wheel in front of her. It had all seemed so logical in her sixteen-year-old mind.

She was suddenly cold. She was shaking so hard because she was cold. She opened her eyes, carefully slid the key into the ignition, and started the car. The engine was still warm. She'd only been in the store ten minutes. Hot air blasted her face.

The image of Billy's car faded in her mind.

She wrapped her fingers around the steering wheel again. She wasn't ready to drive yet, but she was feeling better. More in control.

Billy, the car, her breakdown—that was in the past. Long in the past. She wasn't a sixteen-year-old anymore. Charles Gaitlin couldn't hurt her. Not if she wouldn't let him. She had to take legal steps to protect herself. That was what she always recommended that her clients do.

She glanced at the clock on the dash. It was only three-forty. If she hurried, she could get to family court before it closed.

Taking a deep breath, she glanced in her rearview mirror and carefully eased out of the parking space. Billy might have won, but Charles wasn't going to.

"So there's no way I can file for a restraining order?" Casey pushed the hair from her eyes in frustration.

"Not here. Not you." The young black clerk leaned over her desk. "To get what you're askin' for, an emergency order of protection from abuse, this guy, the respondent, he's got to be your daddy, your husband, your baby's daddy, something like that," she ticked off on her long, curled fingernails stenciled with snowmen. "And if he was one of them, you'd have to be able to convince the judge that he could hurt you. Usually they got to threaten you." She sat back in her chair matter-of-factly. "Most women who come in here, they got bruises. They got broken arms. Busted-out teeth. And tears. They always got plenty of tears."

Casey should have realized before she raced over here that she couldn't file a PFA. She knew from experience with her clients who it protected and from what. But hearing someone say it out loud still angered her. "Ah, so if he's my boyfriend and he breaks my arm, then I can legally require that he stay a certain distance from me? What if he kills me? Does he have to stay fifteen feet from my coffin at all times?"

The young woman frowned, crossing her arms over her large breasts. "I ain't sayin' it's right," she said under her breath. "Just sayin' how it is."

Casey sat in the chair for a moment staring at the floor. The clerk was right, of course. She looked back at the young woman. "Okay, tell me something. If I file this petition anyway, even though you and I know it won't go through, what happens?"

"You got to say what the relationship is. If I see it ain't your boyfriend, your daddy, or your husband, I can't accept your petition."

"What if I lie?" she asked desperately. "What if I say he's my boyfriend?"

She wrinkled her nose. "I ain't never heard that one. I wouldn't suggest it, though." She pointed one long nail at Casey. "Contempt of court is what you might get, wastin' the court's time. You might be the one endin' up in jail, 'stead of that pond scum who won't leave you alone."

"So what do I do?" Casey opened her arms. "What does someone like me do? What would you do?"

The clerk snickered. "Me? I got two brothers size of re- frigerators. Linebackers when they was in high school. I'd sic Tashawn and Dontrelle on 'im, is what I would do."

Casey almost smiled. She didn't condone violence of any sort, but right now, a big brother would come in pretty handy. "So what if I don't have a big brother?" she asked. "What other options do I have?"

"Might try the court of chancery, where you can some-times get a restrainin' order, but that's expensive. You got to have a lawyer, and really I don't think what yer talkin' 'bout applies. They take mostly civil matters, people walkin' 'cross your property thinkin' they have the right and other nonsense like that." The clerk leaned forward. "And you said you already been to the police, sugar?"

"They won't do anything. They say they can't, not with-out any proof."

"Figures." The clerk scowled. "Always seems that's the way it is. Least in my neighborhood."

"But it's not the police's fault." Casey gathered her coat and bag to go. "They're just following the law; unfortu-nately, the law isn't on my side this time."

"I hear ya, sister," the clerk said kindly. "Just wish I could do something for you."

"Well, I know you want to go home." Casey rose. "Thank you for being so helpful. You're very knowledgeable about the law. You should be a lawyer."

The young black woman beamed. "Not me. I got two babies, responsibilities, but my sons, now they're gonna be lawyers, both of 'em, I have my way. Maybe even judges."

"Thanks again." Casey managed a grim smile. "Have a good evening."

That night, Casey was doing laundry when Adam re-turned her call. She picked her cell phone up off the kitchen counter and walked back into the laundry room. "Hey," she said when she answered.

"Casey, Adam. I apologize for not calling you back yester-day," he said. "Crazy day in court and then my grandfather had an episode last night. I stayed all night at the nursing home." He sounded tired.

"I'm sorry to hear that." She stretched out a pair of her father's pants on the dryer and slipped her hand into the front pocket. "Is he going to be okay?" She pulled a balled-up paper napkin from the pocket.

"His oxygen level is back up again. The doctor doesn't seem to know what caused the drop. He's still intubated, so it really doesn't make sense." She heard him exhale. "It doesn't sound good to me."

"No, it doesn't," she admitted sympathetically. From the other pocket of her father's pants, she pulled out a piece of paper that had been folded multiple times. She set it on the dryer and tossed the pants into the open washer. "Look, I don't want to keep you—"

"Actually, it's nice to hear a friendly voice."

She smiled to herself. He really was sweet. What had made her think he was playing her? He was just busy. And dedicated—to his job and his family. "Listen, the reason I called was to see where we are on the Gaitlin case. I know you warned me it could take some time, but . . ."

She hesitated, feeling guilty for confiding in Adam when she hadn't confided in the guy she was dating. She still hadn't said anything to Lincoln about Gaitlin following her because . . . she wasn't sure why. Maybe because she wasn't ready to share her past with Lincoln and Gaitlin was stirring up so much of it. Maybe she didn't tell Lincoln because she just wanted to be normal. Feel normal. Have a normal relationship. Billy had prevented that for many years. She didn't want Gaitlin to do the same.

"What's the matter, Casey?"

She started to tell him it was seeing her client in the hospital right now that had prompted the call. What had happened to Tiffany had reiterated in Casey's mind why she wanted to see Gaitlin behind bars. But she couldn't find the words. Instead, she quickly told Adam about the additional drawings Gaitlin had sent. She told him about her visit to the police station, the run-in at the grocery store, and her failed attempt to file a petition for protection from Gaitlin.

"Casey, why didn't you tell me this was still going on?" Adam questioned when she was done. He really seemed upset.

She poured laundry detergent into the washer and turned the dial. "I don't know," she confessed. "A lot of reasons. Number one being that I'm a big girl. This kind of thing goes with the job. Gaitlin's not the first man to try to intimidate me."

"Casey, this goes beyond intimidation."

She started the washer and leaned against it. "I keep thinking I'm making more of this than it is, but . . ." She thought about Billy. "But I have to confess, he's got me a little spooked. I just wish there was something I could do. I just want to make him stop."

"Why not let me see what I can do. I know a few cops."

"Adam, no. You can't do that."

"Sure I can. I'm not talking about anything physical. Just a friendly off-duty chat. I can make a couple of phone calls—"

"And put the case against Gaitlin at risk?" she interrupted. "Absolutely not, Adam. I refuse to allow you to do that. I shouldn't have ever told you about this in the first place."

"I'm not talking about doing anything unlawful. And these cops are discreet, Casey. No one will—"

"I'm serious, Adam. I don't want you to tell anyone about this. I don't want to give a judge any possible excuse to throw out the case against Gaitlin. I won't do that to Linda," she said firmly.

He was quiet on the other end of the line for a moment. "Casey," he finally said, "you're one hell of a tough cookie."

She found herself smiling. When she had decided she wasn't really interested in dating Adam, it hadn't occurred to her they could be friends. Tonight, he felt like a friend.

She walked into the kitchen to get away from the sound of the washing machine. "I'm going to take that as a compliment," she said.

"I meant it to be."

In the dark kitchen, she sat down in a chair at the breakfast nook. There was another silence, but it wasn't an uncomfortable one. It felt good to talk to someone about Gaitlin. Someone who didn't think she was blowing the situation out of proportion. If only she'd had someone like Adam to listen to her when she was sixteen. "I appreciate you taking the time to listen to me, Adam. I think that's all I really needed."

"Don't tell me the boyfriend doesn't have an ear?"

His words took her by surprise. Obviously, he was referring to Lincoln. How did he know about him? She'd certainly not mentioned him. "So you've heard," she said, feeling a little bit like a girl caught with her hand in the cookie jar.

"It's a small county," he said good-naturedly. She could almost imagine him shrugging his broad shoulders. "Lincoln and I bump into each other in the courthouse once in a while."

"And he told you we are dating?"

"Nah, but I heard. Lincoln's too 'cool' for that, but lawyers and judges are the worst gossips around. We don't have a life, for the most part, so we're all fascinated when one of us does."

"Well, to answer your question, Lincoln's an excellent

listener. I haven't told him about Gaitlin because his law firm is representing the creep."

"Ah, conflict of interest. Right," Adam said.

"Not that I think Lincoln would, in any way, allow our relationship to affect his firm's client's relationship . . ."

"No, of course not. Lincoln's a stand-up guy. Ridgeway, Barton, and Bailey is an excellent firm. I think you're probably smart to keep this to yourself, though."

She straightened the napkin holder on the table. She was glad Adam had called. He made her feel much better about the whole Gaitlin thing. He made her feel empowered. "I won't keep you any longer. I appreciate you returning my call and listening to me whine."

"You're certainly welcome. And I didn't even answer your question because, unfortunately, I don't have an answer for you. As far as recharging Gaitlin, we're still waiting on the lab. But my office is on this. I swear we are."

"I know you are. I shouldn't even have called."

"Don't be silly. I like to see the Department of Justice kept on its toes."

He had her smiling again. "You take care, Adam. I hope your grandfather improves."

"Thanks. You have any more problems with Gaitlin, you call. I don't mind making those contacts. I really don't."

"Night, Adam." Casey hung up the phone, smiling.

Leaving it on the counter, she stuck her head through the doorway. Ed was sitting in the dark, the dog at his feet. They were watching The Weather Channel, of course. "Need anything, Dad?"

"Need to play cards at the senior center!" he shouted belligerently, without turning his head to look at her.

She smiled again. The doctors had warned her that Alzheimer's patients could deteriorate and then improve. It was all part of the complicated disease. He was definitely on the upswing this week, whether it was the new drug or the rhythm of the disease. "We'll talk about it," she called back. "Let me get the clothes out of the dryer. You can help me fold."

Returning to the laundry room, she opened the dryer door and swept the warm, spring-fresh-smelling clothes into the laundry basket on the floor. She spotted the piece of paper she had removed from her father's pants and unfolded it.

It was a drawing, which was unusual. Dr. Edward Mc-Daniel had always been a man of words rather than images.

She smoothed the paper out on the dryer to get a better look. It was a drawing of a window with a sticklike figure that appeared to be looking through it. The stick figure had pistols.

Chapter 19

The next morning Casey got up thinking about Gaitlin. By the time she had finished her shower, she'd moved on to her more immediate concern, her father. Casey really felt as if she and Jayne needed to discuss the matter. On the way to work she called her sister and Jayne agreed to "squeeze her in" that day.

At twelve-thirty, Casey went down to the hospital cafeteria to meet Jayne for lunch. She waited until one for her, and then, when Jayne was a no-show and didn't answer her cell phone, Casey got in line for a bowl of Sarge's soup.

"Haven't seen ya in days," Sarge commented. He sniffed.

"Guess I've been busy. Packing lunch or just eating crackers. You have a cold?"

"Must be workin' on one." Despite the line of OR nurses behind her, he took his time ladling out a portion of minestrone for her. "You too busy to see old Sarge? I wait every day to see your pretty face. You don't show up, you disappoint old Sarge." He actually seemed put out.

"I didn't realize I was so important to you," she said, reaching out for her bowl.

"Prob'ly a lot a things ya don't know about me." He held the plastic bowl just out of reach and sniffed again.

When she made eye contact with him, there was something in his facial expression that she didn't like. She instantly remembered seeing him in the parking lot the same day Gaitlin had come to her office. Where else had she seen Sarge lately? She saw so many people she knew from work outside of the workplace. She wracked her brain. The minimart where she bought gas? Wal-Mart?

"Thanks for the soup." Casey reached over the counter to take the bowl from him.

"Have a nice day." He watched her as she carried her tray away.

Casey realized when she got to the cashier that she had forgotten to ask for crackers, but she didn't want them bad enough to go back to see Sarge.

She paid for her soup and bottle of water and walked to the windows. Her favorite table was taken. She took the closest vacant one.

Sarge had kind of creeped her out. Had he really been acting strangely, or had it just been her imagination?

She had eaten half her soup when Jayne showed up flustered, wearing a heavy winter coat, trailing a long wool scarf behind her. "So sorry," she said, plopping down in the chair across from Casey as she unbuttoned her coat.

"I called, but you didn't pick up."

Jayne set her enormous purse on her lap and dug through it. "Put it on vibrate earlier. Guess I forgot to turn it back on."

"You want to get something to eat? I've only got about twenty minutes." Casey dipped her plastic spoon in and out of her soup. She wasn't that hungry. "I have an appointment with a patient's family at one forty-five."

Jayne was still digging through her purse. "I'm not hungry. Had two donuts and about a gallon of coffee in my morning meeting. Aha." She lifted her phone out of her bag. "I can only stay a minute anyway. Tons of work at the office. You know how it is; the faster we go, the further behind we get. So, let's see this drawing." She punched buttons on her phone and it chirped in reply.

Casey removed the piece of paper from her bag hanging on the back of her chair, unfolded it, and pushed it across the table.

Jayne studied the picture Casey had found in their father's pants pocket. She looked up. "You think that's a window? Looks sort of like jail cell bars to me."

Casey frowned. "Yes, that's a window. It's the French doors in my dining room, and my concern is not that Daddy's a bad artist. My concern is that he's seen a man holding two guns staring in my window."

Jayne set her phone down, taking a closer look at the picture. "There's a palm tree in it." She pointed.

"It's still a man holding two pistols," Casey responded tersely.

Jayne sat back in her chair, removing her wool scarf.

"I'm worried about Charles Gaitlin," Casey said.

Jayne wrinkled her nose. "Why?"

"Because I think he's been following me and I think he's sending me drawings in the mail. I've been to the police."

"What? Why haven't I heard about this before?"

Jayne sounded suspicious. As if she didn't quite believe Casey, which was exactly why Casey *hadn't* said anything before.

"The problem—and the police confirmed it—is that I don't have a case. No real proof."

"What makes you think he's been following you and sending you drawings in the mail?"

"I don't know. Because he's a mean, nasty, vindictive man who beats women and murders his girlfriends."

Jayne gave her one of her looks.

Casey groaned. She hated feeling as if she was always on trial with her sister. "I guess he's afraid he's still going to be arrested for his girlfriend's murder and I could play a part in his conviction." She sat back in her chair, folding her arms over her chest, then added, "And he should be, because if I have anything to do with it, he's going to jail for the rest of his life for what he did."

Jayne frowned. "So what's Daddy's picture have to do with all this? You think he saw Gaitlin in the window point-ing pistols at him?" She leaned over the paper again, squint-ing. "They look like six-shooters. Like in the cowboy and Indian movies." She glanced up at Casey. "No one has guns like that anymore. Criminals shoot automatics, semiauto-matics at least."

Casey glanced out the window. The trees beyond the parking lot were gray and lifeless, their thrust-out branches looking like open, empty arms to her. She turned back to her sister. "I'm very concerned."

"You think you should show this to the police?" Jayne smoothed the paper with her hand.

"What's the point?" Casey shrugged. "They're going to say the same thing they said about Gaitlin's little pieces of art-work. It doesn't prove anything. It doesn't look like Gaitlin, or anyone else for that matter. It's a stick figure. And maybe Dad didn't see a man in the window; maybe he drew some-thing he saw on TV." She opened her arms. "Who knows where he got the image."

"Did you ask Dad what he'd drawn?"

"Of course I did. He said he didn't draw it and he didn't know how it got in his pocket." Casey pressed her fingertips lightly on the table. "I'm just not sure what to do. I'm won-dering if it's time to start thinking about sending him to day care when I'm at work, or bringing in a sitter."

"He's totally opposed to that."

"I know he is."

"He told me he wanted to go to the senior center and play cards."

Casey frowned. "When did you talk to him?"

"He called me on the phone yesterday."

"He called you? He never calls you."

"Well, he called me, Casey," Jayne said with a little bit of a tone again. "He said he wanted to go to the senior center and play cards, but you didn't think he was capable of riding the bus or playing cards."

"I never said that." Casey reached across the table and retrieved the drawing. She couldn't believe her father had called her sister to complain about her.

"So let him go."

"I'm not even sure they'd take him."

"Have him evaluated. I can make the appointment with the senior center if you don't want to."

"It's not that I don't want to, Jayne. It's just that . . ." Casey met her sister's gaze. "You don't live with him. You don't understand. . . ." She let her sentence trail off into silence.

"You know what I think?" Jayne said quietly in her psychologist's voice. "I think Daddy's right. Your intentions are well founded, but you're smothering him."

Casey was surprised by the tears that stung the backs of her eyelids. "I'm not trying to smother him. I'm trying to keep him safe."

Jayne returned her angora scarf to her neck. She had never taken her coat off. "Let's call the senior center, get an appointment, let them evaluate him and see if they're willing to let him come on the bus to play cards. It will get him out of the house—what he wants—and you'll know he's safe. It's door-to-door service."

"Coming and going on a bus, alone?" Casey ran her fingers

through her hair. "I don't know. I'm surprised he's willing to even consider leaving Frazier. I guess we could give it a try."

"Great. I'll call the senior center." Jayne got up.

"No, that's okay. I'll do it."

"I don't mind." That tone again.

"I know you don't." Casey rose, grabbing her purse and then her tray. "It's just that it will be easier for me to make the appointment from my desk where I can see what else I've got going on."

"Super. Gotta run." Jayne lifted her hand. Her cell phone rang and she dug into her purse. "Bye," she mouthed, with a wave, as she drew the phone from her bag to her ear.

"Bye," Casey whispered, walking in the opposite direction.

"I think your father going to the senior center is an excellent idea."

"Of course you do. Traitor," she accused. "Traitor Lincoln." Stretched out on her side facing him, on the rug, Casey picked up her wineglass. Her father had gone to bed and they had the dark living room all to themselves. Lincoln had lit a fire in the rarely used fireplace and he and Casey were now lying in front of it.

"I'm not a traitor. What makes me a traitor?"

"Everyone thinks it's a great idea but me, which makes me look like a jerk."

He chuckled, smoothing her hair, looking into her face. "It doesn't make you look like a jerk. You have most of the weight of Ed's care on your shoulders. You're protective of him. There's nothing wrong with that."

"My sister thinks I'm being *overly* protective." She shifted her gaze, meeting his.

"So maybe you are," he said gently. He leaned forward and kissed her. "That makes you a good daughter, not a bad one."

She kissed him back. "You really think so?" His mouth felt good against hers. Warm. Firm. "Or are you just saying whatever you think I want to hear so you'll get invited upstairs?"

"I truly believe you have your father's best interests at heart. Always," he said firmly. Lincoln's voice got huskier. "And yes, I'm hoping to get invited upstairs." He kissed her again, this time touching the underside of her upper lip with the tip of his tongue.

"Mmm," she murmured, closing her eyes. "You taste good."

He took the half-full wineglass from her hand and set it aside, then scooted closer so they were lying on their sides face-to-face. "You taste better."

He kissed her again, slowly, taking his time. As he pressed his mouth against hers, he cupped one of her breasts. Through the fabric of her sweater and bra she felt a trill. She leaned into him, opening her mouth to his kiss.

Lincoln slipped his hand under her sweater. Casey reached behind her and unfastened her bra. She sighed with him as his warm hand found the weight of her breast.

Still mouth to mouth, he pushed her gently onto her back. Casey wrapped her arms around his neck and pulled him closer as he pushed up the hem of her sweater. Her voice caught in her throat in a jagged gasp as he closed his hot, wet mouth over her nipple.

Casey groaned. "We should go upstairs."

"Mm-hmm."

She rolled her head back, closing her eyes, savoring the sensation as he sucked gently. "I'm serious." She lifted her head off the carpet. Let it fall.

He released her breast. "So am I." He rubbed her taut nipple with the pad of his thumb.

She grabbed his hand. Lying in front of the fireplace making love sounded romantic, but Casey yearned for the privacy of her bedroom. Not just because her father was sleeping thirty feet away, but also because she felt exposed here, even with the shades drawn. She felt vulnerable.

She tugged on his hand as she rolled up on her knees. He faced her.

"Come on," she whispered. They touched hands palm to palm. Kissed.

"Should I bring the wine?" He got to his feet and offered his hand to her.

"Sure."

"First one upstairs gets to undress the other," he whispered in her ear.

Casey took off.

Angel stared at the pieces of paper that Charlie had pushed in front of her on the dinette table. She was so tired she could barely keep her eyes open. All she wanted to do was climb into bed under the old quilt her granny Naomi had made and go to sleep. She had to be at work at seven tomorrow morning. But it wasn't often that Charlie actually wanted to talk to her and he was being so nice. He'd even made her a cup of tea.

"So the police questioned you. So what? They didn't arrest you. They didn't even take you in for questionin'. I don't understand why you care what she says." She grabbed the tea bag, lifted it up, then lowered it again. She liked her chamomile tea strong with lots of sugar. Real sugar. None of that stuff out of the pink packet. "You ain't been nowhere, and Sweet Jesus knows you ain't been sendin' any drawings in the mail. I've seen how bad yer drawin' is."

"This is about my rights. The police, that bitch, she don't

have the right to harass me. They came right here to my home."

She wanted to remind him that it was *her* place, even if it wouldn't be for long if she didn't get caught up on the rent, but she kept her mouth shut.

"How am I supposed to find a decent job when I'm afraid any minute she's gonna sic the police on me?" he ranted, sounding like James.

"It's not the police or that woman keepin' you from gettin' a job, Charlie." She knew she shouldn't push him, but it was true. "You can't find a job because you ain't tried."

"This could mean a lot of money for me, baby. *For us.*"

"I don't know about a lawsuit." Angel lifted the tea bag out of the hot water, dropped it over her spoon, and used the string to strain the tea from the bag. This all sounded way too complicated to believe Charlie had come up with the idea. She looked up at him suddenly. "Is this another one of your brother's stupid schemes to make money, because if it is, Charlie, you're gonna lose out. You always—"

"Why do you always think everything is James's idea? You got no confidence in me, baby."

She glanced at him out of the corner of her eyes. She knew that look. Something wasn't right here. Charlie could "baby" her all he wanted. He was lying. She could tell by the way he squinted. He always did that when he was lying.

But it wouldn't do any good to accuse him. He'd just lie some more. And she didn't want to pick a fight with him. Not tonight. She was too tired. Too tired of fighting. Too tired of getting hit.

Besides, she didn't want to waste the one night she had alone with Charlie fighting with him. They hardly ever had any privacy anymore. Most nights, James slept on the couch, but apparently he and his girlfriend were trying to patch things up, or something. Nights James was here, Angel usually just let Charlie climb on top of her and rut away to keep the peace. She just told him to be quiet. But tonight . . . tonight maybe there'd be a little something for her if she didn't piss him off too bad.

"I don't understand who these people are. They don't know you." She rested her hand on the papers on the table. "Why do they care if yer rights been violated? What are they gettin' outta all this? How much they chargin'?"

"I told ya, baby, it's free. It's a *citizens' rights activists organization*."

Now she *knew* he was lying. Where would he come up with "citizens' rights activists organization"? Certainly not from his pea-sized brain.

Angel sipped her tea and glanced at the papers again. Rights for the People was what the group was called. It said so right across the top. Charlie said they had offered a lawyer to him free of charge. A whole bunch of lawyers did this kind of thing all over the country. All he had to do was sign the papers and they'd sue for him. They'd sue everyone: the bitch from the hospital, the police, even the state. Charlie said they said it could be done. He said there was money in it. Free money.

Angel knew better than to think there was any such thing as free money. "I don't know," she said suspiciously. "If it don't sound right, it usually ain't. There's gotta be some catch."

"There's not, I'm tellin' you. In this country, you're innocent until proven guilty. They couldn't prove I was guilty for killin' Linda so they let me go. They can't follow me around after they let me go. It says so in the Constitution."

She pushed the papers away and took another sip of tea. "So, fine, sue 'em. Sue everybody. I hope you do get rich. I do." Putting the mug down, she got up from the table. "And

when you do, I want a new red car. A Hyundai with a
sunroof."

"I'll get you two. One for you, one for Buddy for when he
can drive." Charlie got up and put his arm around her.

"You get a million dollars, you can pay for Buddy to go
to college 'stead of buyin' him a new car. No sixteen-year-
old boy needs a new car."

"Whatever you want, baby." He kissed her. "We'll live in
a mansion and we'll have a maid. We'll hire James's girlfriend to scrub our toilets."

She laughed with him. "I'm goin' to bed. You comin'?"

He reached up and tweaked her nipple through her sweatshirt. "Sure, baby. I'm comin' if yer goin'."

Casey had switched her bedside lamp on to low so the
room was bathed with golden light. Lying on her back, Lincoln above her, she could see his eyes in the semidarkness.

He held her gaze as he thrust into her. She pressed her
kiss-bruised lips together in a soft moan and lifted her hips
to meet his again.

Lincoln was a good lover. At least she thought so. She'd
only ever had sex with two other men, so it wasn't like she
was much of a comparison shopper. And really, Billy didn't
count as a lover, did he?

Half closing her eyes, Casey ran her hand down Lincoln's
lower back and over his butt cheek. It was nice. Like the rest
of him, firm but not too muscular. He didn't work out at a
gym, but he did enough chores around his grandparents'
farm that he stayed in good shape.

He leaned over and kissed her, stilling his hips. "Hey," he
whispered in her ear. His voice was thick. "Where are you?
You seem like you're a million miles away."

"I'm right here," she breathed. She stroked his cheek with her palm, gazing into his eyes.

"Yeah?"

She raised her hips, taking him deeper. "Yeah."

He smiled. Kissed her.

She lowered her hips, raised them again, and he grunted in pleasure.

He thrust into her again. Casey slid her arms around his back, pulling him deeper.

He kissed her forehead, pushing away the damp wisps of her hair. He smelled so good. Clean, but with that scent of masculinity that made every woman's knees a little weak.

Casey pushed harder upward against him. She could feel the tension building deep inside her. Sex was about trust, her therapist said. Orgasm was about ultimate trust.

Casey didn't know if she was ready to hand Lincoln her ultimate trust, or any man for that matter, but she was on board with the orgasm.

Lincoln moved faster over her and she dropped her hands to the bed, grasped at the sheets. She felt every muscle fiber in her body tense.

She was overwhelmed by the smell of Lincoln, who was all deliciously hot and sweaty. By the weight of his body on top of hers. She was so close. . . .

She raised her legs and wrapped them around his, straining, her hips to his. The orgasm hit, sudden and sweet, and Casey cried out loud, raising her arms off the bed to hug him tightly. Lincoln dropped his head to the crook of her neck, thrust twice more, and he was done for.

Breathing hard, Casey relaxed, letting her arms fall to her sides. Her whole body had been so tight a minute before and now it was like she was floating, floating on a raft in a pool.

Lincoln kissed her cheek tenderly and hovered over her.

She waited for him to roll off, and when he didn't, she opened her eyes to see him gazing intently at her. "What?"

"You," he whispered. "You're so beautiful . . . and *loud*."

Mortified, she squeezed her eyes shut. "Oh, God. You don't think he could hear me?"

Lincoln laughed and kissed her again before rolling onto his side beside her. "Nah, you weren't *that* loud. Door's closed. So is his."

She brought her hand to her face to cover it.

"Don't be embarrassed." He drew his hand over her bare belly. "I like to hear you. I like to know you're enjoying yourself."

"Oh, I'm enjoying myself, all right," she said from behind her hand, giggling.

He was looking at her again. Waiting.

She slowly lowered her hand and gazed into his eyes.

"I'm glad we met, Casey," he whispered. He brushed his knuckles against her cheek and she turned her head, enjoying the feel of his hand on her skin. "I'm glad you've let me into your life. I . . . I feel like we have something special here. Like . . . I don't know."

She smiled up at him. She was glad he hadn't said he loved her. She didn't know if she was ready for that. But she liked the tone of his voice. She liked the idea that maybe what was between them scared him a little, too. Casey had always dreamed of marrying, of having children. That dream had seemed dim in the last year, but now her life seemed full of possibilities.

Chapter 20

Adam leaned back in his chair in his home office and rubbed the back of his neck. He'd been working on a case for a couple of hours. No matter what angle he'd attacked it from, he'd come to the same conclusion. The case, due to be heard in court Monday morning, was screwed. The first assistant deputy who'd been assigned to it had failed to provide discoverable evidence to the defense in what anyone in the courtroom was going to consider a timely fashion.

He glanced at his Rolex. A gift from his grandfather when Adam had graduated from law school. It was his most prized possession and not because it was a Rolex, but because it had come from his grandfather with a word of praise. Could have been a Timex for all Adam cared; it was the approval.

Still, the Rolex had been a pretty impressive gift, coming from Adam Preston Sr., who would have been considered a bit of a miser in his time; a cheapskate nowadays. He had lived frugally his whole life, spending little, saving much. He knew a good deal when he saw one and often took advantage of people down and out on their luck, especially in real estate. Over the years, he had accumulated homes and property.

That was why he was so rich, Adam's mother used to say, albeit a little bitterly. Because he was so stingy. As Preston Sr.'s health had begun to decline, he had insisted that Adam sell the property; he wanted to see the big numbers on bank and investment statements before he died, he had said. And big numbers there were. The sale of the old man's last condo in Florida had just gone through. The only property left was a farm in Roxana, minutes from the beach, which his grandfather, in an unusual act of generosity, had deeded to Adam.

The farmhouse was in a sad state of repair, but the land was worth a fortune. Adam knew he should sell it while the market for development was hot, but sentimentality had kept him from doing so. As a child, he had spent summers there, puttering in the garden at his grandfather's side, learning the secrets of growing the juiciest tomatoes and the sweetest corn. At fourteen, Adam had gotten his first job busing tables in a Fenwick Island diner and had pedaled his bike the six miles in each direction each day. His mother had protested it was too far for a boy to ride his bike, but Preston Sr. had prevailed and Adam had kept his job. His grandfather had never once offered to drive him to or from work that summer, not in the early morning rain or the heat of midday. It was the best summer Adam remembered. In August, he and his grandfather had harvested their tomatoes and canned them in Ball jars. They had made the sweetest tomato sauce Adam ever remembered tasting.

Something rattled against Adam's office window and, startled, he looked up. He'd never gotten around to window coverings anywhere in the house but the bedrooms. Despite what his mother thought, he liked them bare. He liked the way the light spilled through to the sand-colored hardwood floor and travertine all over the house. Even in the winter, it was pretty. Maybe even prettier in the winter because the light seemed so . . . cool.

Adam heard the rattle again, rose from his chair, and walked to the window. With the light from his desk behind him and the beach dark, he couldn't see anything. But something didn't *feel* right. He rubbed the back of his neck again and wandered out of the room, down the hall.

The house had a reverse plan from most residential homes. The living quarters—the spacious kitchen, living room, and office—were all on the second floor, with a massive wraparound balcony. The four bedrooms and media room were on the first floor, and there was a laundry room, a shower, and storage on the ground floor. Because the house was built on pilings, the second-floor living quarters were actually three stories up, giving a spectacular view by day.

He walked into the kitchen and flipped on the light switch. The kitchen echoed with his footsteps. It was after midnight, too late for snacking, but the memory of his grandfather's homemade tomato sauce had made him hungry. The dry, tasteless tuna wrap he'd had at the nursing home at seven seemed only a distant memory. Opening the refrigerator, he glanced toward the French doors that led to the upper balcony.

The flapping sound again. A loose shutter maybe? Shingle? Adam had no clue. He was by no means a handyman.

After grabbing a square of Gruyère wrapped in plastic and a green apple, he closed the refrigerator door and set the snacks on the marble countertop. As he walked to the far counter to pull a cutting board from a slot, he stared at the black span of glass windows and doors.

Was someone on the deck?

He left the bamboo cutting board and knife on the counter and walked to the door. He rested his hand on the doorknob. Twisted it. It was locked.

He resisted the urge to open it. If someone was on the

deck, three stories off the ground, he had no business open-ing the door to the intruder. Instead, he reached out and flipped the switch on the wall. The lights went out in the kitchen, leaving him in perfect darkness.

As he waited for his eyes to adjust, he realized the hair on the back of his neck was prickling. He rubbed it. He wasn't easily spooked, but he was definitely feeling apprehensive. He stared through the glass.

Light from the security lamp along the side of the house gave the deck a dark gray hue. Slowly, silhouettes emerged. On the balcony he could make out the chairs stacked and covered with plastic. The barbeque covered and lashed to the railing. There was a table in the corner.

He looked back toward the stack of chairs. Then, realiz-ing he'd seen movement, he fixed his gaze on the table again. There was something there. Against the railing. A person crouched down maybe? Shoulder-length hair . . . He squinted.

There *was* someone there. His or her hair—it seemed kind of long—was blowing in the wind.

Adam's heart was suddenly beating double time. Keeping an eye on the figure on the deck, he sidestepped to the wall and slowly lifted the phone off the receiver. He eased back in front of the door and glanced at the lit buttons on the handset.

But he had to know what he was looking at before he called the police.

Heart thudding in his chest, phone in his left hand, he reached with his right. He tried to recall which switch in the row of four turned on the balcony lights. He didn't want to make a mistake and turn on the lights in the kitchen.

He flipped the second switch. Light immediately illuminated the deck . . . and the mop leaning against the railing, its cotton tendrils whipping in the wind.

Pressing the phone to his chest, Adam managed a chuckle.

He turned off the balcony lights and turned on the kitchen lights.

A mop. He didn't even know he owned a mop. The cleaning girl must have left it out there the other day and he just hadn't noticed it.

Feeling silly, he returned the phone to the wall cradle and retrieved the cutting board to cut up his snack. He heard the rattle again but continued to slice his apple. It had to be a drainpipe or a loose shutter. He'd call the handyman service tomorrow.

As Adam shut out the kitchen lights, taking his cheese and apple with him, he glanced over his shoulder one last time toward the windows. He still felt as if someone was there. As if someone was watching him.

It was ridiculous, of course. There was no one there. Just a mop.

When Casey came downstairs Monday morning at six-thirty, her father was already in the kitchen. He was still bundled in his coat and hat from taking Frazier outside. "You're up early."

"Got a busy day." He unbuttoned his coat. "Bus is coming for me. I'm going to play cards. And swim. They have a pool, you know. They swim on Wednesdays."

"Dad, keep in mind, it's just a trial basis. We'll have to see about Wednesday when Wednesday comes." When Casey had called the senior center on Friday, Mrs. Poppy, a staff member, had said they'd had a cancellation that afternoon and would love to meet her and her father. It was their policy to not have a doctor evaluation unless they felt it necessary. They liked to draw their own conclusions, Mrs. Poppy had explained.

Ed had been on his best behavior at the senior center that

afternoon. He identified the day, the date, the current president of the United States, and the warm air mass passing
through the Texas Panhandle. Mrs. Poppy had found him
charming. She accepted him on a trial basis for a program
they called "semisupervised." He would check in and out
each day at the front desk. He'd be encouraged to attend pro-
grams and activities and would be monitored by a team of
employees.

Casey hadn't been able to decide if she felt relieved, or
more worried than before. He father had been acting so normally the last few days that she was beginning to wonder if
Jayne was right. Maybe the medication really was working
and maybe she was overprotecting him, overstating his
shortcomings.

Maybe Casey was just crazy.

"Would you like some coffee?" she asked.

"Nope. Gotta check the weather." He walked out of the
kitchen, carrying his coat. "Peanut butter and jelly air system
off the Carolinas."

So she wasn't *completely* crazy.

Casey had called midmorning to check on her father and
had been informed by Mrs. Poppy that he was in the craft
room making a Christmas gift and that he was having an excellent first day. When she'd called Jayne with an update, her
sister had fed her an "I told you so" line and then invited them
for a birthday dinner for Joaquin Friday night. She was making
his favorite enchiladas and Lincoln was invited as well.

Now, Casey stood on the front porch, freezing to death,
watching for her father. The wind whipped around the corner
of the house, blowing her scarf across her face. Frazier paced
at her side, seeming as eager to see Ed as she was.

At last, she spotted the white minivan coming around the

corner. It pulled into the driveway, and Casey, with her boxer escort, went out to meet her father. The van stopped. The door slid open and Ed appeared.

"Have a good evening, Mr. McDaniel," the driver said. Ed didn't reply.

"Thank you," Casey said to the driver and waved. She shut the van door behind her father, looped her arm through his, and led him toward the front porch. "So, Dad, how was it?"

"It was all right." The dog bounced up and down in front of him and Ed patted him. "We didn't play cards."

"Oh, that's disappointing."

"Cards are on Tuesdays and Thursdays. That's what Kate said. They don't let you change the channel on the TV. Haven't seen the forecast all day."

"We can fix that. Who's Kate?"

"Have to have a partner to play bridge. Not to play poker. Kate says she'll be my partner if I want to play bridge. I told her I'd think about it."

Casey laughed. Her father was so talkative. He was never this talkative. They crossed the porch. "Dad, who's Kate?"

He looked at her. "Kate who? It's cold out here." He stepped in front of her, opened the door, and waited for the dog to bound in before going inside.

"So you want to go back again? Tomorrow?" she asked.

"Cards on Tuesdays." He shuffled toward the laundry room, unwinding his scarf, removing his wool cap. "Kate says she'll be my partner."

Tugging off her hat, Casey got in front of her father and put out her hand. "Here, give me that. And your coat. You and Frazier go check out the forecast. TV's already on. There's chili for dinner. I put it on this morning."

The phone rang.

"Phone's ringing." Ed shuffled away.

Casey stood there for a second. "Thanks, Dad." On her

way toward the laundry room, she grabbed the phone off the kitchen counter. "'Lo."

"Hey." It was Lincoln.

"Hey, yourself. You're not home from work already, are you?" She smiled, tickled to hear his voice. They hadn't talked since last night.

"No, still at work."

She detected something in his voice. "What's going on?" She hung up her Dad's clothing, one piece at a time.

"I shouldn't be making this call. I'm standing out front on the sidewalk, freezing my ass off."

He was obviously upset. He never cursed. "Okay." Now he was starting to scare her a little. "So make it quick. What's wrong?"

"You *absolutely* cannot tell anyone. Not *anyone*. Not even your assistant deputy buddy. You have no idea what lines I'm crossing here. I did *not* make this call."

That was the first time he'd ever acknowledged she even knew Adam Preston. The reference to him being her "buddy" was a little odd. Was he jealous of their friendship? "I get it, Lincoln." She slipped out of her coat. "You didn't make this call."

"There's a lawsuit in the works. A big one. You're named as one of the defendants, along with the Delaware State Police, the Georgetown City Police, the hospital, the State of Delaware, you name it."

"You've got to be kidding. Who's suing me? Who's suing me *and* the state?"

"We were notified as a courtesy because our firm defended the client in the state Linda Truman case."

"Gaitlin is suing *me*? For what?"

"Harassment, basically, but he's claiming you've prevented him from obtaining a job. Ruined his relationship with his girlfriend. Caused insomnia. There's a long list of complaints, apparently. He wants damages."

"*I'm* harassing *him?* You've got to be kidding me." She was so angry that she practically shouted into the phone. "And what does this have to do with the hospital? This makes no sense."

"These things don't have to make sense. But in this case, it's actually good news for you because the hospital's lawyers will be defending you."

"Lincoln, I still don't understand. I made a complaint about him to the police. How can I be harassing him?"

"You didn't tell me he's been harassing you," Lincoln said into the phone. "What's he been doing? When did you go to the police?"

She exhaled, dropping her coat on a hook. "Long story. I didn't want you involved. I still don't. Your firm will probably end up having to defend him in court again on the Truman case, so let's not go there." She walked into the kitchen; it was filled with the spicy aroma of tomato, cumin, and chili pepper. "How soon will I officially learn I'm being sued?"

"Midweek, probably. Wednesday. Thursday. But I'm serious, Casey. This could be a mess. He's somehow got the RP people behind him. Two attorneys flew in from Dayton this morning."

"RP?" She lifted the lid on the Crock-Pot and the aroma got stronger.

"Rights for the People. A citizens' rights activist group."

Casey grabbed a wooden spoon from the drawer. "You've got to be kidding me. I think my sister sends them money."

"Look, I have to go. My secretary is waving at me through the window. I just wanted to give you a heads-up. Call you tonight?"

"Sure." Casey hung up. Like Lincoln, she didn't curse often. She hadn't been raised in a household where either of

her parents did. Her father always said there were more elo-
quent ways to express oneself. But sometimes there was
nothing that sounded right like a good swear. She dug into
the pot of thick chili beans and chunks of beef and pork.
"You son of a bitch," she muttered.

Angel tiptoed out of Buddy's room, closing the door
behind her. He'd been running a fever since yesterday afternoon. When she'd picked him up at Shonda's last night, it
was like his skin was on fire. Then she'd arrived home to
find out that Charlie hadn't paid the electric bill or the
phone bill, but that he *had* taken the money she'd left him
on the table.

Buddy was better today, but Angel still had to keep him
home; she didn't want to get Shonda's little girl sick. Angel's
sister hadn't been happy about Angel calling in sick with
only two weeks left before Christmas, but when Angel had
agreed to work extra hours over the weekend, Amber had
calmed down a little.

Beat, Angel walked down the hall and through the living
room. She didn't look at James lying on the couch as she cut
between him and the TV. He'd come home about three. Said
he didn't know where Charlie was and he didn't know anything about the bill money.

Angel didn't really care where Charlie was, but when he
did come home, she was going to have it out with him. He
was either going to straighten up or get out. Him and his
brother. She wasn't going to live this way. Wasn't going to
raise her boy this way.

"Turn it down or turn it off," she told James. He was
watching a monster-truck race.

He picked up the remote, but she didn't hear the volume

go down. She leaned over to pick up a plastic mallet that went to Buddy's tool set. "You hear me? I said turn it down."

"I'm turnin' it. I'm turnin' it," he grumbled. "Hey, you heard anything from Charlie?"

She tossed the mallet into the cardboard box at the end of the couch that served as a toy chest. Angel had picked out a nice red and blue toy chest at Wal-Mart that she was hoping she could get Buddy for Christmas. Missing work today would kill her budget for the week, though. It might mean no toy chest now. "Have I heard from him? You heard the phone ring? Hell no, I ain't heard from him."

"You got a lotta mouth, you know that, Angel? I tell Charlie all the time, he *oughta* make you watch your mouth."

Angel bit back a response. She had a feeling she had to be careful alone around James. Charlie might give her a smack once in a while, but she knew he'd never hurt her bad. But James? James was hard to read.

God, she never should have gotten drunk that night. Never should have slept with James.

A monster truck on the TV revved its engine.

"I said, turn it down." She walked into the kitchen. Dirty dishes littered the table and the counter. James had made himself spaghetti for dinner last night when she had refused to cook. He'd sprayed tomato sauce all over the stove, the wall, and the counter.

The truck on the TV grew louder. There were sounds of fans screaming and an announcer whooping it up.

At the kitchen sink, Angel soaked a dish rag with warm water. She had just wiped down the counters and dropped the dirty dishes into a sink full of hot water when she heard someone bang on the door.

"I got it!" James hollered over the TV.

Dishrag in her hand, Angel went to the window and peeked out. She groaned. It was Drina, James's sometimes girlfriend.

Angel didn't like her much. Not that she had anything against Latinos, but Drina was as two-faced as they came. She could be all sweet and nice to your face and then call you a whore to your friends. Angel had warned Drina weeks ago to stay out of her face and out of her house. Angel was surprised she was here.

Angel dropped the curtain and went back to the dirty dishes. She heard James let Drina in.

"What are you doin' here, honey? I was gonna call you later."

"Don't you honey me, chico," Drina said above the drone of the trucks.

Angel couldn't see them from where she stood, but she could imagine Drina all up in James's face. Latino girls were good at that, especially the bad-assed ones, and Drina was definitely a badass.

"Hey, the baby's sleepin'," James said.

"Well, my *niños* are in the car, so you listen here. I want my money."

"What money?"

"The money you stole from me. The money you took out my bag while I was takin' a pee after you got your rocks off the other night, *chico.*"

"Shhh. Lower your voice."

"Don't you touch me! Don't you do it!"

Angel slowly lowered a cereal bowl into the dishwater as she listened.

"I told you, you don't take what's mine. You don't take what I earn to feed my babies. You understand that? I don't scrub people's toilets so you can have my money. You hear what Drina is sayin'?"

"Drina, I swear—"

"I'm not jokin', chico. You do it again, and you'll wish you hadn't."

"What are you gonna do, call the police?" James said in that snotty voice of his. "'Cause you do, and I'm gonna tell them all about you workin' in those rich people's—"

"No, *loco,* I'm not goin' to call the police," Drina interrupted haughtily. "But you're gonna wish I had."

Angel heard the door open and then slam. A minute later, the monster trucks got louder. She smiled to herself. Maybe she liked Drina better than she'd thought.

Chapter 21

I wait for him on the boardwalk. It's cold and there are few people to be seen. Those who do face the elements walk with their heads down, hurrying along, bundled in coats and hats and hoods that obscure their vision.

No one will see me. No one will notice me. I look like them.

I sit on the bench facing the ocean. The waves rise up and crash down in thick white mountains of foam. There is a cold-pressure zone moving in. I have seen it on The Weather Channel. Like Ed, I like to watch The Weather Channel in the morning when I drink my coffee. I like to know what the temperature will be for the day so I can dress accordingly. I like to know the temperature in Puerto Vallarta. No reason in particular. I am just curious. I am a curious man.

I hear footsteps behind me, but I don't turn around. He knows to stand behind me. He knows not to look too closely beneath my hood. Despite how stupid he is, he seems to sense that I am dangerous. Rodents are like that—not smart, but they recognize danger. I think of him as a rodent. A rodent with thinning hair.

"What do you think you're doing?" I say.

"Don't know what yer talkin' about." He sniffs.

My fists clench at my sides inside my leather gloves, but I don't raise my hand to him. I know better. I am still in a public place. "Stealing from houses."

"I didn't—"

"Silence," I order in a deep voice.

He is silent. He knows that I am angry. He knows that he is expendable.

"You do what I hire you to do and you stay out of trouble. You understand?"

"I understand."

I relax my hands. Flex my fingers. Anger is bad for one's blood pressure. It serves no purpose. I like to always act with purpose. Speak with purpose. I speak to the knucklehead now with purpose. "Who have you told about me?"

"No one."

"Your girlfriend?"

"I don't tell her shit."

I wince at his bad language. "You recognize you have a good thing here, right? I pay you well."

"Yeah. Sure." He sniffs again.

I consider offering him my handkerchief, but the thought of his snot on a piece of my clothing so disgusts me that I don't. "I pay you enough? Enough to support your drug habit?"

He hesitates. Shuffles his feet. I imagine that he is wearing a hoodie and that his hands are stuffed down in his pants pockets; he is not smart enough to wear a coat or gloves.

"You pay enough," he says.

"You understand that you can't tell anyone." I try to speak plainly so that he understands me, even with his limited IQ. "If you tell anyone, you know what will happen?"

"Won't get paid." His voice is nearly lost in the howl of the wind.

"No," I say. "I'll kill you."

He walks away. I let him go.

I sit a minute longer, waiting until he has made his way down Rehoboth Avenue. To his vehicle. To a bar. Anywhere away from me. He is filth and I hate the idea that I have to deal with people like him every day.

I turn my thoughts purposely to something more pleasurable. I think about Maury and how our relationship is evolving. From the time I first learned of his accomplishments, I have admired him. Wanted to meet him. Maybe, on some level, to *be* him, at least when he is at work.

Now that our friendship has been established, I want so badly to pay him a visit. And I know that he wants to see me. I can tell by his letters that he is eager to meet me. That he sees me now as a worthy student, if not an equal.

I could visit him easily enough. No one would be suspicious.

But I know that I must be patient. That there must be no physical contact as long as he remains incarcerated. It's not safe for him. Certainly not safe for me.

That doesn't mean I can't pick his brain.

"What's this I see in the paper about you getting your butt sued, sis?" Joaquin, who'd just come through the front door, walked up behind Casey and placed his hands on her shoulders.

She looked at him over her shoulder. "You believe everything you read in the paper?" She pulled him down so she could kiss him on the cheek. "Happy birthday, birthday boy."

Lincoln rose from where he'd been sitting beside Casey. "Happy birthday. Thanks for having us." He shook her brother-in-law's hand.

"Thanks for coming." Joaquin walked around the couch,

picking up a cracker and a piece of cheese from a plate Jayne had placed on the coffee table.

Lincoln sat again. "Hey, I never miss an opportunity for birthday cake."

"Hi, Ed." Joaquin munched on his cracker. "I hear you had a nice week at the senior center."

Ed stared at the big-screen TV he had pulled his chair in front of. Casey could tell he had heard Joaquin; he was just ignoring him. Her father hadn't wanted to come for the birthday festivities. He said he wanted to stay home with Frazier. She was beginning to wonder if she should have let him.

Joaquin turned back to Casey and Lincoln. "Jayne's in the kitchen?"

Casey nodded. "But we're not to go in. She and the kids are preparing your birthday dinner. I understand the cake has lavender icing and a green dinosaur on top. Your son and daughter's creation."

"Long as it tastes good." He reached for another cracker. "So seriously, what's up with the lawsuit? Paper made out like it was a big deal, constitutional rights being violated Innocent man being persecuted and so on."

What's up? Why don't you ask your wife, she wanted to say. *She supports RP.* As she contemplated a better reply, Lincoln jumped to the rescue. "It's not a good idea for Casey to talk about it, Joaquin. The hospital is representing her; this is really more run-of-the-mill than you probably realize. Happens all the time to professionals like Casey, but she still needs to keep the details to herself. You understand."

"Sure, sure." He worked as a counselor for troubled teens, many headed for incarceration. He probably did understand. And he was far less left wing than Jayne. He was a psychologist because he wanted to help people, but he wasn't so

naïve as to believe that *everyone* was innocent, or even able
to be saved. Casey thought it was interesting that Jayne and
Joaquin were able to make their marriage work when they
often had such opposite views. But Joaquin was easygoing.
Like Casey, sometimes he just agreed to disagree with Jayne.

A loud clatter came from the kitchen and Joaquin looked
at Casey and Lincoln. They could hear Jayne chastising one
of the kids.

"Need some help in there, honey?" Joaquin called.
"Dinner smells good."

"Stay out!" Jayne yelled from the kitchen.

There was another clatter as if something hit the floor.
This time, it was followed by the sound of breaking glass.

Casey rose off the couch. "Jayne?"

"Don't you dare come in here," she threatened. "I can do
this. I know you two don't think I'm capable of putting on a
nice dinner, but I am."

Casey sat back down, looking wide-eyed at Joaquin.

Lincoln smiled, easing off the couch. "How about if I see
if she needs an extra hand? She won't kick me out. I'm still
considered a *guest*." He waggled his eyebrows.

"If she throws anything, duck," Casey warned, leaning
over the end of the couch to make sure she'd left her cell
phone on ring. She was on call this weekend and Friday
nights could be busy, especially in December. Unfortunately, emotions ran high around Christmastime, which
meant an increase in alcohol-related car accidents and do-
mestic violence.

The episode of *Storm Stories* got louder on the big-screen
TV. "Dad, turn it down," Casey said.

Ed held the remote firmly, but the volume didn't go
down.

Joaquin just smiled. "Hey, you want to see what I bought
myself for my birthday?"

She shruggcd. "Sure."

She followed him down the hall into the small room they used as an office. Like every other room in the house, every surface—the floors, too—was stacked with papers, bags, toys.

He went behind the desk to a metal gun cabinct where she knew he kept the rifles and shotguns he used in hunting. He took a key off the top, over his head, and Casey watched him unlock the sturdy door.

She didn't like guns, but she knew Joaquin loved hunting. She reasoned she could admire his passion, if not the sport.

He removed a wooden box from the top shelf, set it on top of a pile of *Reader's Digests* on the desk, and opened it. "A guy in my hunting club has been bugging me for months to try target shooting."

She stared at the handgun he liftcd out of the box. "That's nice."

"It's pretty simple, a Ruger Mk 2. A .22 semiautomatic. A good pistol to start out with."

"So you want to compete in target shooting?" She stood back, arms crossed over her chest. She was keeping one ear on what was going on in the other rooms. Lincoln had disappeared into the kitchcn, there had been no more shattering of glass and he hadn't come out, so she figured he was probably safe. The TV continued to blast. "I didn't know you were interested in that," she said.

He shrugged, turning the pistol over in his hand. "I don't know. I was a good shot in the army. I thought it might be fun. And the guys are nice out at the club. A lot of retired military guys and retired cops."

She nodded. "Could be fun."

"Maybe. We'll see." He reached behind him and pulled out a little cardboard box. "See, you shoot .22 Long Rifle bullets. They give you tighter groups at standard velocity."

Casey had no idea what he was talking about, but again,

she nodded. He seemed tickled with the handgun. "But it stays locked up, right?"

"Oh, sure. I bought one of the best gun cabinets they make." Joaquin put the box of bullets back, then tucked the pistol into the box. "Kids aren't even allowed in this room, and they wouldn't dare get near the cabinet." The pistol back in its box, he returned it to the top shelf, closed the metal cabinet door, locked it, and placed the key on top again.

"Shouldn't the key be stored somewhere else?" she asked. "You know, just to be safe?"

"Yeah. But where would you put it in this room?" He looked around, giving a laugh. "I guess when the kids get a little older, I need to find a place for it. They couldn't reach the key right now, if they tried." He came around the desk. "Should we go see how dinner is coming along? I'm starved."

"Sure." She turned around and almost ran into her father, who was standing in the doorway. He had the TV so loud in the living room that she hadn't heard him come down the hall. "Dad."

"Expecting icy rain, sleet tonight," he told her. "We should go."

"Dinner first, Dad." She straightened the collar of his shirt beneath his sweater. "Cake and presents and then we'll go home."

"Sleet can make the road slick, Freckles. You remember that accident you had when you were in high school? You slid right through the stop sign into the intersection."

Casey followed Ed down the hall. Joaquin closed the office door behind him.

"That was Jayne, Dad, and her accident was in July. You used to call her Freckles, not me." She rubbed her father's shoulder. "And she was changing a CD in her stereo when she went through the stop sign."

"Daddy!"

"Daddy!" The children met them in the living room.

"Come see your cake in the dining room, Daddy." Annabelle, dressed in a pink tutu over purple tights and body-suit, beamed.

"Daddy! Daddy!" Little Chad bounced up and down like a pogo stick.

"You sure it's okay?" Joaquin asked. "Mommy says I can go in the dining room?"

"It's okay, Daddy." Annabelle took her father's hand. Chad took the other.

Lincoln joined them in the living room. "Coast is clear, at least as far as the dining room."

Casey watched the children lead Joaquin into the other room. "So, everything going okay in there?" she asked Lincoln softly.

Her father was in front of the TV again, remote in hand.

"Dinner looks great." He leaned over and kissed the top of her head. "How are you with this lawsuit nonsense? You doing okay?"

She looked up at him. "I haven't done anything wrong, Lincoln."

"I know you haven't."

"The police say they can't do anything without any proof."

"Well, what's Gaitlin been doing?"

She shook her head. "I really don't want you to get involved."

He exhaled. "You know, with the RP breathing down their necks, the police will have to be careful. There's nothing his attorneys would like better right now than a false arrest to add fuel to the fire."

"This is a man who should be in prison, Lincoln," she said steadily. "You don't understand what a monster he is. He *has* to be prosecuted for Linda's death."

"I've already told the partners that I don't want to see anything that should cross their desks concerning his case."

"They're not getting involved in the suits, are they?" She looked up into his blue eyes.

"I don't think so." He rubbed the small of her back in a soothing circular motion. "In fact, between you and me, if he's rearrested on the Truman case, I doubt we'll represent him."

She lifted her brows.

"Various reasons."

"None I need to know about." She nodded. "I understand."

He rested his hand on her hip, holding her against him. "So, you okay? I mean about Gaitlin. Is there something I can do? Something to make you feel safer."

She lifted up on her toes, smiling, and kissed him. She liked the idea that he cared enough to ask. "Nothing you can do. I can handle it, counselor."

He leaned over. "Can I have another little taste of that?"

"This?" She kissed him again, this time darting her tongue out to tease him.

"Mmmm."

"Okay, enough of that, you two. This is a G-rated home." Joaquin walked out into the living room clapping his hands together. He was wearing a pointed paper party hat, as were his two accomplices trailing behind him. "Shall we eat?" He walked over to his father-in-law. "Dinner's ready, Ed." He took the remote from him and shut the TV off. "Let's go," he said, not giving him a choice. "Jayne has made my *abuela's enchiladas pollo* and I know how you love them."

"I hate enchiladas," Ed grumbled, getting out of the chair.

Casey laughed. "Dad! You just asked me to make enchiladas the other day. I use Joaquin's grandmother's recipe."

He shuffled into the dining room behind them. "I don't like enchiladas," he complained under his breath. "And I don't like the *birthday boy*. Jayne should have married Lincoln. I told her to marry him and not this one."

Casey met Lincoln's gaze, and the look on his face was one of such amusement that she had to cover her mouth to keep from laughing out loud.

"Quite a family you have here," Lincoln said above the sound of the tooting paper horns Casey's niece and nephew now possessed.

"Gotta love 'em," she whispered, grasping his hand and squeezing it before she let go.

"Gotta love 'em," he repeated with a grin.

The sleet hit the windshield and beaded the way Carmen's mother's candy used to bead on the wax paper she dropped it on. Some people tested the temperature of candy by dropping it into water, but not her mom. She liked to see it, touch it. She made it the same way her grandmother had always made it.

Carmen's mom could make all kinds of candy. Used to be able to. Brittles, taffies, divinity. Carmen loved the fluffy white divinity made every Christmas. Carmen and her little sisters and their mom would all gather around the kitchen table and make the divinity with its stiff white peaks like snowy mountaintops. Then Carmen's dad would come home and he would snitch pieces and her mom would playfully slap at his hand. Everyone would laugh, and Carmen's dad would pull her mom into a big bear hug and kiss her with his sticky-candy mouth.

A tear slipped down Carmen's cheek. There would be no more sticky-mouth kisses. Her father had passed away two years ago from lung cancer. Never smoked a day in his life.

And now, the doctors said her mom wouldn't make it out

of the hospital this time. They weren't even sure she would make it until Christmas.

Carmen rubbed her blurry eyes and turned up the speed of the windshield wipers. She hadn't meant to stay at the hospital so late, but the room had been warm and quiet and her mom had been sleeping peacefully, for once. Carmen just hadn't had the energy to get up and go home to her two sisters. Tomorrow she would have to talk to them about the situation before she took them over to the hospital after school.

And soon they'd have to talk about what life would be *after*. After Mom died. Because Carmen had just turned twenty-one, she would be able to be her sisters' legal guardian. Her mom had made sure of that before she went into the hospital for her last surgery.

Carmen had left college in Virginia, midterm, a month ago when her mother had called with the news that she was no longer in remission. Her mother hadn't wanted her to come home; she'd been angry when her eldest daughter had shown up with her car full of her belongings. But Carmen was glad she had done it. Glad she could be here for her sisters.

No one had expected the breast cancer to metastasize this fast.

Carmen shifted in her seat, gripping the steering wheel a little tighter. The road was slick and the sleet was making it hard to see. She cranked up the fan on the defroster.

At a light, she glanced down at her sweater and the "mosquito bumps" under it. She tried not to be selfish, not to think about it, but she wondered if she would get breast cancer, too. They said it was hereditary.

Carmen signaled. Turned. The traffic light on the next corner was green and she was tempted to step on the gas, but she knew her Honda might slide. She was the head of the family now. That was what her mother said. She couldn't take chances like that.

The light blinked yellow in front of her. She touched the brake lightly, just the way her dad had taught her.

Both of her parents dying of cancer in two years' time. What was the possibility of that? She would have to ask her sister Hannah sometime. Hannah, a tenth grader, loved numbers. She loved statistics. She would know what the odds were.

Carmen eased to a stop at the white line and took her hands off the wheel to rub them together. She'd lost one of her gloves. Had to be somewhere in the house.

She was cold. She shouldn't have taken her coat off and thrown it in the backseat. The heater in the Honda didn't work all that great, and the defroster did nothing to help the matter.

Carmen's gaze was fixed on the red light in front of her when she heard a noise to her left.

It happened so fast.

The car door jerked open and a guy reached in and yanked her by the arm. She didn't see his face under the hood. Only the red skull and crossbones on the sleeve of his black sweatshirt.

Carmen screamed, hanging on to the steering wheel with one hand. All she could think of was that if he killed her, who would take care of Hannah and Molly? She had to fight. She had to hang on.

Carmen's foot came off the brake and the car began to slowly roll forward. There wasn't another car at the intersection. No one coming in either direction. Who would be out on a night like this? Cold. Sleeting. Most people had better sense.

There was no one to hear her scream.

Carmen gritted her teeth so hard that her jaw hurt. He was so strong that she couldn't hold on. She cried out as her hand slipped. She hit the wet road hard. Water splashed up, cold on her face, soaking her jeans. "Let me go!" she screamed, beating him with her free hand.

He kicked her hard in the small of her back and Carmen's whole body jerked in response to the pain. He let go of her and she fell hard, her face hitting the ground. She slid a little and something burned her cheek. Instinctively, she covered her head with her hands. She'd seen a show the other night on TV with her sisters where a mountain lion had attacked a woman riding her bike and she had saved her own life by protecting her head.

Thankfully, Carmen's attacker stepped over her, but he started to give her one more kick. She was able to curl into a ball quickly enough so that his sneaker made contact only with her buttocks. She grunted as his foot connected with her tailbone.

Carmen rolled onto her back in the street and watched him get into her Honda. Her car? He wanted her old Honda? He could have the hunk of junk.

But her purse was in the car. Not her purse!

Carmen knew she should just lie there on the ground. Let him go. It was just a car. Just a purse. She could get another.

"No!" she screamed through tears. As she tried to get up, she squinted in the sleet, hoping she would at least be able to get a good look at him so she could identify him if she saw him again. But the hood of his sweatshirt obscured his face.

"Not my purse, you bastard!" she hollered. On her feet, Carmen almost made it to the car door before he slammed it, nearly catching her fingertips between metal.

He hit the gas. The car lurched forward, fishtailing. The side panel hit Carmen hard in the hip, nearly sending her to the icy road again.

She watched as the taillights glowed, trailing across the intersection. Still not another car in sight.

"Not my purse," she sobbed, rubbing her cheek where it now felt as if it was on fire. But it wasn't the purse she was crying for. It was her mother's wedding ring, tucked inside it.

Chapter 22

"No change?" Adam stood over his grandfather's bed, his hands resting in the pockets of his gray flannel slacks. The ventilator clicked and whooshed. It was a sound he had come to detest.

The private nurse looked up from the paperback novel she was reading and shook her head sympathetically. "I'm sorry, Mr. Preston. There isn't."

Adam just stood there looking down at the tiny, shriveled man in the bed. This wasn't how his grandfather wanted to die. Adam couldn't imagine *anyone* wanting to die this way.

But Adam's father had been insistent that all efforts be made to sustain life, no matter how feeble that life might be. Last night, they had had a tense discussion on the phone; his parents were now in Budapest.

Adam had tactfully tried to suggest that perhaps his grandfather's status should be reevaluated. If there was no chance of recovery, of him ever waking up, perhaps it was time to look at other options. What he had not said was that he thought they should just pull the plug on the ventilator. He knew better than to come right out and say it. His father, Adam Thomas Preston Jr., was a man of euphemisms. He was a soft man, a man who avoided not only confrontation, but the making of decisions, at almost any cost.

It was that weakness in his father that Adam had come to despise over the years. Preston Junior had never been the man *his* father had been. Perhaps that was why it was so important to Adam that he live up to the Preston name, that he make his grandfather proud.

His jaw clenched, Adam looked down and smoothed the pristine white sheet that had been folded neatly beneath his grandfather's chin. If it were up to Adam, he would not let him suffer this way.

But, the decision was not his to make, and no matter how much it pained him, Adam had no choice but to wait and watch as this great man wasted away.

Lying on his back on the narrow bunk, Maury munched on the Snickers bar he'd gotten from one of the vending machines at mail call. Lights were out and it was pretty quiet on tier D. One of his roommates had escaped today, so there were only five of them in the room tonight. Carlos apparently had clocked in at his landscaping job, clocked out at the end of the day, and walked away. He wasn't the brightest kid, so everyone was taking bets as to how long it would be before he'd be back. Stupid thing was, he had less than three months to serve. When they caught him—and they would—he'd do a nine-month mandatory in prison whites for the prison break, and then he would *still* have to serve the last three months on his old charge.

Maury took another tiny bite of the candy bar. He always tried to make it last. Draw the pleasure out of it.

He'd gotten mail from Danni again today and a newspaper clipping from the local *Police Beat*. This one was about a carjacking. A young woman had been attacked, her car stolen on her way home from seeing her dying mother in the hospital. The girl hadn't been hurt. According to the paper, it was the third carjacking in the last month, but the only one in which the car was found locally. Odd.

The carjacking was in bad taste, really.

Maury was worried about Danni. What kind of person carjacked a young woman on her way home from the hospital where her cancer-ridden mother was rotting away? There was a side note in the article stating that some local church was taking up a collection to aid the victim and her younger sisters . . . to help them have a brighter Christmas.

Maury wished he had enough money to send the girls something, but most of his money was still being banked for legal fees.

The chocolate in the Snickers was creamy. The nuts crunchy. The patterns of texture in each bite were totally unpredictable. He was enjoying it tremendously.

He thought about Danni again. What was he up to? Surely he hadn't jacked all three cars. Not in a month. That would be too dangerous. And Danni didn't fit the carjacking profile.

So what was he up to? The B&E; the robbery of the minimart, where he shot the boy in the balls; the carjacking . . .

Odd. Very odd. And a little disconcerting.

Maury wondered if Danni was a nut. If he was, it wasn't safe for Maury to associate with him. Not in any way. Not and jeopardize his own future.

But Danni didn't strike him as a nut job. So what was he?

It was a very interesting question.

Casey checked her watch on her way upstairs. Frazier bounded playfully after her. She had enough time to retrieve the Christmas boxes before going outside to meet the van that would bring her father home. She felt guilty for having waited so long to put up the tree that had been delivered from the nursery Friday afternoon, but tonight was the night.

Last night Lincoln had helped her lug the heavy, balled tree into the living room, and it was now standing bare, but proud, on the opposite side of the fireplace from the TV. Lincoln was coming over for homemade vegetable soup, and they and Ed were going to trim the tree.

At the end of the hall, Casey entered the access door to the attic of the Cape Cod. The dog followed curiously. She flipped the switch, and the bare bulbs screwed into utilitarian sockets illuminated the eaves. She rested her hands on her hips as she gazed over the maze of stocked boxes, plastic containers, and furniture. Frazier whined and slid his bottom to the floor as if he was suggesting he was there to support her, despite the obviously daunting task ahead.

When Casey and Jayne had sold their parents' house, they had sold or donated most of their parents' belongings, but there were some items neither had been able to part with. There were an antique couch, some rosewood tables, English china, and books. Boxes of books. Even some first editions. Because Jayne's house was already so cluttered, her attic and garage already packed, Casey had agreed to store the things until they came up with a better solution.

When the movers had delivered her parents' belongings, Casey had been so distracted by dealing with her father and getting him settled into the house that she had told them to set the stuff anywhere in the attic. Now, staring at the mess, she wished she had had more forethought. She had no idea where her Christmas boxes were. Nothing looked the same as it had six months ago. Everything had been moved or shifted.

But she was no grinch and Christmas could not be halted, or even slowed, by a few misplaced boxes. Grabbing her flashlight out of her back pocket, she scooted between a stack of boxes and a chair draped in a flowered sheet. Frazier followed.

"Okay, boy," she said, trying to sound upbeat. "Clear boxes, red and green snap tops. Fetch, boy. Fetch."

Ed shuffled down the sidewalk studying the line of white vans. Old farts were climbing aboard for the ride home. One of the vans was his; the one with the driver with the long nose hairs. That was the van that would take him home to Joe Frazier.

People pushed past him. Bumped into him. An ambulance with spinning lights and a loud siren had just carried someone off. She had fallen at the front door; she was probably dead. She had looked dead to him when he had stepped over her.

Everything was a mass of confusion on the sidewalk now. Loud noises, people hurrying . . . like they could get away from the woman who had croaked and cheat death, somehow. Ed knew better. When it came, it came.

There were cars parked erratically at the curb and the buses didn't seem to be in the right order. Not like usual. Ed liked things the same way. On TV, channels were always the same, always in the same order. It made them easier to find. He remembered that one of the white vans had moved to make room for the ambulance and the guys in the truck with the medical kits. *Para-matics,* he thought they were called. It was a word something like that.

It was cold out and Ed pulled the collar of his coat together. It was windy. He wished he'd worn his hat with the fuzzy earflaps. They were made of fur. Some kind of animal, but he couldn't remember which right this minute. Didn't really matter what animal had died to give him warm earflaps because he'd left the hat on the shelf in the laundry room.

He stuffed his hands in his pockets and walked to the next van. The driver looked fourteen and had pimples all over his face. That wasn't the right van.

Feeling something wet on his face, he looked up at the sky. Snowflakes? *The only other sound's the sweep of easy wind and downy flake.* The words drifted in his head. *Robert Frost.*

The forecast had called for a winter mix later tonight, but no snow. Ed liked snow. He lifted his chin toward the sky with delight and watched as the glittering flakes drifted downward from Jesus. One hit him on the end of the nose and he laughed. He stuck out his tongue. The snow was cold and tingly.

"Ed?"

Ed tilted his head forward. There was a man standing next to a blue car. *A stranger.*

"Hey, Ed. There you are. I was looking all over for you."

Ed stared at him. He didn't remember the guy, but the guy knew him. That happened to Ed a lot these days. It was embarrassing. Getting old was hell. Getting old and crazy was worse. Like being caught in Dante's Ninth Circle when you hadn't even committed the sin.

"Casey sent me to pick you up."

Ed still didn't say anything. He was suspicious. He was supposed to ride the bus. Casey said she would see him when he got off the bus.

"You *are* Ed McDaniel, right?"

Ed looked back toward the "old farts' center." They called it the Modern Maturity Center, but he knew better. It wasn't a place for modern, mature people. It was where the young people parked the old farts during the day so they could go to work.

The sidewalk was beginning to clear. White vans were pulling out. What if he had missed his van? He didn't always remember the address at the house. It was confusing. Numbers similar to his house in Maryland, but not the same. It would have been easier if the numbers were the same. He looked back at the stranger.

"Ed?" the man said.

Ed nodded.

"Come on, man. Jump in."

The guy was wearing a black sweatshirt with the hood up. He had his hands stuffed in his jeans and he looked cold.

"You know Casey?" Ed questioned.

"Sure. We work together. Remember?" The guy opened the car door. It squeaked loud like it was going to fall off. Ed wondered why Casey would send someone from work in a car with a squeaky door.

"Come on, Ed." The man had his hands in his pockets again. "It's cold out here. Let's get you home."

Ed took one last look down the sidewalk. The last van was pulling out. He got into the car. The man closed his door.

Ed struggled to get his seat belt on as Casey's friend from work got in the other side. The buckle wouldn't reach. Ed let it go and then tried to pull it across his lap again. A car like this, you couldn't be too careful.

"Need some help?" The man took the buckle from Ed and pushed it into the slot. It clicked.

Ed tugged on the belt to be sure it was secure.

Casey's friend didn't buckle his. They pulled out, fishtailing a little at the exit.

Ed pushed his hands down on the seat trying to steady himself as they went around the corner. Damned young folks. All crazy drivers.

Ed stared straight ahead. Snowflakes hit the windshield

and flattened into little wet puddles. The man turned on the wipers, which whisked them away. Ed watched as they passed houses. A mini-mart. Some things looked familiar. Sort of. But nowadays, everything looked the same, didn't it? A mini-mart on every corner?

They drove in silence for a couple of minutes. The windshield wipers clicked as they went back and forth. The defrost fan hummed.

Ed saw fields now, but they hadn't passed the pizza place. When Casey drove home, they usually passed the pizza place. But it was dark out now; things never looked the same in the dark. He looked at Casey's friend.

"Where are we going?"

"Told you. I'm takin' you home."

Ed looked out the windshield again. Even though it was dark, he was pretty sure this wasn't the right way. He didn't want to be in this car. He wanted to ride home in the van. That, or he wanted to drive himself.

Ed missed driving. Jayne and Casey said he wasn't allowed to drive anymore, just because he got lost a couple times in all that crazy traffic in College Park, but Ed still had his license. He'd hidden it from them and said he'd lost it. Maybe tomorrow he would drive to the old farts' place.

He glanced at Casey's friend again and rested his hand on the seat belt buckle. It was cold. His hands were cold. His ears were cold. He wished he had the animal fur hat.

The car was going faster. The road was slippery. Ed could see the slush from the wet snow on the pavement. It wasn't safe to drive this fast.

"What did you say your name was?" Ed asked.

"Ronnie. Ronnie Reagan." The man grinned.

Ed started to feel all prickly inside and he didn't like the feeling. Not one bit. His heart was beating a little faster. "This isn't the way."

"How would you know? You can barely find your way to the shit house."

Ed's lower lip trembled. He looked quickly at the man and then back at the road again. He *did* look a little bit like Ronald Reagan. But Reagan never wore a hooded sweatshirt.

"I want to get out of the car."

"Why would you want to do that, Ed? I'm taking you home. Remember? Or did you forget already? Casey says you're a forgetful man. Actually, she says you're a pain in the ass."

Ed was cold before, but now he was hot. Sweaty in his green sweater and overcoat. He could feel his armpits getting wet. He hated sweaty armpits. Lorraine would never tolerate a man with body odor.

Ed swallowed hard and looked at Ronald Reagan in the hooded sweatshirt. "I want to get out of the car."

Ronald Reagan hit the gas and the car slid one way and then the other, picking up speed. "So go ahead. Get out, Ed."

Casey located two of the five Christmas boxes and lugged one down the stairs and then the other. As she set down the second box, she checked her watch. "Shoot. We almost forgot Dad, Frazier! Let's go get Ed."

The dog followed Casey into the laundry room, where she put on her coat and hat. They went out into the yard through the garage. Fortunately, the van was late. Casey looked up at the sprinkling of snowflakes falling from the dark sky. The roads were wet; the driver was probably taking his time.

Frazier ran over to the nearest bush and lifted his leg. Casey wandered down the driveway, spotting a Coke can on the front lawn. Better than a beer bottle. Done with his business, Frazier raced around the front yard.

"Pretty spry, for such an old man," she called to the dog.

She picked up the soda can and a gum wrapper. On her way toward the green trash barrel beside the house, she spotted a plastic bag caught in an azalea bush.

Casey picked up a half dozen pieces of trash and then got the tennis ball off the front porch and threw it to Frazier a couple of times. Eventually, he tired of playing fetch and lay down in the driveway. Casey checked her watch again. Her father was now a half hour late. She went into the house to check her voice mail on her cell and the house phone. No message from the senior center.

She went back out through the garage. Frazier had moved into the garage and lay down again, staring down the driveway, his head resting between his paws. Casey was beginning to get worried. She walked down the driveway, then up again. It was cold out. The snow had stopped.

She went into the house and dialed the senior center. The elderly woman who answered the phone said there had been a slight delay in the van departure. She told Casey not to worry, that it was snowing out. Her father would be along soon.

Casey waited fifteen more minutes and then called back, asking Mrs. Polaski, the evening receptionist, to contact the van driver and see how late he was running. Casey was concerned that the van had broken down. If it had, she would just go meet it and get her father. She knew sitting in a van beside the road would irritate him.

Mrs. Polaski called back ten minutes later. Casey was standing in front of the living room window. Frazier waited by the front door. Mrs. Polaski confirmed that her father had been there all day, but said that the van driver had already completed his route and had just returned the van. According to the bus driver, Casey's father hadn't taken the van home.

"You're sure he was there?" Casey asked, gripping the phone, her heart pounding.

"All day," Mrs. Polaski said, seemingly annoyed. "I saw

him go out the door this afternoon myself after he signed out. Nice-looking man, your father. Very dapper."

"So he was there all day, signed out at the front desk, left the building, but didn't get in the van? And he didn't get on the wrong van?" Casey questioned.

"All of the vans are accounted for. No one's seen your father since he left here, Miss McDaniel. You sure he didn't go home with a friend?"

"He doesn't have any friends." Casey hung up and dialed the police.

Ed stared at Ronald Reagan for a minute. He was scared, but he was angry, too. Casey's friend wasn't very nice. Certainly not very presidential.

"What? You don't want to jump?" the guy cackled.

Ed covered the seat belt buckle with his hand and slowly lifted it. "I want you to stop the car."

"And I want your daughter to lay off."

"Lay off what?" Ed said it loud enough so that Ronald Reagan couldn't hear the seat belt buckle unlock.

"Casey knows."

Ed didn't like the way he said it. He didn't like the way he said her name. He wondered if this Ronald Reagan was friends with Richard Nixon, who stood in the flower beds sometimes. He didn't like either of them. He rested his right hand on the door handle and checked to be sure it was unlocked. "Stop the car and let me out."

"Told you—you want out, you'll have to jump."

In Ed's lifetime, he hadn't been forced to make many split-second decisions, but in his heart, he knew he had to now. He just hoped he wasn't going to break any bones.

As the car went into a curve in the road, Ronald Reagan decelerated. Ed pulled on the door handle and pushed with his elbow. The man behind the wheel yelled, shooting his hand out to catch Ed.

But Ed was too fast for him. Too smart. Ed threw himself out of the seat, pushing his right arm back so he wouldn't get caught up in the seat belt strap. His shoulder hit first, then his face. Mostly his chin. He slid in the wet, crackly grass, the toes of his shoes dragging on the edge of the road and then through the gravel.

As he hit, he tried to roll in a ball the way John Wayne did when he jumped off his horse, but it didn't work all that well.

Pain shot through Ed's shoulder. His chin burned.

Behind him, he heard the car speed away, Ronald shouting obscenities.

Ed lay there beside the road in the dark for a minute, trying to catch his breath. His heart was pounding and he was scared so bad that he had to urinate. But a part of him felt good. He'd gotten away from the presidential kidnapper. Just like the Duke, he would live to fight another day.

Ed sat up, rubbing his chin. He was wet and cold and he didn't know where he was. Slowly he got to his feet. His shoe had come off. He found it in the ditch beside a Kentucky Fried Chicken box. He didn't like Kentucky Fried Chicken. He liked Casey's crunchy baked chicken. A lot less saturated fat.

By the light coming from a house across the street, Ed studied his brown loafer. It was really scraped up on the toe. He wasn't sure he could polish that out. He put the shoe on the edge of the road and slipped his foot into it. He looked up at the house. He could go over and knock, but he was still a little shook up. What would he say?

No, it would be better if he just walked home.

He looked up the road, then down the road. The question was, which way?

He thought for a minute and then decided that he should

go the opposite way of Ronald Reagan. He didn't want to run into him again tonight. Maybe if he walked back into town, he would recognize something. If he could just find the pizza place.

A car approached from the direction of Georgetown and Ed got well off the road. It was slippery. He'd already taken one tumble tonight. He didn't need a car careening off the road taking him out. The car passed and he moved onto the loose gravel next to the road again, where it was easier to walk.

He had money in his pocket. Twenty dollars. He always kept it there with his picture of Frazier and the grandbabies. Jayne had put the grandbaby pictures in. She said he didn't need money, but Ed liked having it. It would come in handy if he found the pizza place. He was hungry. If he found the restaurant, he would have a piece of pizza and a cola. Maybe even a beer. Light. Then he would walk home.

Ed shuffled along the side of the road. He'd walk home tonight, but tomorrow when he went to the old farts' place, he was definitely driving himself.

Chapter 23

Lincoln arrived shortly after Casey called the police. She wanted to drive around looking for her father, but Lincoln insisted she stay at the house and wait for the police to call. What if Ed tried to call, or showed up, Lincoln reasoned with her.

Casey told Lincoln she was afraid that if Lincoln did find her father, he wouldn't get in the car with him. Lincoln countered by offering to take Frazier with him, and Casey ended up standing on the front porch, fighting tears, waving as Lincoln backed out of the driveway with the boxer in the tiny passenger seat of his Mini Coop. *Good boyfriend,* she thought. *A good guy.*

Jayne called twice. She was at Annabelle's Christmas dance recital, but she swore she would be at Casey's within the hour. An hour and a half and two calls from Lincoln but no word from the police, Ed, or Jayne and Casey was beside herself. She had *known* her father shouldn't go to the senior center.

When the phone rang again, she pounced on it.

"Casey McDaniel?" the official-sounding voice on the other end of the line said.

"Yes, yes, this is she."

"This is Officer Boden with the Georgetown police. We spoke earlier."

Casey took a deep breath. She was sick to her stomach. "Yes, sir."

"I have your father here, at Bob's Pizza Palace on one-thirteen."

Casey heaved another breath, this one of relief. "You found him. Oh, thank you. I can't tell you how much I appreciate this."

"He was just sitting here having a beer and a piece of pizza. Another officer came in to pick up dinner and thought he recognized him from the description that went out. I can bring him home —"

Casey heard another voice in the background. It was her father interrupting Officer Boden.

"But it seems Mr. McDaniel is unwilling to accept our hospitality," the officer said. "Would you like to come pick him up or should I try to persuade him—"

"No, no. I'll be there. Five minutes. Thank you so much!"

Casey flew out of the house, taking her coat with her, but not taking the time to put it on. Her father had to be so scared; she just wanted to reach him. Later, she'd get the details of what had happened. In the car, on the way to the pizza place, she spoke with Lincoln on the phone, who agreed to meet her back at her house. Casey got Jayne and Joaquin's answering service on their cells, so she left a message.

Casey rushed into the restaurant to find her father sitting at a booth in front of a grease-stained paper plate. He was rubbing his mouth with a napkin. She glanced down at the empty beer mug. He didn't appear to be all that frightened.

A police officer stood nearby, talking to a busboy.

"Daddy." She tried not to sound too upset, but when she

saw his bloody chin and his damp clothes, she had to choke back her emotions. "I'm so glad to see you."

He glanced at her. "I told the police you would come for me. I was going to walk home, but it's cold out. Did you see the snow?"

She slid into the booth to sit beside him. "Yes. It snowed at home."

"Nothing stuck, though." He wiped his mouth with his napkin again. "Freezing rain tonight. There'll be no snow for Christmas."

Casey tried to get a better look at his face. "Dad, what happened?"

"This?" He stroked his chin. "You probably don't want to know."

"Of course I do."

"It was stupid. My fault. Ruined my shoe." He pointed under the table. "Don't know if it will polish up."

"It's okay, Dad." She covered his hand with hers, noticing that it was also scraped up.

"Miss McDaniel." The officer approached the table.

Casey rose. "Officer Boden, thank you so much." She glanced at her father. "He seems okay, just beat up a little. I have no idea how he got here."

The officer crooked his finger, and Casey stepped closer he could speak without Ed hearing him. "Ronald Reagan," he said.

"Excuse me?"

The young officer cut his eyes in Ed's direction, then back at Casey. "He said that Ronald Reagan picked him up at the Modern Maturity Center."

Casey didn't know what to say.

He smiled kindly. "I'm assuming he has some dementia. He does pretty well for himself, though. Very polite. He tried to buy me a beer."

Casey put her hand to her forehead. So now it was Ronald Reagan coming to the senior center? Okay, so he made that up. Had he made up Nixon looking in the windows, too? But her father had obviously gotten here somehow, and she doubted he walked all this way in this weather.

She looked up at the officer. "I apologize for bothering you like this. Thank you so much for finding him. There was some confusion at the senior center and they thought he caught a ride with someone."

"Then maybe forgot where he lived." Boden nodded. "My Aunt Tillie's got dementia. Forgets where the refrigerator is all the time. Puts her milk in the linen closet. No apology necessary." He walked away, headed toward the door. His car was parked in the no-parking zone out front, engine running. "It's just nice to see a story with a happy ending. See you around, Ed." He waved.

Ed tipped his mug and finished his beer.

Casey slid in beside him on the bench again. "Dad . . . how did you get here? Did you walk?"

"I don't want to talk about this." He reached for his coat. "Road's getting slippery. We have to go home."

"We'll go," she said firmly, "but I have to know what happened. You really scared me, Dad. No one knew where you were. You can't do that."

He stared at the napkin crumpled in his hand. "I made a mistake. I should never have gotten in the car with him."

"With Ronald Reagan?" She waited.

"He said he knew you. Said you sent him to pick me up, but I knew better." There was a break in his voice.

Casey's eyes suddenly burned. She hated to see her father like this, so . . . vulnerable. But there was something else in his voice that tapped her attention. "You really did get into a car with someone, Dad? Who? And for the love of God, please don't tell me Ronald Reagan or Richard Nixon."

Ed twisted the napkin and a little piece of paper broke off and fell on the table. "He looked a little bit like Ronald Reagan and he said he was your friend from the hospital. He said you sent him."

Casey grabbed her father's hand. "He knew you?" She looked away. She had assumed that if he hadn't walked, he'd simply accepted a ride with some other senior citizen, then got turned around. Too embarrassed to admit he couldn't find the house. She had assumed he'd ended up here because he recognized the place. "Dad, listen to me. Did this man know your name?"

Ed nodded.

"And mine?"

He nodded again. "Chin hurts." He rubbed it. "High-pressure zone in the Rockies."

"Dad, this is really important. You didn't recognize him?"

"He was wearing one of those sweatshirt things with the hood." He motioned with the napkin. "I couldn't see his face very well."

"Was it the same man you saw looking in our windows?"

"That was Richard Nixon," he snapped. "You think I'm too stupid to know the difference between Tricky Dick and Dutch?"

"No, I don't think you're stupid. I'm just trying to figure out what's going on. Dad . . ." She hesitated. "I think someone might be stalking me."

He began to roll the napkin. "You should call the police."

"I have. But I have no proof the man is doing it."

"Innocent until proven guilty," Ed said in a far-off voice.

"Exactly. Now tell me about the man who picked you up. What kind of car was he driving?"

"Old. Blue."

Casey slammed her hand on the table. "That son of a—" She cut herself off.

Ed had jumped at the loud sound and now was picking up the little pieces of napkin on the table, pinching them between his wrinkly fingers.

Casey was so angry that her vision blurred. It was Gaitlin. Had to be. She looked back at her father. "Did he say anything? I mean, like why he wanted to give you a ride?"

Ed looked down at the crumble of paper between his knobby fingers. "He said you should back off."

"How did you get these scrapes? Did he . . . did he hit you, Dad?"

Ed continued to hang his head. "I fell."

"And he just let you off here?"

"I knew the pizza place. I like mushrooms." Ed didn't say anything else for a moment, then continued, "Chance of a wintry mix tonight. Low around thirty."

After a moment of silence, Casey stood up. There was no reason to question her father any longer right now. Maybe he would be able to tell her something else later, but now, he was shutting down. She could see it in his gray eyes. She could see it in the way his hands were beginning to tremble.

She reached past him for his coat.

She would kill him. She would kill Charles Gaitlin, and then this would be over. "Dad, let's go." She motioned for him to slide out of the booth.

What made Casey angriest of all was the fact that she couldn't do anything about this and Gaitlin knew it. Her father had told the police that the fortieth president of the United States had given him a ride to the pizza place. Who was going to listen to her when she said it was actually Charles Gaitlin?

She helped her father into his coat and linked her arm through his. "Come on, Dad," she said. "Let's go home."

* * *

On the way home, Casey finally reached Jayne on her cell; Jayne had gotten the message that their father had been found and that he was safe. The sisters agreed that there was no reason for Jayne to come over tonight. The children needed to get to bed after their busy day. Jayne and Casey could talk tomorrow afternoon at Casey's when they met for Christmas Eve dinner before going to church.

Casey also called Lincoln and told him that Ed had gotten into a car with someone he didn't know, but she didn't give him too many details. She didn't tell him about Ronald Reagan or who she suspected had actually picked up her father.

Lincoln and Frazier were waiting in the yard when Casey pulled into her driveway. Frazier bounded up to his master as Ed got out of the car in the garage.

"Hey, Ed." Lincoln stood casually as if they had not been in family-crisis mode an hour ago. "Looks like your buddy missed you today."

Ed gave the dog a big hug and then went into the house. Frazier followed.

Lincoln remained in the garage, waiting for Casey. She put down the automatic door, walked over to him, and rested her head against his shoulder. He put his arm around her and kissed the top of her head.

"He seems okay," he said.

"He's okay," she repeated. "Scraped up a little. Wet. Apparently he fell at some point, but he didn't want to tell me what happened. He's embarrassed, I suppose."

"I'm just glad he's home safe." He kissed her again. "I hope you're not going to be too hasty in making a decision on the senior center."

"Of course he can't go back."

"But he likes it there," he said gently. "He told me he had a *lady friend*."

Casey didn't even want to broach that subject. "He can't go if he's wandering away. It's not safe. Getting into cars with strangers. This could have turned out very badly, Lincoln."

"I'm sure you could make arrangements to see that someone escorts him to and from his van." He walked her toward the door to the house. "Surely he's not the only old man who gets confused as to which white van is his. I'm not sure I could do it," he jested.

Casey took a breath. One of the nicest things about being with Lincoln was the different perspective he offered on so many subjects. He saw the world so differently than she did. "You're right. I know you're right." In the laundry room, she locked the door behind them. "He has been happier since he started going. And he's been . . . better. But something has to be done differently. Maybe Jayne and I need to take turns driving him back and forth."

"I'm sure something can be done," he assured her. "Maybe I could even help out."

They walked down the hall, past the kitchen, into the living room. Ed sat on the couch, but uncharacteristically the TV was off. "Give it to me. Give it." He held out his hand and the big brown dog reluctantly turned over his stuffed squeaky toy, a big pink hot dog in a bun. Ed tossed the hot dog and it bounced off the fireplace hearth. The dog lunged for it.

"Want the TV on, Dad? We can check on that high-pressure system in the Rockies."

"Tired. Think we'll go to bed." As he rose from the couch, he put his hand out to Frazier. The dog danced in front of him just out of reach. "I can't play fetch if you don't hand it over," he chided.

Frazier trotted around some more, and when he drew closer, Ed grabbed the hot dog. The dog squeaked the stuffed toy noisily between his jaws and then surrendered it.

Casey followed the two down the hall. "I'll be right back," she called to Lincoln over her shoulder. "There's a bottle of wine on the counter."

Frazier nudged Ed's pant leg as Ed held the toy over his head. "I don't think so, boy." He stuffed the toy hot dog into the rear of the waistband of his pants. "You don't want to give it to me? Two can play that game."

Casey halted in the doorway of her father's bedroom. *Two can play that game. . . .*

"You need anything?" she asked.

Two can play that game. The words went through her head again. "I can get your pajamas for you."

"Can get my own," he grumbled, hand on the doorknob.

"You should clean up that scrape." She reached out but then pulled her hand back before she touched his chin. She was hovering. He hated it when she hovered. "The one on your hand, too."

"I'll wash it up." He looked up, seeming to want to say something more.

She waited.

"Just wanted to tell you thank you," he said haltingly. "For, you know, coming to get me."

"Of course, Dad." She looked into his eyes. "I'd do anything for you."

"And I'd do anything for you," he said roughly. "You know that, don't you, Freckles?" He looked up at her and then down at the dog as if he couldn't bear to meet her gaze. "I would never let anyone hurt you. Never again."

"I know." Her smile was sad. She rubbed his arm. "Good night, Daddy."

The door closed behind her and her father's previous phrase went through her head again like words on a ticker tape. *Two can play that game. Two can play that game. . . .*

Talk about an epiphany. That was it. That was the answer

to her problem with Gaitlin. If she could prove he was following her, mailing her those drawings, she could have him
arrested. All she needed to do was catch him in the act. Get
the evidence. Photographs. Whatever.

Casey walked into the kitchen with a smile on her face.
"Your dad's okay?"

She walked over to Lincoln, at the counter. He was pour-
ing them both a glass of pinot noir. "I think he'll be fine."

"And how about you?" He pushed a glass of dark wine
into her hand.

"Me? I'm fine." She sipped her wine, then smiled up at
him. Even though she didn't know exactly how she was
going to follow Gaitlin, how she was going to catch him, the
plan made her feel good. As if she finally had a way to fight
back. "In fact, I'm pretty great right now."

He leaned over and kissed her.

He tasted of the savory pinot noir: earthy, smoky—rich.

"Yeah?" he said.

"Yeah." She kissed him back, sliding her hand over his
chest and then his shoulder. She parted her lips, darted her
tongue out to taste more of him.

"Thought we were going to put the lights on the tree," he
teased.

"We are." She set her glass down, slipping her other arm
around his neck. "But first I need a kiss. Maybe two."

"Guess I'll be forced to comply." She could hear his
desire for her in the timbre of his voice.

She loved that sound in his voice. He made her feel so . . .
empowered. For so many years, Casey had fought her sexu-
ality. Like most victims of sexual abuse, she had, on some
level, no matter how illogical, blamed herself for what had
happened. Even her relationship with John had been affected
by it. Casey had never been able to give herself to him completely. Never been able to take from him. As the relationship

had slowly petered out, so had the sex. Or maybe the sex had petered out and then the relationship. Either way, in the end, he was getting it somewhere else and she wasn't.

But with Lincoln, it was different. From the beginning, Casey had *felt* different. For the first time in her life, she felt like an adult and not a sixteen-year-old fumbling in the backseat of her older boyfriend's car. She felt capable of choosing her own sexual path. She felt as if she was in control, and that control was so positive that she could actually hand it over to Lincoln if she so chose.

Holding her in his arms, Lincoln deepened his kiss. He slid his hand down the small of her back and over her gray dress slacks, cupping one buttock. She thrust her tongue into his mouth greedily, pressing her groin to his. He shifted, pushing her up against the kitchen cabinet. The marble countertop pushed into her back. Hard. Solid. Like Lincoln.

Her fingers found the buttons of his oxford and she hastily undid them and pulled his shirt out of his khakis. She slid her hand under his T-shirt and glided her fingertips over the small patch of hair on his chest.

But feeling his bare chest with her hand wasn't enough. She needed skin to skin. With his help, she pulled off his shirt and T-shirt.

"Your dad?" he whispered in her ear.

"Never comes out once he goes in," she assured him.

The truth was, she didn't really care. The chance of getting caught having sex in the kitchen just wasn't as important at this moment as feeling Lincoln's hands on her naked body.

She shed her sweater, and when Lincoln didn't unhook her lacy pink bra fast enough, she helped him out.

"What's gotten into you?" Lincoln whispered in her ear. "I like it." He kissed her bare shoulder and lowered his head.

She arched her back, thrusting out her breasts, making it

easier for him to catch her nipple between his lips. She threaded her fingers through his shaggy, dark hair.

The truth was, Casey didn't know *what* had gotten into her tonight. Usually, she liked sex controlled. Neat. In a bed on clean sheets. She wasn't a roll-in-the-hay kind of woman. Or a do-it-on-the-kitchen-counter kind of woman. At least she hadn't *thought* she was.

So maybe this was the new Casey. The empowered Casey. Maybe this was the Casey who could outwit Charles Gaitlin and set her life, which seemed on tilt right now, level again.

Lincoln pressed both of his hands on her hips, and without him speaking, she knew what he wanted. She half jumped, half let him lift her onto the counter.

She shimmied out of her dress slacks, then the pink panties, and let them fall carelessly to the floor. She tugged at Lincoln's belt buckle, released it, and unhooked his pants. Pushed them down. Looking into his half-closed blue eyes, she slid her hand into his knit boxer briefs.

She had never disliked a man's genitalia. Never been afraid of it, as some women were, but she had never really *liked* it before. She cupped his balls in her hand. But she liked Lincoln's.

Their mouths met again, more insistent. He nipped at her neck, her earlobe. Not hard, just enough to send ripples of sensation to every pore on her skin. She usually needed plenty of foreplay, but tonight something pushed her outside her usual comfort range. She needed Lincoln now. Hard. Inside her.

Stroking him, she wiggled toward the edge of the counter. He kissed her bare shoulder, her arm, the swell of her breast. By the only light in the kitchen, the bulb over the stove, she could see his face. His eyes were nearly closed, his face calm, almost dreamlike.

"Come here," she whispered.

"Not sure I'm tall enough," he said huskily in her ear. "But I was an Eagle Scout, you know. Ingenuity is my middle name."

She laughed and she liked the sound of her own voice, deeper now too. "Meet you halfway," she breathed.

Half on the counter, half off, she opened her legs to him further. He grunted as he pushed into her. She moaned.

He whispered her name. Told her she was beautiful. She clung to him, digging her short fingernails into his bare back. She pushed against him, arching her hips again and again.

"You can slow down," he suggested, his tone a mixture of amusement and ardor.

She shook her head, fervent now. The pleasure came in waves, mounting higher.

"Casey . . ."

He was close.

Still propped against the counter, she wrapped her legs around his hips, resting her head on his shoulder, letting him take much of her weight. She strained against the oncoming flood. Her muscles tightened, loosened, tightened again. When she came, she pressed her mouth to his shoulder, trying to muffle her voice.

Lincoln followed a stroke behind her. He thrust, groaned, and then pulled back.

Laughing, realizing what she'd just done on her kitchen counter, with her dad in the other room, she scooted back, using Lincoln's shoulders for support.

He dropped his head, resting it against her bare breasts, her nipples still hard. "What's so funny?" His voice was muffled, but he was chuckling too.

"I don't know." She laughed harder. Tears welled in her eyes. "I don't know," she repeated. "I think I love you."

Chapter 24

The minute the words came out of Casey's mouth, she wished she could snatch them back. Her hands on Lincoln's shoulders, she jumped down off the counter and began to pick up her clothes. She pulled her sweater on first, sans bra, suddenly feeling vulnerable. So much for the empowerment.

The silence in the room was brittle. *He didn't say it back.* Why would he?

"God, that was awkward," she heard herself say after another second, which seemed like an eternity, passed. She grabbed her panties off the floor and stepped into them. A woman needed panties to fortify herself at times like this.

"Casey—"

"No, it's okay. I—" She didn't know what she was saying, what she *should* say. She stopped herself before she made things worse.

Leaning over, hair concealing her face, she picked up his boxers and pants and held them out to him. He took them, but set them on the counter, then grabbed her wrist.

"Casey."

She resisted, tugging back.

"Come here," he said. He pulled harder.

She was so embarrassed that tears burned the backs of her eyelids. If she cried, she'd be mortified. What had she been thinking when she had said she *loved him?* Was she out of her mind?

She hadn't been thinking at all. That was what was scary.

"Look at me," he whispered.

She let him pull her into his arms, but she still couldn't bring herself to look at him.

"I didn't mean to—" He stopped, then started again. "You took me by surprise, that's all." He caught her chin between his thumb and forefinger and lifted it.

She closed her eyes.

"I just want to take things slowly, that's all. I care about you. I care about you deeply. It's just that I royally screwed up a marriage once and I want to be sure—"

Marriage? She barely heard what else he said. He was thinking about *marriage?*

Of course that wasn't what he meant. Was it?

She certainly hadn't been thinking that far down the road. Still, somehow the word made her feel better. . . .

"I want to be sure. You know what I mean?" he said gently.

She made herself open her eyes. Made herself look into his. She still didn't know what to say and that seemed to be all right with him.

He pulled her against him and they stood there, hugging in the semidarkness of the kitchen, she in her panties and sweater, him in nothing but a pair of brown socks.

He hugged her for a long time. Long enough that when she lifted her head from his shoulder she was smiling. She was hopeful. "Want to help me put the lights on the tree?"

"Like this, or you want me to get dressed?" He grinned.

* * *

Angel looked at herself in the bathroom mirror, the tiny Ziploc baggy of white stuff she'd found under the sink in her hand.

Her eyes were bloodshot. She'd had too much to drink. First the six-pack of beer, then the shots of Jack Daniel's that Charlie had insisted she do. But it was Christmas Eve, right? She deserved to relax a little.

The JD was her Christmas present. She almost laughed out loud. A bottle of whiskey for Christmas from her old man? A bottle he and his brother had already half finished off. And she'd been thinking maybe a promise ring or something stupid like that.

She studied the face of the woman in the mirror. She looked older than twenty-six. More tired than any twenty-six-year-old ought to look. She turned her face so that the light from the only bulb, of the three, still burning over the mirror shone on her chin. The bruise was fading. With make-up on, you could hardly see it. A leftover from a fight a week ago. Charlie'd barely caught her with his fist. She'd been too fast for him.

Or he'd been too high or drunk to take good aim.

She looked down at the baggy in her hand. She didn't know what to do. She told Charlie no drugs. He hadn't used them when she'd met him. This was something new. This was James. Charlie had been spending a lot of money the last week or so, like he had it. He had this idea in his head that he was going to get rich because of the lawsuit. She tried to tell him it would take years to get any money, if he got any at all, but he wouldn't listen to her. James told him everyone would settle. He'd get a million or two easy.

She fingered the baggy. *No drugs.* Not with the baby. What if she got arrested? Buddy could get put in foster care. Angel'd lose her subsidized-housing privileges if she got caught with that shit here. It didn't matter if it was hers or not; it'd be a good excuse for them to kick her out. Especially since she owed rent.

But it was after midnight. Christmas Eve. Did she really want a knock-down blowout on Christmas? Did she want to spend Christmas alone? Charlie wasn't much, but he was better than nothing, wasn't he?

She looked in the mirror again. Her roots were showing.

Pushed around. Beat up. She didn't deserve this. *But nothing would ever change unless she changed it.*

Angel jerked open the bathroom door and charged down the short hall, keeping quiet until she hit the living room. "Get out," she said.

Charlie and James were sitting on each end of the couch, a can of beer in their hands. Professional wrestling was on TV.

"Get out," Angel said to Charlie. She looked at James. "You too. Out of my house."

"Come on, baby, get out of the way." Charlie craned his neck. His face was red from the booze. She needed to give him a haircut. Thin, the way his hair was, as soon as it got long, it looked like he had a comb-over. James's was even worse because she wasn't cutting that son of a bitch's hair.

"I told you no crack, no weed, Charlie." She threw the bag of tiny powdery chunks at him.

He picked it up. "Where'd you get this?" he said in a pissed-off voice.

He didn't deny it was his.

"Under the sink, in the shaving cream cap. It fell over when I was trying to get toilet paper, 'cause it seems like I'm the only one on earth who puts a new roll on!"

"She's snoopin' in your shit?" James asked Charlie.

"It friggin' fell out! And it's *my* place!" Angel crossed her arms over her chest. "My name's on the lease and I bought that shaving cream. 'Less of course you stole it from the shop!" She stared hard at James. She was fired up. Enough was enough.

Charlie looked at James. "Man, I told you not in the house. We got a baby." He gestured drunkenly in the direction of Buddy's bedroom.

She couldn't believe Charlie was actually taking up for her.

"So you're gonna take her side?" James flew off the couch, heaving his beer at Angel.

She dodged the can. The last of the beer sprayed as the can hit the corner of the TV stand.

Charlie staggered off the couch.

"Brother against brother?" James demanded.

"Get out! Get out!" Angel shouted, turning on him.

James shoved her, but he was drunk, so he didn't shove too hard. She caught her balance before she went down. She charged forward, pushing him back.

Charlie punched James in the shoulder. Just a nudge. "Hey, man, keep your hands off my girl!"

James took a swing at Charlie. Charlie never moved until James's fist connected with his chin.

"Ow! Son o' bitch." Charlie worked his jaw, massaging it with his hand. "Now yer really pissin' me off. Get out."

There was a loud thumping on the living room wall from the unit next door. "Quiet down, you assholes!" Angel's neighbor barked, his voice muffled by the wallboard.

"I can't believe yer actin' like this, Charlie." James began to back toward the front door. "All pussy whipped. We're brothers, man." He thumped his chest with both hands. "It's Christmas. Where am I supposed to go?"

"Hell, where you belong!" Angel shouted, picking up the empty beer can and throwing it at him.

Charlie put his arm around her shoulders and gave her a hard squeeze. "Settle down, baby, he's goin'."

"I want him out," she said. "Now. Outta my place, and I

never want him back here again. Bringing crack around my baby!"

"All right, all right. Let me handle this." Charlie let go of her and walked toward the door. He grabbed the winter coat she had bought him that he'd left on the floor. "Come on, James. You better go for tonight," he said.

"I know when I'm not wanted." James jerked open the front door.

"You're right! You're not wanted!" Angel shrieked. "Worthless, limp-dicked—"

"Angel, shut up," Charlie snapped.

He said it in that voice she knew meant she was pushing too hard. Even drunk, she knew to step back. "I want him out," she said more quietly.

"And he's goin'." He held up his hand. "Now stay here and shut your mouth. Go get the toys and we'll put 'em under the tree. 'Kay? I'll be back in a minute and we'll get the stuff ready from Santa for little Buddy."

Angel watched James and Charlie go out the front door. Charlie was still trying to get his brother to take his coat. It was sleeting outside last time Angel looked. She didn't want Charlie to give James the coat. They'd never see it again. James could freeze solid for all she cared.

She walked into the kitchen. The room was spinning. She felt slightly nauseous. She couldn't drink the way she used to. She'd have a bad hangover tomorrow.

She went to the sink, got a glass of water, and walked over to the window. She pulled back the curtain over Buddy's high chair. Out front, one of the lights was burned out, but the other one was still lit up. She could see Charlie and James talking. Arguing. James was gesturing toward the house. Cussing. Talking smack about her, for sure.

Angel was tempted to open the window and yell to Charlie that he could just go with James. She knew very well he'd been smoking it too. And even if it wasn't *his* crack, he knew about it. Stuck in the lid of his shaving cream? That was their secret hiding place? How long would it take a cop to find that? Even a stupid one?

She let the curtain fall and drank the glass of water. As she walked into the kitchen, Charlie came in the front door. He slammed it behind him.

"There. He's gone. You happy now, you stupid, ugly little bitch?"

She stood where she was. Charlie got mean when he got drunk. He said things he didn't mean. Did things he'd apologize for later. He almost always apologized for hitting her, later.

He stood there staring at her for a minute and then stomped off down the hall. Tears filled Angel's eyes. All she wanted was to be loved. Why couldn't Charlie love her?

Why couldn't anyone?

Adam sat back in his office chair and glanced at his watch. It was after midnight. Christmas Day and he was sitting in his office going over a deposition. It didn't really even need to be done. Not this week. He just didn't want to go home.

He threaded his fingers and rested his hands behind his head. The nursing home had been cheery in a dismal kind of way tonight. So cheery, so gloomy that he'd felt even more depressed than usual when he'd left his grandfather. There were lots of visitors because it was Christmas. Everyone was laughing, talking, pretending people weren't wasting away and dying in the long hallways. Nurses and patients wore red Santa hats. There were a few sporting brown felt antlers.

A Brownie troop had been there caroling and had stopped in his grandfather's doorway. They sang "Frosty the Snowman." Adam had smiled, nodded to the music, but he had only done so to be polite. He didn't enjoy the holidays particularly, especially not with his grandfather so ill. If he had a girlfriend, a wife . . . children, maybe it would be different, but Christmas carols only reminded him how alone he was in his life right now. They forced the truth upon him. For all his accomplishments, he was at work at midnight on Christmas Eve.

He reached for his cup of coffee, took a sip, and spit it back into the mug. It was way past lukewarm, bordering on cold.

He wondered what Casey had done this evening. While Adam was eating a tuna salad wrap beside his comatose grandfather, had Casey been sitting down to ham and a sweet potato casserole? Had she gone to the midnight service at her church surrounded by her family?

Had Lincoln been there?

Lincoln Tyndall was becoming a sore spot, like one that slowly wore on your heel until one day you woke up and it was a blister. When Adam had first heard from one of the court stenographers that Casey was dating him, he had been happy for her. Maybe a little jealous, but happy she had found someone. Happy she was happy. He did like her, but with the Gaitlin case still pending, and his personal life being what it was, he really didn't have time to date her. Not date her properly. Not . . . woo her.

It just wasn't the right time in his life.

But he wanted her. And he felt guilty for wanting her.

The thing was, he didn't quite trust Lincoln Tyndall. There was something about him. . . . Sure, he played a good game. He was a decent lawyer and performed well enough in the courtroom. He had that slightly scruffy, tree-hugger look that was so popular in Hollywood right now. Him with his corduroy blazers and his economical little car.

But there was something about the way he looked at people. Watched people. Women in particular. He didn't like the idea that Lincoln watched Casey that way. Casey was someone special.

On impulse, Adam tapped his mouse and his computer monitor lit up. He entered a Web site accessible only to certain employees of the state. It was used mostly by the police and occasionally by correctional facilities. It displayed statewide arrests and allegations against a person back to the time when the state first computerized its records.

He typed in Lincoln Tyndall and a driver's license photo came up. Right guy. Stupid grin. He scrolled down.

One speeding ticket. Caught in a speed trap in South Bethany. August 2006. Idiot. Everyone knew not to speed there. Adam chuckled. Read on.

And . . .

He read a line in a block at the bottom-right corner of the screen. He reread it, thinking he had read it wrong.

Nope. The charges were dropped. Lack of evidence, most likely. This kind of charge could be hard to prove, as Casey was discovering. He read the notation again.

Twelve years ago, Lincoln Tyndall had been charged with stalking.

Chapter 25

Casey sat in the parking lot of the flea market and watched the door. She had followed Charlie from his girlfriend's house to a mini-mart, where he had bought cigarettes and a candy bar, to here. The blue car wasn't his, she'd learned, but the girlfriend's. He'd now been inside the flea market about twenty minutes. She was debating whether she should go in and see what he was up to and risk losing him when he left, or sit in the parking lot and wait for him.

She was amazed by how easy it was to find someone. Shocked, really. Because she didn't want to abuse her position at the hospital, she hadn't used any source there to find Gaitlin, even though she was quite sure that Linda would have provided information about him to hospital staff or the police. And she didn't call Adam's office.

Casey couldn't let anyone know what she was doing. Not Adam or Lincoln, for legal reasons. Not her sister, because . . . Jayne wouldn't understand.

Not to mention that it was against the law. If she got caught, not only could the state lose the case against Gaitlin, but Casey could lose her job.

It had taken less than three hours to find Gaitlin, and that had included phone calls, driving time to the post office, and a stop at the grocery store to buy Cap'n Crunch.

She had read in the newspaper article reporting on the lawsuit that he lived in Georgetown. While pretending to address an envelope, Casey had asked a postal worker for Gaitlin's address. It seemed that Mr. Gaitlin had become a celebrity of sorts, and the federal employee had been eager to chat about him. His mail, according to the "Chatty Patty," was being forwarded to an apartment complex nearby, in care of an Angela Carey.

Casey drummed her thumbs on the steering wheel, feeling only slightly guilty for being there. She had dropped her father off at the Modern Maturity Center with instructions that he was to wait inside the lobby for her and that she would be there to pick him up at the end of the day. He hadn't asked where she was going and she hadn't offered to tell him. She hadn't told anyone she was taking vacation time. She was giving herself a week to tail Gaitlin and then she would reassess the plan.

Following Gaitlin evenings would be harder. And she knew she couldn't follow him twenty-four hours a day, but right now, she was just trying to get a feel for where he went, what he did, what his routine was. He had never let a week go by without making contact with her in some way, whether it was standing in her flower bed peeping in her window or mailing one of those stupid drawings. Surely in a week she could catch him at something.

She had helped one of Gaitlin's neighbors, a young single woman with two small children, carry groceries into her apartment. The woman had provided Casey with plenty of information about Charlie, including the facts that he didn't work and that his brother, James, sometimes stayed there with him and his girlfriend, but the woman hadn't seen the brother in a few days.

Another ten minutes passed and Gaitlin still hadn't come
out of the building. Needing to use the restroom, and a little
curious, Casey decided to go inside. The flea market, apparently once a warehouse, had been cleverly turned into a
mini-mall of sorts.

Inside, she discovered that the "stores" were makeshift
rooms constructed of chain-link fencing lining both sides of a
track that went around in a circle in the center of the structure.
She was amazed to see that a person could find almost anything in the shops, and at a discounted price. There were hard-
ware and kitchenware, a music store, a Hispanic food market,
a newsstand, and even a barbershop. Following the signs for
public restrooms, she located a food court where deli meats
were sold in one place, pastries, pizza, and ice cream in others.
When she came out of the restroom, she halted in front of the
Amish deli trying to decide if she should go back to her car or
walk around and look for Gaitlin.

Out of the corner of her eye, she spotted a familiar face,
but it wasn't Gaitlin's. It was her old "buddy" Sarge, from
the hospital cafeteria. He was seated at a table at the food
court, drinking from a Styrofoam cup and eating a muffin.
He must have taken time off from work for the holidays, too.
She turned away, hoping he wouldn't spot her. She didn't
want to get stuck talking to him, for a variety of reasons.

That was when she spotted Gaitlin buying a piece of
sausage pizza. She hung back until he paid and then followed
him, past shop after shop, and watched him enter a dollar
store. A blond woman in her late twenties, maybe early thirties, worked the cash register. She gave a customer his
change and the man exited the store. Casey stood one store
over pretending to look at pink candles shaped like seashells
that smelled strongly of gardenias. She watched Gaitlin and
the woman through the fence that served as the store side.
Plastic snow shovels, knit scarves, and flyswatters, of all

things, hung on the fencing, but from where she stood, she had a good view of Gaitlin.

Casey didn't remember the young woman who had picked him up that day after court very well, but she suspected this was the same one.

"You still here?" the woman asked Gaitlin. She began to dump pencils from a cardboard box into a plastic bowl next to the cash register. "I thought you were goin' to apply at the Exxon."

"I was hungry. That a crime?" He stuffed pizza into his mouth.

She looked at him, hand on her hip. "You bring me any?"

He kept eating.

She finished dumping the pencils into the plastic container with an obvious gesture of annoyance. He chewed. A Hispanic family stopped in front of the store to contemplate the purchase of one of the snow shovels. Casey tried to breathe through her mouth; she hated the fake smell of gardenias.

"Want the crust?" Gaitlin asked finally. His lips were wet with grease from the sausage.

"No," she answered testily.

The family decided against the purchase of the snow shovel and moved on.

"But you like the crust," Gaitlin said.

"What I'd like is a piece of pizza of my own, only I can't spend two twenty-five on a big ol' slice of hot pizza because I got to stop at the grocery store on the way home and buy bread and peanut butter."

He shrugged and pushed the crust into his mouth.

She reached under the counter and came up with a brown napkin that looked as if it had come from a dispenser in the ladies' room. "Wipe your face."

He snatched the napkin from her hand and blotted the grease on his mouth.

"You were supposed to be returnin' the car. That's why you're supposed to be here. You take my car again, you gotta swear you'll be back at six. I promised Shonda."

"I swear." He raised both hands as if she were holding him at gunpoint.

"And you swear you'll go by the Exxon when you leave here and drop off your application? It's on the seat of the car. I filled it all out."

"I swear."

She crossed her thin arms over her chest. Like Linda, this young woman had probably been pretty once. But her hair was overbleached, she had on too much eyeliner, and she looked tired. "Rode hard and put up wet" was the sad phrase that came to Casey's mind.

Casey felt a pang of compassion for Angela Carey. She was tempted to wait until Gaitlin left and then go inside and talk to her. Tell her what Gaitlin was, warn her she needed to get out of the relationship before it was too late.

But Angela already knew who Gaitlin was. She had picked him up the day he was released from jail.

Casey had learned the hard way that you couldn't help people who didn't want help.

As Gaitlin walked out of the dollar store, Casey turned away, facing the pink candles. The gardenia scent was so strong that it was making her nauseous.

Gaitlin didn't notice her. Allowing him to get a safe distance in front of her, she followed him into the parking lot. Out on the highway, he drove past the Exxon gas station. A few miles up the road, he pulled into the parking lot of a dumpy bar that advertised lottery tickets, Budweiser, and "Country Karaoke" every Saturday night.

Casey slipped into a spot on the side of the gravel parking lot under a faded yellow banner that read, "Welcome Race Fans." She cut the engine and checked to be sure her car doors were locked. Then she fished a pen out of her bag and picked up the crossword puzzle page of the newspaper off the front passenger seat.

She had a feeling it was going to be a long, boring afternoon.

"You going to eat your Jello, Professor?"

Ed looked at the old woman seated next to him in the dining hall that also served as the rec hall. *Kate.* He liked her. She had once been a teacher too. Chemistry, in high school.

She was nice to him. She didn't mind when he occasionally used the wrong word, like this morning when he said *tulip* instead of *ace* at the card table. But she was still old. Ed didn't know how he felt about old women. In a way, they made him feel old.

I felt my life with both my hands
To see if it was there—
I held my spirit to the Glass,
To prove it possibler —

Something Emily Dickinson had once written about getting old. Ed didn't like the word *possibler.* It wasn't even a real word, but who was he to tell Emily Dickinson that?

"You going to eat it?" With her plastic spoon, Kate poked at the plastic container on his tray.

He frowned. "It's red."

"Christmas Jello," she told him. "We didn't eat it all before Christmas. I suppose that makes it New Year's Jello." She chuckled as she took it off his tray.

"I don't like Jello," he said. "Frazier and I like pudding. Chocolate."

"You should bring this Frazier fellow one day. He can play cards, too."

Ed chewed his meatloaf slowly. It was all right, but not as good as he got at home. "Frazier doesn't play cards often."

"Neither did any of us, before we got walkers." She cackled at her joke, elbowing Ed in his side.

She had pointy elbows.

"I don't want to talk about Jello." He took another bite of meatloaf. "I want to talk about my daughter."

"Freckles? Yes." Kate peeled the foil on the snack container and dove in with her spoon.

Ed tried to concentrate on what he wanted to say. It was so difficult for him to focus his thoughts. One word and he'd find himself flying off in another direction, forgetting the original path he had sought. It was frustrating. Even frightening sometimes, because often he got lost. Lost in his own mind.

He set down his fork. "Kate, I'm worried about her. Someone is watching her. He's following her."

Kate sucked the red wiggly gelatin off her spoon. "That could be bad. My son Eli, he had a friend mugged in Trenton. They stole her pocketbook. Muggers follow you."

Ed stared at the meatloaf, which no longer looked all that appetizing. There were mashed potatoes, too, with gravy. He liked chicken gravy better than beef gravy. There had been a little diner he and Lorraine used to take the girls to whenever they went to visit Lorraine's family in—

Ed squelched the thought. He pushed gravy out of his mind. "This is a bad man. I know he is."

"So call the police." Kate zealously scraped the bottom of the plastic container with her plastic spoon. "That's what they're there for. Catch muggers and such." She gestured with the spoon.

Ed shook his head. "No, this is a very bad man. Worse than a mugger who takes a pocketbook. He might hurt her."

He looked at the wizened old lady with the ruby red lips beside him. She was so tiny that she looked like a dwarf or maybe one of those lady yard gnomes. "I can't let that happen. You understand, don't you? You understand I have to protect her?"

Kate suddenly put the spoon and the empty container down on her tray. She took one of Ed's hands between her tiny, wrinkled ones. "I understand, Professor. You have to protect her. We have to protect those we love."

"No matter what the consequences," he said. He shook his head. "It could get messy."

"No matter what the consequences," she repeated, looking into his eyes.

She had pretty eyes. Pale blue. They looked even bluer contrasted against her white hair and ruby lips. Kate listened to him. She understood him. That was another reason he liked her.

"You need help protecting her?" Kate asked, still giving him her undivided attention. "I'm slow on the walker, but I've still got something upstairs." She let go of his hand to tap her temple.

"I don't need any help," he said. "I can do this. I can protect her this time."

"Good thing these kids have got us, that's all I have to say, Professor. You need Katydid, you just give her a call." She turned to the old woman sitting on the other side of her. "Janice, you going to eat that Jello?"

Ed picked up his plastic fork again. His appetite was beginning to return. He felt better having had this talk with Kate. He had been thinking for some time that he needed to make preparations . . . in case Freckles needed him. It was reaffirming that Kate agreed.

* * *

"He just said he wanted to come over?"

Jayne stood in her cluttered foyer with Casey, a lavender tutu in one hand, needle and thread in the other. Apparently, Chad had been wearing the skirt on his head and had somehow torn off a row of tulle ruffle. Jayne had told Casey that he was currently in a time-out, although it sounded to Casey as if he was running around in the kitchen screaming for juice.

Casey shrugged. "He asked yesterday, too, so apparently it's been on his mind. He said he hadn't been over to visit lately and he wanted to come."

Casey had kept her coat on. She was going to do "the loop" to check up on Gaitlin, and then, as she had promised, she was going to drop by Lincoln's place. It wouldn't take her long to find Charlie if he was following his usual pattern. She had learned over the last five days that he was only ever at one of four places: his girlfriend's; the honky-tonk bar; the flea market; or his brother's girlfriend's place, in the same trailer park where Linda had lived.

The trailer park was always the last place Casey looked for him because she hated going there. She hoped he'd be at one of the other places tonight. Every time she pulled onto the gravel road, she imagined that flash of emergency vehicles the night Linda had died. She remembered the somber faces of the police officers and EMTs. Every time she saw Linda's old place, she fought the same feeling of helplessness that she had felt that night.

Casey glanced at her father seated in the chair in front of the television. Joaquin was watching college basketball. Ed was on his best behavior tonight; he hadn't told Joaquin to change the channel or demanded control of the remote. "Dad, you want to take off your coat?"

"No," Ed grunted, staring straight ahead at the TV. "Cold in here. Always cold in this darned house."

The sisters looked at each other and smiled.

"He say *why* he wanted to come over?" Jayne asked Casey. "Did he want to talk to me? See the kids?" She waved the tulle tutu in the direction of the family room. "Wanted to watch basketball with Joaquin?"

Casey shrugged, chuckling with her. "He didn't say. But he's been pretty good this week. Not real talkative, but"— she nodded—"good. No complaints so far about me dropping him off and picking him up at the senior center instead of letting him ride the bus."

"I'll definitely help out with that as soon as I can, but with the school holidays, our schedule is just crazy." Jayne opened the front door. "So you'll be back at nine?"

"Yup." Casey buttoned the top of her green wool peacoat. "Just going to run a few errands."

Her sister raised an eyebrow. "That what we're calling it these days? 'Running errands'? I'll have to remember that when the kids get a little older. Right now, 'Mommy and Daddy are having a tea party in their bedroom' seems to be working."

Casey laughed as she stepped out of the warm house, into the cold. "Back in a little while."

Ed pretended to watch the TV. Basketball. Tall, young, black men in tank tops. He had never quite understood the game, even back in the days when he could have. Now, he just didn't care enough to try.

He could hear his daughters talking, but he couldn't quite hear what they were saying. Didn't matter; they were talking about him. About how crazy he was. They always were.

He sat back in the chair.

"Dad, you want to take off your coat?" one of them shouted.

Did they think he was hard of hearing? Well, he was, a

little . . . but it was the darned basketball game so loud on the TV that made them have to shout. Not him.

"Cold in here," he called back. "Always so darned cold in this house."

He kept his gaze fixed on the TV the way he did when he was really interested in the forecast. He had to play this right. Make sure no one was suspicious.

Freckles was the one he had to watch. She was the sharp one. Jayne was too self-centered to pay close attention. Always running here and there. Scatterbrained. Hyper. She'd been that way since she was a kid. Not that he didn't love his Jayne . . . but it was different between him and Jayne and him and Freckles. Always had been.

Ed heard the front door open and he relaxed a little in the chair. Freckles was finally leaving. Once she was gone, he'd have a better chance. The son-in-law would be busy watching the game. The grandkids would be running disruptively all over the house. Jayne would be doing her little projects, talking nonstop on the phone, not paying attention to her wild Indian children, or him.

Ed just had to be patient. Be patient and try not to fall asleep watching this pointless game on the TV.

Chapter 26

Angel was waiting for Charlie when he pulled into the parking lot of the apartment building.

He had picked her up after work tonight, on time, like he had been all week, and he had been in a good mood. Yeah, he smelled like beer, but he had been nice to her. He even mentioned how great it had been New Year's Eve to hang out together and not go out partying.

After work, they had gone by Shonda's, picked up the baby, and come home. Only once they were in the house did Angel realize she'd forgotten to get milk. Buddy needed his milk. The little bugger drank it the way Charlie drank beer.

Charlie had offered to buy the milk. With his own money. He had said his granny had given him money for Christmas. He knew Angel hadn't gotten her WIC coupons for juice, milk, and cereal yet for January, so she had thought that was real nice of him to offer. He had promised he would be back in ten minutes and bring home Chinese takeout for dinner.

That had been four hours ago. Angel felt like one of those cartoon characters with steam coming out of their ears. From the window, she watched Charlie walk across the parking lot, drinking out of the plastic half-gallon container of milk.

Buddy was long in bed. He'd had a juice bottle tonight instead of milk. Angel had eaten a packet of instant oatmeal for dinner. She'd cleaned the refrigerator out, which wasn't hard because there was no food in it. Then she'd picked up Buddy's toys and put them in his new toy chest under the tree. She was proud of that red and blue toy chest. It had been expensive, but her overtime had stretched far enough for her to pick it up from layaway on Christmas Eve.

Tonight, after Angel had put Buddy to bed, she had been so tired that she had fallen asleep on the couch, but she was awake now. She was ready for Charlie.

He walked into the house without the takeout, carrying the milk. He had a milk mustache like you saw in the magazine ads. "I'll put this in the fridge," he said, trying to slip by her.

She snatched the milk out of his hand. "Where you been?" She leaned closer to him and sniffed his coat. "You been in that bar, haven't you? You were supposed to bring dinner home. You said you was bringin' home dinner four hours ago!"

"You little bitch," he slurred.

He hit her so hard that her head whipped around and it felt like something in her neck cracked. His fist just seemed to come out of nowhere. One minute she was standing there giving him hell, and the next minute it was like her jaw was going to split in two.

Blinding tears filled Angel's eyes as she tried to stay upright. He swung again, knocking her against the wall. Her head hit with a sickening clunk and she felt blood trickle down the back of her neck. *He's going to kill me,* she thought. *No he's not. He's not!* She heaved the plastic container of milk and it hit him right in the chest. The green plastic cap flew off and milk sprayed everywhere, soaking them both.

"Cunt," Charlie grunted, looking down at his new coat, covered in milk. He lunged at her.

Angel knew when to stand her ground and when to run. She ran.

I open the dryer door and savor the rush of warm air that comes from it. The Downy Fresh Scent wafts in the heat. I reach in and pull out one white undershirt. I pinch it by the shoulders and snap it. Hard. I do it a second time, hoping to release some of the tension in my own shoulders.

I am out of sorts tonight. I've been so all day.

I lay the shirt on top of the washer, enjoying the feel of the warm fabric on my fingertips. I fold one side over, carefully straightening it. I run my thumb along the fold to make a nice crease.

There are many thoughts weighing heavily on my mind tonight. Thoughts that have become worries. I am not usually a worrier and I don't like the feel of it. I don't like my lack of appetite, my inability to sleep soundly, or the fact that I can't concentrate properly. I do not like the tightness I feel in the pit of my stomach when I turn my worries over in my mind.

I fold in the other side of the undershirt. Crease it. Smooth the warm fabric.

I wish I could talk to Maury face-to-face. He would be a good sounding board.

I am worried about Casey. About Angel. About Drina. Oddly enough, I am worried about Linda. I know she is dead, but I think about her. About what she must have experienced those last seconds of her life. The terror. The pain.

I fold up the bottom of the shirt, flip the shirt over, and smooth it. It's perfect. I reach for another T-shirt in the dryer.

I have other concerns.

There are solutions to my concerns. I have come up with several solutions for each. What I must do now is decide how troublesome each matter is and what I am willing to do . . . what I am willing to risk . . . to implement these solutions.

Her screaming baby in her arms, Angel somehow managed to get the car doors locked. Charlie was like a wild man. He was out of his skull, furious. He pounded on the passenger-side window as she laid Buddy on the seat of the car beside her. There was blood everywhere. All over Angel. All over the blanket she had wrapped Buddy in. Charlie had hit her a couple more times before she'd gotten her boy and run out of the house. Her nose was bleeding like crazy.

Charlie pounded harder on the car window. Buddy screamed louder.

Angel ignored both of them as she tried to get the key in the ignition. Thank God the keys had fallen out of Charlie's pocket when he'd hit her in the living room; otherwise, she'd be running down the street right now trying to carry Buddy and his diaper bag.

But the key wouldn't go in the ignition, her hand was shaking so bad. It wouldn't go in!

Charlie was cussing her. Still beating on the window. If he broke it, Angel knew she was dead. Charlie was that out of control this time.

"Come on, come on," Angel groaned, trying hard not to cry. She couldn't breathe when she cried. It was just a bloody nose, but it hurt bad. Probably broken. She knew how that felt. She'd had it broken once before. An old boyfriend.

Buddy sat up and crawled across the seat toward her. He was completely awake now and he put out his little hand to her. He needed to be in his car seat. She knew that. But if she could just get out of the parking lot, get far enough from Charlie, then she could stop and put Buddy in his car seat, calm him down. She had some juice in the diaper bag. She'd give him a bottle; that would make him stop crying.

But first she had to get out of here.

"Sit down, Buddy. Sit next to Mommy." She patted the seat with her hand and the key. "Right here."

But he was scared. He was just a baby. He couldn't help it if he was scared.

"Ma-ma!" Buddy blubbered.

"Stop it! Stop it, Charlie!" Angel screamed at the window.

Finally, the key went in and Angel twisted it hard and rammed her foot down on the gas pedal. You had to give it a lot of gas when it was cold, or else it wouldn't start.

Blood dribbled over her lips and she wiped at it with the sleeve of her already bloody sweatshirt. A nose could bleed a lot. Plus, she had a cut under one eye. She could tell by the way it stung. And her head, maybe. She touched the back of it as she shifted into reverse. Her hair was wet too. More blood.

The car lurched backward.

Charlie backed away from the window.

It was a wonder the police weren't already here, the way he was carrying on. Surely one of her neighbors would have called the cops. Toto, in the next place over, had already threatened to call them earlier in the week, and that night Charlie had hardly gotten loud. Tonight . . . tonight he was like a psycho in a slasher movie.

Angel shifted the car into drive and it shot forward. As she pulled away, she saw Charlie running after her carrying a cement block.

Shit! If he hit the window, the glass might bust.

Angel hit the gas hard. Out of the corner of her eye, she saw the cement block hurling toward the car. But he must have missed the window because all she heard was a big clunk above the sound of Buddy's wailing. One hand on the wheel, she reached out to comfort her baby boy and sped away.

Several blocks up the street, Angel realized she was crying almost as hard as Buddy. She couldn't see through her tears and she couldn't catch her breath. Looking in the rearview mirror to be sure Charlie wasn't running down the middle of the street after her, she pulled over.

Her nose wouldn't stop bleeding. She had to stop the bleeding.

Holding Buddy in one arm, she dug into his diaper bag and pulled out a cloth diaper she used to wipe his boogies. "It's going to be all right. Stop cryin', baby," she soothed. "We're gonna be fine. We don't need him. I swear to God, we don't."

And this time, she really meant it.

Casey cruised by the public-housing complex; no sign of the blue car, which was odd for this early. She sipped her coffee, warm air from the heater blasting her face, a classic-rock station tuned in on the radio.

She had left her father and Frazier in front of the TV eating Cap'n Crunch cereal and watching *The Man Who Shot Liberty Valance* on DVD. Casey found it interesting that his whole life her father had always eaten sensible bran cereals, and now suddenly he had decided he wanted the sugary kids' stuff. Last week it had been Cocoa Puffs; this week it was the Cap'n, with crunch berries.

Casey circled the block. Although it wasn't even eight in the morning yet, Angela Carey's car definitely wasn't there.

The flea market didn't open until ten. Maybe she'd gone in early, left Charlie with the cute little boy Casey saw her loading into the car seat each day.

The thought that Gaitlin might be the little boy's babysitter turned the coffee sour in her stomach. What if he got angry with the child? She was frightened for him. Men who hit women hit children, too.

Casey took another turn around the block, debating whether or not she should pull into the parking lot or go to the flea market. One curtain in the living room to Angela's unit appeared to be open . . . or maybe torn down. Casey might be able to see through the window if she pulled into the handicapped spot.

Casey's phone rang and she tapped the Bluetooth earpiece in her ear. "Hello?"

"Casey, it's Rose O'Shannon. From the ER."

Casey eased into a parking spot across the street from the housing complex. "Hey, Rose."

"I know you're not on call."

"Actually, I'm on vacation until Wednesday," Casey said apologetically. "I think Alberta's on call all weekend. You should have her number."

"Yes, that's right. It is Alberta, but . . ." Rose hesitated.

Casey liked the fifty-something Irish woman. Rose had a no-nonsense manner in the ER, but she could be amazingly compassionate. Word around the hospital was that she'd never missed weekly mass since her first communion. Casey didn't know if it was her strong religious beliefs that made Rose so capable, but the woman was an amazing emergency room nurse.

"Casey, I probably shouldn't be making this call," Rose said in a low voice.

Casey rested her hand on her earpiece to block out the sound of a car passing on the street.

Rose didn't give Casey time to speak. "I've got a patient here. Lacerations to the face. Broken nose for sure, possible fractured eye socket. She says her boyfriend did it."

Casey groaned inwardly. Everyone in the ER knew her pet cause was battered women, but she really didn't know if she was up to tackling a case today. She felt as if the time she had to try to catch Gaitlin in the act of harassing her was running out. Five days had passed and he had never once gone near her, her house, the senior center, or even a mailbox, to her knowledge. "Rose," Casey started.

"Casey, her name is Angel. She says her boyfriend is Charles Gaitlin. She says Gaitlin is the one who beat her up."

Casey reached for the steering wheel and gripped it solidly. How many Charles Gaitlins could there be? She glanced in the direction of the sagging living room curtain. "You said her name is Angel?"

"Yeah. Well, it's Angela, Angela Carey, but she says everyone calls her Angel. I've got her in a treatment room right now, but I'm not sure how long I can keep her."

Casey's throat constricted. "Her baby? She has a little boy."

"She says he's with a friend. He's fine. Apparently this happened last night. Angel came in this morning only because her friend made her. They couldn't get her nose to stop bleeding."

Casey looked at the living room window of the town house again. At the pathetic, hanging curtain. *Gaitlin could be inside right now,* she thought. *Inside gloating.* "Keep her. Whatever you do, don't let her leave. You hear me, Rose? *Don't let her leave.* I'll be right there."

Casey closed the curtain to the treatment room, turned around, and practically bumped into Rose.

"How'd it go?" Rose asked. She wore blue scrub pants and a scrub top with yellow Tweety Birds all over it.

"Pretty well," Casey whispered, then walked down the hall crooking her finger to indicate that Rose should follow. They halted near the ladies' room door, out of earshot of Angel. "She's pretty scared, but I think she has a good head on her shoulders. She seems like a good mom. She wants to do what's right for her little boy."

"Officer Mendez said Angel wouldn't talk to her. Said she gave the usual story about how she fell. How it was all her fault." Rose held on to the stethoscope dangling from her neck. "You think she'll go back to the boyfriend?"

"I've been here long enough, seen enough of this to know better than to place any serious bets, but I have a good feeling about this girl. She's gutsy." Casey looked back at the curtained treatment room. "Of course, the place is hers, not his. I'm trying to convince her that she should go to a shelter and then have the police remove him from her property."

Rose frowned. "That only works until the next time she opens the door for him. She needs to have him arrested."

"I know." Casey smiled grimly. "But maybe a few days in a shelter and she can get some perspective on this. Some time away from him and some counseling and she might realize that she has to get away from him, at any cost. Him in jail would be the best bet, but I'm trying to look at this from her point of view. I understand why these women don't want to prosecute. Angel seems, at least right now, to at least want to get away from him." She threw one hand up in the air. "I know the apartment is hers, but if it comes down to having to move to get away from him, we have to convince her that it's worth it. No one wants to see Gaitlin in jail again more than I, but I have to help Angel. She has to be my priority right now."

"You talk to her about the last girlfriend? About what he did to her?"

Casey grimaced again. "She doesn't think he did it, of course. Even after this, he's still got her snowed into believing he's a decent person."

"Just like the one he murdered." Rose touched the tiny gold crucifix she wore around her neck.

"I'm going to make some phone calls to see if I can find a place in a shelter for Angel."

"She can't stay with the friend who's watching the baby?"

"She says not." Casey started to walk down the hall. "How long do you think we can keep her here?"

"At least another hour, hour and a half. Her nose is definitely broken, and the laceration on the back of her head needs a couple of stitches."

"Can you stay with her?" Casey asked. "I swear, I'll be back in ten minutes."

Rose smiled sympathetically. "I'll be right here."

Fifteen minutes later, Casey returned to the ER floor. The curtain to Angel's treatment room was half open, so Casey knocked on the wall. "It's Casey, Angel. Okay if I come in?"

"Sure," the woman called, her voice nasal.

Casey waved to Rose, who was at the other end of the hall. She mouthed "Thank you," knowing the nurse was way too busy to be baby-sitting. Casey found Angel lying on her back on a gurney, gauze packing protruding from her nostrils.

"Good news." Casey walked to the woman's bedside and laid her hand on her arm. "Sunrise has an opening for one woman with one toddler. It's a small private shelter on the south side of town." She tried to sound upbeat and positive. "Buddy's walking, right?"

Angel nodded and then reached up to cover her nose with her hand. "Bleeding's stopped but I know I look stupid." She half smiled. "Buddy's real smart. He was walking by his first birthday. He's eighteen months now. He can say a bunch a words."

"I know you must be proud." Casey pulled a chair up beside the bed. "Do you want to do this, Angel? You want to tell the police the truth about who did this? You want to go to the women's shelter and break this cycle of abuse? You have to be very strong, but I know you can be."

Angel shifted her gaze to the white wall in front of the gurney. "I'll go because I've had enough of his shit, but I ain't talkin' to the police. That would look bad for him." She turned to Casey and looked at her more closely now. "You're that woman, aren't you? The one Charlie's suin'. I knew I knew you from somewhere, and then I remembered it was in the parking lot the day he got out of prison. You guys were talkin'."

Casey looked down at her hands, folded in her lap. "Would you like me to find someone else to help you?" She lifted her gaze to look at the woman. "I didn't mean to deceive you, Angel. I just wanted to help. This is my job. I help women like you."

Angel looked at her for a long moment. "Nah, I don't want nobody else. I can tell you know how it is, what it's like. I 'preciate your help. You're wrong about Charlie, though. He ain't no murderer. But I don't care about him suin' you." She shrugged. "It's all another one of his brother's stupid schemes anyway."

Casey wanted to ask what she meant, but she reminded herself that right now this had to be about Angel and not Gaitlin. And certainly not about herself.

"You can't go back to your house if he's there. You can't even go back to your job. Not unless you report Charlie. If you report him, the police will arrest him and you can go home. You can go back to your life before Charlie."

"I know." Moisture gathered in the corners of Angel's eyes. "But I can't do that. I love him."

Casey felt a pang of pity for the young woman. It was the same story she'd heard dozens of times. Even after they beat their faces in, the women still loved them.

"Don't matter anyway." Angel rubbed her nose with the back of her hand. "I didn't make rent last month. Already late this month. We was gonna get kicked out anyway. I just hadn't told Charlie so he wouldn't get mad."

"You sure you don't want to talk to Officer Mendez?" Casey asked, trying one last time.

"Nope. But you can tell me about this shelter." Angel rolled her head to the side so she could look into Casey's eyes. "There other kids there for Buddy to play with?"

Chapter 27

"You can't stay here no more, chico. I don't want you here." Drina threw James's sweatshirt and jean jacket down on the floor in front of the door.

She paid the rent on this trailer every month by scrubbing other people's toilets. The place wasn't much, but she was proud of it because it was hers. Because *she* made the rent payments, *she* had the right to say who stayed here, and James wasn't staying here anymore. Not him or his woman-beating brother.

"Get out." She pointed to the door.

"Where we supposed to go?" James got up off the plaid couch, opening his arms. "Come on, Drina, baby girl."

"I don't care where you go. Just so you go, chico. And you take your *hermano* with you." She eyed Charlie, who sat on the end of the couch, half lit on the twelve-pack of beer the two men had brought home. *"Now,"* she said loudly. She scooped the keys to James's truck off the top of the TV and tossed them to him.

He'd just pulled it off the blocks the day before. New fuel pump. There was a big shed out back that a couple of people in the park used. Drina paid an extra twenty-five dollars a month to keep the kids' bikes and a lawn mower there. James wasn't supposed to have a car in there; she'd gotten in trouble with the landlord over him using other tenants' space. It was a good thing the truck was running, though; otherwise, James and his brother would be walking in the rain tonight.

"Hey, you hear me, chico?!" Drina hollered to Charlie. He looked like he was about to fall asleep with his head cocked to one side and drool in the corner of his mouth. She turned the TV off. "I washed your coat. It's in the kitchen. Now go on. Out."

"Come on, Charlie." James jerked his hoodie over his head. "We don't need this shit."

Charlie still looked confused, but he got up, pulling his flannel shirt down over his fleshy, white belly. James went into the kitchen and brought out the coat Drina had washed the milk out of. She didn't know what had happened between Charlie and his girlfriend the other night and she didn't want to know. But James said Angel and the boy were gone, and along with the soured milk, there had been blood on Charlie's coat. Drina didn't want Charlie or James in the house with her children. Not anymore, she didn't. Maybe Charlie didn't kill that woman, maybe he *was* falsely accused. But the way Drina saw it, as mean as he got when he was drunk, it was only a matter of time before he *would* kill someone. She didn't intend that someone to be her or one of her kids.

"We're goin'?" Charlie asked. "Yer lettin' her put you out?" He looked at James, then at Drina, then at James again.

If he came at her, Drina had already decided she was going to shoot him between the eyes. She might have to spend a night in jail, her kids might have to go to their *abuela*'s for a few days, but no one would find Drina guilty. Not a poor, young, working Hispanic girl trying to live the American dream. Not when Charlie was a known abuser.

She inched her way toward the bookcase on the far side of the living room. She kept the gun up there in a shoebox. Nobody knew she had it except her brother, who had given it to her. Not the kids. Not James. Nobody. If Drina pulled the trigger, it would be in self-defense. *Dios Mío,* she might have to kill both of them in self-defense.

James pushed the coat into Charlie's arms and grabbed his sweatshirt and jean jacket off the floor. "Come on. Why you doin' this, Drina?" He came toward her.

"You know why. I told you to stay away from the houses I clean. I told you I could lose my job."

"And I didn't go there. I ain't been to any of them houses in weeks."

"You lie." She reached over her head for the box. "I saw you talkin' to him."

"Drina, you don't understand. I—"

She pulled the pistol out of the sneaker box and he shut right up. She didn't even have to aim it at him. "Get out," she said quietly. "Get out and never come back, chico."

"What about my things?" He sounded all manly, but he was moving for the door. His brother, a bigger coward than he was, was going to beat him there.

"You can come back for them. Some day when I ain't here. But I'm warnin' you." This time she did point the gun at him.

James went out the door, following his brother.

Drina smiled to herself as she locked it behind them. She hadn't even had to load the pistol. . . .

Adam lay in the bed with his hands at his sides and listened. He heard voices. Women. He had always loved the sound of women's voices. Like songbirds, some of them.

He wondered if it was day or night. It was hard to tell

because he couldn't open his eyes. They were frozen shut. Just like his arms. Frozen at his sides. His legs were also frozen, like the sticks he had used at the farm to tie up his tomato plants. Only those sticks had been useful. These . . . These sticks attached to his body were useless. He was useless.

He heard the click and whirl, the whoosh of the respirator. He knew it forced air into his lungs. Life-sustaining oxygen. He knew it kept him alive, along with all the other tubes that had to be going in and out of every orifice of his body.

Adam felt trapped. Trapped by his useless limbs, by the respirator. By the female voices that spoke so gently, so kindly to him. They thought they were doing the right thing, keeping him alive like this. A vegetable. That's what they used to call it before the term became "politically incorrect."

There was only one person who seemed to understand Adam's pain, and that was his grandson.

When Adam thought of the young man, emotion swelled inside him. He was so proud of the boy. Adam III was smart. Better yet, clever. A far better man than his worthless father had been. They say certain traits often skip a generation.

The boy understood the ways of the world. He understood politics. He knew how to *be* politic. He would be far more successful in his political career than Adam himself had been. His grandson was better looking, better educated, and knew how to play the game. The boy knew what was expected of him and he knew how to give it while still keeping his own objectives. Adam had high hopes for his grandson's political career.

Adam wished desperately that he was able to talk with him. The boy came regularly. Talked for long periods of time—so long that Adam drifted in and out of awareness listening to him.

He wished he could speak, could give advice. The boy

was doing well in the attorney general's office, but his job wasn't easy. It was stressful. What he needed was a woman, a woman to come home to, to share his life with. Lately, he had been talking about someone. Casey. Casey was her name. He mentioned her casually, but Adam could tell that he really liked her. That, at times, he was concerned for her welfare.

If only Adam could verbalize his thoughts. Support the boy. Do something—*anything*—other than lie here and rot.

The ventilator clicked, whirled, whooshed, each rhythmic sound reminding Adam of his helplessness. The sounds were nails in a coffin that never sealed. This had become Adam's private hell.

He wished that he was back on the farm, that his grandson was young again and they were picking tomatoes. Adam's worthless son had never understood the hard work one had to put into a garden to get decent tomatoes. His son had whined about the heat and about the bugs, but not his grandson. The boy had ground the bugs with the heel of his sneaker without so much as a complaint. He had helped his grandfather grow the tomatoes, pick them in the sweltering heat. He had helped can them. They had lined the jars up on the shelves in the cool cellar. Adam recalled the last time he had been at the farm, only weeks before he had had the stroke. There were still jars in the cellar. Plump, red Roma tomatoes bobbing in Ball mason jars. They were too old to eat, but he hadn't been able to bring himself to throw them away.

Adam heard footsteps and listened carefully. This was all he had left. Sounds and the thoughts in his head that didn't always make as much sense as they once had.

The person who walked into the room was not female.

He waited for him to speak. A male nurse maybe? A doctor? His grandson? No, his grandson had come earlier today. Or was that yesterday? Whoever it was, he would speak. They usually spoke, even though they knew Adam couldn't answer. It was one of the perks of staying in a nursing home that cost the amount of a new sedan each month.

But he didn't speak. Adam heard sounds beside the bed.

Adam heard the click and then the whirl of his respirator . . . but then it didn't whoosh.

Where was the whoosh?

He suddenly felt as if there was something on his chest. Something big. Heavy. Like the freezer they had kept in the cellar of the old farmhouse. He struggled, not with his body, because he couldn't, but in his mind. In his mind, he twisted and turned and shouted. He begged. He had thought he was ready to go. He had lain here for hours on end, weeks, months, wishing he could die. But not yet!

Where is the whoosh? he wondered frantically.

There was no whoosh because the ventilator had stopped. The someone standing beside him had stopped it. It was no longer forcing oxygen into his lungs. It was no longer sustaining life.

Why would he stop the ventilator?

The freezer on Adam's chest grew heavier until it seemed as if the weight of the world was balanced there. Adam knew that he was suffocating. He was now getting lightheaded. Images drifted in his head. His grandson as a baby sitting on his chest. Not so heavy.

Tomatoes on the vine. In jars on the shelves.

The weight began to lighten. He did not hear the click, whirl, whoosh again, but he knew it didn't matter. It was too late.

Adam wondered with his last, dying cognitive reason if Saint Peter would really be at the Pearly Gates. He wondered how he would explain why he had been such a terrible man. . . .

* * *

Casey stood in the kitchen in her flannel pajamas and sheepskin slippers dunking a chamomile tea bag in a mug of hot water. It had been a long, but productive day. After dropping her father off at the senior center, she'd had breakfast with Angel at the shelter.

The young woman still refused to report her boyfriend's abuse, but she had asked her sister, who employed her at the flea market, to give her a few days off to think and heal. Angel seemed to be enjoying the companionship of the other women in the shelter, and she was meeting with a counselor every day as well as attending a daily group session with other abused women. One of the staff members had gone to the house when Gaitlin was out. Using Angel's keys, she had gotten the young woman and her little boy some clean clothes and personal items. Angel had talked to her friend, the one who baby-sat for her, and had learned that Gaitlin was looking for her. He had asked the friend to pass on the message that he was sorry for what had happened and wanted her to come home. Casey had learned from Angel that Charles was now using his brother's pickup, red with a blue tailgate, as his new mode of transportation since Angel had taken her car.

Casey had followed the red Ford pickup with the blue tailgate for a while today. The Gaitlin brothers had gone from Angel's place to the flea market to another public-housing complex in town to the bar. Charles was still following his same pattern, just in a different vehicle, and now, with his brother. Charles had not contacted Casey in any way since she had begun tailing him. She wondered if it could be that easy. Had he seen her somewhere, realized what she was doing and just stopped his harassment? It seemed far-fetched, but certainly prudent.

Somehow Charles Gaitlin didn't strike her as the prudent sort.

The downside of her day had been a conversation with Lincoln. He had called to break their date this evening saying he had too much work to do. When they had talked, he had seemed distracted. She had wondered if he had somehow found out that she was helping Angel, or maybe even that she was following Charles, and he was just waiting for her to tell him. Casey did feel guilty about not discussing either matter with him, but she *was* the prudent sort and she still thought she was making the right choice. She didn't condone secrecy between a man and woman establishing what could potentially be a long-term relationship, but right now, she felt she had to stay quiet about it.

Casey lifted her tea bag out of the mug and tossed it into the trash can. She was just taking her first tentative sip of the hot tea when her cell phone rang. She glanced at the kitchen clock. It was 11:10. Was Lincoln feeling guilty about breaking their date? Sometimes he did call late when he was working.

She picked up her cell from the counter. The ID screen identified the caller as Adam Preston. Surprised, she answered.

"Casey." He almost sounded out of breath.

"Adam?"

"I'm sorry about it being so late."

She could tell by his voice that something was wrong. "It's not a problem, Adam."

"My grandfather . . ." He sounded close to tears. "He . . . he passed away tonight. A few minutes ago. They can declare him there, but they asked if I wanted to come and see him. My parents are in Prague, or Barcelona. I'd have to check the itinerary."

"You want me to go with you, Adam? I can meet you there," she said, her heart going out to him. She knew this was probably best for the elderly man, but she also knew that didn't make it any easier for his loved ones.

"I hate to ask you to come out so late." He hesitated. "I'll be fine. I just . . . I guess I just wanted to talk to someone. Tell someone." He half laughed. "This is a little embarrassing. A couple of months ago I admit to you I can't get a date. My grandfather dies, and now I'm telling you I don't have anyone to call. It's not that I don't have friends, but—"

"Adam, I don't mind coming." And she honestly didn't. She was already headed up the stairs to change. This was something she was good at—tragedy, death. It was her gift. One she didn't always relish, but a gift nonetheless. "Tell me what nursing home and wait there in the lobby for me."

"You don't have to—your father."

"My father will be fine. He's sound asleep. I always leave him notes on his bathroom mirror when I go out. He checks them when he can't remember where I am. I'll just leave a note. If he wakes up, he'll see it. I'll be back before he even knows I'm gone." She walked into her bedroom and flipped on the light switch. "Now tell me where you'll be."

Casey met Adam in the lobby of the nursing home and immediately hugged him. It just seemed like the right thing to do. He wasn't crying, but his eyes were red. He was obviously relieved to see a friendly face.

"I'm so sorry," she whispered.

He hugged her tightly before letting her go. "I really appreciate you coming. I was hesitant to call, but—" He stopped, then started again. "I'm glad you're here." He stepped back, looking down at his running shoes.

Casey guessed that the nursing home must have called him after he had gone home from work. He was wearing sweatpants and a long-sleeved T-shirt under his black wool dress coat. He'd probably worked out this evening.

A nurse entered the lobby but stood back at a respectable distance. "We're ready for you, Mr. Preston, but, please, take your time."

Casey looked at Adam, resting her hand on his forearm. "You want me to go in with you?"

He shook his head. "No . . . I just . . ."

"I know. You just needed a friend here. That's fine. There's nothing wrong with that, Adam. Some things we just shouldn't do alone. How about if I have a seat and wait here for you? If you need me, I'll be here. You go see him and then we'll find out what paperwork needs to be done to have his body released."

Adam worked his hands together. "They said his heart rate had been dropping on and off all day. I knew he hadn't long when I left this evening. Then . . . he just . . . died. I knew it would happen, sooner rather than later. The doctors warned me," he said. Then he added quietly, "I just didn't expect . . . I didn't expect it to be tonight."

Casey squeezed his hand and released it. "Go see him. I think you'll feel better. They will have unhooked him from the ventilator and the monitors and other equipment. He'll still be in his bed. His eyes will be closed. He'll look very peaceful."

Adams eyes filled with tears. "Thank you for this, Casey. I won't forget it."

She smiled sadly. "You're welcome."

She took a seat alone in the quiet, dimly lit lobby. Adam was gone no more than ten minutes. She rose as he entered the room. He looked better than he had when he left. He looked relieved.

Casey hugged him again and, again, he hugged her, and

she felt a connection to him that she believed only those who have lost loved ones could share. "You okay?" she asked.

"I'm fine. You were right. I do feel better, now. He looked so peaceful. Finally."

She smiled up at him. "I'm glad. I'm glad you could see him that way once more."

"I already signed what needed to be signed." He hooked his thumb in the direction of the hallway he'd just come from. "All done. We'd already made arrangements for cremation. The doctor on duty pronounced him, so he can go directly to the funeral home."

"Right. Good."

He stood there for a minute, his hands clasped. Then he released them. "So I guess that's it. I really appreciate you coming over, Casey; I mean it. You should go home now."

"You sure?" She looked up at him, not sure she should leave him quite yet. "You don't want to grab a cup of coffee or something first? You look like you could still use a minute."

"I . . . I hate to keep you. There *is* a little break room always open for patients' families." He pointed down the hallway. "If you want, we could just grab a cup."

She looped her arm through his and they started for the hallway. She felt good knowing she could help him. "One cup," she said, "and then I'll be on my way."

I sit at my desk and I stir my cup of coffee and listen to the clink, clink of the spoon. I am annoyed by what I have read in the paper. I stir faster and coffee splashes up over the rim onto the newsprint, smearing it.

I like to remain in control and it seems as if the Charlie situation is getting out of control. At first, the whole lawsuit with Rights for the People backing him amused me, but now his case is getting too much publicity. The story has been picked up by the Associated Press and is gaining momentum. A couple more weeks and he'll be a hero.

Charlie is many things and he has served his purpose well—in ways he will never know—but he isn't a hero.

I sip my coffee.

Something needs to be done about Charlie, if for no reason other than he annoys me. I've grown bored with the stalking game, anyway. I've learned from it, but I am ready to move on.

Besides, I am beginning to feel guilty. I like her more than I realized. I am seeing more potential in her. Seeing her not as a pawn, but perhaps a queen.

I went to the post office this morning hoping for a letter from Maury, but there was none. He hasn't written in a week and I am worried. Have I lost favor? I want to go and see him. I want to ask him. If I've said something to offend him, I want to know. I want to apologize. It took me a long time to find Maury. I don't want to lose his friendship now. Not now, when I might need his help.

I wonder if he is angry about the drawings I have requested. Or perhaps the news clippings I have sent him. I don't want him to think I am, in any way, competing against him. I simply want to possess the knowledge he possesses.

Chapter 28

Drina heard the knock on the door as she was picking up dirty clothes off the bathroom floor in the back of the trailer. It started again as she came down the hall. "Coming!" she called.

She flipped on the front light before unlocking the door. She wanted to be sure it wasn't James. He'd been there four times in the last three days since she'd kicked him out, begging her forgiveness, begging her to let him come back. Promising to get a job and bullshit like that. He'd said he loved her. He'd told her he couldn't live without her, that he'd die without her. Drina had heard that line before.

She pulled back the curtain on the window. It was the manager of the park. She opened the door and let him in. Last time Getty had been there, it was to chew her out about James's stupid truck parked in the shed.

"I made him pull that truck out a couple days ago. He's gone, him and his crappy truck. I swear."

Getty tipped up his yellow Makita ball cap and looked at Drina. He was an okay guy. Just trying to do his job. Drina knew that.

His eyes crinkled. Something was wrong.

"I paid my rent," she said suspiciously. "Put the envelope in the box, just like I do every month. Didn't you get it?"

"Drina, honey, has he been here?"

"Who?" she said. But she knew who he meant. "James? No . . . well, he came this morning before I left for work, but I told him to get his white ass off my property. I told him not to come back. That we were done."

"You didn't see him tonight?"

She shook her head. "Came home from work. Fed my *niños* and we played Candyland. We had baths and I put them to bed. Nobody's been here tonight." In the distance, she could hear a police siren. Maybe an ambulance. Police cars and ambulances came to her neighborhood more often than she liked.

Drina was beginning to get a weird feeling. Like something was *really* wrong. Like the time her baby sister drowned in the pond on the Fourth of July. But her babies were safe. She knew they were safe; she'd tucked them into their beds.

Blue lights flashed behind Getty in the open doorway. She could hear people outside. Hear voices.

Panic fluttered in Drina's chest. "*Dios Mío,* what's wrong, Getty?" She turned for the open door.

He put out his hands to stop her. "You shouldn't go out there."

"What is it? Who is it?" She stared at his pudgy middle-aged face. "James? *Ay Dios!* Not James!" she shrieked, grasping her head with both hands.

Getty tried to prevent her from getting out the door, but she pushed past him and ran down the concrete steps in her socks with no shoes. There were people walking through her yard. Neighbors. A police car had stopped between her trailer and the next. She heard the wail of an ambulance as it approached.

Drina ran past her neighbors, around the back of the trailer. "James! James!" she screamed.

Her stockinged feet slid in the partially frozen muck.

Her neighbors were gathering near the back shed where her *niños* kept their bikes and their wagon. Where James had parked the truck.

"Drina," someone said.

"Drina, no."

They had flashlights. Beams flashed in the darkness illuminating the run-down, tin-roofed shed that wasn't much more than a lean-to.

"You'll have to step back. Sir, ma'am," the police officer was saying behind her.

Someone drew a flashlight beam across the end of the shed where James had parked the truck. Drina half expected to see the truck again. No truck. Just a silhouette. Something hanging . . .

Drina grabbed a flashlight from a woman standing next to her and centered the beam on the silhouette, starting at the bottom and slowly raising it. First she saw the legs, then the black, hooded sweatshirt. A sob erupted from Drina's throat as she raised the flashlight higher until the beam of light encircled James's face. More light appeared around his head as others raised their flashlights until it looked as if he wore halos. Like an angel floating. Only there was a rope around his neck leading upward into the rafters.

Drina screamed, fell to her knees on the cold, wet ground. The flashlight rolled away as she grabbed her hair, in handfuls, shrieking. The last thing she saw as she lowered her head to the ground was her son's red trike under James's dangling boots.

Angel lugged another bag of rock salt from the storeroom area behind the curtain, out front, all the way to the door. "Stack them where people can see them," her sister had ordered before taking off to have lunch with her new boyfriend. "People don't buy what they don't see," is what her sister had said. Amber was smart like that. A good business-woman.

The county had been pelted by icy rain this morning. Angel had had a hard time getting out of the parking lot at the shelter. That big ol' car of hers with the bald tires didn't ride so well on ice. She might just buy herself a bag of the rock salt and throw it in her trunk for emergencies. She wouldn't want to get stuck somewhere with little Buddy in the car, not the way the heater was acting up. With the em-ployee discount, it would only come out to $1.50.

She dropped the bag of rock salt on top of the two she had already carried out and went back for another. The flea market was quiet today. People were staying inside, or just driving where they had to: school, work, the doctor's.

If Angel had any sense, she'd have stayed home too. Only she couldn't go home. She was still at the shelter. No money, no other place to go. She really wanted to go home, at least until the eviction notice was served. But a week had passed and Shonda said Charlie was still in the house. He and his brother. Shonda had offered to send some of her cousins to put them out, but Angel knew those guys. They carried tire irons when they evicted people.

Angel didn't want to make trouble for Charlie. She just wanted him out of her house. She just wanted him out of her life.

At the shelter, the counselors had warned her she shouldn't go back to work, or go to any places her boyfriend might be. But Angel had been working since she was four-teen and she couldn't *not* work. She was going crazy just sit-ting around watching soaps on TV and listening to other people's troubles. She was used to keeping busy. Besides, she couldn't just keep accepting handouts from the nice people at the shelter. Buddy needed his milk. He needed his vitamins. Angel had gotten herself into this mess with Charlie; Buddy shouldn't have to pay for it.

Angel had talked to another girl at the shelter about getting a place together. Tammy had two kids, but she had a good job. The place where she'd been living had been her boyfriend's, so she had to get a new place. She knew where there was a trailer for rent that she could afford if she had a roommate. She had suggested maybe they could live together, maybe even share babysitting so each of them could go out once a week and meet a decent man who worked. Angel and Tammy had laughed about that idea. Like there was such a thing as a decent man.

Angel liked Tammy and she liked her two little girls. She thought maybe they could get along pretty well living together. But to move in with Tammy, Angel had to have her half of the deposit, and the only way to get it was to work. So, she'd come back to work. It wasn't like Charlie was going to come here and hit her or anything. He never hit her in front of anyone. He was too chicken he'd get in trouble.

Angel returned to the front of the store with another bag of rock salt and dropped it on the pile. As she straightened up and rubbed the small of her back, she saw Charlie standing there. He was wearing one of James's black sweatshirts, his hands thrust in the front pockets.

"Angel."

"You shouldn't be here." She walked back toward the cash register wondering to herself how she had ever thought he was good-looking. "I gotta work."

"Angel, please," he said pitifully.

Charlie could be good at pitiful when he wanted to be. But she wasn't falling for it. Not this time.

"Angel, didn't you hear? About James?"

"What?" She went around the cash register to put some

distance between them, just in case he tried to get all huggy with her. "He finally get picked up for stealing shit from the houses where his girlfriend works?"

"No," Charlie rasped. "He's dead."

"Oh, God." Angel looked up from the counter. "Charlie, you're kiddin'." But she could tell by his face that he wasn't. "I'm so sorry. What happened?" She came back around from the cash register.

"They say suicide," he sniffled, "but I don't believe it. James wouldn't do that. He wouldn't." Charlie looked at her. "I think somebody hanged him and made it look like he did it himself. He was into some stuff he wouldn't tell me about. It happened right in Drina's backyard where the kids coulda seen." He raised his hand and let it fall. "James'd never do that. He'd never kill himself."

"Ah, Charlie." Angel put her arms out to him and he wrapped his arms around her waist and lowered his head on her shoulder.

"You gotta come home, baby. I need you right now. I got the funeral and Granny to worry about. She's not takin' it well, I'll tell you that."

Angel didn't say anything. She felt just awful about James. Sure, she didn't like the bastard, but he was still Charlie's blood.

But Angel was dug in. She wasn't going back to the house with Charlie. She had plans now. Plans with Tammy. Plans that didn't include Charlie. She felt bad for him, but not bad enough to put herself back in front of his fists again. And she knew that's where she'd end up. No matter what. He'd hit her again. Men like Charlie always did.

"So you comin' home, baby?" He sniffed, looking down at her.

Angel let go of him. Backed up. "I can't do that, Charlie." She folded her arms across her waist. "You know I can't."

She touched her nose. She'd just gotten the splint off the day before. "You know it and you know why," she whispered.

"Ah, I'm sorry, baby. I just got drunk. I got mad. I won't no more; I swear I won't. I turned a new leaf, now with James gone. I'm a new man." He put out his arms to her. "Come on, baby. Please? I need you, baby. I . . . I don't think I can live without you."

Tears filled Angel's eyes and she took another step back. This was where her boyfriends always got to her. This was when she crumbled—when they said they needed her. Then she thought about Buddy. About what Buddy needed.

"I'm sorry about James, Charlie—I swear I am—but I can't come back. And you're gonna have to find another place to live. My eviction notice ought to be comin' any day 'cause I ain't been makin' the rent."

He sniffed and wiped his nose with the back of his hand. He was definitely playing the pitiful card. "You're not comin' home, baby? But my brother is dead."

"I'll come to the funeral if you want me to. Me and Buddy. You just tell me when and where." She shook her head sadly. "But I ain't comin' back to you, Charlie, not ever. You hit me. You've hit me time and time again, and I can't let you hit me no more. I can't let Buddy grow up thinkin' that's how a man ought to be."

Charlie stood there looking at her for a minute, his hands hanging at his sides. He looked like he'd lost weight and he needed a shave. "You're not comin' home?" he whispered, seeming bewildered now.

She shook her head.

As she held her breath, Charlie slowly turned around and walked out of the shop.

Angel hoped she would never see Charlie Gaitlin again.

* * *

"Why are we here?" Ed demanded from the passenger side of the car. "I thought we were going out for pizza."

"We are going out for pizza, Dad. We're meeting Jayne and the kids in half an hour. I'm just . . . checking on someone. A client."

Casey had called the shelter to speak to Angel only to find out that she had gone to work, against the director's recommendation. Casey had left a message, but Angel hadn't called her back.

Casey had read about Gaitlin's brother's suicide in the paper this morning and she was worried about Angel. Worried that Charles would use his brother's death as a way to lure her away from the shelter and back into his web. Men like him don't hesitate to take advantage of women any way they can.

Casey cruised down the street in front of the public-housing complex, and then, seeing only a dim light from Angel's unit, pulled into the parking lot.

"We're having pizza here?" Ed grumbled.

"No, Dad. We're having pizza at Bob's Pizza Palace. That's where you said you wanted to go."

"Should have driven my own car." Ed crossed his arms over his chest and stared out the window.

"You sold your car, Dad," she said gently.

"Then I should have driven yours. This is taking too long. I'm hungry."

Casey wanted to remind him that he no longer had a license, that he wasn't capable of driving, but when she looked at her father in the seat beside her, something told her that he knew that. He just wasn't happy about that one more step in the loss of his freedom, and for that, she couldn't blame him.

So, Casey kept quiet as she drove slowly through the parking lot. She was relieved not to find Angel's car. She did, however, see James's old red pickup with the dented blue tailgate. It was parked in the handicapped parking space right outside Angel's door. The same place Charlie had often illegally parked the car.

As Casey headed for the parking lot exit, she thought about Charles Gaitlin sitting alone in the apartment. His brother was dead. His girlfriend was gone. He was probably sitting there getting drunk this very moment, feeling sorry for himself. She wondered how long it would take him to find another woman to beat on.

Casey needed to talk to Adam about Linda's case. She needed to find out what was taking so long. He had sworn it wouldn't be long before Gaitlin would be arrested again. Even though she had talked with Adam every day since his grandfather had died, she didn't feel as if she could bother him about it this week. He had enough to deal with, with his parents returning from Europe and having to make the arrangements for his grandfather's memorial service Saturday. But next week, they would definitely discuss the issue. Casey felt as if she had been patient long enough with the legal system; it was time to start pushing someone.

"Where we going now?" Ed asked as Casey pulled out onto the street.

"We're going to have pizza with Jayne and the kids, Dad."

"It's about darned time."

She smiled to herself, feeling better than she had in days. Gaitlin appeared to have lost interest in harassing her. Angel seemed to be safe, at least for the time being. Despite his grumpiness, her father's mental state was relatively clear. And her relationship with Lincoln was on track. Life was good.

Chapter 29

Ambient music played softly in the entryway where Casey and Lincoln waited in line to sign the guest book. They'd arrived fifteen minutes early for the memorial service and still had to wait in line in the cold to get inside. The funeral home was going to be packed. Adam Preston Sr. had apparently been a well-respected man in the state political arena at one time. Someone had told Lincoln in his office today that the lieutenant governor was expected to make an appearance.

Casey and Lincoln inched forward in the line.

"Just so we get this straight, now," Lincoln whispered in her ear, "I don't want any of this nonsense when I die."

She lifted her brow.

Lincoln gazed at the white walls in the entry hall, hung with religious paintings. Mourners were dressed in dark suits, dark dresses. Women wore dark hose and black pumps. The place smelled thickly of lilies. *Flowers of death.*

"No service for me, religious or otherwise. I want to be cremated and have my ashes spread on my grandparents' farm."

"Lincoln, that's not legal," she admonished. Secretly, she

was pleased. Pleased that he wanted to tell her what he wanted her to do with his ashes. Conversations like this suggested he wanted her around long enough that they would grow old together.

"You don't have to tell anyone that's what you did with me," he teased in her ear. "Right by the pond, under the silver maples, that's where I want to spend eternity." He gestured as if sprinkling salt on his plate. "Maybe a few ashes in the pond. I bet I'd make good fish food."

"Lincoln." She had to cover her mouth to keep from laughing. Several mourners looked her way, frowning. She turned her back to Lincoln and inched forward.

Adam walked through a doorway that led from the main chamber of the funeral home, where the service would be held. He walked from the podium where the guest book was, down the line toward the door, shaking hands. Speaking in a hushed tone. He looked as good in his somber black suit, white shirt, and dark red tie as he had the night he had worn the tux to the DuPont Hotel. When he reached Casey, he put out his arms. Casey hugged him, feeling just a little uncomfortable doing so in front of Lincoln.

She had told Lincoln that she had met Adam at the nursing home the night Adam's grandfather had died, and she had mentioned that she had talked to Adam a couple of times this week. Lincoln hadn't seemed pleased, but if he was jealous, he hadn't said so.

"You okay?" Casey asked as she stepped out of his embrace. He was wearing his usual cologne.

"Hanging in there." Adam grimaced.

"You know Lincoln Tyndall."

"I'm very sorry for your loss." Lincoln offered his hand and the men shook, their gazes meeting.

They clasped hands just a second too long and it seemed awkward. Casey could almost feel the testosterone building in the stuffy room. She was flattered that Lincoln felt the need to be jealous, flattered that Adam liked her well enough to get his tail feathers ruffled, but really, this was the twenty-first century, and they were at a memorial service.

"Are your parents here, yet?" Casey asked, turning her back slightly on Lincoln. "I'd like to meet them."

"Yes. I'll introduce you when you come inside, but I hope you'll join us at their house in South Bethany afterward. Both of you." He offered a quick, politic smile. "Just a small reception for family and close friends."

"Adam, I'm so sorry." A thin, elderly woman with yellow-blond hair walked up to him, arms outstretched, her hands like claws. Her cheeks were bright red with rouge. One of the grandfather's cronies, no doubt.

"Excuse me," Adam whispered. He clasped Casey's hand, then released it and walked away. "Mrs. Clendaniel."

Casey and Lincoln faced forward again and he leaned over to whisper in her ear. "Do I need to be concerned that he might be trying to cut in on my girl?"

She glanced over her shoulder at him. "I'm your girl?"

"Of course you are." He ran his hand down her back. "I don't know. He smells awfully damned good. What do you think he pays for that fancy cologne? Think it's Parisian?"

She faced forward again. "I'm dating *you,* Lincoln. Not Adam."

"That doesn't exactly answer my question," he said under his breath.

His tone surprised her. It was a little . . . aggressive. Lincoln was always so calm, so easygoing. She reached back and took his hand, squeezing it as she accepted the pen the gentleman ahead of her offered. She leaned over the podium to sign her name in the guest book. She and Lincoln would definitely *not* be attending the reception at Adam's parents' house. The last thing she needed right now was Lincoln getting into a cockfight with Adam.

"This is good, Shonda, real good." Angel dropped a couple of noodles on the high chair tray for Buddy. "It's good, ain't it, big boy?"

"Just macaroni and cheese outta the box with tomato soup stirred in," Shonda said, taking a bite from her plastic bowl. "You don't add the water for the soup. Makes it creamy."

It was Sunday night and they were seated at Shonda's kitchen table—Angel, Shonda, Buddy, and Shonda's little girl, Toneesha. Toneesha, almost two, was cute as she could be. So cute that she made Angel almost wish she had her own little girl to dress up and do her hair.

It was nice coming over to Shonda's at night, not having to hang out at the shelter. Usually, Shonda was busy with her on-again, off-again boyfriend, Darrell, but this week they were off again. Earlier tonight, on the phone, Angel had heard Shonda threatening to cut Darrell's balls off if he stepped in the house, so she was guessing he wouldn't be back tonight.

Angel hoped Shonda would invite her and Buddy to spend the night. Maybe they could sleep on the couch or something. It just depended on whether or not Shonda's sister was crashing there tonight. The house had only two bedrooms, so it could get crowded on a weekend. Everyone at the shelter had been real nice to her and Buddy, but it just wasn't the same thing as having a real friend. Shonda was a real friend.

"Biscuits are good, too," Angel said.

"I like my baby to eat good food." Shonda slathered margarine on her own biscuit.

Buddy popped the last piece of macaroni in his mouth and tossed his plastic sippy cup on the floor. Shonda's dog sniffed it.

"Mama," Buddy said, clapping his cheesy hands together.

"All done?" Angel got up to get the dishcloth and wipe her little boy's mouth. By the time she came back, Shonda was already letting Toneesha out of her booster seat. Angel wiped both kids' faces and hands, and the children toddled off into the living room talking gibberish.

Angel flopped back in her chair to finish her macaroni and cheese.

"Want a beer?" Shonda pulled a can out of the refrigerator and popped the top.

Angel shook her head. "Nah. I been tryin' to lay off. Seems like I always get myself into trouble when I drink too much. Seems like I always get myself hit when I drink too much."

"I'm not gonna hit ya," Shonda teased, pushing away her bowl.

Angel grinned and licked her finger, then picked up the last crumbs of biscuit off the table. "You know what I mean."

"Yeah. Good for you. Seems like I always let Darrell back in the house when I been drinkin'." Shonda tipped her can.

"This week at the shelter's been good for me." Angel gingerly touched her still-tender nose. A lot of the swelling had gone down; it actually looked like her nose again. "Made me think a lot. I'm done with Charlie." She looked at Shonda across the table. Shonda had a big, bushy Afro these days. It looked so good on her that Angel wished she had one. "I'm serious."

"I'm sure you are." Shonda cocked back in her chair.

"No, really. That girl at the shelter I told you about? We talked again this morning. She thinks we can get into that trailer the first of February. We show the lease to Juanita, who runs the shelter, and we can definitely stay there the rest of the month."

"Where's Charlie going to go if yer gettin' evicted from housing?"

Angel shrugged, then took a sip of red punch from a plastic cup with "Dora the Explorer" on it. "Don't know. Don't care."

"He tell you when the funeral was?"

"Nope." Angel set her cup down. "I told him I'd go, but I ain't heard from him since he came to work the other day. And that's okay with me, 'cause I wasn't going for James—stupid bastard—for killin' himself. I just offered on account of I thought Charlie might want me there. I ain't heard from him, so I'm thinkin' he's finally got it through his thick skull that I ain't comin' back. He's too busy with his fancy lawsuit, thinkin' about all that money he's goin' to be comin' into, to care about me."

"Sounds like you got yer shit together, sista." Shonda raised her beer can in toast.

"Yeah, things are comin' together good." Angel fiddled with the empty cup. "I just wish I had more of my stuff." She looked up. "You think he'll hock my stuff?"

Shonda shrugged. "He's a man. I wouldn't put nothin' past him."

"It's not that I got that much. He can have the stupid TV. I just want Buddy's clothes and toys." She glanced up. "I want the toy box. It's a Little Tykes. It cost me sixty-three dollars."

"You ain't thinkin' about goin' back to the house, are you?" Shonda got up to get another beer.

"I don't know. Thinkin' about it." She shrugged. "He probably won't even be there. He's probably at the stupid bar. He and James always liked to play pool Sunday nights."

"You want me to go get it? He gets in my face, I'll kick his ass." Shonda leaned on the open refrigerator door and popped the top on a fresh beer.

Angel looked at Shonda. She had no doubt her friend could kick Charlie's ass, but she didn't want to put her in the middle of the mess she had created.

Angel thought hard. Casey McDaniel had warned her not to go back to her house. The director at the shelter had warned her not to go. They said arrangements could be made at a later time to pick up her stuff. But what if Charlie hocked the toy chest? What "arrangements" could anyone make, then?

"Could Buddy stay here for a while?"

"Don't do it, sista," Shonda warned, shaking a finger at her. Then she tipped her beer.

Angel got up, taking her and Buddy's bowls with her. She put them in the sink and ran the faucet. "What would you do?" she asked.

"Me? I'd go get my shit," Shonda said. "But me, I'd have killed the bastard the first time he hit me. Darrell might give me shit, Toneesha's daddy might've given me shit, but don't nobody hit Shonda."

Angel walked back to the table and picked up the other dirty dishes and utensils. "Can he stay here or not? I won't be gone an hour."

"'Course he can stay here. He can stay here anytime you want. I love Buddy like he's my own boy." Shonda closed the refrigerator and fingered the gold necklace she always wore that spelled out her name in cursive. "You want me to call Darrell, tell him to meet you over there with some a his boys?"

"I thought you told Darrell you'd cut his balls off if he came around."

"I call him, he'll do what I tell him."

Angel shut off the faucet and wiped her wet hands on a bath towel hung over the chair. "I can do this myself. Charlie was tame as a lamb last time I saw him. I think James's dyin' might have taken the fight outta him."

"Do what you gotta do." Shonda held up one hand as she walked out of the kitchen into the living room with the kids. "You call me if you need me. Shonda will be there."

"You shouldn't be going out this time of night," Ed chastised, changing channels on the TV.

Frazier lifted his head off the carpet and looked at Casey with his big brown eyes as if in agreement with his master.

Casey stood in the living room, her coat on, keys in her hand. Angel still hadn't called her back and she was worried. She hated to keep calling the shelter and bugging them. She was just going to do the loop, just check on Gaitlin's whereabouts, and be right back. "Dad, I'm too old for a curfew."

"That boy ought to come here." Ed reached into the bowl on the end table beside the couch. He tossed a kernel of popcorn into the air.

Frazier's jaws opened. Clamped shut. He scooted across the floor closer to Ed.

"My day, a boy had to come to a girl's house. She didn't go to his."

Casey wanted to argue that she wasn't going to Lincoln's. He was preparing for a trial. He'd been at the office since noon and would probably be working until midnight, he'd told her. But obviously, she couldn't tell her father where she was going.

"I'll be right back." She walked away.

"Casey."

She was surprised to find that when she turned back, he

was looking at her. "You have to be careful," he said, his voice strange.

She studied him for a moment. "Sure, Dad. Why do you say that?" she asked hesitantly. "Has . . . have you seen something? Have . . . any of the presidents been around?"

He suddenly seemed agitated. He turned back to the TV. "I'm just telling you, Freckles. You have to be careful."

"I will, Dad. See you in a few minutes." Casey walked past the kitchen into the dark laundry room, the hair on the back of her neck prickly. The sensation was so eerie that she almost turned around. Almost tossed the keys on the kitchen counter and called it a night.

But her fear for Angel was stronger than her fear of the unknown. She locked the door behind her.

Ed got up from the couch, set the remote on the end table, and walked to the front windows in the living room. Frazier stood beside him as they watched the headlights of Casey's car back down the driveway.

Ed was nervous tonight and he didn't know why. He wished he had someone to talk to. He wished Kate could remember the phone number at her daughter's house. Then he could call her. She had said she was going to give him her number. She had said they were going to go out on a date. Ed had told her he didn't have a car, but she had told him not to worry, that her '84 Mercedes convertible was parked in the garage.

Ed didn't know about driving Kate's car, but he wasn't that worried about it. If she couldn't remember her phone number, how could he call her and take her on a date?

Ed walked through the dark living room, illuminated only by the light cast from the TV. *Storm Stories.* He'd already seen this episode. Already seen the Coast Guard's daring rescue.

He shuffled down the hall, not bothering to turn on the lights. Ed wasn't afraid of the dark. He wasn't afraid of the boogeyman or Ned Pepper. They weren't real. It was real men Ed was afraid of. And not for himself, but for his daughter.

He had never been a man of feelings. He didn't believe in ESP or creatures from outer space. But something didn't *feel* right. He could *feel* a tension building around him, and he didn't yet know the source, but he knew he would know it when he saw it. In the meantime, he'd continue with his preparations.

In his bedroom, he flipped on the light. He opened the closet door and pulled down several shoe boxes. He had kept his black dress shoes for funerals. Could be for someone else's, or his own. Also a brown pair of dress shoes and a pair of boating shoes that were too new to give away. In the back of the closet, behind the box with the Cole Haan funeral shoes, was the box that usually contained his golf shoes. Jayne had insisted he donate them to a local charity, but as Ed saw it, people taking charity shouldn't be on golf courses. Besides, he liked the shoes. Even if he wasn't ever going to play golf again, a man needed to keep a little dignity. Sometimes a man just needed his golf shoes. But right now, the golf shoes were hidden behind a laundry basket in the closet. There was something else in the box.

He carried the box to the bed and sat down beside it. Frazier dropped his bottom on the floor and waited, watching the box.

Frazier disapproved.

Under normal circumstances, Ed would have disapproved as well. But Frazier didn't understand. He didn't know the history. He didn't know how Ed had failed as a father to protect his daughter from Billy in the white car. Frazier was a good dog, but he didn't understand the guilt Ed had carried all these years. He didn't understand why Ed had to protect Freckles this time, at any cost.

Ed would make it up to the dog later. Maybe get him an iPod or something. He had been watching advertisements and thought Frazier might enjoy his own personal MP3 player.

Ed took a deep breath and removed the lid from the shoe box. He carefully took out the left shoe. From inside the shoe, he removed the loaded pistol and checked the safety.

Chapter 30

Angel drove around her apartment complex once, then a second time. She recognized most of the vehicles. James's piece-of-shit truck wasn't there.

Cautiously, she pulled into the parking lot and backed into a space only two spaces down from where she had been the night Charlie had beaten her. Her heart pounded in her chest as she got out of the car, leaving it unlocked. As she crossed the parking lot, she kept looking at the street, at her living room window, and back at the street again. If Charlie pulled in, she'd just leave. With or without the toy box.

But she really wanted Buddy's toy box. No one understood how important the toy box was to her, not even Shonda. It was like a symbol to Angel of what she could accomplish if she tried hard enough. It was a symbol of what she was capable of doing for her son. And she didn't want Charlie hocking it for beer or crack money.

Light shone through the curtains in the living room, but that didn't mean Charlie was there. He always left the lights on. Said *he* wasn't paying Delmarva Power. He didn't seem to care that Angel was.

She walked cautiously up the sidewalk. It was cold out

and she hadn't worn her coat. Just the sweater Shonda had
given her for Christmas. Angel loved the sweater; it was her
favorite piece of clothing. It was a white turtleneck with embroidered white snowflakes on it. Brand new when she got
it, still had the tags on. It was the only present she'd gotten
for Christmas.

At the front door, Angel stopped and listened. She could
hear the TV next door. She also thought she heard the TV
on at her own place. No surprise there, either. Charlie was
always walking out the door leaving it on.

She rested her hand on the doorknob. Turned it gingerly.
It was unlocked.

Crap. Was Charlie home? Had the truck broken down
again already? James hardly in his grave and his truck had
already crapped out. It was sad, kind of, when she thought
about it.

Angel chewed on the inside of her lip. She thought about
knocking next door, ask them if they'd seen Charlie. But she
didn't want to get them involved. All she wanted to do was
go inside, get Buddy's toy box, and get out.

She stood there another minute, but it was so cold that she
couldn't stand it. She knocked on her own door and then
pressed her ear to it. If she heard Charlie, she'd just run back
to the car, get in, and take off.

She didn't hear anything. Shivering, she knocked again.
Then louder. The dog next door began to bark. Still nothing from inside her own apartment.

Glancing over her shoulder, she turned the knob on the
front door and pushed the door in a little. She peeked around
the corner. The TV was on, but not real loud. Cartoons. The
couch was empty.

She tiptoed in, almost tripping over a little red snow boot.
She picked it up, wondering where the other one was. Buddy
loved his red boots. He was always taking them out of the

cardboard box by the door and putting them on. He'd need his boots if it snowed.

"Charlie?" she called.

No answer.

She wondered if he was on the can.

She glanced down the hallway. No lights on down there. Charlie always turned on the lights when he went to the bathroom. From where she stood, she could see the living room littered with take-out boxes and beer cans. Beyond the living room, she could see the empty kitchen.

Closing the door, stuffing her keys into her jeans pocket, Angel breathed a little easier. He wasn't home. She'd be quick. She'd grab Buddy's toy box and be out of there. The red boot dangled from her finger.

Maybe she should take Buddy's boots, too. The question was, What had he done with the other one?

She ran into a beer can with the toe of her sneaker and it rattled, startling her. Looking down, seeing the can, she felt stupid. She kicked it out of the way and walked over to the toy chest, opened it, and dropped the boot inside. Turning around, she surveyed the mess.

It didn't look like Charlie had done a thing since the night she'd left. The glass she had been drinking water from that night was still on the plastic milk crate she used for an end table. There was a blanket on the floor near the end of the couch. He'd been sleeping there. There was an ashtray on the arm of the couch. He was smoking again. The place stunk of cigarette smoke and sour Chinese takeout.

She dropped onto her knees and thrust her hand under the couch. She pulled out two more beer cans, a flattened plastic baseball, a little blue sock, and an empty chip bag. No boot.

She surveyed the living room floor, then checked the kitchen. No red boot. "What'd you do with your boot, Buddy?" she said aloud to the empty house. "Yer feet are gonna be cold in this snow, you with no boots." Hearing her own voice calmed her a little. She was alone. She was safe.

She checked the living room window for headlights and then went down the hall. First, she checked Buddy's bedroom, which was closest to the bathroom. She tossed some clothes into his crib and yanked off the sheet, wrapping the clothes inside. She knew she shouldn't take the time to gather everything, but at least she'd have a few things. She dropped the bundle in the hallway outside his door and added half a bag of diapers. She glanced over her shoulder again in the direction of the living room windows. Headlights?

She waited. Nothing.

Must have been her imagination.

Angel entered her bedroom next. Someone had slept in her bed, but she wondered if it had been James. Charlie would never have slept there without her. The idea that a man who was now dead had slept in her bed creeped her out a little. Then she realized *she'd* slept with a man who was now dead and *that* really creeped her out.

Suddenly, Angel just wanted to get out of the house.

She dropped to her knees and poked her head under the bed. Charlie's sneakers, a pink thong—

She heard a sound behind her and instantly froze. Waited. Nothing.

Then the sound again. No mistaking it this time.

The front door had opened. It had closed.

Angel's hand trembled as she dropped the panties on the floor. Her pounding heart felt like it was in her throat. She had told Shonda she wasn't afraid of Charlie, but she had lied.

No . . . it wasn't so much she was afraid of him as she was the pain.

Her nose was just starting to feel better. She wasn't getting the stitches in her head out until tomorrow afternoon.

Now what? She couldn't climb out the window. She had

a ground-floor unit. There were bars on the windows to keep people from breaking in. The only way out of the tiny apartment was through the front door or the back door in the kitchen. To get to the kitchen, she had to go through the living room.

Right where Charlie had to be standing.

Angel didn't know how long she stood there listening. Two minutes? Ten? It felt like an hour.

He was being very quiet. She couldn't see from where she stood in the bedroom at the end of the bed, but he had to be in the living room. He had to know she was there. Her car was in the parking lot.

She stared at the pink thong at her feet.

She thought about hiding in the closet, waiting until Charlie fell asleep and then sneaking out. But what if he'd just gone out for more beer? What if he was sitting on the couch right now watching *SpongeBob SquarePants* and getting liquored up?

Besides, the closet wasn't big enough for her to hide in. Not stacked with boxes the way it was. Back here in the bedroom, she was trapped. Trapped like the mouse she had cornered in the kitchen a few weeks ago with a broom. She'd beaten the mouse to death with the broom.

The only way out was the front door.

Angel eased her way to the bedroom door. From there, she could see the front door. She heard nothing. He hadn't changed the channel.

Squidward was talking about entering a parade. An underwater parade. Angel had seen the episode. It was funny. Kind of. In a been-at-work-all-day, Spongebob kind of way.

She took a breath and slid one sneaker across the dirty blue carpet. Then the other. Slowly, soundlessly, she took one sliding step at a time down the hall.

Despite how cold she had been a few minutes ago, her armpits were wet. There was sweat above her upper lip.

She hated feeling this way. Hated waiting for the fist.

Never again, she vowed silently. Never again would she let a man raise his hand to her.

Somehow, Angel made it all the way to the end of the hall. The front door wasn't more than five feet away. Getting up her courage, she quietly peeked around the corner at the couch.

Charlie wasn't there. She waited, peeked around the corner again, getting a better look this time.

He wasn't in the kitchen either.

For a second, she was totally confused. She looked back down the hall, and suddenly she was so scared she thought she might pee her pants.

The bathroom light! The bathroom light was on.

Only five feet to the door. To hell with the toy chest.

As Angel darted for the door, she heard his footsteps behind her. Out of the corner of her eye, she saw the black hoodie sweatshirt.

She never saw his face. He had the hood up. He hit her so hard that she fell sideways and smacked into the wall, then fell to the floor. She curled into a ball, trying to protect the top of her head where the stitches were, but he grabbed a hank of her hair and yanked her head upward, exposing her throat.

Angel opened her mouth to scream as she saw the knife, but she was silenced by fire. The blade seared her neck and suddenly she was wet and warm. He released her hair and her head dropped, bouncing on the carpet. She choked. She was covered in blood. The carpet was covered in blood, pooling under her. Her beautiful white snowflake sweater was now red with blood.

He'd slit her throat.

She screamed, but the only sound that came from her throat was a muffled gurgle. She was too weak to move so she just lay there.

She thought about the toy box. About the red boots. About Buddy. What would Buddy do with no daddy and now no mommy? It wasn't right; it wasn't fair. Tears sprang in her eyes, the pain in her heart greater than the pain from the neck wound.

Angel tried to catch her breath, but she couldn't. It was like someone was holding her under water. Bubbles of blood came out of her mouth, the hole in her neck.

She didn't want to die. In a last futile effort to save herself, she lifted her fist and hit it as hard as she could against the wall. If only she could get the neighbors' attention.

He grabbed her foot and dragged her on her belly away from the wall. Angel watched as her body left a trail of red smears behind her. She was dizzy. She could still hear herself gurgling, gasping, but the sound in her ears was dull now.

He left her by the toy box, and she stared at the blue front panel as she heard him walk out the door and close it behind him. Paralyzed, her head swimming, all she could do was stare at the toy box as her vision slowly faded. The last thing she saw was the flash of headlights as he pulled out of the handicapped parking spot near the front door.

Chapter 31

Casey was surprised to see Adam walk into her office less than ten minutes after she arrived Monday morning. He'd never come to her office before and she felt a little uncomfortable. Had Lincoln been right? *Was* Adam trying to cut in on him on the dance floor?

Then she realized, by the look on his face, that something was wrong. She pressed her hands to her desk. All she could think of was her father. She'd dropped him off at the senior center only half an hour ago. But if there was something wrong with Ed, the senior center would have called her or Jayne. How would Adam know anything about it? This had to be about the case.

"What's wrong?" she asked.

"I'm sorry, I didn't mean to scare you by walking in on you like this. But . . . I wanted to tell you in person before you heard elsewhere." He stood beside her desk and looked down. His expression was grave.

She rose out of her chair. "Adam, what is it?"

"Angel Carey is dead."

Casey covered her mouth with her hand.

"I'm sorry," he whispered.

"What happened?" She was shocked, although why, she didn't know. In her business, with the things she saw in the ER, nothing should shock her anymore. Women like Angel got themselves into bad situations all the time. Auto accidents in unsafe cars. Hitchhiking with the wrong man.

"The police are still at the crime scene, so I don't have all the details, but I came over the minute I heard. She was murdered, Casey. Stabbed to death in her apartment," he said quietly.

Casey stared at him. "She was stabbed to death?" she repeated. "In . . . in her apartment?"

"I'm so sorry, Casey. I know you were trying to help her. I know you found her a shelter. I know—" Adam turned around, pressing the heel of his hand to his forehead. "God, I feel so bad. I knew this was going to happen if we didn't get him back behind bars." He clenched his fist. "I knew it." He turned back around and gestured toward her. "You knew it, too. We've both dealt too long with this kind of thing not to see the reality of the situation."

His words slowly sank in. "The police think Gaitlin did it?"

"They know he did. They arrested him just before eleven last night. Apparently her girlfriend found her, but it was too late. Too late to save her," he said, his voice thick with emotion. "She was pronounced at the scene."

"They arrested him at eleven?" She was trying to wrap her brain around what he was saying. "How—when did he kill her?" *It doesn't make sense. What Adam is saying doesn't make sense.*

Casey's phone on her desk rang, loud and shrill. She could've just ignored it, letting the caller leave a message, but by the second ring, she couldn't stand the sound of it any longer. She picked up the receiver.

"Casey McDaniel," she said into the phone, trying not to

reveal in her voice any of the emotions she was feeling right now.

"Casey, it's Lincoln."

She glanced at Adam. "Lincoln."

"Have you heard?"

She looked at Adam again. "About Angel Carey," she said softly. She looked away from Adam, not sure why she felt guilty having him here in her office right now. It just felt . . . weird. "Yes, I heard." She hesitated. "Adam's here," she said, not completely sure she should have offered that information.

There was a pause on Lincoln's end.

"He . . . wanted to tell me in person. He knew I was involved with her case at the hospital," she said into the phone. "He wanted me to know before . . . you know, before I heard it elsewhere."

"Before *I* told you?" There was no mistaking the anger in Lincoln's voice.

"Lincoln . . ." Again, she hesitated. She didn't want to have this conversation right now, not with Adam there. Lincoln had no need to be jealous, not on her account, but this wasn't the time to discuss it. "Can I call you right back? Or lunch maybe? Can you meet me for lunch?"

"Call me back, Casey. I'll see what I can do." He hung up before she could answer.

She set the receiver on its cradle, embarrassed that Adam had heard that conversation. Even though he couldn't hear what Lincoln was saying, he couldn't miss the gist of it, or the tension in her voice. But that wasn't what mattered right now; what mattered was Angel.

She turned to Adam, looking up at his handsome, chiseled face. "You said the police arrested Gaitlin at eleven last night? What time was she killed?"

"Around eight-thirty, they think. The girlfriend called it in. Apparently, Angel left the girlfriend's house around eight to get something at her apartment—where Gaitlin was still living—and when Angel didn't come back within an hour, the girlfriend went looking for her. Gaitlin was already gone, but she told the police where to find him. Sure enough, he showed up at some bar and they arrested him."

Casey steadied herself by resting her hand on her desk. "What did Gaitlin say when they arrested him?"

"What do you think?" Adam grimaced. "He said he didn't do it. He said he was innocent."

Casey looked down at the floor, at Adam's shiny, black leather shoes. "He's right, Adam. He didn't do it." She suddenly felt dizzy at that thought.

"What do you mean, he didn't kill her? Sure he did. He stabbed her with a knife. Just like Linda Truman."

"No," Casey said softly. "Charles Gaitlin didn't kill Angel Carey last night between eight and nine. He couldn't have." She met his gaze. "He couldn't have because I was with him, Adam."

For a moment Casey's office was dead silent. Down the hall, she heard footsteps. Muffled voices. The whirr of a photocopier.

"You were with him?" Adam finally said. "*With* him?"

"Well, no. Not *with* him." She stepped back, sitting heavily in her chair. Her legs were feeling a little weak. "But I know where he was between eight and nine because . . . because I was following him."

Adam was silent.

"I know, I know. It was stupid. It seems really stupid now." She held her hand up and let it fall to her desk. "You knew I thought Gaitlin was following me. Harassing me. I couldn't get the police to do anything about it because I had no proof."

"So you *tailed* him?" he asked incredulously.

She leaned forward, dropping her face into her hands for

a moment. She was trembling. All she could think of was that if Gaitlin hadn't killed Angel . . . what if he hadn't killed Linda, either? Had Jayne been right? Had they been persecuting an innocent man?

"Casey?"

She looked up. "Okay, I admit it. It was stupid on my part. It's just that I didn't want to be a victim. I know this is hard for you to understand, but I . . . I had something happen to me a long time ago. I swore I would never be victimized again."

He shook his head as he sat down in the chair in front of her desk. "Casey . . . do you have any idea what a mess—" He halted midsentence.

"It's going to complicate the case, isn't it?" She felt like an idiot. But how could she possibly have imagined anything like this could happen? What were the odds that Gaitlin's latest ex would be stabbed to death and he *wouldn't* be responsible?

"So, what do I do now? Whom do I go to?" she asked. "The police? Gaitlin's lawyers?" She grabbed her head again. "Lincoln's not going to understand."

Adam sat back in the chair, opening his coat. "You should do what you think is best, but do you know what I think you should do?"

She rested her hands on her desk. Took a deep breath. "Of course I want to know what you think. I highly respect you, Adam."

He half smiled. "You even like me a little, don't you?"

She smiled back but didn't say anything. Considering the circumstances, she had no business flirting with him or anyone else.

"Okay, here's what you do." He got out of the chair to pace behind it. "Nothing today."

"Nothing?"

"The police may be calling you, interviewing you, but that will take a day or two. That will give us some time. Me some time."

"Some time?"

"To find out the timeline. You need to write down for me exactly where you were at what time last night. Where Gaitlin was. *Exactly*. We may be fine. You may have come in before or after the fact. The girlfriend could just have the times wrong. The cop I spoke to was at the scene last night. He said Angel's friend was out of her mind, screaming. She'd been drinking. They had to have a patrol car take her and the kids home."

"That's where Angel's little boy is? With the girlfriend?"

"That's what I heard." He stopped, settling his hands on the back of the chair. "We're not doing anything illegal here. You're just waiting to answer the questions when they're asked."

"But you shouldn't be here," she said.

"I shouldn't be here."

"You haven't told me anything I won't be able to find out myself if I go down to the ER," she assured him. "And you know I would never tell anyone anything you had told me."

"Okay, so for now, you say nothing. To *anyone*."

"Meaning"— she nodded her head—"Lincoln. Right. Of course. I don't want to screw up his law firm's defense if Gaitlin really is innocent."

"Exactly. That and . . ." Adam hesitated.

Casey looked up at him. "That and what?"

He was silent for a moment. "I shouldn't tell you this."

"Tell me what?"

He held out his hand, looking immensely guilty. "I shouldn't even have brought it up."

"You have to tell me now," she insisted.

He was still hesitating.

"Adam, please."

"I'm embarrassed to admit to you that I even looked up his record, but . . ."

"You looked up whose record?"

"Lincoln's."

She stared at him.

"Casey, I really don't think your problems had anything to do with him, but . . ."

She waited, holding her breath.

"Lincoln was accused of stalking a girlfriend. The charges were eventually dropped." He held up his hands. "But there were definitely accusations."

Casey sat back in her chair, taking a shuddering breath.

"As I said, it's probably nothing."

"But if Gaitlin wasn't the one sending those drawings, if he wasn't the one looking in my windows?" She looked away, then stared at her desk, her eyes losing focus. The idea was preposterous.

"But, I saw Gaitlin's blue car," she rationalized. "It had to be him. I ran into him and his brother in the grocery store. They were obviously following me."

"This is why this kind of thing is so hard to prove, Casey, just as the police explained to you," he said gently. "Coincidences can be combined with events that are, well, not quite so coincidental."

Casey thought out loud, "I followed Gaitlin for a week and he never went by my house, near a post office, near my office or the senior center." She paused. "And whoever's been harassing me made no attempt to contact me all week. I just assumed Gaitlin was on to me, but what if Lincoln knew I was following Gaitlin? A couple of times this week he asked me where I was going, what I was doing."

"Casey, I'm not saying it was Lincoln. It wasn't. He's a member of the bar, for God's sake. I know him. He's a good guy. A stand-up guy. I'm just saying, give me a day or two. We wouldn't want to screw up his firm's case. If Gaitlin didn't do this, he's going to need those attorneys to defend him, because my office, considering the circumstances, will be going for the death penalty. I can guarantee it."

Casey just sat there. She didn't know what to say. Didn't know what she thought.

"Casey," Adam said gently, "I really need to get to my office."

"I shouldn't tell Lincoln," she said softly.

"You can do what you think is right, but I'd hold off."

"You'll call me?"

"I'll call you."

"Thank you." She looked up. She didn't feel steady enough to walk him to the door. She didn't want him to think that she couldn't handle this, that she was some kind of emotional basket case.

"I'll call you later, to check on you." He stopped at the door. "You going to be okay?"

She exhaled. "I'll be fine."

She waited until he was gone and then got up and closed the door. It wasn't until she heard the click of the knob that heat rushed to her face and her knees went weak. A sob rose in her throat as she slowly slid to the floor, resting her back against the office door.

The memories came in flashes. The white car. Billy cajoling her. The rain. Her getting into the car.

She had trusted him. Maybe loved him.

She thought she was in love with Lincoln. Had she chosen the wrong man *again?*

Chapter 32

When Casey picked up her cell phone off the car seat and saw that it was Lincoln, she was tempted not to answer. They'd had a very brief, tense phone conversation when she'd called him back after her little breakdown in her office. He didn't meet her for lunch. He'd called twice later in the day, but she hadn't called him back or listened to his messages.

Now he was calling again. Was it to apologize for his tone of voice earlier? Or was it for his questions about why Adam was there this morning, why he hadn't just picked up the phone? They hadn't really discussed Angel's death or Gaitlin's arrest. The conversation had been of a purely personal nature.

All day she'd been going over in her head the details of the contact she'd had with whoever was stalking her. Not once could she disprove the theory that it could be Lincoln. Of course it didn't work that way. There were 200,000 people in the county, but since it could only be *one* of them, it could *still* be him.

She just couldn't believe Lincoln could do something like this. And why would he? Adam hadn't given her any details of what Lincoln had done in the past, or exactly what the circumstances of the charges had been, or why they had been dropped. It might not even be true.

The phone continued to ring. She didn't know what to say to him.

She tapped her earpiece. "Hello."

"Freckles."

"Dad?" Her grip tightened on the steering wheel. "Dad, why are you using Lincoln's cell phone?"

"I'm calling on Lincoln's phone."

She tried not to sound exasperated. "Why are you using Lincoln's cell phone? I just left the office to pick you up. I'm only going to be a few minutes late."

"Lincoln picked me up. He called you to tell you. Left a message. You want pizza? We got pizza."

Casey was annoyed that Lincoln would pick her father up, but she had listed him, at his suggestion, as an emergency contact person or a person permitted to sign her dad out at the end of the day. It had seemed like a good idea at the time because Jayne and Joaquin were always so difficult to reach by phone.

"I'm on my way home. I'll see you at home. You're going right home, right?" Her voice sounded shrill. She had no reason to doubt that Lincoln *wouldn't* take him home.

But she was full of nothing but doubt, and for the hundredth time she wished her therapist weren't on maternity leave. She wished she could talk to someone. All these years, all this time she'd been working on trusting herself and her instincts, and in one day, it all seemed to be swirling in the toilet bowl. She couldn't really have been this wrong about Lincoln, could she?

"Dad?" she said.

"Pepperoni," he answered.

* * *

Lincoln must have taken her father directly home after their pizza stop; his blue Mini Cooper was in the driveway when she pulled in. He had considerately parked to the side to allow her to enter the garage.

She was hanging up her coat, stalling, when Lincoln walked into the laundry room.

"Hey," he said. He sounded contrite.

Casey was so confused. Angel was dead. And she knew Charlie didn't do it. Now she was second-guessing herself on virtually every and any subject. She felt like crawling into bed and pulling the covers over her head.

"Hey," she said, not looking at Lincoln. She passed him in the hall.

"I'm sorry about the phone call today," he said, following her. "I brought you eggplant parmesan because I know you get sick of pizza. Ed wanted pizza."

She walked into the living room. Her father was seated on the couch, the TV on. Frazier was lying on the floor chewing on a piece of pizza crust trapped between his two front paws.

"Dad," she said.

He lifted a Coke can in her general direction. She turned and walked into the kitchen.

Lincoln followed. "Casey, what do you want me to say? I'm sorry. It was a bad day for all of us. I'm jealous of him. His friendship with you. I admit it."

She leaned against the kitchen counter, still not ready to speak.

"Don't you understand why I'm upset? It's not about Gaitlin," Lincoln continued. "It's not about *a case.* It's about you. About you and me. I don't want him coming to your rescue. I don't want him *being there for you* every time I turn around. I don't want him calling you in the middle of the night when he has a family tragedy. I'm sorry, but that's how I feel. I'm not saying he can't; I'm just saying I wish he wouldn't. I don't want to share you with him. Is that so wrong?"

"I don't need anyone to come to my rescue," she said, looking at the tile floor. It needed to be mopped. There were paw prints everywhere. "I can take care of myself."

"Of course you can. You know what I mean." He stood there in front of her, one hand in his pocket.

She finally lifted her gaze. Looked at him. He'd gotten a haircut last week, but his hair still managed to somehow appear shaggy. She loved his shaggy hair, his warm blue eyes and easy demeanor. He was certainly not as polished as Adam, maybe not as handsome, but he looked like a people's attorney. He looked trustworthy. He didn't look like a stalker. He didn't look like he could harm a kitten.

"Casey, what's wrong?"

"What's wrong?" He reached for her but she batted his hand away. "What's wrong? Why didn't you tell me you were arrested for stalking?"

She didn't mean to say it. It just came out.

"What?"

"So you're denying it?"

"Whoa. Easy." He reached for her again; she pulled away. "This is about my arrest over a decade ago? How did you even—" He halted before he finished his sentence, then said snidely, "That slick bastard."

"It doesn't matter how I found out." She leaned back, pushing the heels of her hands on the kitchen counter. "I want to know why you didn't tell me."

He stared at her for a moment. "Because maybe I was embarrassed?" He tilted his head. "Because maybe it happened when I was a stupid kid who made a stupid mistake? And exactly what does this have to do with us, now? What does Adam—"

"This has nothing to do with Adam. It's about me and you

and . . . and . . ." She groaned with exasperation. "Lincoln, you should have told me. You *knew* I had trust issues."

He ran the fingers of one hand through his hair. "You didn't tell me why you had *trust issues* and I didn't pry. It never occurred to me that something I did in college could come between you and me."

"Someone stalked me once," she said. Her voice sounded hollow. "It turned . . . ugly."

"Ah, Casey." He stepped toward her, wrapped his arms around her. She didn't hug him back, but she didn't push him away.

"I'm sorry," he said, then kissed the top of her head. "I should have told you. You're right. But, honestly, I didn't think it mattered that much. Not after all this time. Let me explain what happened."

"You don't have to."

"Yes, I do." He rubbed her arm. "It's really not that complicated. See, I went out with this girl, and I thought I loved her. She broke up with me and I went a little crazy. I sent her notes. Called her a lot, even when she asked me not to. I showed up at a party she was at—the wrong party—and she called an uncle who was a cop. He arrested me on harassment charges."

"Not stalking?"

"No. We didn't even have stalking laws in those days."

Tears burned the backs of Casey's eyelids. Now she was even more confused. Adam had said *stalking* charges, hadn't he?

"I'm sorry," he said again. "And I'm sorry about Angel." He stepped back, catching her hand in his. "And I wanted to tell you in person, but I've agreed to work on the team that will be defending Gaitlin on the new murder charge. Casey, I don't know what's going on, but something isn't right this time."

She looked up at him. She was overwhelmed by emotion. She believed his story about stalking the girlfriend; it was too common for kids that age not to believe. As for Adam, he obviously wanted to go out with her. Maybe he had played up the story because he was jealous of Lincoln in the same way Lincoln was jealous of him.

Casey didn't know for sure, but what she did know was that Lincoln hadn't been stalking her all these weeks. She didn't know who it was, but she knew in her heart that it wasn't Lincoln. It was only her lousy self-doubt that had made her suspect him. It was the craziness of the day.

She studied his face; he was so earnest.

She hesitated. Adam asked her not to tell Lincoln what she knew about Gaitlin. Adam worked in the district attorney's office. He was a powerful man. Had he been using his power in a personal way to cause Casey to alienate Lincoln? To make her doubt Lincoln and herself and go running into his arms?

Trust. It was about trust. And more about trusting herself than either of the men.

"If we're making confessions tonight, I might as well jump in." She walked to the dinette table and sat down. The lamp over the table cast soft yellow light on the wood surface.

Lincoln took the chair beside her. "Okay," he said quietly. He waited for her to speak.

Casey pressed her lips together as she looked down at her hands on the table. "When Adam was in my office today and he told me about Angel and about Gaitlin being arrested . . ."

"Yes."

Casey heard tension in Lincoln's voice.

"We had a conversation about her murder and then Adam asked me to not tell you something."

"About him?"

She shook her head, then made herself look up at him. "About Gaitlin. You see, I told Adam that I knew Gaitlin didn't kill Angel because I was following him when the murder took place. During *the hour* the police say it took place."

"You were *following him?*"

"In my car," she explained. "Long story, but I thought he was harassing me. I was afraid he was stalking me, and the police couldn't do anything about it, so I thought I would try to solve the problem myself."

"So *you're* Charles Gaitlin's alibi," Lincoln said slowly, as if trying to process the information.

"Yes. I followed him to his brother's girlfriend's place, where he sat in her empty driveway for a good hour. Waiting for her to get home, I guess."

"The same hour that Angel was apparently murdered?"

She nodded.

"And Adam didn't want you to tell me because he wanted a head start on the case?"

"No," she defended. "Well, I'm not sure why. He thought maybe the time frame was off. Maybe—"

"What an ass. Everyone says you need to keep an eye on the Prestons. I knew he had political aspirations, but it never occurred to me he'd purposely withhold evidence—"

"He didn't tell me I *couldn't* tell you, Lincoln. It wasn't like that. I just asked him what he thought I should do—"

"About me," he interrupted.

She closed her eyes for a moment. "No, not about you." She reached for his hand and squeezed it. "I was worried about jeopardizing the case . . . the cases. Linda's . . . Angel's. Now I'm afraid I might have"—her voice caught in her throat—"accused the wrong man. Charles Gaitlin didn't kill Angel; I know that for a fact. What if he didn't kill Linda, either?"

He looked at her hand resting on his. "What a mess."

Casey laughed. She didn't know why, but she did.

"That funny?" He half smiled, not sure if he should be smiling.

"No." She laughed again. "Not even a little bit."

He took her hand in his and lifted it to his mouth to kiss her knuckles. He kissed her fingertips one at a time. "Don't worry, we'll figure this out."

"I know," she said, once again close to tears. "But you have to swear to me you won't tell anyone about Adam's breach of confidentiality."

"He shouldn't have run my record," Lincoln said quietly.

"No, he shouldn't have," she agreed. "But we've all done things we shouldn't have based on emotion. No one was hurt here."

He was quiet for a moment. "I guess you're right. What's most important right now is that you know I'm sincere when I tell you that I would never do anything to harm you. To scare you."

"I know."

"Do you?" Now he was smiling. He looked at her with his big blue eyes, a twinkle of amusement in them. "Do you also know, Miss Know-It-All, that I'm in love with you?"

Chapter 33

I have taken a chance in coming, but I knew yesterday when Casey told me that she could vouch for Gaitlin what had to be done. It's a shame, really. The relationship was developing nicely. She really cared for me.

I have to admit she surprised me. Took me off guard for the briefest moment. It never occurred to me that she would have the balls to follow Gaitlin or that she would fight back the way she has. In a way, I am proud of her. Still, I can't let her get in the way of my scapegoat. I must cover my tracks. I can't jeopardize my own career, not even for sweet, tougher-than-I-expected Casey.

I wait at the table that's specifically set up for client/attorney meetings. The room is small. Cold. Bare. I don't mind. Tax dollars pay for it. It is not meant to be a Marriott meeting room.

Maury will be here any moment.

I try to imagine the surprise on his face when he was notified that he had a visitor. That an attorney was here to see him. He isn't expecting me.

I suddenly find myself nervous, and I tug at the collar of my dress shirt. It feels tighter than usual.

I have waited a long time to meet Maury in person. I hope he isn't angry that I have come. But no one will question my presence. No one did when I came in. No one will at a later date. There will be no connection to this event and the events that will follow.

I know that I can do this on my own, without Maury's assistance. But he is the master of body disposal, so I have taken this tiny, calculated risk of meeting him in person.

And the true fact of the matter is that I seek his approval. I am entering a new realm. I am smart. Smarter than those around me. I can do what I set my mind to, but at this moment, I need a confidence boost.

Or maybe I am here to reward myself for my decision. For what I am about to do.

There's a knock on the door, it opens, and Maury walks in. He is dressed in a khaki uniform with the name of the chicken plant he works for embroidered above his left breast pocket. He waits until the door closes before he looks at me.

I gesture to the chair. He sits. I am amazed by the way my heart rate rises at the sight of him. My pulse quickens. I am in the presence of a true master. I liken it to meeting a rock star or a movie star, only I am far more interested in conversing with this man than Lindsay Lohan or even Mick Jagger.

"Maury," I say. It isn't a question. I have seen photos of him. I have seen his criminal and FBI files. Although he has been questioned numerous times by the FBI in the disappearance of different women, he's been in prison only twice before. Once when he was eighteen, for stealing a car, and again in his late twenties, for another petty crime. He is forty-two and, perhaps, at his prime.

"Your time's almost up. What? Another fifty days?" I say, wanting to make idle conversation for a moment.

"Forty-one," he says. He leans back in his chair. He is pleasant enough looking. Average height. Brown hair. Blue eyes. At a bar, in a grocery store, I would not notice him beyond thinking he was a pleasant enough looking fellow. Which is, of course, one of the reasons he's so good at what he does. He blends in well.

"I have to leave for work in forty minutes, but you already know that, I bet." He watches me. "So what brings you to my neck of the woods so early in the morning . . . Danni?"

I see a certain magnetism in his cool blue eyes. Another reason why he's so good at what he does.

Maury plucks a pack of gum from his breast pocket. I know that he has a sweet tooth. I read it in his FBI file. He leans forward and offers the pack to me first.

He is polite, has such good manners.

"No, thank you," I say.

He slides a stick of tangy cinnamon flavor out of the paper package, unwraps it, and curls the stick of red gum into his mouth.

"I don't care for—"

"No need to explain yourself," he interrupts me as he rests his forearms on the table.

Not quite as polite as he should be. But I remind myself that he has been in prison for more than a year.

"I'm curious," I say, smelling the cinnamon gum on his breath. "Why were you selling oxy? That was a foolish gamble to take, and lose."

"You're right." He shrugs. "Obviously, I didn't intend to get caught." He sits back in the chair again and stretches out one leg. "It was part of another 'project' I was working on."

"I see," I say. I am curious about this "project," but I know it would be poor manners to ask about it.

"You should come out to the ranch sometime and visit my sister and me," he says. "You would like her."

I feel that he is assessing me. Despite our correspondence, I know that face-to-face first impressions are important. I cannot help but hope he finds me . . . acceptable. "I'm not sure it would be prudent for me to visit you, Maury."

He shrugs again.

We both sit there for a moment, him still sizing me up. "How do you know me?"

"As I've told you before, I'm a fan."

He narrows his pale blue eyes.

"I work in the justice system," I say. "People talk. Because of my *'interests,'* I've done some reading. Quite a few women have disappeared in the tristate area over the last decade."

"I've never been arrested in connection with any of them," Maury defends.

"No, but you've been questioned." I watch him. "There are a couple of FBI agents keeping an eye on you; you should be careful."

"I *am* careful." He chews his gum for a moment. "Your letters were interesting. It was nice to keep up with what was going on on the outside. With our poor cousin . . ." He searches for the name.

"Dylan," I offer. I am relieved that he's satisfied with my answer as to why I contacted him. How I know what he is. What he does.

"*Dylan,*" he repeats. "I'm curious. A B&E, robbery, carjacking. Quite a . . . what do you call it?" Maury asks, chewing the red gum. "Repertoire?" He waits and then goes on when I just smile. "My guess is copycat. We get the paper in here. We hear things. Talk. Every time you sent me one of those articles, something like it had happened before then." He nods. "Pretty smart. Good way to cover your tracks. I've been known to do the same. . . in certain phases. What I want to know is, why?"

I consider telling him I'm not comfortable answering his question, but we don't have a lot of time. I have to be in court in an hour and I must, sometime during the day, find time to go to Lowe's, to purchase my supplies for my kit. If I am to get something from Maury, I know I must give him something. It seems a small price to pay, a simple explanation.

"Why?" I say philosophically. "Why not?"

He studies me. I know that he and I are different. That the needs that drive him are different from mine. His are cruder. I suspect that my simple, yet complex, explanation might be difficult for him to understand. "I do it because I can," I say, an air of mystery in my voice. "Because I can get away with it. Because others will have to take the fall for it."

I think about James. About the things he did for me, knowingly and unknowingly. I think about the surprised look on his face when he saw the noose. Even as high as he was, he knew he was in trouble.

But how could he not have known how it would end? When he agreed to follow Casey, when I gave him the money for drugs, surely he knew it would not end well.

"So that's how you get your thrills, huh?" Maury asks, drawing me back to the conversation at hand. "Seeing other people go to jail for what you've done."

It's my turn to shrug. "I don't care who goes to jail as long as I don't."

"Was that why you asked me to draw those pictures? So I could take the fall for you?"

"Certainly not. It was perfectly safe. And fun, don't you think?"

"So that's it? You do these things because you can? Because you think you're smart enough to get away with them?"

"In a nutshell," I conclude, trying not to sound haughty. "But don't worry. I'm not going to become the competition. I don't see myself getting into your line of work."

He nods thoughtfully, chewing his gum, which no longer

smells of cinnamon. Then he leans forward and rests his
forearms on the old table, making eye contact with me.
"Okay. So what can I do for you, Danni?" A faint smile.

Casey was packing up the Christmas ornaments in the
dining room, placing them into boxes, when the phone rang.
Her father was watching *Rooster Cogburn* on DVD.

Casey checked the Caller ID screen. It said "Unavailable."
She was tempted not to answer it. But at any given time, several of her clients had her cell number. It could be someone
actually calling for her, and not another telemarketer.

"Casey McDaniel," she said into the phone.

Ed tossed a piece of popcorn to Frazier. He was having a
hard time concentrating tonight even though he liked the
movie. He liked the people in it. Rooster J. Cogburn and Eula
Goodnight. The bad guys had killed her preacher father, and
the marshal and Eula were teaming up to track them down
and see justice done.

It had been a long day. Kate had been on Ed about going
out on a date, him driving her Mercedes. Freckles had been
acting odd; she was worried about something. He had asked
her about it in the car on the way home from the old farts'
center; all she had said was that something bad had happened at work this week. She hadn't trusted him enough to
tell him what was going on, or why Lincoln and Adam were
both calling her.

Ed had a bad feeling. Frazier did, too. He was hardly interested in his popcorn.

Ed half listened to the TV, half listened to Freckles, who
was talking on her cell phone.

"Hey," she said. "Where are you calling from? You didn't
come up on my Caller ID."

She paused to listen.

Ed guessed it was Lincoln. She liked Lincoln. Ed liked him. She was having sex with him. Ed was not.

Ed tossed another kernel of popcorn and Frazier caught it in midair. They were eating low-fat popcorn because Ed was trying to trim his waist. If he and Kate were going out on a date, he needed to take a few pounds off.

"Oh, okay," Freckles said. "Now? Sure."

Again, she let Lincoln speak.

"See you in a couple of minutes."

She hung up her cell phone and went back to wrapping ornaments in pieces of used wrapping paper they had saved from Christmas. She didn't call out to tell him who had called. Who was coming over. Or why he was coming. That meant she thought it was none of his business, or she didn't want to worry him, but he could guess.

It was Lincoln, and he was coming for sex.

She wrapped a couple more glass ornaments and then went to the front door, unlocked it, and switched on the porch light. On her way back, she glanced in the gold-framed mirror that had hung in their living room in College Park. Ed had always liked that mirror. He remembered Lorraine's beautiful face in it. She always checked herself in mirror before they went out the door.

Freckles gazed into the mirror now. She smoothed her honey hair with its red highlights. She was primping. Lincoln made her happy. Ed was glad; she deserved to be happy.

Ed tossed another kernel of popcorn to the dog.

"I'm going to make some tea. You want some, Daddy?"

Ed ignored her. She knew he didn't like tea. Did she think he was so old and feeble that he couldn't remember he didn't like tea? He turned up the volume on the TV, trying to block out some of the thoughts bouncing around in his head.

The iPod.

Freckles said she'd think about getting Frazier an iPod. Ed

had his own money. He told her he could pay for it, but she said money wasn't the issue. She said she didn't know if she agreed Frazier needed an MP3 player.

Tea? The thoughts in his head were rebounding so haphazardly tonight that what he wished he had was a dry martini. Lorraine had always made the best martinis.

The front door opened and Ed glanced over his shoulder. He watched Richard Nixon walk through the door. Only it wasn't the same Tricky Dick Ed had seen standing outside the window.

Frazier barked and Ed turned and grabbed Frazier's collar. "Sit, boy," he whispered, unsure of why he needed to be quiet. The hair on the back of Ed's neck stood up and he ran his hand over it. The hair was prickly under his fingertips.

"In the kitchen," Freckles called. "I'm making tea."

Ed glanced toward the kitchen. Something wasn't right. He had been wrong about the phone call. Apparently, it had not been Lincoln who had called, but Richard Nixon. It was all so confusing. Lincoln had been a president once, too. Gettysburg Address. *Four score and seven years ago our fathers brought forth, upon this continent, a new nation, conceived in liberty, and dedicated to the proposition that all men are created equal.* November 1863.

Ed slipped his fingers through Frazier's collar and stood, his knees creaking. It was time to get ready, though for what, he wasn't entirely sure. What he did know was that he needed the gun. What he also knew was that Lincoln belonged in the house and Richard Nixon did not.

Chapter 34

"Hey," Casey said, her back to him as she measured loose tea into the white teapot with painted lilacs. The teapot had been her grandmother's. "I wasn't expecting to hear from you tonight. I thought you were working late."

When he didn't answer, she turned around. "Didn't you—" Her throat constricted until nothing but a croak of sound came out.

A man stood in her kitchen. A man wearing a black sweatshirt and a full latex Richard Nixon mask.

Casey's thoughts splintered into a hundred pieces as her pulse shot up, adrenaline rushing.

Her father hadn't imagined Richard Nixon in the window. The man spying on them had been wearing a mask!

Staring at the intruder, Casey slipped her hand behind her, hoping to locate something on the counter to defend herself. A knife, a glass pitcher. Anything.

He lunged for her. "Don't scream," he warned, clamping his hand painfully over her wrist. "I've only come for *you*." Catching her other hand, he then pulled both of her hands forward. "Make a sound and I'll kill your father now. He's watching TV. He can sit there and continue to watch TV or I can slit his throat. Your choice."

Casey shook with fear. She didn't recognize his voice, which was muffled by the latex mask. Why was this man wearing a Nixon mask? This was all too bizarre. It shouldn't be happening. It couldn't be. It had to be a dream. She thought she was making tea, but actually she was asleep. She was having a nightmare. A bad one. Any minute, Linda would appear from the dark corner and start shrieking at her. Maybe Angel, too.

He pulled what looked like a long, plastic zip tie out of his sweatshirt pocket and secured her wrists together in front of her. Zip-strip handcuffs.

"I . . . I don't understand," she mumbled.

"It's not important that you understand." He nudged her forward. "What *is* important is that you understand that if you do anything to attempt to attract anyone's attention while in the yard, or once we're on the road, I'll come back and kill your father and you'll have to watch. Then I'll kill you. Do you understand me?"

Casey fought the sob that rose in her throat. She nodded, terrified out of her mind.

"Do you understand?" he repeated, pushing her into the hall, shutting off the electric teakettle on the counter as he went by. "Tell me you understand."

"Yes," she managed. "I . . . I understand. But why—"

"You're not talking now, Casey. I'm talking and you're listening. You're listening and you're walking out the back door into the garage, and you're getting into the car parked in the driveway. I have a gun in my pocket. Would you like me to show it to you? It's a Glock 9 millimeter similar to one carried by many law enforcement agents. It's a gun designed to kill humans."

Casey walked through the laundry room feeling as if she

were a zombie. She was so terrified that she couldn't get her mind around what was happening.

"Wait. It's bitter out."

She heard him take a step back and then felt the weight of her winter coat on her shoulders.

"I don't want you to get cold."

Ed was digging in his sock drawer for his brown argyles when the house phone rang. He ignored it. He never answered the phone. It was never for him. But then he heard Freckles's cell phone ringing in the dining room.

She didn't answer that one either.

He glanced at the pistol on his bed and shuffled down the hallway. Frazier loped behind him. The cell phone was on the dining room table, next to a blue glass ornament. It had stopped ringing. Now it chirped. *A message.* He stared at it for a minute. Then it rang again. Ed leaned over the table and stared at the phone. He had left his glasses somewhere. He couldn't read the screen.

He debated whether or not to answer it. He didn't like cell phones. He found them annoying. Always ringing in purses, in pockets. People answering them in line at the grocery store while you were trying to talk to them.

The cell phone kept ringing. He glanced in the direction of the kitchen. Freckles always answered the phone. She must have gone somewhere. He picked it up and hit the green button on it. It wasn't that he *couldn't* use a cell phone; he just didn't like them.

"Hello," Ed said.

"Ed?"

"Yes, this is he."

Frazier sniffed under the table. He was looking for a tidbit of food he'd missed but didn't appear to be having any luck. "Check the kitchen," he told the dog.

"What?" the voice on the phone questioned.

"Talking to Frazier," Ed said. "No crumbs under this table. He wants crumbs, he needs to go into the kitchen or in the living room near the couch. We don't eat much in the dining room, Freckles and I. She's a busy woman, you know. But she keeps the dining room clean—not like Jayne. Have you ever seen Jayne's—"

"Ed, why are you answering Casey's phone?"

Ed walked through the dining room and looked down the hall into the laundry room. The door to the garage was open a crack. That wasn't like Freckles leaving the door unlocked. He suddenly felt strange. Like something bad was happening right in front of him only he couldn't quite see it.

"Ed, where's Casey?" the voice on the phone repeated.

"Don't think she's here." Ed walked past the empty kitchen into the laundry room. He stared at the partially opened door. He was beginning to get a little scared.

"Did she go out somewhere?" he asked.

"Yeah," Ed said.

"Where?"

"Get an iPod maybe?" Ed was trying hard to remember what had happened in the last hour or two. He remembered Marshal Rooster J. Cogburn. Richard Nixon. The Gettysburg Address. He opened the door to the garage wider. "She didn't take the car," he observed.

"Casey's not there, but her car is?" He sounded scared now, too. "You're sure she's not somewhere in the house? Maybe in the yard?"

"I know when my daughter is here and when she's not," Ed snapped. Freckles and Jayne were always saying he was grumpy. How could a man not be grumpy always being asked questions like this? "She's not here."

"I'm coming over, Ed. Stay where you are. Do you understand, Ed? I'll be right there."

"I can't find my socks." Ed hung the cell phone up and
closed the door to the garage. He still wasn't sure what he
was supposed to do, but he was glad the car was there. It
would have been a long walk if he'd had to borrow Kate's
Mercedes.

Ed finally found the brown argyles. He had his socks and
shoes on by the time the doorbell rang. He shoved the pistol
under his pillow and went out into the living room. Frazier
danced around Ed's feet as Ed peered out the window. If it
was Ronald Reagan, he wasn't letting him in.

It wasn't the president. Ed opened the door.

"Casey?" He brushed past Ed.

"I told you she wasn't here."

"Casey?" He frantically checked the kitchen, the garage,
down the hall, and then he hollered up the steps before he
returned to the living room. He came back carrying her cell
phone, which Ed had left on the dining room table. "She's
not here."

"Nope."

"She's gone, but she didn't take her cell phone and she
didn't take her car." He grabbed Ed's arm. "Did she *tell* you
she was going somewhere? You said something about an
iPod."

Ed looked at his arm where Lincoln was touching him.
He looked hard.

Lincoln let go.

"She didn't tell me she was going anywhere." Ed hesitated. Then he remembered the front door opening while he
was watching Rooster and Eula. Ed had been expecting Lincoln, but it had been Nixon. "I thought maybe she went to

get an iPod." He spoke slowly as he thought out loud. "But I'm not so sure."

"What makes you say that?"

Lincoln stood in the middle of the living room floor, hands in the pockets of his black coat. He looked warm. Nixon had been wearing only a sweatshirt. He had looked cold.

Ed thought hard. He didn't believe Freckles had gone for the iPod. He just couldn't quite think *why*.

"Why don't you sit down, Ed?" Lincoln suggested, walking into the dining room. He pulled out a chair.

Ed sat down.

"Ed, you have to think. You said Casey didn't go to the store. What makes you think that if she didn't tell you where she was going?"

Ed was quiet for a second. Thinking. Then he looked up. "Because Richard Nixon was here."

Lincoln made a loud groaning sound, walked away, and then came back.

"I know you think I'm crazy," Ed said, remembering more clearly now. It was like TV used to be when there was an antenna. Sometimes the picture was clear, sometimes it wasn't. Certain pictures in his mind were getting clearer. "Sometimes, maybe I *am* confused," he continued, "but I'm sure Nixon came in the house and he walked right into the kitchen where Freckles was making tea."

"You're sure there was a man here?" Lincoln questioned.

Ed nodded, relating the events in order as he remembered them. "Freckles was packing up Christmas tree ornaments." He pointed to the box on the table. "Then her phone rang and she told him he could come over. She went to make tea and I looked up when he came in the door. I thought it was you. I thought you were coming over to have sex with Freckles."

Lincoln made a face that Ed couldn't interpret.

"But it was Nixon," Ed continued. "And he went into the kitchen."

Lincoln looked at Casey's cell in his hand and pushed some buttons. It beeped. "Someone called her around seven-thirty?" he asked.

"I don't know what time. I'm not so good with time," Ed confessed. "I have Alzheimer's. I would think you people could remember that."

Lincoln grabbed a chair and sat down next to him, then slid the chair closer. "I know remembering is hard for you, but this is important. I'm afraid Casey could be in danger. Someone *did* call her, but according to her phone, it wasn't someone she knew. See, Ed, you can check the number that calls in. Her phone says someone dialed from an 'unavailable' number. It was someone she didn't know."

"She doesn't know Nixon," Ed explained.

Lincoln took a deep breath, the same way Freckles did sometimes when she was talking to him. Ed knew people got frustrated with him, but there was no reason to huff and puff. Didn't they know he got frustrated with himself?

"But . . . I'm sure she knew the person who called her," Ed said. "She told him he could come over. She doesn't invite strangers into our home. Freckles is very safe. You're not supposed to invite strangers over." He looked at Lincoln. "Should we call the police?"

Lincoln looked at him. His face was sad. Scared and sad.

Ed lowered his gaze, embarrassed. Ashamed. "No one will believe me because the man was Nixon. No one will believe there *was* a man because that's crazy. I sound crazy."

Lincoln pressed the heel of his hand to his forehead. "Ed," he said in a kind voice, "I believe you. I believe there was a man. Casey thought someone was following her. She thought it was a man she knew through work, but it couldn't have been him because he's in jail tonight."

"My Freckles," Ed said quietly. "Someone has kidnapped my Freckles. It happened before, you know." His voice cracked.

"Casey was kidnapped before?"

"I can't let this happen again." Ed gripped Lincoln's hand. His own hand looked so old and wrinkled on the younger man's. "Do you understand?"

Lincoln was quiet for a second. "Is there anything you can tell me about the man who came in who looked like Richard Nixon? What he was wearing? What he sounded like?"

"He didn't speak to me," Ed explained. "I didn't hear him and Freckles because I went to my room." He closed his eyes for a second and then opened them. "He was wearing a sweatshirt like the kids wear, with a hood. Black, I think." He shook his head. "That's all I remember."

Lincoln exhaled. "It's okay." He patted Ed's hand.

"Oh," Ed said suddenly. "I do remember something else about him."

"What's that?"

"He smelled good."

Chapter 35

Casey stared out the window as they sped down the road. He had snapped the seat belt around her, trapping her in the rear passenger seat of a car she didn't recognize. He had made a point of warning her that the child safety locks had been activated, so even if she could manage the door handle in the handcuffs, there was no way for her to escape.

Tears stung her eyes. Her stomach flip-flopped and she feared she might get sick. How could this be happening?

Cars sped by in the opposite lanes, headlights flashing. She knew where they were, but not where they were headed. She wondered if a police car might pass them on the highway, which was busy even this time of night.

Memories of that night with Billy flashed in her head. The car on the highway. The headlights. The images were in black and white. Why were they always in black and white?

The white car. The black dashboard. Her naked skin had looked so pale in the backseat of the car. His hands, his silhouette.

That night when Billy had refused to take her home, she

had prayed for a police car. Billy hadn't handcuffed her or activated childproof locks. Her pride, then her shame, had kept her from attempting to flee.

"Why are you doing this, Adam?" she said when, at last, she found her voice. "*What* are you doing?"

He was silent.

She made herself look at him. He didn't appear as if he belonged here, in a blue Honda with a cardboard air freshener hanging from the rearview mirror. Wearing the black hooded sweatshirt. He looked so out of place that she was having a difficult time connecting this man with the man she had met at the attorney general's office three months ago. The man she had flirted with. Gone on a date with. Trusted.

The bastard.

"Where are you taking me?"

Glancing in the rearview mirror, he held up his finger as if she were a naughty child. "You're not speaking."

Her cheeks flushed with anger. She leaned forward. "Yes, I *am* speaking, Adam. I'm asking—*no*—demanding to know—"

She saw the flash of his arm. She felt the impact of his fist as it connected with her chin and the side of her face. Her head snapped, her jaw exploding in pain. Tears filled her eyes as she choked down the bile that rose in her throat.

"You're not speaking," he repeated.

"You did it," she said through her tears as she leaned back against the rear seat, as far away from him as she could possibly get. "You killed Linda and Angel and you tried to frame Gaitlin. That's why you're doing this—because I'm his alibi. You killed them both."

"I didn't kill them both."

* * *

I grip the wheel of the stolen car, hesitant to speak, but wanting to. I don't know if I want to explain myself to justify what I have done. What I will do. Or if I just want to brag.

Bragging is dangerous.

In the backseat, she makes a little whimpering sound and I feel the smallest inkling of guilt. This isn't what I had thought would happen between me and Casey. I had fantasized that we would date and she would fall in love with me. I had imagined what it would be like to marry her, have a reception at the DuPont Hotel in the Golden Ballroom, and bring her home to my house in Bethany Beach to bear my children. I had even put thought into which spare room we could make her father most comfortable in. After seeing my own grandfather in a nursing home, I could never do that again to a family member.

Had Ed become my father-in-law, I would have killed him with my own loving hands before I would have put him in a nursing home. I would have made it appear as if someone else had done it, should anyone look too closely, as I had done with my dear grandfather. There had been no investigation with my grandfather. I had reattached the vent properly. But had there been any suspicions, they would have led to the man who had hanged himself in his girlfriend's garage. Poor, tortured soul, James Gaitlin.

I glance at Casey in the rearview mirror. Street lamps illuminate her beautiful face, her red-blond hair. Her lower lip is bleeding. It runs to the corner of her mouth. My heart softens. "It's complicated," I say.

She stares at me coldly.

"You may not believe me, but I didn't kill Linda. Charlie did it. His brother told me he did it. Charlie admitted it to James. In a drunken rage he stabbed her to death."

"You knew James?" she asks softly. I can tell she is caught

between her fear and her curiosity. Humans are always so curious.

"Because of the case?" she asks.

"No, it was purely coincidence that I knew James and was later called on to prosecute his brother. I caught James attempting to rob my house last summer and learned that his girlfriend was my maid. He was using her to case homes in my neighborhood, so it was easy enough to convince him to work for me. I allowed him to continue his petty thievery as long as he did my bidding when I asked him."

"So *he* followed me, in Angel's car, not Charles? He sent me the drawings?"

"He followed you." I smile, feeling a boyish flush of pleasure. "But I sent the drawings. I thought it would be funny if you thought Charlie was stalking you."

When she says nothing, I go on. I see no harm in filling her in. It actually feels good to talk about it. It makes me flush with pride.

"Charles knew nothing about his brother's relationship with me," I explain. "I insisted it had to be that way. With me still handling Linda Truman's case, you understand?" I signal and turn off Route 113 in Dagsboro. My car is home in my garage. I will lose the stolen car later.

"James was my errand boy," I say.

She stares straight ahead.

I offer her a tissue from a box on the floor. "You have blood here," I say, looking in the rearview mirror at her, touching the corner of my mouth.

She cautiously lifts her handcuffed hands and takes the tissue. She awkwardly blots her mouth. "You . . . said Charles killed Linda. But you killed Angel?"

"When Charlie got the backing of the Rights for the People, I started to get nervous. They play dirty. Charlie killed Linda and he deserves to die. He may have had a chance to get off on a technicality once, but I will not let it happen again. I intend to manipulate the case so that Charlie will end up on death row for Angel's murder."

"But the RFP was supporting him because I thought he was stalking me. You were stalking me. You're the one who was responsible for making me think it was Charlie. You were the one who caused the activists to come to his aid," she says.

"I told you it was complicated. I think on multilevels. I like the way the events overlap sometimes, but it makes them tricky. It makes my task more difficult."

"Your task?"

"To keep from getting caught. For the robberies, the B&Es . . . other things."

She's quiet for a minute, staring ahead. When she speaks, her voice is dull. Reality is setting in. She's beginning to lose hope that she will escape. "You've been committing all these crimes I've been reading about in the paper and no one has any idea?"

"I don't commit *all* of them. I am very selective, so that I fit into other criminals' MOs."

"Other people go to jail for the crimes you've committed."

"Not really. What's the difference if a criminal goes to jail for committing two mini-mart robberies or three?"

"And what about *this* crime? If James is dead, you're taking a chance in kidnapping me yourself."

"Well, I did have a little help from a friend," I say, glowing with pride when I remember my meeting with Maury. "He was unable to make it, though. Not that he didn't want to be here . . ."

I see, by the light from the dashboard, that her lower lip is trembling. She is quite pretty, even frightened as she is. Her hair is silky. Her complexion is smooth. Two spots of color circle the apples of her cheeks.

"Why are you telling me all this?" she asks in a shaky voice.

I grip the wheel. There is sadness in my voice when I speak. And I truly am sad. "You know why I'm telling you, Casey. I'm telling you because in a very short time, it won't matter what you know."

"Because I'll be dead," she whispers in the smallest voice.

I make the turn onto the road to Roxana. It is deserted, as I knew it would be. "Because you'll be dead," I confirm.

"What are we going to do?" Ed asked Lincoln.

Lincoln sat in the dining room, still wearing his coat, staring at the wall. Trying to think. He was so scared for Casey that his thoughts were bouncing around in his skull, crisscrossing, rebounding.

Adam Preston has kidnapped Casey.

It made absolutely no sense.

Yet, in his gut, Lincoln knew it to be true. The moment Ed had mentioned that the intruder smelled good, Lincoln had made the connection. He didn't know why Adam had done it or what he intended to do with her, but he knew he had her.

Which was all the more reason why he couldn't call the police. They'd be more likely to believe Ed's story about Richard Nixon than the fact that Assistant Deputy Attorney Adam Preston III had stalked and kidnapped a woman. Lincoln didn't have time for any long explanations or interviews; he didn't have time to justify his wild hunch with law enforcement officers. Casey didn't have the time.

So Lincoln figured he was on his own. At least for now.

He rose out of his chair and began to pace.

"We have to do something," Casey's father said.

Lincoln's heart went out to Ed. He didn't know exactly

what had happened to Casey in the past. Ed said she had been kidnapped. She had alluded to Lincoln that someone she had trusted had harmed her. Whatever had happened, Ed obviously felt at least partially responsible. The poor man was worried to death. Scared to death.

Probably not any more scared than Lincoln was right now, though.

"We're *going* to do something. *I'm* going to do something," Lincoln told Ed. "Just give me a minute. Where would he take her?" he thought out loud. "Where would a man of prominence like Adam take a woman if he kidnapped her?"

"To his house," Ed said. He stroked his dog's head. "Billy took her to his house."

Lincoln halted beside the table. He looked down at the glass ornaments, placed carefully on a stack of wrinkled Christmas paper. If Adam harmed Casey, Lincoln would never forgive himself. He had been suspicious of the man, but he hadn't listened to his own instincts. He had just assumed he was jealous of Adam, of his model good looks, his wealthy family, his career, his relationship with Casey.

"You think he'd take her to his house?" Lincoln said doubtfully.

"Don't know," Ed grunted. "Good place to start."

It was as good an idea as any right now. Only Lincoln didn't know where Adam lived, and he knew very well that he wouldn't be able to get a phone number or address from Directory Assistance.

"I'm going to make some phone calls, Ed, and I'm going to find Casey."

Ed pressed his hands on the table and got to his feet. "I'm ready. Let's go."

"No. You stay here." He put his hand on the old man's

shoulder. "You and Frazier stay here and wait in case Casey comes back, or she calls or something."

"I don't think Nixon is going to bring her back," Ed said.

"Please, Ed. Just stay here and wait for me." He squeezed the old man's shoulder and headed for the door. "Lock up behind me."

Ed didn't even wait for Lincoln to get out of the driveway. He went down the hallway, retrieved the gun from under his pillow, and grabbed his coat on his way out of his room. "Come on, Frazier," he called. "Let's go get Freckles."

Chapter 36

Casey shivered in the dampness. Her coat was around her shoulders, but she was still cold. Cold to the very bone.

"That too tight?" Adam asked, securing her feet to the legs of an old wooden chair he had sat her in.

She just glared at him. He was a madman.

He frowned and tore another strip of duct tape off the roll. He was working by the light of a shop lamp hanging from a hook in the rafters of the low ceiling.

Adam had taken her out into the country somewhere near Roxana. They had followed a long farm lane and parked behind a run-down frame farmhouse similar to many that dotted the local countryside. When they had driven up, Casey had thought it was abandoned, but it had turned out the electric was turned on inside. Someone was using it, though not living there. It appeared as if nothing had changed since the 1950s, including the kitchen appliances.

Adam had led her through the kitchen, into a hall, to a doorway under the front staircase, and down rickety wooden stairs, festooned with banners of cobwebs, into a cellar. She had stood a moment in inky blackness before he had found the hanging lamp and snapped it on. The bulb was low wattage, so the light did not reach the far corners of the large, cluttered room. An area had been cleared where he had sat her, but she was surrounded by berry baskets and half-bushel baskets stacked in towers, skeletons of furniture, and lumpy cloth feed sacks. She could see the silhouettes of more junk outside the ring of light, and the dark rectangular shadows of small windows high on the walls at ground level.

"That okay?" Adam asked, adding another strip of tape around her ankles. He rested his hand on her knee as he rose.

She turned her head away . . . just as she had done that night in Billy's car. He had parked in the backyard of his house, of all places. She remembered a dog barking. She remembered him forcing her into the backseat.

Billy had made her take off her shoes, then her jeans, then her shirt and bra. When she had resisted him, he had ripped off her panties.

They had been lavender cotton with pink hearts. "Happy drawers," Jayne had called them when their mother had bought multiple pairs for the sisters.

Casey still remembered the panties on the floor of the car. She remembered them more than the pain. She had gone home without her panties and wondered later if they had been in the car the night Billy had driven off the bridge in the white LeSabre and drowned in the river.

Would he even have been on the bridge if her father had believed her when she had said Billy had raped her? If he had been less concerned about his reputation and allowed her to go to the police? What if Lorraine had spoken up in her daughter's defense? Could Billy's arrest have put him in jail and saved him from going off the bridge that night? Or was it fate? Had Billy been doomed to his wet grave the moment he had picked up Casey, walking back from the library in the rain?

Tears filled her eyes, not because Billy had drowned, not because Adam was a madman who was about to murder her, not even because Billy had raped her, but because she had become a victim once again.

She took a shuddering breath.

She had *sworn* she would never be caught in this position again, and now, here she was, all these years later. Everything had changed. Yet nothing had changed. And this time, it would mean her life.

"Adam, *please,*" she begged. "You can't—"

"I *can* do it and I *am* going to," he said sharply. "And I'll get away with it, just as I've been getting away with things for years. Now shut up and sit there. I hope you'll excuse me, but I'm not quite ready yet." Adam's tone had changed; now he suddenly sounded as if he had invited her to lunch and the meal wasn't prepared.

Who *was* this man? How could Casey have misjudged him so greatly? How had everyone around him misjudged him?

"I've got some things to do upstairs. But I'll leave the light on. There's nothing that can harm you here, so you needn't be afraid."

He walked to a workbench and flipped on another hanging shop light. Behind the bench were shelves lined with fruit and tomatoes canned in dusty glass jars. On the bench were pieces of mechanical equipment. Tubes. Wire. Some sort of timers.

Adam picked up something off the bench and turned to her. He was holding a white plastic tube with wires and a device attached to it.

Casey's mouth went dry. She'd never seen a bomb in her life, but she knew that's what it was.

"A little project I've been working on, weekends." He squatted in front her. "There's mercury in this little glass vial. If you jiggle it, the contents of the tube will mix and explode. I haven't had a chance to use it, but my suspicion is that *you'll* explode." He used the tape to attach it somewhere under Casey's chair. "I know you promised me you wouldn't try to get away, but this is assurance for me."

"How do you know I won't blow myself up to save myself from you?" she asked, looking down at him.

"Because you won't. Because you're human, and until the very last second, you will believe there is some chance you'll escape, be saved, or I'll change my mind about killing you and hiding your body parts so that they'll never be found."

Satisfied with the placement, he stood up. "I'd blow myself up to escape, but not you, Casey." He tried to stroke her chin but she turned sharply from him.

He walked out of the circle of light and toward the stairs. "Sit tight. I'll be back." He winked. "Promise."

Lincoln gripped the steering wheel. It had taken him three calls before he had found someone willing to go into the Delaware Criminal Justice Information System and look up Adam Preston III's home address. Lincoln owed the detective a big favor.

Lincoln was surprised that Adam had two addresses listed. The first one was on the ocean side in South Bethany Beach. He went there first. He looked in the windows, found the BMW in the garage, but saw no lights on inside except for one that he guessed glowed in a hallway.

Lincoln had gone there first because it was closer, but he hadn't been hopeful. For whatever depraved reason Adam had kidnapped Casey, Lincoln doubted he would take her to such an obvious place. Now Lincoln was headed for an address in the countryside near Roxana. He had used his cell phone to map it. It was out in the middle of nowhere. It was the kind of place you would take a woman if you wanted to—

Lincoln refused to allow his thoughts to go there. What mattered right now was finding Casey. Nothing else.

He made a turn at the intersection, following the mapping software on his phone. He glanced in his rearview mirror. It was a cold, windy night. There were few drivers on the country road. Right now, just one, half a mile or so behind him.

Lincoln began to slow his car. According to the map, he was 200 feet from the address. He peered through the windshield. In the distance, across a field, he saw the outline of a two-story house. Light glowed behind shades in some of the windows.

He almost missed the dirt lane. He cut his headlights and made the turn into the driveway, then pulled over. He waited until the car that had been behind him went by and disappeared into the woods. Then he got out of the car and walked up the dark driveway, adrenaline rushing.

There was definitely someone home in the old farmhouse. Lincoln went up on the front porch and tried to look in the windows, but the lamp glow was from rooms in the back of the house. He heard music from inside. One of the Three Tenors, he believed.

He couldn't see anyone or anything. He walked around to the back to find a light blue Honda that he didn't recognize.

Had he made a mistake? If he was peering in the windows of the wrong house, he might end up getting arrested or shot. But the cop said this property was owned by Adam. Not his father or grandfather. The third. And if you were going to commit a crime, would you use your own car if you didn't have to?

Lincoln stood in the driveway, undecided as to what to do.

There was a back door, which probably led to a kitchen. Knock? No, that would be crazy.

He needed to get a look inside.

He glanced at the car. On impulse, he opened the passenger-side door, not really sure what he was looking for. A flashlight maybe? A tire iron to use as a weapon? Light flooded the interior and he quickly climbed in and flipped the overhead light off.

The car smelled like Casey! It smelled like her hair. . . .

Lincoln's throat thickened with emotion. He had no doubt Casey had been in this car.

He had his cell phone in his pocket. He should just call the police. He knew he still had no evidence Casey was even inside, but he pulled it out of his pocket and dialed 911.

The screen on the cell flashed a message: "Loss of Service."

Damn! It had been working a few minutes ago when he'd used the mapping service. But there were a lot of places in southern Delaware where there was weak or no cell phone service because there were too few towers. He fought the urge to throw the phone as far into the field as he could. He would have to walk back to the main road.

But walking to the car would mean leaving Casey.

Finding nothing of use in the car, he got out and eased the door shut. He walked around the other side of the house, still hearing the music faintly through the walls. He debated again whether or not he should hike back to the car.

On the south end of the house, he noticed a feeble light coming from the ground. Tiny, darkened, rectangular windows. Lincoln crouched in front of one of the windows. If you kidnapped someone, where would you take the person? A cellar in an old farmhouse was a pretty good hiding spot.

Unable to see anything, Lincoln stuffed his cell into his coat pocket and dropped to the wet, cold grass. The window was painted over. Barn red. He rubbed the glass with his hand. Nothing. Then he tried to scratch it. To his amazement, paint peeled away and a thin line of light seeped through. It had been painted on the outside instead of the inside!

He scrubbed vigorously with his fingertips, making a peephole, not caring that shreds of paint jammed under his fingernails sent shooting pains through his fingers. Then he lowered his body flat on the ground. He eased forward.

It was a cellar very similar to his: whitewashed brick walls, dirt floor. Except that this one didn't appear to have changed in the last fifty years. Cobwebs hung everywhere. He saw stacks of baskets, feed bags, even home-canned vegetables.

Then he saw her and his chest tightened so quickly that he had to gasp for air. Casey was sitting upright in a chair in the middle of the room, her back to him.

He couldn't fit through the window, even if he was willing to take the risk of Adam hearing the glass breaking. Lincoln didn't know where Adam was, but he didn't appear to be in the cellar.

Many of these houses had outside entrances to the cellars, as well as inside entrances. Adam had to be in the house.

Lincoln leaped to his feet and ran for the aluminum door that led underground.

Ed didn't take the dirt road up to the house. Instead, he and Frazier trekked across the fallow cornfield.

Ed had parked in the woods down the road. He'd been nervous when he'd backed out of the driveway. He'd been afraid he wouldn't remember how to drive, but his hands and feet had remembered.

When Lincoln had turned into the driveway at the old farmhouse, Ed had been afraid to pull in behind him. He had been afraid Lincoln would make him go home. Lincoln didn't understand that Ed had to be here. That Ed had to save Freckles.

It was a longer walk across the field than Ed had thought it would be, and he was getting hot in his coat. He unzipped it. Frazier trotted beside him. Joe Frazier was a good dog. He heeled without a leash. Joe Frazier had been a good boxer, too.

At the house, Ed walked around to the back. He could hear music. Pavarotti's Rodolfo in *La Bohème*.

Ed didn't know what he was supposed to do. He just figured he would get Freckles and then they would walk back across the cornfield to the car. Now that he could prove to her that he was capable of driving, maybe she would let him drive home.

Lincoln believed in God, but he was not typically a man of prayer. He prayed as he tugged on the handle of the cellar door and God smiled upon him. It creaked so loud as the hinges gave way that he froze for a heartbeat. Two. He held his breath.

After a moment, when he heard nothing from inside, when Adam didn't burst out of the darkness, Lincoln pulled harder.

He only opened the door far enough to climb through the opening and step down into the stairway. He eased it closed over his head and fought the urge to run down the steps to Casey. Instead, he crouched there listening. He heard nothing. How could she not have heard the door? How could anyone within a mile radius of the house not heard it? As he eased down the steps, he guessed why.

There was music coming through the floorboards overhead. A rich tenor voice. He didn't know enough about opera to identify the tenor.

He peeked around the corner, and as he did so, his hand brushed against a glass jar, causing the jar to slide and make a scraping sound. He stared at the jar with tomatoes bobbing in it.

"Is someone there?" Casey whispered. She didn't turn around. She didn't move.

Seeing no one, Lincoln made a run for her. He would just sweep her up in his arms and carry her out of there. He had seen the keys dangling in the ignition of the Honda. They would take the Honda. They would drive away, and the minute he had phone service, he would call the police.

"Casey," he whispered. When he reached her, he rested his hand on her shoulder and stepped around her to see her face.

"Don't touch me," she warned in a voice that didn't sound like her own.

Lincoln let go of her at once. All he could think of was that Adam had already raped her.

"Casey . . ." He gazed into her tear-stained face. Her hands were cuffed in front of her.

"Get out of here," she whispered harshly. "Go, Lincoln. Run."

"Casey . . ." He put his arms out to her. He didn't care what Adam had done. He loved her. He wanted to marry her. He wanted to have babies with her.

"Under the chair, Lincoln." She was nearly hysterical. "A bomb under the chair."

He lowered his gaze, her words barely sinking in. *A bomb?*

Then he saw it. Wires. A tube. Crude. Homemade, but almost surely a bomb.

"Call for help," she whispered, her eyes pleading. "Your cell."

"No service here. I tried." He crouched down in front of her.

"You can't touch me," she warned. "Or the chair. He said it

would be triggered by movement. You have to go for help if you can't use your phone. You have to go now before he comes downstairs." She pointed with her chin to a narrow wooden staircase without railings that led upward into the dark.

Lincoln looked down at the device looped in wires under Casey's chair. This just got crazier and crazier by the moment. "You think he's capable of—"

"I *know* he is!"

The outside aluminum door creaked and Lincoln shot to his feet. Had Adam slipped out of the house and come around to the outside? Had he realized Lincoln was there?

The door creaked again and Lincoln and Casey both cringed.

"Lincoln," she whispered, her eyes filled with tears.

He lunged for the closest object he thought he could use as a weapon, a long wooden handle that had once been attached to a rake or a shovel. He put himself between the back of Casey's chair and the outside staircase.

He heard footsteps and something shot out of the dark. Lincoln reacted without thinking, swinging the stick.

Fortunately, he wasn't a good aim. He missed Frazier's head by a foot.

"Oh my God," Lincoln muttered as the dog skittered around him.

Two steps behind, out of the darkness, Ed appeared.

"Ed, what are you doing here?" Lincoln begged.

"Came to get my daughter." He walked around her. "What's she—"

"Shhh," Lincoln warned, grabbing his arm and pulling him back before he touched Casey or the chair she was tied to. "He's upstairs."

"Nixon?"

"Adam Preston."

Ed stared at his daughter. "I saw Nixon." He pointed at Lincoln. "Tell him I'm not crazy."

Casey was smiling and crying at the same time. "You're not crazy, Daddy. He was wearing a Richard Nixon mask. Now listen to me. You have to get out of here. You have to go for help."

He looked down at her. "I'm not going without you. I'll just get a knife and cut that tape."

Casey looked to Lincoln for support.

Lincoln took Casey's father's arm and tried to steer him toward the door. "Even if we cut the tape, she can't just get up. We have to get the police. We probably need the FBI."

"I don't understand." Ed struggled to escape Lincoln's grip. "Why can't she get up? If she can't walk, I can carry her. I'm still strong. I'm strong for an old man."

"Ed," Lincoln said as gently as he could, "listen to me. He's tied a bomb to her chair. If she tries to get up, it will explode."

Ed turned to stare at his daughter's back. "A bomb?"

"Yes. So you see, I need you to take my cell phone"— Lincoln pulled it out of his coat pocket and pressed it into Ed's hand—"and go to the road. Go as far as you have to until the phone works, and then you have to call nine-one-one and tell them where we are. The address is here in my phone. You don't even have to remember. You can just read it to them."

Ed halted halfway to the staircase. Lincoln tried to push him, but the old man wouldn't budge. He was strong for his age.

"There's a bomb under my daughter's chair?" he said in a small voice.

"Yes."

He looked up at Lincoln. "Then what would make you think I'm going anywhere, boy?"

Chapter 37

The End of the End

I check the contents of my duffel bag one last time, dragging my fingers lightly over my tools. Maury explained the use of each item as I wrote them down.

I am, frankly, delighted with myself.

She never saw me coming. They will never suspect me. I am too smart for all of them.

I have duct tape and a spool of #4-gauge wire, for securing items; a box of disposable latex gloves, to keep myself tidy; wire cutters, for cutting tendons. Then there are garden shears, for snapping small bones; hand towels, to sop up blood; disposable coveralls, to keep my clothing clean; a drop cloth, for the dirt floor. I cannot carelessly leave trace evidence behind, even though there isn't a chance anyone will ever come here looking for it. I also have a hacksaw, for cutting the larger bones, and then there are the disposable shoe covers.

The shoe covers are a clever idea. In my haste, I might not have thought of them. But Maury is an experienced man.

I dig to the bottom of the bag: a hunting knife, for the

obvious; plastic sheeting, to contain blood spatter; zip-strips, for tying more than wrists together; a blue bandana, for a gag.

Beside me, leaning against the old kitchen table, is a shovel. The correct term would be a *spade.* Good for digging. Good for burying. There are twenty-seven acres here, plenty of room. But I won't bury her body parts here. I'll take a trip to Maury's ranch, instead. Just to be on the safe side . . .

The last item I pick up off the kitchen table is the Glock 9 mm. I tuck it into the back pocket of my khakis, singing along with Pavarotti.

"Casey, talk some sense into him," Lincoln said. "Make him understand that he has to go for help."

"Daddy, *please,*" Casey begged. "You're the only one who can do this." She was scared, trying not to move. She didn't even turn her head. Ed and Lincoln walked around her so that she could see them without shifting in the chair. Frazier had sat down on the dirt floor very close to her, but not touching her or the chair.

"I'm not leaving you," Ed insisted, looking down at her. "I wasn't there when you needed me once. You know when I mean."

He seemed perfectly cognitive at this moment. His old self. He was just being stubborn. "I know," she whispered, looking up at him lovingly through teary eyes.

"I'm sorry for that, Freckles. For all of it." Tears welled in his gray eyes. "I was wrong. I was very wrong. I need you to forgive me."

"It's okay, Daddy. I forgave you a long time ago." She sniffed. "But right now I do need you. I need you to go for help."

He shook his head. "Sorry, I can't do that. Whatever

happens this time, I'll be here." Hc looked at Lincoln.
"He'll have to go."

"Ed—Casey, we don't have time for this." Lincoln looked
up at the ceiling. The music was still playing.

A voice had joined the tenor. Adam was singing. Hc had
an excellent voice.

"I think you should both go." She looked down at the
boxer at her feet. "And Frazier, too," she added sentimen-
tally. "You should all go for help."

Lincoln turned to her father. "Ed, I don't mean to be dis-
respectful, but I'm younger than—"

"Oh, so you want me to traipse across that field again?"
Ed threw up one hand.

"Ed," Lincoln said, his voice amazingly calm, "we're
trying to think what's best for Casey right now, and it's best
if I stay here to protect her."

"With what?" Ed scoffed. "A hoe handle? I can protect
her as well as you can."

Her father reached into his pocket and Casey gasped as
he pulled out a pistol.

"Oh my God, is that loaded, Daddy?"

Lincoln took a step back.

"Yes, it's loaded," Ed said incredulously. "It wouldn't do
much good if it wasn't loaded."

Casey stared, as horrified by the thought of her father
being in possession of a handgun as she was of anything that
had happened tonight. "Daddy, I don't know where you got
that, but you need to give it to Lincoln."

"None of your damned business where I got it," Ed said
gruffly.

"Casey," Lincoln murmured.

"I know, I know." She looked back at her father, taking
care only to shift her eyes. Despite the chill of the damp
basement, she was sweating profusely. She wanted someone

to take her coat off her, but she was afraid to let them for fear it might jiggle the chair.

"Give Lincoln the gun, Daddy."

"He hates guns," Ed protested. "Never fired one in his life."

"Have *you?*" she managed. All she could think of was that Ed would accidentally pull the trigger and shoot himself or Lincoln.

Ed hesitated. Casey could tell he was considering turning the weapon over.

"Daddy, please. You can't legally have that handgun," she said, trying a different approach. He had always been a law-abiding man. "Not with your diagnosis."

"But I wanted to help." Ed's voice was thick with emotion. He sounded scared, for the first time tonight. "I got the gun to protect you. I don't want to get in trouble with the police. I just want to protect my daughter. I just want to protect you," he insisted to her through tears.

Casey felt as if her heart was splitting in two. She loved her father so much. She loved both of these men. She didn't want this life to end. She thought about what Adam had said about the bomb. What he would do in her situation. About what *she* would do. He had been right. She wouldn't blow herself up, because she still had hope. She had hope that she and the men she loved would get out of this alive. She had hope and now she had a gun.

"Give the gun to Lincoln this minute, Daddy. Take Frazier and run for the car. Call the police. Do it now, Daddy," she snapped.

Ed stared at her for a moment and then lowered the gun. "I guess he should take it," he conceded. "He probably has steadier hands. My hands aren't as steady as they used to be."

Lincoln gingerly took the handgun from Ed. "You have

to go for help," he said gently. He handed him the cell phone. "You have to go *now.*"

A sound coming from the direction of the inside staircase made all three of them and the dog focus. There were footsteps coming out of the darkness. Light. Then, Pavarotti's singing got louder.

"Go, Ed," Lincoln insisted, giving him a push toward the outside door.

Ed moved amazingly quickly, the phone clutched in his hand. "Frazier."

The dog bounded after him.

Every muscle in Casey's body tightened as she stared straight ahead waiting for Adam. Lincoln moved somewhere behind her, into hiding.

"So here we are," Adam announced, coming out of the stairwell, a green gym bag in his hand.

The moment he stepped into the circle of light that surrounded Casey, she could see that he sensed something was amiss. He set the bag on the ground at his feet and slipped his hand behind him, reaching for something in the waistband of his pants. He gazed around the cluttered, shadowy cellar.

"What have we done, Casey?" There was the slightest sound of surprise in his voice. He looked down at her feet. "You haven't moved. Couldn't have." He made a clicking sound with his tongue. "So what's different?"

Casey just stared at him, afraid to speak. She couldn't tell where Lincoln was, only that he was behind her.

His hand still behind his back, Adam turned his head left and then right, reminding her of a prairie dog, of all things. In different circumstances, she might even have laughed. Adam was uncertain of himself for the first time tonight.

"It's cooler down here than it was," he said suddenly.

He drew his hand forward and Casey saw the gun he had

warned her of. He pointed it at her face. "The outside door is open, isn't it? Lock's been broken for years. I've meant to replace it, but I never needed to." He took a step forward, still aiming the gun at her face. "Why is the door open, Casey?"

She heard something move behind her.

"Because I opened it," Lincoln said.

Adam took a step back, swinging the gun in Lincoln's direction. "How did you get here? How did you find us?" He was almost childlike in his astonishment.

Lincoln was so scared for Casey, so scared of Adam and the guns in both their hands that he could barely put one foot in front of the other. He had never held a gun in his life. He had hoped he never would, and now, he was pointing one at someone's chest. But he had realized at the instant that Adam had appeared out of the dark that he would do anything to save Casey. He loved her and he would do anything to spare her life, including sacrificing his own.

What he wasn't sure of—even at this moment—was if he could kill another human being.

"Lincoln," Casey whimpered.

"Put down the gun and deactivate the bomb," Lincoln instructed.

"Or what?" Adam challenged. He was still backing up, still aiming at Lincoln.

"Or I'll shoot you."

"You won't shoot me," Adam scoffed. "Mr. Gun Control, Mr. Guns Should Only Be in the Hands of Law Enforcement Agents," he taunted. "You don't have the balls."

"*Please,* Adam," Casey begged. "He'll do it."

"He'd let me kill him before he'd pull that trigger," Adam taunted.

Lincoln moved closer. His intention was to put himself between Casey and Adam. He was afraid if he didn't do it quickly, Adam would just shoot her in the head. Lincoln didn't know anything about handguns, but from the look of the shiny metal and the shape of the one Adam was holding, he had a feeling that Adam knew how to handle it. If he shot at Casey, he wouldn't miss.

Adrenaline pumping, Lincoln slid another foot forward. "You don't want to do this," he told Adam.

"Sure I do. At this point, what do I have to lose?"

Lincoln didn't really see Adam turn the gun on Casey so much as he felt the change in the air. Without thinking, without taking aim, Lincoln squeezed the trigger.

The cellar echoed with the shot, which sounded like the crack of a whip. Casey screamed. There was smoke and the acrid smell of gunpowder as Adam went down on one knee.

Lincoln had shot him! He'd hit him!

Adam slowly lowered his gaze to his upper thigh, which was gushing blood. "I can't believe you just did that," he said in awe. "I know people. I know what makes them tick. Odds were a million to one that a man like you would shoot a man like me."

"Drop the gun," Lincoln ordered, fighting the urge to vomit. "Drop it and push it this way. You're losing a lot of blood. I'll put a tourniquet on it for you, but first you have to give me the gun."

Adam looked at the blossoming red wound and then slowly lifted his gaze to meet Lincoln's. "You've got to be kidding. You don't really think I would let anyone take me alive."

Lincoln lunged for him, but it was too late. Adam raised his gun to his mouth and Lincoln turned away at the sound of the shot.

Casey screamed again. Lincoln closed his eyes for a second and turned away, staggering. There was no need to check Adam. He had heard his brain splatter.

"Casey." The pistol now hung at Lincoln's side and he was fighting a sob in his throat.

"Lincoln. . . Lincoln, look at me." Casey's voice pushed through Lincoln's haze.

"Look at me. This wasn't your fault. You did what you had to do. You saved my life and you saved your own."

When he opened his eyes, she was smiling. She was crying, but she was smiling. Tied to a chair. A bomb under her. And Casey was still smiling.

Lincoln leaned over, carefully laying the handgun on the ground. "I want to hug you," he said, feeling light-headed. He stood upright again. "I wish I could . . . I think maybe . . ." He gazed into her eyes. "I'd like to ask you to marry me."

That was when he heard the first wail of the police sirens. Ed had come through. Somehow, Ed had found a cell phone signal and he had come through for his daughter.

"I think I'd like you to propose to me," Casey said, still looking up at Lincoln, still smiling through her tears. He knew she heard them, too. "But maybe we should wait until the police get this bomb out from under me, okay?"

Chapter 38

Maury lay on his bunk, stalling. He would have to go in a moment, but not yet. He was giving himself a second to calm his nerves and prepare what he would say to the *authorities*. He chewed his gum slowly, savoring the minty sweetness of it. With his eyes, he traced the pattern of the ceiling tiles.

He was not entirely surprised when he was told the Delaware State Police were there to speak to him. He did not have to ask what matter it concerned.

Maury had read the headlines of the newspaper all week. Assistant Deputy Attorney Adam Preston III had committed suicide. It had made national press. He had *allegedly* kidnapped a local woman named Casey McDaniel. He had held her hostage, tied her to a chair with a bomb, and then, when cornered by another attorney, the woman's fiancé, Preston had put a gun to his head and killed himself.

The assistant deputy attorney had allegedly been involved in additional crimes, including the murder of a local woman. It was believed, at press time, that Preston had been trying to frame a man named Charles Gaitlin who had previously been accused of killing a girlfriend. The case was still under investigation.

There had been press about Charles Gaitlin, as well. It was believed that the attorney general's office had information exonerating Gaitlin from the second murder, but indicating guilt in the first. Gaitlin had been out of jail only two days before he was arraigned again for the first murder. Some citizens' rights group was up in arms about the arrest, but apparently the charges were going to stick this time. *Poor, sorry sucker.*

Maury had been disappointed when he had heard that Adam Preston III had committed suicide. Danni had had potential. But he had never been in Maury's league.

And now the police were investigating every step the assistant deputy attorney had taken in the weeks leading up to his death. This was where the matter got a little sticky.

When Preston had come to the work-release building to visit Maury, he had signed himself in at the front desk. That meant he had left evidence behind, linking him to Maury. The police were interviewing everyone who had had contact with the assistant deputy attorney in the last days of his life.

Of course, the police couldn't ask Maury about what Preston and he had spoken of. Well . . . they could ask, but Maury was under no obligation to answer. Attorney/client privilege.

"Pinkerton!" a CO summoned from the hallway.

Maury climbed down off his bunk and spat his gum into the trash can. The sweetness was gone.

This interview with the police was nothing but a technicality. He would not tell them about the drawings he had sent to the assistant deputy attorney, per his request. He would not tell them of the small role he had played in stalking Casey McDaniel, or about the information he had provided Preston on how to prepare the perfect "murder kit."

As Maury walked out of his stark room, he glanced at the calendar on the wall. He thought about the woman in the barrel.

Thirty-six days.

He would be released in thirty-six days.

It would be good to see her again.

It was time she had some company.

"This is so nice, Lincoln, but really, you didn't have to go to all this trouble." Casey set her wineglass on the coffee table. Dinner had been amazing: lamb chops, parsley potatoes, asparagus, and homemade applesauce. Lincoln hadn't let her do a thing to help prepare the meal or clear away the dishes and now they were seated comfortably together on his couch in front of a blazing fire. "I feel silly about all this fuss. I'm fine."

"There's been no fuss." Lincoln took her hand and pressed it between both of his.

"There's been a great deal of fuss. Everyone's treating me like I'm spun glass; the police, the people at work, Dad, you. Even Jayne's been unreasonably accommodating."

"Well, you *were* kidnapped from your home less than two weeks ago. You *did* have a homemade bomb strapped to your tail-end."

She groaned and laughed, but didn't pull her hand from his. She wasn't scared anymore. In fact, surviving her ordeal with Adam had made her feel empowered. She was *not* a victim. She would never be a victim again. That didn't mean she didn't want to keep Lincoln close. Her near encounter with death had not only made her feel stronger, it had also made her amazingly thankful for what she had. Family. Friends. And Lincoln. Especially Lincoln.

"I just want to get back to my life before all this," Casey said, trying to find the right words to explain how she was feeling. "I want to get back to work. Back to fighting with my sister. Back to chasing Dad in the yard, him dressed in my bathrobe. The way things were before Adam and Gaitlin."

"Before me?" He lifted one eyebrow.

"No. Of course not. Not before you." Casey leaned toward him, meeting him halfway for a kiss. His touch was warm and comforting, but there was still that thrill of sexual attraction.

"You want to stay again tonight," he whispered, his voice deep.

"I shouldn't." Looking up at him, she stroked his cheek with her fingertips. "Dad—"

"Your dad's in his PJ's and his own robe watching TV with my grandparents. There's a John Wayne marathon on TNT tonight. Grandma already had me come set the DVR for them. Let your dad spend another night. My grandparents are tickled to have a guest in their spare room." He gestured. "Frazier's already adopted them as his second family."

"I have to go home sometime," she insisted, gazing into his dark eyes.

"No, you don't."

She kissed him again, lightly this time. "Yes, I do. There's no reason for me to be afraid and no reason for you to be afraid for me. They're gone—Gaitlin, his brother, Adam, Billy. They're all gone." In the hospital, Casey and Lincoln had had a long talk about her past, about Billy, with her father. He'd been a good listener.

"You really don't have to go home if you don't want to." Lincoln let go of her with one hand and slipped it into the pocket of his jeans. "I was thinking maybe we could make other arrangements."

The walkie-talkie on the kitchen counter squawked and they both looked up and laughed.

"Base Camp Two, this is Base Camp One, do you read? Over."

Lincoln removed his hand from his pocket with a groan.

"Base Camp Two, come in," Lincoln's grandmother said, via the walkie-talkie. "You there, son? Over."

Lincoln closed his eyes.

"Go ahead." Casey was still laughing. "You might as well answer her, otherwise she'll be here in five minutes banging on the front door."

Lincoln got off the couch. "This'll just take a second. I swear."

Casey smiled, settling back on the couch as she reached for her wineglass.

"Base Camp Two, this is Base Camp—"

Lincoln snatched the walkie-talkie off the kitchen counter and walked back into the living room, holding his finger on the transmit button. "Grandma, are you on fire?"

"Ah, that's a negative, Base Camp Two," his grandmother said. "Base Camp One is not on fire. Over."

"Is there blood, Grandma? And I mean arterial blood. Is one of you bleeding, Grandma?" Lincoln released the transmit button.

Casey took a gulp of wine to keep from laughing aloud.

The walkie-talkie crackled. "That's a negative on the blood, as well, Base Camp Two. You're supposed to say *over* when you're done. Over."

"Grandma, you swore to me that you wouldn't bother us tonight," Lincoln said, obviously trying to be patient. "You promised me three hours of peace. All I asked for was for three hours." He let go of the button.

"You better say *over*," Casey suggested.

Lincoln shot her an evil look. "Over," he said into the walkie-talkie.

"No need to get your boxers in a twist, Base Camp Two.

We were just checking in. Wanted to see if you had popped the question yet."

Lincoln suddenly looked as if he wanted to kill or be killed.

Casey almost spat her mouthful of wine back into her glass.

"Grandma," Lincoln moaned into the walkie-talkie. "She can hear you, you know." He let go of the button, looking to Casey. "I'm sorry," he said. "I really wanted this to be a special evening." He started to fish in his jeans pocket with his free hand. "I wanted to do this right."

Casey got off the couch and crossed the room to Lincoln. Her heart swelled. "It's all right."

"No," he said. "It's not. I—"

"Base Camp Two. Is that a negative on the marriage proposal, then? Over."

"Grandma—"

"You have to get on your knees, son. Get down on your knees and ask her. A girl can never say no to a man who proposes on his knees. Over."

Lincoln met Casey's gaze, looking sheepish. "I didn't mean for this to be a group effort."

Laughing, Casey wrapped one arm around his waist, taking the walkie-talkie from him. "Base Camp One, this is Base Camp Two. Over."

"Go ahead, Base Camp Two," Lincoln's grandmother said cheerfully. "Over."

"That's a yes on the marriage proposal. Now if you'll excuse us, I'm going to have a look at the ring he's got shoved in his pocket." She brushed her fingertips over the front of his jeans. "Over."

"Affirmative, Base Camp Two. She said yes!" his grandmother said, obviously directing her comment to Lincoln's grandfather and Casey's father in the room with her. "This is Base Camp One, out."

"Base Camp Two, out," Casey echoed. She tossed the walkie-talkie on the couch.

"I really am sorry," Lincoln apologized again. "I wanted it to be a surprise."

"How big a surprise could it be? I asked you to ask me to marry you, remember?"

He laughed and lowered his head until their lips met. "I love you," he said.

"I love you." She kissed him and leaned back, still in his arms. "So let's see it." She held out her hand.

Lincoln pulled a ring out of his pocket. "Let me put it on you," he said.

Casey held out her left hand.

"It might be a little big, but we can have it sized." He spun it on her finger and the diamonds caught the light from the fire on the hearth. "It was my great grandmother's wedding ring, but I thought you might like it as an engagement ring."

"Oh, Lincoln," Casey said, surprised that she couldn't catch her breath. The ring was perfect, an antique setting in platinum with a row of sparkling diamonds. "It's beautiful," she added, tears filling her eyes.

"So is that a yes?" Lincoln closed his arms around her. "Will you marry me, Casey? Will you and your dad become a party of my crazy family? Will you consider having my children?"

Casey's eyes clouded with concern and she caught both his hands in hers, taking a step back so she could look up at him. "Are you sure about this? Dad's disease is progressive. Caring for him might require more than either us realizes right now."

"My eyes are wide open, hon. Whatever comes, we'll face it together."

"Do you mean that?"

He squeezed both of her hands, his dark eyes sincere with just a twinkle of humor. "That's affirmative, Base Camp. Over."

Casey threw her arms around him. "Then, yes, yes, yes! I'll marry you. We'll have a baby." She was laughing. She was crying. It had been a long time in coming, but she was happy at long last.

Nail-Biting Romantic Suspense
from Your Favorite Authors